W9-AOC-996

INNOCENCE BETRAYED

Sinking to the bed, she lifted her arms to her husband, and Lance came to her. Their lovemaking was an exquisite torment, and when it was over Lance took her again, quickly, hurriedly, as though she might slip away from him.

"I love you," he said huskily, and Raine nodded in total contentment.

"It's all I've ever wanted, and it's all I'll ever need," she whispered in return. Then she lowered her eyes in shyness. "I shall always love you, my darling. I have never loved any man before you, and I shall love only you until I die."

Lance's eyes filled with pain. "When the day comes I'll remind you of your promise, and I shall ask you to honor it. . . .

Other Leisure books by Constance Conant:
SOUTHERN STAR
FALLING STAR

STAR
OF THE
WEST

Constance Conant

LEISURE BOOKS ∞ NEW YORK CITY

A LEISURE BOOK

Published by

Dorchester Publishing Co., Inc.
276 Fifth Avenue,
New York, NY 10001

Copyright © 1988 by Constance Conant

All rights reserved. No part of this book may be repro-
duced or transmitted in any form or by any electronic
or mechanical means, including photocopying, record-
ing, or by any information storage and retrieval system, without the written permission of the Publisher,
except where permitted by law.

Printed in the United States of America

For
Nellie and Maggie

1

San Francisco, 1853

Lance Randall sipped the burning liquid that was only half jokingly referred to as 42-caliber whiskey. In his line of work, he could not afford the slowed movement or blurred vision that came from consuming too much alcohol. And he definitely could not afford the addled brain that accompanied hard drink.

Sorely tempted though he was to erase this latest assignment with oblivion, he pushed the half empty glass aside. Still, he chaffed under the fool errand his father had given him, an errand any gun-slinger could have carried out.

But, no. His father had insisted that a *Randall* must exact punishment from the men who had dared touch what was his.

Only a member of the family could seek vengeance and execute it in such a way that no one would ever forget the cost of stealing from the Randall empire.

A weary sigh escaped his lips. It was a damned good thing he wasn't married. A man with a wife and family could not go chasing all over the world intimidating and killing those who defied his father's will.

His body jerked in silent, humorless laughter. Someday the tables would be turned. He would be the one to die.

Shrugging away the thought, which had become increasingly persistent, he gazed idly in the direction of the whores, card sharps, miners and just plain lonesome men in search of female companionship. Everyone in San Francisco, it seemed, was looking for something. It was a city where the strong and the shrewd survived. The less able were left lying by the wayside, destitute and disillusioned.

"Five years," he thought glumly, for already five years had passed since that day in 1848 when his father had first heard the rumors of gold in California.

Few other men of substance had thought the wild stories credible, but his father had taken a chance. At the first quiet whisper of gold, he had sent men and equipment to the sleepy town once known as Yerba Buena.

From here they had fanned out across

the hills and valleys and had explored along the rivers. And they had found gold. Thousands of tons of ore had been mined. Huge nuggets had been scooped up from creek and river beds. And for several years the Randall family had bought up other claims along the mother lode, claims to mines that adjoined their own properties. Another great fortune had been amassed because his father had gambled on a rumor and had won. As usual.

Now, when most of the easy gold had been stripped from the original digs, a new hydraulic system was being brought in. It was a system that would wash away the rolling hills of the countryside—a system that would forever change the face of mountain and meadow, of swift-running creeks and of rivers swollen by the cold waters of a spring thaw. Lance detested it.

His brooding was interrupted as his attention was briefly diverted by the sound of the roulette wheel. He was tempted to make a bet or two himself but decided against any of the games of chance this establishment offered, games that picked the pockets of fools and desperate men.

Then, with an unmistakable air of finality, Lance placed a wide-brimmed hat on his head and turned to leave. Just as he took his first step, a slight figure, drenched to the skin from the cold November rain, drifted into his range of vision.

Lance stood rooted to the spot as his

eyes followed every step the girl took. She walked as though in a trance, not noticing the streams of water that ran down her face from hair that was sopping wet. Nor did she seem to feel the water in her shoes, which made squishing sounds as she walked. Slowly, she made her way toward a portly man standing a few yards from Lance. Her eyes never left the florid face.

"Claire," Lance whispered in disbelief, and his face paled. Then he blinked as though by doing so he could chase the disturbing apparition away.

As he watched in fascinated silence, a sudden chill of apprehension shivered through him, for in her hand the girl carried a pair of scissors. Instantly Lance understood: the young woman had stopped to confront the man she intended to kill.

Her voice was beguilingly soft. It was the voice of a child, lilting, musical. But the words that came from that soft sweet mouth were deadly in their condemnation. And in them Lance heard utter desolation.

"You drunken fool. You killed him. You killed my father. You let him bleed to death and came here to get even drunker."

Before Lance could move, before the accused man could answer, the girl's hand darted and the scissors flashed in the lamplight. Finally, Lance broke the spell that had kept him paralyzed with hope and with fear.

"Claire! No," he hissed, and lunged for the young woman.

But Lance was too late. He had stood mesmerized for too long. The weapon found its mark in the paunchy stomach. The victim's face mirrored shock and disbelief as the point of the scissors pressed heavily into his vest, then penetrated the flesh itself.

As the scissors were pulled out of his body, the man stood gaping at the blood that slowly spread in a widening stain on his expensive vest. He did not see the girl lift her arm, shifting her grip on the deadly weapon, preparing to plunge the sharp point into his throat. Nor did he see the tall, muscular man step between him and the girl.

It was not Lance's habit to interfere in troubles that weren't his own, but he made an exception in the case of this small creature who reminded him so strongly of Claire. It was this striking resemblance that caused him to break a lifelong habit.

The split second in time it took him to reach her seemed much longer as Lance maneuvered to grab the girl's wrist without getting stabbed himself. But there was never any danger of that happening, for the girl was intent only on the man she had come to kill.

As Lance yanked the scissors from her hand, he let out a shrill whistle, which was a signal for help. Zeke and Bart Hubbard turned their heads sharply in the direction of the sound that meant they were needed in a hurry.

Despite their size, the men moved with

all the speed and grace of an alarmed mountain cat. Drinks were left on the table; the whores they had chosen for the night were left sitting in their chairs. Their one mission now was to get to the man who paid them, the man who was also their lifelong friend. Patrons who were unaware of what was happening only a few feet from them were rudely pushed aside as the two men hastened to the bloody scene.

"Get her to the boat," Lance ordered quietly as he gave the girl a shove that sent her sprawling into the arms of Zeke Hubbard.

Neither Zeke nor his brother asked a question or so much as raised an eyebrow. They had no idea what had happened, but they saw the middle-aged man hold a hand to his midsection, and they saw the blood seeping between his fingers. None of that mattered: Lance had given an order and they obeyed without question.

As Lance lowered the wounded man to the floor, Zeke and Bart hustled the unresisting girl out into the pouring rain and made their swift way through treacherous, muddy streets.

The shortest route to their destination took them through the dangerous section of the city known as Sydney Town, an area along the waterfront that was inhabited by a gang of renegades who had come from Australia to make their fortunes. Most of them, though, had found that preying on the weak and helpless was much easier and sometimes more profitable than bending over a creek panning for gold.

As they hurried past the noisy saloons and raucous bordellos, the girl faltered, but before she could fall, Zeke scooped her up in strong arms and carried her past thugs awaiting their chance to encircle the two men burdened by a helpless girl. However, the pistols hanging heavy in the well-worked holsters each man wore discouraged even the most foolhardy, and the three intended victims passed safely from the waterfront.

A few minutes more and they reached a burned-out dock, a stark reminder of the many fires that had ravaged San Francisco in the past. Tied to one of the charred pilings was a rowboat that strained against the rope that held it as it bobbed with each wave of the incoming tide.

Gently, Zeke placed his burden in the small boat and then sat beside her, offering his support should she need it. Bart manned the oars, dipping them into the dark waters of the bay while Raine Louise Colter sat immobile and unfeeling, her hands neatly folded in her lap, unaware of the incessant rain that pelted her uncovered head and of the water in the bottom of the boat that covered her feet to her ankles.

Nor was she conscious of the rain-soaked cape that clung like a shroud to her shivering body. She sat in silent acceptance of her fate. She cared little what happened to her. She only knew that her father was dead—killed by the incompetence of a drunken murderer who dared call himself a physician.

Then her thoughts blurred. She did not know she was being transferred from the rowboat to another vessel that lay anchored far out in the bay, a ship that was almost indistinguishable in the dark of night from the rotting fleet of derelicts that had been deserted by crews seeking their fortunes in the gold fields.

While Zeke took Raine below, Bart hunched deeper into his jacket and kept watch for any sign of pursuit. He saw nothing but the blackness of the water and the beckoning lights along the shore. He sighed forlornly. He had looked forward to a far different night than the one that now stretched before him. Instead of a warm bed and an obliging woman, he would be catching pneumonia looking out for some fool girl Lance had taken a shine to.

But Bart was uneasy. He, too, had gotten a good look at the girl's face. He, too, saw the resemblance to Claire, and he shook his head. He didn't like the situation at all.

Minutes seemed like hours as he waited. The rain increased in intensity as it swept across the deck, sounding the drumbeat of its fury on anything it hit. For a moment Bart listened, sorting out the sounds as the large drops pelted the deck and the hatch covers. He knew which barrels were full and which were empty by listening to the difference in pitch, and he smiled as he heard the changing tune of the empty ones filling with the soft rainwater that would be used for washing both men and clothes.

He hunched his shoulders against the cold and the rain, for both he and his brother Zeke had left their rain gear at the saloon. There had been no time to stop for it once Lance had given them orders.

He cursed silently. It was bad enough that his expensive imported raincoat had been left behind, but his brand-new hat would almost certainly wind up on someone else's head. There wasn't a chance it would still be there when and if he had the opportunity to go back for it.

Then his discomfort was forgotten as his attention focused on the thing he had been waiting for. A shaded lantern, whose light could be seen only from the sea, glowed softly as another small boat approached. Lance nudged the bow of the rowboat against the hull of the larger ship, extinguished the lantern and boarded his vessel without a sound. Stealth had become so much a part of his life that it was as natural as breathing.

As Lance stepped onto the deck, Bart's lips twitched in frustration. Always the cool one, Lance had taken his own sweet time leaving the scene of the stabbing. Not only had he put on his own raincoat, but he had collected his and Zeke's brand-new ones as well. And when he pulled two hats from between the folded raingear, Bart could not help but feel a twinge of envy for the way Lance always handled himself.

"Where's the girl?" Lance asked in the casual tones that were so typical of him.

Bart shrugged. "Where else? In your cabin."

Lance nodded. "Think she'll look like more than a drowned rat when we get her cleaned up?"

Bart decided to chance saying what was on his mind. "Claire always did as I remember."

The subtle change of expression on Lance's face warned Bart that he had stepped onto dangerous territory.

Without another word, Lance headed below, pondering the incident. The saloon where it had occurred was a pleasure palace that raked in a fortune by catering to every perversion imaginable. Its patrons' lust had been heightened by liquor and inflamed by their sensual surroundings and by the skilled whores who serviced them. As the wounded man lay bleeding on the floor, as the smell of blood lay heavy in the air, primitive passions would have been unleashed, and the girl would have gone down like a helpless doe under the vicious charge of a pack of wild dogs. It would have become a game, a game in which each man would have felt compelled to demonstrate the force of his manhood.

He doubted very much that any man would have tried very hard to save a woman who might well be headed for the hangman's noose.

Lance shook his head in disbelief. The girl had not belonged there; that much had been painfully obvious. Not only had she defied the taboos of an increasingly proper San Francisco society, she had actually stabbed a man in the midst of countless witnesses.

She was a fool; that much was certain. There were other ways to kill a man, ways that could not be traced back to the one who had done the killing. But whether the man she had stabbed lived or died made very little difference to Lance. He had plans of his own, and those plans did not include sharing the woman who looked so much like Claire with other men. He shrugged as he admitted the truth to himself. He had interfered, he had rescued the girl only because of her resemblance to Claire.

Lance opened the door to his cabin and only then realized that Bart was right behind him. His pale green eyes narrowed in displeasure, but he said nothing to the younger man who was crowding him more than he liked. What he did with the girl was nobody's business, and Bart had better remember that.

The warmth from the charcoal heater that Zeke had gotten started was beginning to chase the chill from the cabin, but it also filled the room with the unmistakable odor of wool being dried too close to the source of heat.

"Lord, Zeke," he complained mildly, "get that cape away from the heater or we'll all suffocate."

Then, turning to the girl who sat as still and as expressionless as a statue, clutching the blanket Zeke had put across her shoulders, Lance knelt so he could look into her face. Tilting the bowed head up, he stared into the huge emerald eyes. There was no response, and Lance frowned. She'd be no good to him like this.

"Miss," he said quietly. "You're safe here, but we have to know what's going on. Why did you stab that man?"

Slowly and with an effort that was plainly visible to the men, Raine's eyes focused. The soft tone of her voice was coarsened by grief.

"My father and I had just gotten to town from our mining camp. We were going to stay at our usual hotel near Sydney Town, but first we had to get our team to the livery stable and put up our wagon."

A twitching of her mouth was meant to be a smile. "They were as wet as we were, so we had the stable boy rub them down good."

Raine slumped, and Lance caught her before she fell from the straight-backed chair. "Then what?" he encouraged as he supported her.

Raine struggled to recall exactly what

had happened. She closed her eyes and tried to sort out the pictures that crowded her mind.

"Just as we were running from the livery stable to our hotel, two men came crashing out of Jake's saloon shooting at each other. One of the bullets hit my father. With the help of the hotel clerk, I got him to the nearest doctor, who was so drunk he could hardly stand.

"I told him! I told him," she sobbed, "not to touch my father—that I would go for another doctor. But by the time I got back, it was too late. He had already cut the bullet from my father's leg and had left him there to bleed to death unattended. I didn't know where he had gone, but I started to look for him. I looked for a very long time. You know the rest."

There was little Lance could say. It was nothing new. People died under the surgeon's knife all the time. Whether the doctor was actually guilty of botching the job or the girl's father would have died under any circumstances, he did not know.

He studied the huddled figure and wondered if she might not be better off if she could cry out her grief, but the eyes were dry and fevered. Flushed skin stretched taut over the high cheek bones and her shoulders drooped with the effort required to sit up.

As her body convulsed with a violent shiver, Lance looked at Zeke and Bart. "Got to get her out of these wet things. She must have spent hours slopping around in the rain and mud looking for that doctor. Damned fool thing to do."

"Yeah," Bart agreed, "but she did it and now we got trouble."

"More trouble than you know," Zeke commented, and removed the blanket from Raine's shoulders.

Lance blinked in surprise and Bart cursed softly as they both saw the source of Zeke's concern. The blouse that had been soaked through was plastered to her body, revealing the feminine curves of her breasts. It wasn't a kid they had rescued after all, and Lance hid his pleasure.

Bart looked at his brother and pursed his lips. "Well, girl or woman, she needs help and that's for sure. Guess we'll leave it to you, Lance," he stated, only a little ashamed of himself for dropping the delicate matter squarely in his employer's hands. "You got a little sister, at least. Us, we come from a family of boys. We don't know much about takin' care of a female."

A rare smile softened Lance's usually cold eyes at the mention of his sister. Out of habit he looked at Zeke to get his opinion, and Zeke nodded in total agreement. Lance tried not to look smug.

"Guess Bart's right," the older brother concurred, satisfied to leave everything to Lance. "We better get out of here and let you get on with it. At least until we find out if she killed that man or not. No sense bringin' anybody else in on this 'til we know for sure.''

Lance nodded. It suited him just fine. And it didn't matter whether the doctor died or not. Nobody was going to get his hands on this woman, especially not the law. She belonged to him now, and he'd do what he had to in order to hold on to her. He had lost Claire once; he would not lose her again.

"Agreed," he stated. "At least until it's safe to get somebody else to take over." Then, looking at his friends through less than approving eyes, he changed the subject. "And the two of you had better get into dry clothes as well. You look as bad as she does."

"Can't nobody look that bad," Zeke drawled in his dry, humorous way.

But as Lance put his hand to the girl's blouse to unbutton it, and the two brothers turned to leave, Raine made a small sound of protest. "No," she whispered, for the conversation had penetrated her wandering mind. "My father—buried, please. Gold—in the wagon."

Lance steadied her and looked at his friends, who had also understood the plea. "Seems we'll be seein' to a burial. And, Zeke, when the mortician goes for the body have him take a close look at that wound. If the doctor killed a man because of drunkenness it'll be much easier to settle this matter without involving the law—if he's still alive, that is."

Zeke nodded. "I'll take care of it."

Satisfied, Lance turned to Bart. "Search that wagon from one end to the other. There's gold in it somewhere. And if anybody asks, you don't know where the girl got to."

Zeke and Bart understood what was required of them, and they left the cabin each to go his own way. Their assignments would be carried out competently and completely. Nothing would be left to chance.

2

The heavy steps of his two friends receded in the distance, but Lance was unaware of them. His every thought was with the young woman who lay unconscious in his arms, and his eyes devoured the familiar face.

Bending his head to kiss the sweet, soft mouth, he whispered the name of the woman who haunted his dreams. "Claire." It was no more than the soft sighing of the wind, but it drained Lance of his strength and resolve.

Holding the fragile form tighter to him, he pressed another kiss on the unfeeling, unresponding lips, a kiss that became insistent and demanding. "Claire," he moaned as he pressed his cheek hard against hers.

He stood in the middle of the cabin

trembling with emotion, clinging to the girl who had brought so many memories rushing back in a flood of anguish and remorse. Finally, he breathed deeply to cleanse himself of thoughts that surely would drive him mad.

He did not want to release her even though he knew she needed his help. From the moment he had interfered in her affairs, he had made himself responsible for her. Even so, he did not regret his actions. He would do the same thing again.

At last, and with great reluctance, Lance relinquished his burden. Gently he put Raine on his bed, and his arms ached with emptiness. All the yearning and tenderness that he had denied himself for so many years flooded his body with need. His heart yearned for far more than he had allowed himself. Once more Lance felt the faint stirrings of hope as he stood above the girl, studying every line and plane of that hauntingly beautiful face. Then, with unsteady hands, he began to remove the wet, soiled clothing from her small, helpless body.

Though his hands and fingers were large and strong, matching in proper proportion the height and breadth of his muscular build, they were also light and dexterous in their touch. The plain wool skirt presented no problem and was easily discarded. It was not until Lance attempted to remove the wet long-sleeved blouse that clung tenaciously to Raine's skin did the girl moan and try to turn away, but Lance would not allow it.

Almost as though he were handling a child, Lance positioned Raine so that he might balance her against his own body while peeling the troublesome blouse first from one arm and then from the other. It was a frustrating task; it was necessary to change Raine's position several times before the rain-soaked blouse lay like a wet rag on the floor, and he blew out a breath of relief for he had fully expected that he would tear the thin cloth before succeeding in getting it free of her damp and sweet-smelling skin.

It was then that Lance hesitated, not knowing how much more he could endure, for her camisole had become transparent as the wet material molded itself to her breasts, outlining their proud, rounded beauty, the perfection of which was interrupted only by the nipples that hardened under the light touch of his thumb as he unconsciously brushed them in a tantalizing circular motion.

Deliberately, his hand cupped one breast and fondeled the firm yet yielding flesh. He wanted her. He wanted her now. Yet he fought.

Tempted almost beyond endurance, Lance clutched the unconscious girl hard against his chest. His heart raced, and the core of his manhood jerked with the swelling rush of blood that pulsed unrelentingly as it demanded surcease. Rocking back and forth, holding the girl in a grip born of desperation, Lance rode out the surging tide of desire. When it subsided the hissing of his breath being sucked deep into his lungs was the only sound that disturbed the perfect stillness of the cabin as Lance removed the camisole.

Pale green eyes heated with desire. They devoured the woman he held so tightly, and the victory he had won only after a valiant struggle against this terrible temptation crumbled. He clenched his teeth as his body once more reacted to the sight of the woman's partial nakedness, only this time the sight of her bare breasts gleaming with moisture in the glow of the oil lamp taunted and beckoned to him with their beauty.

Slowly, so as to savor the joy more fully, Lance lowered his head to those jutting peaks of palest pink. His tongue touched each one and lingered to taste again. His lips tugged gently, forcing each nipple to grow under his persuasion. His mouth closed around each breast, his teeth barely marking them as he claimed them for his own. No man would ever be allowed to trespass where he had put his mark. She belonged to him, and she would remain his until he decided to let her go. She would renew the past. She would rekindle the flame that had died so many years ago. This girl would be what Claire had never been.

As he fondled and caressed her, as he

buried his face in the hollow of her neck, Raine moaned in her semi-unconscious state, with budding desire, a desire that went deep into her body, where it flicked and sparked and burned her with its fire.

Lance smiled as he heard the soft sound. For now it was enough. And though his resolve was a fragile and tenuous thing, he wanted to wait. He wanted her to come to him for the first time in their marriage bed . . . something Claire had scoffed at.

This time it would be different.

Satisfied that his plans would be fulfilled, Lance continued to disrobe Raine. The petticoat slid to the floor to join the other articles of clothing. Then came the ridiculous ruffled and laced underdrawers. But when Lance slid them down Raine's legs, revealing the silken triangle that was the color of ripened wheat, he feared that their marriage would not come soon enough. He must hurry. He must persuade this young woman to marry him as soon as she recovered her health or all his plans would crumble around him.

Tearing his eyes away from the part of her which held his ultimate joy, Lance concentrated on the contrast between the delicate coloring of her skin and the blackness of the hose that were secured midway up Raine's thighs. He cursed softly. No whore could have been more provocative, and his hands trembled as he traced the soft curves that flowed from the graceful neck to the rounded breasts and then to the narrow waist, which curved again to the barely discernible roundness of her belly to the graceful length of her legs. Slowly, he removed the hose, reveling in the feel of her.

"Jesus," he whispered in the extremity of his distress, but he explored no other part of her body. He did not dare.

Instead he covered her with a quilt and released the tortured breath he had been unaware of holding. She was a beauty, and she was a woman grown. This last fact pleased Lance and brought a gleam of satisfaction to his eyes. He would not have to raise a child to be the woman he wanted. She already was.

As he contemplated the coincidence of her resemblance to Claire, Raine suddenly shuddered against an inner chill. Lance had seen this kind of fever before, and he knew that it would probably get worse before it got better. Despite the blanket, despite the heat filling the cabin, the chill brought on by her illness would invade her body even to the marrow of her bones.

There was one way he could help her and hold what was his at the same time. Having made his decision, Lance bolted the door, turned the lamp low, stripped and slid under the quilt. He cuddled the unresisting woman close against the masculine hardness of his body.

The cabin was in total darkness but for the dim glow of the lamp whose small circle of light barely touched the bed. As he held Raine to him, feeling the heat of her body meld them together as one, Lance allowed his mind to drift back in time to the woman he had so desperately loved, the woman who looked so much like the one he now held in his arms.

Unconsciously, he tucked Raine's body closer into his just as he had done with someone else long ago. He smiled in remembrance as his hand pressed against her buttocks, forcing her tight against his loins. And without conscious thought he caressed her bare back as he buried his face in her damp, clean hair breathing in the special smell of her. He let out a long sigh as his hand slid between the smooth thighs, which he stroked with a gentle touch.

Claire's image loomed large in his mind. The feel and taste of her came back to haunt him again, and Lance's body jerked almost violently, seeking the soft, dark solace that would still the deep needs of his soul.

At that precise moment of pain and physical torment, Raine sighed and snuggled closer to the unknown source of comfort. Her body relaxed even as Lance felt the warning tension mount in his. He fought against the increasing cadence of need, which threatened to gather its forces and surge in uncontrolled passion, a passion that could only be vented on this innocent girl who lay so helpless in his arms.

Lance struggled as he never had before.

He fought back the relentless tide of desire for he was determined to wait, to bind her to him forever by the vows of marriage. It would not be as it had been before.

When the worst of it had passed Lance moved a short distance from the girl and studied her flushed face. Long lashes curled softly and cast their delicate shadows on the smooth, soft skin. The lips, which were gracefully formed, were parted slightly in invitation. The face was serene, and the heat from her fevered body reached out to him, adding to the smoldering fires that might yet consume them both.

Then, without warning, Raine shivered violently against the chill that could not be reached by the heat of fever or by the warmth of the small charcoal stove. She doubled up against the impenetrable cold, trying to curl into a protective ball, and as she did, Lance opened his legs to receive hers between them.

The upward pressure of her thighs against his groin sent a sparking flash of passion through him, and Lance moaned his misery to the empty cabin. He clamped Raine's thighs tightly between his, but he saw and felt only the presence of the woman he had loved.

The apparition vanished as quickly as it had come, leaving Lance weak from his struggle against the woman who still held him captive, bound by a remembered love. Then, almost angrily, he straightened out the girl's legs as his mind clung to reality. She was *not* Claire. Her hair was a little darker, her eyes greener, her body thinner and harder.

The litany of denial that coursed through Lance's brain had a calming effect, and his mind concentrated on the small details of the cabin and on the girl next to him. He sighed as Claire released her hold, and his mind returned from a past that had not lost its sting.

As he relaxed in the warmth of Raine's body, Lance gradually drifted into an uneasy sleep. But Claire haunted even this refuge. And as Raine stirred restlessly against him, Lance shifted positions, forcing a muscular thigh between her legs, pressing hard against her woman's softness, and Claire laughed. In his dream, Claire taunted him.

"No," he sobbed even as he moved to enter the body he had loved and cherished.

Caught tight in Claire's embrace, Lance fumbled with his throbbing, pulsing need. He moaned in surrender as his hardness was drawn deep into Raine's body. He could not resist. He lay helpless, entrapped in the comforting warmth he had thought lost to him forever.

His body twitched with the dream of desire, and he felt only Claire. Then a long-denied anger surfaced, and he took that anger out on Claire. But it was Raine who paid the debt. It was Raine who moaned as Lance thrust to the very depths of her, as he positioned her to accommodate his desires and burrowed deep into her unresisting softness.

And then the anger died, leaving only the gentleness of love. Through her fevered wanderings Raine felt this love and responded. Soft sounds of surrender drifted in the warm air of the cabin. Her body moved in the quiet, tight rhythm of approaching climax. Then she pressed hard against Lance, her fingers brushing lightly against him, as short, desperate sobs of bursting passion that pricked the deepest recesses of her being touched the fragile bubble of Lance's dream. Slowly, reality drifted back to the man who had been held so securely in his lover's arms.

But it was too late, too late to deny his surrender and too late to stem the bursting tide of his seed, which spilled unrestrained into Raine's receptive body. Shuddering under the force of his release, Lance held Raine tight. And he knew that it *was* Raine. The dream was gone. His mind was clear, and he pulled away from the woman he had offended so grievously, the woman he had been determined to take for the first time in a marriage bed.

He was stunned as he recalled the sweet surrender of the woman he held in his arms. Even in her fevered state, she had been touched by the love he had offered her only accidentally, and she had responded.

Unshed tears stung his eyes, and he

clenched his teeth in agony. What he had done was unforgivable. But it was not until Lance slipped from the bed and turned up the lamp that the full consequences of his actions became apparent.

He stared in disbelief at the blood that marked his body. He had punished an innocent, untried child for the sins of Claire Randall.

Fear gripped Lance in its cold, unrelenting hand. Once again Claire had ruined everything. His plans for this girl lay broken like so much shattered glass, for when she regained full consciousness she would know. She would know what he had done while she lay helpless in his care.

Then the pale green eyes glittered as his brain sought a way to circumvent the price he must surely pay for his stupidity and weakness. The answer was clear. Acting with deliberate haste, Lance washed the evidence of his blunder from his own body and then from Raine's. The soiled sheet was stripped from the bed and the quilt was tucked tightly around her.

He stepped back and studied the scene, for the first time noticing the droplets of perspiration that glistened on her skin. The fever was breaking. Had this happened a few minutes earlier, he might well have roused her fully with the force of his passion, but fate had smiled on him. His plan might yet succeed, for the girl would not remember, and there was no longer any visible evidence of his assault upon her. There was only one way she would ever know, and that could be easily remedied. She had responded once, and she would again, but the next time she would be aware.

It was not what Lance had intended. It was not what he wanted, but it was all that was left to him now. He cursed Claire and he cursed himself as he remembered the dream with all its passion and rage, but he knew that he would not give up the woman who had received the love meant for Claire.

"God help me," he whispered to the hollow emptiness of the room as he kept watch over the helpless girl who drifted into a deep and dreamless sleep.

But a subtle change had taken place, a change Lance did not even realize; yet he smiled as he remembered the moment of shared passion. In that moment he had known that it was *not* Claire who clung to him; he had known it was *not* Claire into whom he had spilled the force of his love.

Lance sighed and leaned over the bed. His finger traced the delicate curve of her brow, and he thought that for all her resemblance to Claire, there was something different in that lovely face, something that had not been in Claire's.

3

Lance was dressed and had already disposed of the stained water and the bloody sheet when the knock came on his cabin door. Before he had time to answer, the knob turned as Bart Hubbard pushed at the door. Shifting the burden that bent him almost double under his weight, he stepped back and waited. His eyebrows were raised in speculation, and a small suspicion began to form in the back of his mind. Then he dismissed the traitorous thought.

The door swung open and Bart lurched into the overheated cabin. "Lord," he gasped as he thumped the heavy bundle to the floor, "you tryin' to cook that girl?"

Lance smiled his satisfaction, for Bart had given him the diversion he needed. "Too hot for us, maybe, but it broke her fever. Look for yourself.''

"Later," Bart replied. "Wait'll you see what was in that wagon!"

Without being asked, Bart opened the heavy canvas bag and began to take out numerous smaller pouches. When he had removed almost a dozen he spilled a small amount of the contents from one pouch into his hand. Even in the light from one lamp, the glitter of gold dust was unmistakable.

"And that's not all," Bart continued, bending once more to pull out a long chain made up of nuggets of varying sizes.

Lance stared in fascination as the rope of gold slowly emerged from its hiding place. His eyes marked off each foot of chain as Bart took his time getting to the end of the strand.

When at least three yards of pure gold swung from Bart's hand Lance pursed his lips, contemplating what to do with the treasure that belonged to the girl who was sleeping peacefully in his bed. "Guess we better store it in the assay office as soon as we can. Can't leave it lying around here, not with the kind of men who sail the seas these days," he commented in disgust, referring to the difficulty of finding good men to man the ships. Already he had lost a fourth of his crew to the lure of gold. If he remained here much longer, there would be no crew left for the voyage home. His ship would become just one more derelict rotting along the shore of San Francisco.

Bart nodded in agreement and began to stuff the pouches of dust back in the large canvas bag from which they had come. Before he had finished Zeke strolled through the open door. He was carrying two traveling bags, both of which were stained by mud. "Got these from the clerk at the hotel. Seems he took the girl's luggage in for safekeeping when her father was shot down."

"And the burial?" Lance questioned, anxious to get the remaining details behind him.

"Undertaker's plannin' on puttin' him in the ground at first light if the rain holds off until then. And the girl was right," Zeke continued. "The doctor sliced a vein when he removed the bullet. Cut out a lot more flesh than he should have. The mortician will swear to it, if it comes to that."

"Meanin' the man she stabbed hasn't died yet?"

"Lost a lot of blood, but he'll survive. However," Zeke added innocently, "I did sort of suggest to him that it sure would be a lot healthier for him some place else."

No one had to explain to Lance that Zeke had done a lot more than hint about what would happen to the doctor if he didn't take the suggestion to move on to a friendlier city.

"Be surprised if he's not gone by tomorrow," Zeke concluded.

Tired of the pointless conversation, Bart grumbled, "You want anything else, Lance?"

"Guess not. You might as well get yourself a few hours sleep. And Bart, Thanks. You did a good job. You, too, Zeke," he added, and both men knew they were being dismissed. Zeke added one last bit of information that the usually precise Lance had somehow neglected to ask about.

"Name's Colter. Raine Colter. Father's name was Emmett Colter."

Lance nodded and then waited until his men had closed the door behind them before rummaging through the two valises. The first one, which obviously belonged to the dead man, contained various items of clothing, a few personal papers and two more pokes of dust, which he probably intended to keep out for daily expenses.

The second valise was the one he was looking for. From its jumbled contents he separated a nightdress, a flannel robe and a pair of servicable felt slippers. He draped a dark skirt and white blouse over the chair for future use. Then he sat on the same chair and stared into the sleeping girl's face. "Raine," he said quietly, trying to rouse her from the deep sleep that had replaced the coma that had held her so briefly in its grip, but she was not yet ready to awaken.

So Lance let her sleep for a few hours more until there was no other choice but to rouse the girl. Her fever had subsided, but it was not gone, and as the day wore on, it would rise again. He was not at all sure she should even get out of bed, but he would leave it to her.

When it was time for Raine to wake up Lance put a wet towel to her face and neck. The coolness of fresh water and the dying heat in the cabin served their purpose. She stretched her aching muscles then opened her eyes, and Lance recoiled under the bright, clear reason that shone from them.

For an instant his heart skipped and raced because he was afraid that she would remember. "You feelin' better?"

Raine stared blankly until she remembered. This was the man who had helped her, the man who had knelt by her side before her mind went dark. The dimples that appeared as Raine smiled unnerved Lance. She looked even more like a child now that her pale hair had dried and tumbled wildly over the pillow in tight, deep waves.

"Thank you," Raine answered in the sweet musical tones that somehow made Lance feel uncomfortable. "Thank you for everything."

Her eyes scanned the cabin, and she felt the slight movement of the ship at anchor. The smell of the bay was strong, and though Raine's mind recalled only dimly the outline of the ship in the dark of night, she knew where she was.

Her eyes returned to Lance's face, and she memorized every line and curve of that almost too handsome countenance. Her smile deepened. "I had almost stopped believing."

Lance frowned. He did not understand. "What had you almost stopped believing?"

Guileless eyes locked with his. "In knights in shining armor, of course," she replied softly, ignoring the quick blush of embarrassment that colored Lance's face.

"I don't remember much, but I do know I stabbed the doctor who killed my father, and I remember that I was very sick. You seem to have taken care of everything. You are, indeed, my brave knight."

To avoid having to discuss such a ridiculous notion, Lance ignored the remark. However, he could not help but return her smile, which was probably as sweet as any he had ever seen. "First, you should know that the doctor you stabbed is not dead. As much as you might wish otherwise, he will live. However, he will no longer reside in San Francisco. Also, we've recovered the gold from your wagon, which you asked us to do. And we've taken the liberty of bringing your luggage here. The clerk at your hotel took it in when—" Lance stopped in mid-sentence, cursing himself for a fool, but the girl would have to face up to it. There was no way she could avoid the fact of her father's death.

Raine's eyes closed to hide the pain that flooded them. She had not wanted to talk about her father. She had not yet accepted his death, but she must and she knew it.

With a final shake of her head, a last denial, she raised her eyes and stared into Lance's concerned face.

"I must go," she said wearily and started to get out of bed.

"Wouldn't advise it," Lance drawled in lazy tones. "Especially since you're buck-naked. Besides," he stated firmly, putting his hands to her shoulders, forcing her to stay where she was, "there's no need. I told you we've taken care of everything. You just wait here 'til it's all ready."

Raine's eyes flooded with gratitude as she understood the lengths to which this man had gone for her sake. "You've arranged for my father to be given a decent burial?"

"Couldn't refuse the request of a lady in distress," he quipped, and it was Raine's turn to blush. How very childish she and her girlhood dreams must seem to this man of the world.

"When?" she asked.

"This morning, if the rain doesn't start up again."

"I owe you a great deal, sir," Raine said softly. "Perhaps more than I can ever repay, but at least I can afford the funeral expenses. I won't burden you with that. Lord knows I've been trouble enough," she muttered, and burrowed a little deeper under the blanket so only her head was exposed, for though she tried not to show it, Raine was acutely embarrassed by her state of undress, which her protector had so bluntly pointed out.

"There's nothing to repay," Lance stated as though she already belonged to him. "And I'll take care of the funeral costs."

The puzzled expression on Raine's face warned Lance. She did not remember what had happened to her just hours ago, but if he persisted in actions that took all responsibility from her hands, she'd guess soon enough. He could not afford to arouse her suspicions.

"I don't understand," Raine probed tentatively. "Why should you pay for my father's burial? We're strangers. Do you always do so much for a stranger?"

"No," Lance admitted honestly. "As a matter of fact, I try never to mix in other people's problems."

"Then why mine?" Raine persisted, for there was something here she did not understand and it made her uneasy.

When Lance remained silent the dimples reappeared as Raine smiled away the uneasiness. She chastised herself for doubting the man who had done so much for her. "I don't even know your name."

"It's Randall. Lance Randall, and you must be the only person in San Francisco who doesn't know me or my reason for being here," he answered bitterly.

Raine peered into the self-deprecating eyes and felt a twinge of sympathy. But there was another emotion swirling and taking form in her heart: She was deeply attracted to the handsome man who had helped her in her extremity. And she felt drawn toward him as she never had any other man. She felt a bond between them, and did not know why.

Then she frowned as a more practical matter flashed into her mind. "What time is it? How long have I been here?"

Relieved to have the conversation turned to safer avenues, Lance pulled out his pocket watch. "Almost six in the morning. You've been here about seven hours. My two men, Zeke and Bart, got you aboard ship late last night, and I must say you were a sorry sight. Soaked clean through. I had one devil of a time gettin' that blouse off you."

Lance smiled as Raine blushed. "I'm afraid I've been a great deal of bother, Mr. Randall. I do apologize, but you surely have taken good care of me because I feel so much better. And now," she continued, "if you will be good enough to turn your back, I'll get dressed so I can get on with burying my father."

"We'll escort you," Lance stated flatly, not caring whether his possessiveness frightened her or made her suspicious. "There might be some friends of the doctor who'd take exception to your stickin' him with a pair of scissors."

"I'm really very glad I didn't kill him," Raine admitted slowly, as though testing the truth of her words. "But I'll never forgive him. My father died because of him."

"Your father also died because of the man who shot him," Lance reminded her.

"Yes," Raine responded sadly, and then stared full into Lance's eyes. "You haven't yet told me why you got mixed up in my troubles."

Unable to avoid the question a second time, Lance explained it in terms he would like to believe himself. "There was just something so helpless and so defenseless about you when you dragged yourself into that gambling house. You were soaked to the skin; you looked worse than a drowned alley cat, and something—something I can't explain compelled me to help you."

A gentle smile touched Raine's lips at his foolishness. "Don't you really know what that something is, Mr. Randall? It's called chivalry, sir. And I thank God you were there!"

The soft words of gratitude twisted like a knife in Lance's heart. To her he was a knight in shining armor, a valiant defender, but what would she think when she learned the truth?

Perhaps she would never know. Perhaps he could keep it from her forever. There was no reason he *must* tell her. Not if things worked the way he hoped.

"Thank you," he answered even as the guilt burned like fire in his gut. "I'll try to live up to your opinion of me."

"And now, sir," Raine repeated in laughing tones, "if you would be good enough to turn away, I must get dressed. I see you retrieved my bags—my father's and mine."

Lance turned his back obediently and fumbled awhile with the charcoal heater, trying to forget the sudden tears that had glistened in the girl's eyes when she mentioned her father. It was a heavy burden to be borne on such small shoulders. Then Lance corrected himself. She was small, but she was tough. The body that had fit so obligingly into his may have been skinny, but it was also strong. She was a survivor. She'd make it through the bad times in one piece and be all the stronger for it.

Ignoring the skirt and blouse draped over the chair, Raine rummaged in her bag and pulled out a heavy dark dress that would be more suitable for her father's burial. Holding the quilt around her as best she could, she also searched for an extra set of underwear.

Settling on the edge of the bed, Raine pulled on a pair of hose, then slipped into a pair of lace-trimmed underdrawers. As she stood to pull them up, she saw that her image could be clearly seen in the mirror at the washstand. She cast a furtive glance in Lance's direction, but his head was down. He was not watching her.

Still, Raine was uncomfortable. He might look up at any moment. She turned her back to the mirror and then laughed softly. "I know you must think me foolish," she commented as she buttoned the waist of her drawers and slipped the camisole over her head, "to be so bashful, especially since you're the one who got me out of my wet clothes in the first place."

"Did strike me as a mite humorous," Lance bantered, "though I expect a gentleman wouldn't bring the matter up."

"No sir, I don't expect he would," Raine agreed pointedly as she adjusted the lace-trimmed petticoat and then wriggled into the heavy dress.

"You may turn around now," Raine announced a little too primly, and Lance understood the extreme shyness of this girl who had gone through so much in so short a time.

He watched in silence as Raine struggled to find the right words. Her eyes were downcast, and more than fever heightened the color in her cheeks.

"I don't—I can't—" she faltered, and then sighed heavily before looking directly at Lance.

"Thank you. I am so grateful that it was you who took care of me. I am not so naive that I do not know I could have been in very serious trouble with a man who possessed less honor than you. I cannot begin to repay you, but if there's ever anything I can do for you, anything at all, it would give me great pleasure to oblige."

Only the brief flicking of his eyes hinted at Lance's discomfort, for her faith and her belief in him reawakened a conscience that had been all but dormant for many years. He was tempted, but only briefly, to tell her the truth. But the truth would destroy all his plans. "You're entirely welcome, ma'am, but I think you don't owe me a thing. And now, if you'll excuse me, I'll have my men get to shore and make certain everything will be ready when we get there."

"Mr. Randall," Raine said hesitantly, for she hated to ask any more favors of the man who had already done so much for her. "Would you be good enough to have your men take my belongings ashore with them? I must find lodgings, for I cannot impose on you forever."

The wistful smile on Lance's face made Raine look away. For some reason her presence was causing her benefactor a certain amount of discomfort. And she certainly did not trust her own emotions where he was concerned. Raine almost laughed at herself as she admitted reluctantly that her heart nearly turned flip-flops every time she looked at him. For this, if for no other reason, she must leave as soon as possible.

"You're not imposin' ma'am. And I wouldn't think of lettin' you fend for yourself just yet. You're better all right, but you're still not well. Will you trust me a little longer?"

Some premonition warned Raine that

she would be putting her future into this man's hands if she agreed. "Yes, Mr. Randall," she answered, unafraid.

Before Lance could say anything more, Raine put her hand to her mouth to stifle a cough. Her throat suddenly felt very scratchy, and she coughed again. This time the cough came from deeper in her chest.

She sank weakly to the bed as a brief spell of dizziness made her head swim. The fever was rising, but it was much less fearsome than the one that had so debilitated her last evening. Still, it *was* there, and her bones ached. Even her eyes hurt. And there was a persistent though vague discomfort in her abdomen and private parts. It was almost as though her period were about to begin. She sighed and hoped not, for she had enough problems to deal with.

"You see!" Lance remarked with concern. "You're far from well. Can't we put this burial off for a few days?"

"No," Raine answered stubbornly. "It must be done now. Please," she begged, "we must give him a proper burial *now*. I can't bear to think of him lying all alone in some undertaker's workroom."

There was no use arguing with the girl. Lance agreed, knowing full well that he should keep her bundled up in bed instead of allowing her to go out in nasty weather. "We'll do it your way," he sighed in resignation. "Wait here. I'll be back as soon as I can," he promised as he gathered a few pieces of clothing so he, too, would make a presentable appearance at the funeral. "Is there anything I can get you? Some hot coffee, maybe?"

"No thank you, Mr. Randall. I really don't want a thing." Then, impulsively, she put her hands to Lance's face. "Thank you. For my father and for myself."

Lance turned away abruptly. Those large, trusting eyes defeated him. "I'll be back for you in a few minutes," he assured her before ducking his head so he could get through the doorway.

Raine watched as the door closed behind him. She sat motionless for several minutes, wondering why she was so certain that Lance Randall was going to play an important role in her life. A soft smile curved her lips as she began to brush her hair.

4

It did not take Raine long to bring her hair under control. As she looked at herself in the mirror and patted the tamed tresses, she hoped the rain, which had stopped sometime during the night, would hold off until her father could be buried. Mr. Randall's men had already left the ship to see to the digging of the grave, and Raine knew she must take advantage of even the briefest break in the weather, for she could not bear to think of her father being lowered into a grave that was filling with water.

The wrenching sob that pushed past her clenched teeth told little of the depth of her distress. She was a continent away from any remaining family, and while she had more than enough money to make the journey east, she had no desire to do so. It was not a loving family that waited for her. It was a hateful family, one that had disowned her mother when Jennifer Raine had dared elope with Emmett Colter, a man considered to be far beneath her station. The despicable old man who was her grandfather would not be glad to see her, nor would he welcome her presence in his house. He had made that clear years ago.

Raine put a handkerchief to her mouth to stifle the cough that was growing ever more painful. It was a deep, wrenching cough that tore at her chest. And, again, the fever was rising. She could feel the heat building, and there was dampness all along her hairline. Her knees were weak, and she was exhausted from the effort it had taken to get herself ready. Instinctively, her fingers touched the small white collar of the dark dress that had served her well enough for the occasional camp service her father had reluctantly attended with her.

Raine smiled as she remembered his grumping. Her father had not been a religious man, and therefore never attended services unless badgered into it. But when she had become a woman, his attitude had changed and he had accompanied her wherever she went, for he had not trusted the miners who were woman hungry and not above making cow-eyes at her even during a camp service.

For the last few years of his life, he had

watched over her like a hawk, chasing away the rough, usually good-natured miners who had seen her grow from a spindly legged girl to a woman who could no longer run around in torn britches or dresses that often went askew, showing her underdrawers. That brief time of comradeship had passed all too quickly. The easy familiarity was gone. Even the jovial Frenchmen from a camp north of her father's had treated her differently once she had passed from childhood to womanhood. The transition had been a difficult one, and she had resisted the change.

Suddenly Raine's mind took a sharp turn. She had found her answer. It was so obvious she wondered why it had taken her so long to think of it. She would return to the camp. Her father's partners would buy out his share of the digs and she could continue to live in the cozy cabin she and her father had shared.

There were miners without women who needed someone to bake and cook and wash for them. She had done it in the past and she could do it again. But best of all, she would be among people she loved and trusted. She felt a heavy weight lift from her shoulders. She had somewhere to go after all.

Another spasm of coughing racked her body and again Raine pressed her handkerchief to her mouth. Her head ached and her throat was sore.

She plopped back down on the bed and permitted herself the luxury of feeling miserable. Then she groaned and pushed herself up. She was not quite ready to do what must be done.

Rummaging in her valise, she shook out the knitted shawl, folded the square into a triangle and draped the warm piece of wool over her head and shoulders. It was the best she could do, for the cape she usually wore was still damp, and it smelled awful. Raine wished she owned a hat or at least a mourning veil. Then she wondered why such a little thing was important. Her father would not care that she wore a simple shawl. Nor would he care that she was not dressed in a proper mourning gown. He would know how deep her grief ran, and he would know how sorely she missed him.

Barely able to contain the tears that were dangerously close to the surface, Raine drew in a deep breath to calm herself. She would not shame her father by weeping hysterically as she had seen some do at funerals. If there was one thing her mother had taught her, it was dignity, and she was quite determined to keep her feelings locked inside until she could find the privacy she needed. Despite her feelings of inadequacy, Raine Colter squared her small shoulders and gathered her resolve.

The soft knock at her door threatened to destroy her determination to move through this nightmare with dignified calm. She was not ready. She would never be ready, and the quick tears that sprang to her eyes made a mockery of all her good intentions. She buried her face in her hands. The time had come, the time she dreaded, the time to lower her father into the ground.

Fighting back the terrible ache in her heart, Raine lifted her head. "Come in," she rasped hoarsely.

Lance stepped in and frowned. She looked terrible, and the cough was worse. "Don't you think you should postpone this until you're better?"

Raine knew that she could not go through this again. She shook her head. "No. I must get it done so I can get back to camp before winter really sets in. The high passes are already blocked by snow," she remarked absently, and Lance looked at her sharply.

He was stunned by her careless disregard for her own life. First there had been the open attack on a man in front of a dozen witnesses. Now she would risk the dangerous trails in this time of rain that caused mud slides, flooding, starvation and death. Surely she could not have forgotten so soon the tragedy of last winter's rains. Besides, he could not allow her to leave. If she did, all his plans would be ruined.

Lance protested. "You can't live in a miner's camp by yourself. I won't hear of it!"

Raine smiled forlornly. "Do you have a better suggestion, sir?"

Almost afraid to look at her for fear that she might read his mind, Lance studied the tip of his boot. "Maybe. Just maybe I do," he drawled slowly. And, indeed, it was true, for Lance Randall was determined that Raine Colter would never leave for the mining camp. He could not allow her to go unmarried much longer. If the gods were with him, he might yet carry it off.

He looked into Raine's quizzical eyes and waved the topic aside. "We'll talk about it later."

Raine accepted the delay without question. "Shall we go?" she asked only out of politeness, for she had already started for the door.

Laughing to himself, Lance followed obediently. She might be a little thing, but she had a mind of her own. Courage too. As sick as she was, she was determined to get her father in the ground. She would expose herself to the damp and the chill when she could barely hold her head up.

"Little idiot," he murmured, not unkindly.

Helping Raine into the long boat, Lance sat next to her as the sailors bent their backs to the task of rowing them ashore. The weather was growing ever more threatening, and Lance knew that if they didn't hurry, the burial would take place in a downpour.

The sailors doubled the cadence of their strokes, for they had no real liking for standing around in the cold November rains with their clothing drenched and their boots ruined by mud just to attend the funeral of some man they didn't know. However, they would not complain in front of the man who paid them good wages whether they worked or not. They were pulling easy duty and were being paid for doing little more than seeing to the safety of the ship.

They were relieved when Lance dismissed them as soon as the boat nudged the pilings of the dock. He did not expect them to stand in the rain while a coffin was lowered into the ground. With a grateful, smiling salute, the men headed for the welcome pleasures of Sydney Town while Lance hurried to the funeral carriage that was waiting for them. The closed hearse that carried the casket had already started for the cemetery.

So had the undertaker. Bart and Zeke were also at the graveyard waiting for Raine, who would be the last to arrive. The grave was dug and Lance was sure that every other detail had been taken care of. Even so, he doubted that the rain would hold off long enough to get Emmett Colter buried.

Entering the livery stable and helping Raine into the black carriage pulled by plumed horses, Lance instructed the driver to make all possible haste, but the first large drops of rain began to fall even as the horses jolted them through the cemetery gate.

By the time they reached the newly dug grave where the coffin was waiting to be lowered, it was pouring. Bart, Zeke and the undertaker stood in a forlorn group as the rain pelted their umbrellas. Helping Raine from the carriage, Lance held her close to him so his own umbrella would cover them both, but it was a driving rain with a strong wind behind it and in a matter of seconds they were both drenched from the waist down.

When they joined Zeke and Bart the two men closed in on the side from which the wind was blowing, offering Raine as much protection as they could while the mortician, in lieu of a preacher, spoke in dolorous tones. The man cut the service short and signaled for the plain wooden box to be lowered into the grave.

Before the men who had dug into the raw earth could obey, Raine broke free of Lance's supporting arm and threw herself across the coffin that held all that was left of her father. She wept bitterly.

For six years there had been only the two of them. Now she was alone. He was gone and she was devastated. She poured out all her grief and all her fears. "Papa, Papa," she sobbed broken heartedly.

Then, obeying the gentle but firm pressure at her elbow, Raine stood and leaned heavily against Lance, who half-carried her to the carriage. Huddling in the far corner with her head bowed and her ungloved hands folded in her lap, Raine shivered from more than the cold as she struggled for control. She was painfully aware of what a fool she had just made of herself. Her mother would be so ashamed of her. Jennifer Raine Colter, born and bred in one of the great houses of Philadelphia, would never have approved of such an unseemly display of emotions in public.

"I'm sorry, Mama," she sobbed softly. Then as the grief and the fever overwhelmed her, Raine's mind began to wander. She saw her mother's beautiful face smiling at her, and then she saw her father walking toward her mother. The two of them embraced, waved good-bye, turned and walked away.

"No!" Raine screamed in anguish. "No. Papa—Mama! Wait! Please—wait. Don't go," she sobbed.

Then her voice trailed off and the tear-streaked face that reflected her unbearable grief became serene as she collapsed under the burden that was too heavy to endure. As she slumped, unconscious, Lance moved to her side. Removing his raincoat, he spread it over the young woman who had escaped from the world.

Holding her securely in his arms, Lance thumped his umbrella against the driver's seat. "Hurry up, driver," he shouted above the sound of the wind and the rain, but the man needed no urging. Shrouded in his oilskins, protected by the waterproof hat that spread cloaklike around his shoulders, he flicked his whip above the horses' heads, and the animals broke into a run, heading for the warmth of their stalls and the comfort of a full feedbag.

When the carriage careened around a corner in the more populous area of San Francisco Lance thumped again and ordered the driver to stop at the Parker House. He considered it to be the best place for Raine at the moment. She simply could not endure the trip in an open boat that would be necessary to get her back to his ship. She was much too ill, and Lance blamed himself for allowing her to venture out in the cold rain of November. No matter what she had wanted, he should have put his foot down.

The instant the driver brought the horses to a halt, Lance scooped Raine from the seat and carried her into the well-appointed lobby. He sat on a settee, supporting her, until Zeke and Bart, who had followed in a carriage of their own, strode through the front door, shedding their expensively tailored raincoats.

Lance looked to Zeke for help. "Hire a suite, the best one they have available. And I hate to ask, Bart," he continued, shifting his gaze to the younger brother, "but see if you can find a good doctor. She's going to need one."

"No problem," Bart answered good-naturedly, for he had shed a few tears himself when Raine had collapsed over her father's coffin. "Damn shame," he added sympathetically and headed back out into the driving rain.

Just as Bart had departed on his errand, Raine opened her eyes. She was weak and barely able to push herself upright, but she was determined to do so, for it was embarrassing in the extreme to be held in a man's embrace in public—especially with so many people staring at her.

Expending what little strength she had left, Raine perched primly on the edge of the couch, and it was then that she became aware of her deplorable condition. The skirt of her dress was wet and muddy. She would ruin the delicate fabric of the lovely settee. "Where are we?" she inquired as her surroundings finally registered.

"The Parker House," Lance answered as he crossed his long, powerful legs and relaxed. Raine was sitting as straight as a ramrod, and the effort was costing her the last bit of energy she possessed, but she was carrying it off and he respected her for trying to retain dignity under impossible circumstances. His mother would have done the very same thing. It was apparent that Raine had also been reared by someone who had instilled in her the iron will possessed by all great ladies.

Then he smiled. She was too young yet to have mastered the absolute control his mother had. She was more like a small bird, still flopping around in the nest, still learning all she must know to survive among those of her own kind.

"I thought you would be much more comfortable here," Lance explained as Raine frowned in confusion. "And until you're well I think you should be much closer to a doctor than you would be if you returned to my ship."

Raine's mind was swimming. She could not concentrate. Her head bobbed dangerously, but she jerked it up and stared straight ahead without seeing anything. Then she closed her eyes as a great wave of nausea washed over her. A soft moan escaped her lips as she struggled to stay awake until Lance showed her what she was supposed to do.

At that moment Zeke walked toward them and presented a room key to Lance. "Presidential suite," he said, and smiled at the unlikely thought of any president risking the trip to California.

Lance took the key and stood waiting for Raine to make the effort required of her. She had struggled so courageously to maintain her dignity that Lance could do no less than give her the chance to see it through. He would not turn her hard-won victory into defeat by lifting her into his arms and carrying her to her room.

Raine was so weak she wasn't sure she could stand. She gathered all her strength and pushed herself up from the sofa until she stood wobbling, waiting for Lance to tell her what to do next. Her eyes were unfocused as she looked up at him, and Lance took her arm, tucking it under his. "We're going upstairs now. Can you make it?"

Totally unable to make an intelligent decision, Raine nodded. ''Yes,'' she whispered weakly and took a step forward as Lance increased the supportive pressure under her arm and kept pace with the agonizingly slow progress as she put one uncertain foot in front of the other.

When they reached the stairs Lance made sure Raine was on the railing side so she could use it to steady herself. With deliberate and measured steps, Raine made her way painfully to the second floor, where Lance turned her to the left, put his arm around her waist and assisted the all but unconscious girl to the Presidential suite.

''One more step,'' Raine thought as she struggled against the enfolding dark. ''Just one more step,'' she whispered, and fainted.

As she folded toward the floor, Lance tightened his grip and held her against him until he fit the key in the lock and opened the door. ''Come on, little girl,'' he said softly, and picked her up in his arms.

Once inside the room, Lance pushed the door shut with his foot and placed his light burden on the sofa. Walking into the bedroom, he splashed a little water into the basin and wet a towel. Returning to Raine, he sat next to her, leaned her against him and put the cooling cloth to her forehead.

Struggling to open her eyes, Raine looked up into Lance's face. She wanted to say something, but she couldn't remember what. Finally, after concentrating for what seemed an eternity, she thought of it. "My clothes," she whimpered, for she had intended to return to the ship just long enough to collect her belongings and then rent a room in the hotel where she and her father had always stayed when in San Francisco. She had caused enough trouble. She had inconvenienced Lance far beyond the realm of propriety. And what was worse, she had become a nuisance. Even her handsome, chivalrous knight must be tired of her and her troubles by now. And that was the last thing she wanted.

"Shh," Lance soothed. "We'll take care of everything. In the meantime I know someone who might let you borrow some things until we can get your valises to you."

"Yes, please," Raine whispered through the increasing soreness of her throat, and then she began to weep.

"I'm sorry," she apologized abjectly as she struggled to control the tears. "I don't know why I'm doing this. Mama certainly would not be pleased," she rambled, and Lance frowned with growing concern. The fever was affecting her now. Soon she would be incoherent.

Where in the hell is that doctor? he wondered silently. Aloud, he simply stated the obvious. "I've got to get you out of that dress. You're running a fever again and we must get you dry and warm."

Raine nodded. She really couldn't comprehend what Lance was saying, but whatever it was it was all right with her. She felt safe and she knew that Lance would take care of her. She sighed and wondered what she would do without him, and when she looked up into his face her eyes spoke more clearly than words. Trust and a childlike adoration radiated from them. "Yes, help me," she requested with absolute faith in the man who held her.

Stunned by the love that reached out to him from that lovely face, Lance blinked once as he fought the wave of guilt that threatened to overwhelm him. His hand trembled as he unbuttoned the heavy wool dress and slipped it from her body. The bottom of the petticoat was soaked. The camisole and underpants, however, were dry, so they stayed, but the ruined shoes and the hose had to go.

When he was finished Lance propped her up in the corner of the sofa and hurried to the other room, where he turned back the bed. Then he returned for Raine, settled her in the bed, adjusted the pillows under her head and covered her.

Not five minutes later, just as Raine was dozing off, Dr. Redding, a recently retired army surgeon, entered the room. From what he understood from the man who had summoned him, the girl was critically ill, but the symptoms he observed seemed to suggest little more than a good old-fashioned chest cold. She was running a fever, but a good dose of willow bark tea would fix that.

Then, as he put the stethoscope to her chest and back, he frowned as he heard the congestion gathering in her lungs. Blowing out a concerned breath, he took a bottle of vile-looking liquid from his bag. "See that she takes two spoons of this every three hours. Give her all the willow-bark tea she'll drink. We'll also need one of those new-fangled vaporizers. Just bought a couple from a drummer. Never thought I'd get any use out of them, but if what he says is only half true, it might do the trick. Think you can run back to my office and get one? I'll also need the creosote," he continued without waiting for an answer. "Ask my wife for it. She knows where I keep everything."

"And your address?" Lance asked.

"Montgomery Street. Can't miss it. There's a big white sign out front."

"I'll be back as quickly as I can. Give her whatever she needs," Lance said as he looked down at Raine. "The cost doesn't matter."

Dr. Redding gave Lance a disgusted look. "I'm a physician, sir. The oath I took said I was to heal the sick. It said nothing of caring only for those who could pay."

Lance inclined his head in a silent apology, then walked from the room, stopping in the lobby only long enough to talk to Zeke, who had waited to see if he would be needed. Lance got straight to the point. Zeke was to ask Tess, one of the women who worked in the pleasure palace where he had first seen Raine, to come to the hotel.

"Ask her to bring some suitable night-clothes. Then get back to the boat and bring everything of hers here."

"The gold too?" Zeke asked uneasily, for so much money should be put in a safe place, and they never had gotten it to the assay office.

"The gold too," Lance confirmed. "I want everything she owns off the ship. She's not to go back there."

Zeke pursed his lips but said nothing. He suspected his friend didn't quite trust himself with the girl. Not alone with her in his cabin, at any rate. *My, my, my*, he thought as speculative eyes searched Lance's face for a clue to the truth. Just maybe his companion and employer was falling in love. But it wasn't good. She looked too much like Claire.

Not the least concerned that he was being sent back out into the vilest weather he had encountered since arriving in San Francisco, Zeke nodded and went his way. Soon after, Lance slapped the wide-brimmed hat back on his head, hunched inside his raincoat and followed. He hurried to Montgomery Street and immediately spotted the large white sign swinging from its crossbar.

His urgent knock was answered by Mrs. Redding, who knew exactly what Lance was talking about. She went directly to her husband's office, where she opened a large drawer at the bottom of a tall cupboard with glass doors. Handing Lance a tripod complete with pan and a small oil lamp that had been sized to fit under the pan, she unlocked one of the glass doors and took out a jar of cresote. "This goes in the pan," she instructed. "Try to keep the fumes contained so they do the girl some good. Some folks use blankets to form a kind of tent over the bed. That's best if you can manage it. New-fangled gadgets," she humphed in indignation.

"Thank you, ma'am," Lance replied, cutting her short, and hurried out into the street. Within minutes he was back in Raine's bedroom, watching carefully as the doctor demonstrated what his wife had already explained.

"Think you can handle it, son?" Dr. Redding asked.

"I understand what to do," Lance confirmed, "but I'd better get more blankets if I'm to make the tent your wife suggested."

"Be a good idea," the doctor agreed. "My Sarah has probably nursed more sick folks than I have. Whenever I'm not sure about a treatment, I always listen to her advice. Her mother was a granny lady back in the Appalachians, and I've learned over the years not to argue with something my wife says will work. Including cobwebs," he added, grinning broadly.

Lance smiled and dropped a mixture of

coins into the doctor's hand. There were several English shillings, a Mexican double real and a Peruvian doubloon. To the pile he added a twenty-five-dollar gold slug minted by the assay office. "That should cover the vaporizer and your services," Lance explained. "Mrs. Redding didn't ask for any money."

Doctor Redding laughed. "She never does. Still thinks a chicken or a bag of potatoes is payment enough. One of her biggest faults."

Lance studied the trim, wiry man who was at least thirty years his senior and nodded in understanding. Neither the doctor nor his wife worried about money. They did what they could for those who needed them and got by on whatever money came their way. They were a far different breed from most of the physicians in this town, who charged exorbitant fees for even the simplest of remedies.

Lance held out his hand. "Thank you, doctor."

Dr. Redding's blue eyes twinkled as he grasped the large, powerful hand in his smaller one. It was nice to be appreciated *and* paid, both at the same time. "If she takes a turn for the worse, come for me. And don't delay. Everything depends on whether she has the strength to fight. If the fluid continues to build up in her lungs, I'm afraid there's little more we can do, so keep that vaporizer going. I'll be back in the morning unless you need me sooner.''

Stunned, Lance stood rooted to the spot as he watched the doctor leave. He had known that Raine was far from well, but he had had no idea that he could lose her, that she could die.

The thought terrified him. She could just slip away from him and there was precious little he would be able to do about it. He would lose Claire a second time.

''No,'' he muttered between clenched teeth, and he fretted as the vaporizer began to send its vile fumes into the air, for they were dissipating. They would do no good if they weren't contained. ''Damn,'' he cursed as he waited for Tess. He couldn't leave Raine alone while he went for extra blankets to construct the tent Mrs. Redding had described to him.

Finally the knock came, and Lance opened the door to admit a statuesque red-haired woman. The light from the lamps on the walls accentuated the lines in her face, but skillfully applied powder and rouge hid the signs of dissipation. She was still a handsome woman.

''Glad you're here, Tess. I can use your help.''

Tess heard the anxiety in the usually unconcerned voice, and she bit her lip, for she had never seen Lance concerned over anyone. Now it was painfully clear that he had met a young lady who could make him care very deeply about what happened to her.

She brushed Lance aside and walked directly into the bedroom. Zeke had already told her what to expect, and he had been right. The child who lay so ill was almost lost in the large four-poster bed, but even in the flush of fever she was a beauty, and it was obvious that someone had arranged her hair carefully around her face.

Dropping the valise she had brought with her to the floor, Tess put her hand to the girl's forehead and listened to the labored breathing even as the stinging tears of painful loss filled her violet eyes. Taking a deep breath to ease the ache in her heart, Tess turned her full attention to the young woman whose eyes were closed in something much deeper than normal sleep as she labored to breathe in the life-giving air.

"She looks mighty sick. Had the doctor in?" she asked as Lance hovered over the patient, tucking her in and once more smoothing the hair from her fevered face.

"Dr. Redding," Lance confirmed. "He left medicine and instructions for her care, but I want a woman looking after her, Tess, and I need someone I can trust. I took care of her last night, but I can't do all that needs doin'. Not without embarrassing her to tears."

Some odd, indefinable inflection in

Lance's voice caused Tess to narrow her eyes in a shrewd guess. Zeke had pretty well explained how the girl had gotten here, but he had said little more. As far as Tess was concerned he didn't have to. Lance had slept with this woman. But when? From what Zeke had said, the girl had been sick from the first moment they had run into her.

No, she thought, trying to deny the only conclusion she could reach. But she had to admit it was entirely possible, for this man who could not keep his hands off the girl, who always had to be touching her, tucking her in, smoothing her hair, was not the Lance Randall she knew. This was a man in love. This was a man who was warm and giving, a man totally opposite from the one who had bought her services on several occassions. That man had been aloof, reserved. He had always held something of himself back, even when making love. And now? Tess's smile lay bitter on her lips. Now he was a man who would not be visiting her again.

But that was all right. He had always treated her right, had always been square with her. Right from the beginning, and that was more than she could say about most of her customers.

Shaking herself free from the thoughts that were too painful, Tess asked, "You gonna be bunkin' in here or what?"

"No," Lance answered too quickly and

too emphatically. "I've got to get some blankets to make a tent over her bed, but after that I'll be renting a room for myself."

"Well, why don't you go on then. I'll watch her 'til you get back."

"Yeah," Lance answered absently. "The doctor's wife said the fumes from the vaporizer had to be contained. She's got to breathe them in to fight the congestion in her lungs."

"The sooner you go, the sooner you'll get back," Tess suggested mildly, and Lance grinned at the woman who, if nothing else, was always practical.

"Be right back," he promised, and then hurried from the room.

Tess settled herself comfortably in a chair and watched the young woman who struggled to breathe. She wrinkled her nose at the foul-smelling steam that was rising from the pan and could not see how anything that smelled so bad could do much good. Then her thoughts drifted as she studied the girl's face. She had been that pretty once. Her skin had been as clean and as clear. A twinge of regret pulled her thoughts back to her patient, and Tess smiled as she studied the long lashes that curved gently, casting soft shadows on the flawless skin. The nose was straight and well formed; the brows soared gracefully like the wings of a gull. The chin was firm, the cheek bones high and prominent. And the mouth. The mouth was—Tess searched for a word.

Tempting, she thought. A man only had to look at that mouth and he would need to try it, to possess it. *Yes, tempting's the right word.*

Sighing with regret, Tess walked to the washstand and soaked a towel in water. When she had wrung it almost dry she returned to the bed and placed the cooling cloth on Raine's forehead. Then she sat and waited for Lance to return. When he did she helped tie the ropes to the posts of the bed and drape blankets over and around the girl.

Lance pulled the small table closer to the bed and lifted one of the blankets over it so that it would be inside the makeshift tent. While he was occupied, Tess opened the valise she had brought with her and pulled out a nightgown and robe.

"Nice little filly you've got there," she remarked when he emerged from the tent.

Lance knew she was asking a question, but there was nothing he wanted to say about the situation. "A mite young." He laughed. "No experience to speak of."

There it was. Whether or not he realized, Lance had just admitted to having slept with her. Of course she had no experience to speak of. The girl probably didn't know that he'd started breaking her in. It was an old trick, especially with the more reluctant girls. They were simply drugged. When they came to it was over. Instead of drugs, Lance had taken advantage of the girl's illness. There would be no going back for her. The man who had been so generous with her had found the woman he wanted. And he was going to make sure he got her.

Upset about what she was thinking, Tess inserted what she thought of as humor. "Give her to me," she teased. "She'll get all the experience she'll ever need. Pretty little thing like that? Lot of men anxious to show her the ropes. If she plays her cards right, she could be rich in a year."

Lance's reaction confirmed Tess's suspicions. He was not amused. His pale eyes flicked over her, and there was no doubt what would happen if she introduced the girl to the life she, herself, had led since she had been fourteen. "What she needs, I'll give 'er," Lance said softly, but Tess heard the threat behind the words.

"Kind of touchy on the subject, aren't you, honey?"

"Yeah," Lance admitted, and his face was hard. When he said no more Tess understood that the subject was closed, and she waved him away.

"Why don't you go? I'll look out for her, but you've got to be back by tonight. I've still got a living to make. Nobody's touchy about what I do," she said, and Lance heard the trace of regret in her voice.

"How much you figure you'd earn tonight?" he asked.

The older woman stared straight into Lance's eyes." Are you in love?"

Lance was not pleased with Tess's continued prying, and he hated the way she could cut through to the truth of his feelings, but he needed her, so he would step lightly for the moment. "If you want to earn twice what you'd earn at work tonight, you won't ask any more questions. You're a good woman, Tess, one I'd trust with most anything I owned, but this is personal."

"If you're asking because you want me to stay with her, it'll cost you ten ounces of gold for every twenty-four hours I'm here. Agreed?"

"Agreed," Lance said. He felt lucky. A hundred sixty dollars in dust wasn't too much to have Tess watch over Raine. No amount would have been too much. Besides, Tess wasn't like a lot of her kind. She had class. She didn't drink, so she wouldn't get drunk while she was supposed to be looking after Raine, and she'd earn her money fair and square just as she had always done.

"You want the money in slugs or dust?"

"Slugs will do. Not as awkward as dust. Now don't you worry. She's going to be all right. Look who she's got waiting for her."

Lance looked into the face of the woman who surely had been a great beauty a few years back and hoped she hadn't guessed too much. Lifting her hand to his lips, he pressed a light kiss on it and spoke what to him was the truth.

"You're a good woman, Tess. Too

damned good for most of the men you know.
Myself included. Don't ever let anybody tell
you different.''

An almost radiant smile touched the
whore's face as world-weary eyes followed
Lance's every move until he disappeared
behind the closing door.

5

Raine mumbled incoherently as fever-induced hallucinations crowded her unconscious mind. She thrashed about, throwing off all the covers. Once, the lamp that warmed the evil-smelling liquid in the vaporizer was knocked over, and Tess barely had time to retrieve it before it could do any damage.

"Damn," she muttered in fright. "One thing this town doesn't need is another fire."

After that experience Tess tied Raine's left hand to the frame of the bed with a piece of leftover rope. She couldn't risk having the lamp knocked over again. It was just too dangerous in a town that still had more than its share of ramshackle wooden structures.

When Bart knocked on the door Tess hurried to the other room and opened it, putting her finger to her lips. "That her stuff?" she asked, nodding toward the valises and the seaman's bag with which Bart was struggling.

"Yeah," he answered, easing the duffel bag containing the gold to the floor. "Where you want her clothes?"

"In the bedroom. Just set them down inside the door..I'll sort it all out later."

"How is she?" Bart inquired as he straightened up after shoving the valises against the bedroom wall. To him the bed hidden by blankets was ominous.

"Can't say for sure. Doctor's been here. That's about all I know."

"Anything I can do to help?" he asked, and when Tess shook her head no, he continued. "Tell Lance that Zeke and I will be aboard ship keepin' an eye on things if he wants us. We'll be back tomorrow to see if he needs us for anything."

Tess nodded and followed Bart to the door. After he had gone she returned to her patient. Pulling back a blanket, Tess made sure Raine was still breathing. She checked the vaporizer and added a little more water to the pan. Then she settled back in the chair to wait. It was all she could do until it was time to give Raine another dose of medicine.

As long hours dragged by, Raine seemed to sink deeper into unconsciousness, and

the rattle in her throat became more pro-
nounced. Twice Tess was barely able to
rouse her enough to administer the required
dosage of medicine, and when Lance returned she heaved a sigh of relief.

"I think you ought to get the doctor back
here," Tess suggested, trying to keep her
voice steady, but her eyes betrayed her fear.
"Christ, Lance, I don't think she's going to
make it."

Lance stiffened. She was not going to
die. Pale green eyes glittered with determination. "She'll make it. If I have to breathe
life into her, she'll make it."

The underlying fury in his voice brought
Tess up short, and she knew when to
change course. "Sure she will," Tess agreed
soothingly. "Want me to stay, or will you
take over now?"

Lance did not take his eyes off Raine. He
stood breathing in the vile vapor, holding the
blanket back, just studying the girl who had
gotten worse. The red spots of fever rode
high on her cheeks and her breathing came
with difficulty.

"I think she's gonna need you a while
longer, and you're right. If anything, she's
worse. I'll get Dr. Redding, but before I do,
help me prop her up. When I move her you
put the extra pillows behind her back."

When Raine was resting comfortably
against the pillows that simple remedy
seemed to ease her breathing considerably.
So much so, that Lance managed to let go of

his fear, but not his guilt. He had never stopped blaming himself for Raine's worsened condition, for he should not have allowed her to go out when he knew it was going to rain, when there was a chill in the air that cut to the bone. *Next time she'll do what I tell her,* he thought grimly, and then turned to Tess.

"Watch her until I get back with Doc Redding."

It was an order Tess carried out faithfully, and for the tenth time she put a wet cloth to Raine's face, picked the hair up from the back of her neck and bathed the girl down to her waist, hoping against hope that the fever would break soon. As she wrung out the towel once more, she draped it loosely around Raine's neck to draw the fever out. It was just as she put the blanket back in place that Lance returned with the doctor.

Dr. Redding examined Raine carefully, putting the stethoscope to her chest and to her back. He thumped and listened with a practiced ear. Then he nodded in satisfaction. "Vaporizer seems to be doing the trick. Congestion's a lot looser, and her lungs sound clearer. Keep her propped up, but above all try to get her to cough up the phlegm. I'll have Mrs. Redding prepare a tea she uses for that purpose. Causes a deep cough that helps clear the lungs."

The doctor thought a minute and then nodded. "Guess that's about it, Mr. Randall.

I'll have the tea sent over as soon as it's brewed. Try to get her to drink as much as she can," he added as he repacked his bag and put his hand to Raine's forehead. "Seems to me she's about to come out of that fever. Mighty strong little girl," he said as he smiled down at the patient he wasn't going to lose.

Both Tess and Lance let out long sighs of relief. They looked at each other in mutual understanding. Raine was going to make it. Lance grinned and Tess returned a relieved smile.

After escorting the doctor to the door Lance settled himself in the bedroom, checking on Raine from time to time. The upright position seemed to have done the trick. She was breathing easier and had turned her head on the pillows. She was coming out of it.

"Eaten yet?" he asked Tess, who still hovered over her charge, washing her down again with a wet towel.

"Not yet," Tess answered absently as her skilled hands pushed aside the camisole as she washed the girl, front and back, to her waist.

Lance watched in fascination as Raine's breasts were exposed and the nipples reacted to the cold water, but he drew in a deep breath to control his automatic response when Tess pulled Raine's drawers down to wash the rest of her body. "Then you might as well go on down to the dining room when you get finished with her. I'll stay until you get back.''

"I'll just bet you will," Tess drawled in insinuating tones, but Lance smiled innocently and his pale green eyes revealed nothing.

"Sure will," he drawled in return, but a small smile played at the corners of his mouth.

"Want anything sent up from the bar?"

"Not hardly," Lance replied emphatically, giving Tess a look that said she should know better. "One drunk already killed her father. She doesn't need another one tending her."

Casting a sidelong glance at Lance, Tess nodded. Since she had first met him, she had never seen him drunk or anywhere close to it. In fact, he was almost abstemious. And it seemed that tonight required total abstinence, even to the point where he would not risk so much as a relaxing glass of wine.

Once more Tess glanced toward the makeshift tent that covered the bed. She wondered if the girl inside had any idea of Lance Randall's feelings for her. Then, shrugging away a twinge of jealousy, she left the suite and made her way to the dining room before it closed for the night.

When Tess was gone Lance settled himself comfortably and stared at the blankets that hid Raine from his view, but he did not move them. Instead, he was content to sit staring into space as he recalled every moment of his dream of Claire.

How it had happened he would never know, but he smiled as he remembered Raine's unconscious reaction to his lovemaking. As ill as she had been, she had felt him and she had responded. *So did I*, he thought, and wondered about his deeply distressing betrayal of a young, innocent girl. He could only hope she would never remember.

It was some hours later that Raine gradually became aware of voices. She looked around her small prison in confusion. She remembered little of what had occurred. She could not put the parade of hazy impressions and snatches of conversations into any order or context.

Then the acrid vapor that filled the enclosed space irritated her throat. She was now fully conscious and aware of the burning sensation that came with each breath. She coughed, and instantly the curtain of blankets parted as Lance stood above her, smiling into her open eyes.

"Mornin'."

Raine frowned. "Good morning," she responded uncertainly, trying to remember how she had gotten here. "I still seem to be causing you a great deal of trouble. I am truly sorry."

Recalling the honest and undisguised adoration he had seen in her eyes before the fever had blocked her mind, Lance answered with tenderness. "No trouble, Muffin. No trouble at all. You feelin' well enough to eat somethin'?"

For a moment Raine thought about the question and then realized that she was famished. "I could eat a horse," she admitted, smiling up at her protector with absolute confidence.

Tess watched in fascination. Outside of a whorehouse, it had been a long time since she had seen such blatant invitation in a woman's eyes, and Lance had fallen for it hook, line and sinker. Tess followed each coy expression, each pleased smile and each flutter of lashes as natural and unselfconscious love radiated from Raine's face.

"I think we can do a little better than that," Lance responded, warming to the unaffected display of trust and affection. "How about something more practical, like steak and eggs?"

"Two soft-boiled eggs and some toast will do. And a pot of tea. I'm *so* thirsty."

Lance raised his eyebrows. "Thirsty? After all that tea we poured into you? I think you'd better let Tess help you to the commode while I'm gone." Tess grunted in disgust when Raine's eyes widened as she blushed in maidenly modesty.

But it was no act. Lance had never discussed the details of his care for her when she had been so ill aboard his ship. Now, for

the first time, Raine realized that there
might have been a lot more involved than
simply the removal of rain-drenched clothing.

"Yes," she whispered in embarrassment as she turned her head away from him.
"I would appreciate your absence while I get
washed and dressed."

Lance's eyes twinkled. "Your wish is my
command," he intoned as seriously as he
could and bowed in deference to the lady's
shyness.

The instant he was gone, Raine struggled to get her legs over the side of the bed.
She was still weak, and the blankets were
an obstacle she could barely overcome. Tess
was alert to the problem and pushed the
blankets out of the way. Then she removed
the vaporizer, for she was convinced that
clean, fresh air was what the girl needed.

"Stay where you are," Tess instructed
the younger woman. "I'll bring everything to
you."

Raine nodded in mute obedience. Tess
did not see her compliance as she disappeared behind the ornate Chinese screen
and dragged the commode to the side of the
bed. After helping Raine settle herself on the
necessary, Tess diplomatically turned her
back and waited. Then she helped Raine to
the edge of the bed and put the commode
behind the screen.

Smiling as she returned with the wash
basin, Tess waited until Raine wiped her

face, neck and hands. When Raine asked for her toothbrush, Tess obligingly rummaged in the valise. Finally, Raine felt ready to face the world.

Her interest picked up at once as Tess put aside the basin and took a lovely silk nightgown from the bag she had brought with her. Raine stared covetously at the beautiful crimson gown with strategically placed panels of matching lace. There was a matching robe that had large ruffles that served as a flouncy collar and went the length of the garment to the floor.

"It's beautiful," she said longingly and could not take her eyes from the brilliant red gown and robe.

"Would you like to try them on?" Tess asked as though it would be the most natural thing in the world.

"Do you think I dare?" Raine questioned seriously, for she knew that neither her mother nor her father would ever have approved of such attire.

"Why not?" Tess asked. "Hell, this is the kind of thing a man likes to see on his woman."

The sudden surge of heat that heightened the color in Raine's already flushed cheeks caused Tess to laugh raucously. "Course now, if you don't *want* to encourage him, you'll wear something plain."

Lifting her downcast eyes, Raine studied the provocative gown and robe. A look of daring pushed aside the shy embarrassment in those large emerald eyes. She was considering the possibilities.

"I'll try them," she said, her spine stiffening with resolve as she glanced from Tess's low-cut dress back to the risque nightclothes. "If that's the kind of thing Lance likes, then that's what I'll wear."

"Well," Tess drawled thoughtfully, "I've never seen him with any Sunday school teachers, that's for sure. In fact, I've never seen him with any of the gentry who hold their skirts in when passing one of us girls on the sidewalk. As though we might poison them or something," Tess added bitterly.

Raine's eyes never left Tess's face, reading each emotion in turn.

At first, when the young men had rushed to California to make their fortunes, women had been scarce. There had not been nearly enough of them to go around. Then came women like Tess—women who made their fortunes in their own way, and the men had loved it. They had fallen all over each other in their eagerness to swap gold for the ladies' favors. In fact, even the wealthiest of the miners, businessmen and saloon owners had proudly escorted the prostitutes down the main street of town.

Now all this was changing. Decent women had joined their husbands. Families had arrived, and suddenly the attitude of those who had enjoyed the services of the women who worked the whorehouses of San Francisco changed drastically.

Some patrons had stopped coming altogether. Others arrived only under cover of night, and still others sneaked through the back doors of such establishments. But there were still one or two pleasure palaces gentlemen entered with pride and more than a touch of arrogance.

Studying Tess, Raine decided that she was undoubtedly one of those high-priced prostitutes and had probably earned a great deal of money during the years she had serviced the more prosperous and generous men. Neither was there any doubt in Raine's mind that Tess had been one of the beauties who had been so proudly escorted by men of wealth and power into the finest establishments San Francisco had offered.

Yes, she thought with the instinct of one woman sizing up another, *there are a great many things Tess can teach me about men like Lance Randall.*

"Are you sure that's the kind of thing Mr. Randall likes?" she asked, eying the crimson garments with a twinge of doubt.

"Sure, honey. Why, I wear gowns just like this when he comes calling. They never seem to bother him any," Tess remarked, and then laughed.

She couldn't help it; the look on Raine's face was one that always gave a whore a moment of spiteful satisfaction. It was an expression of shock and self-conscious embarrassment when a wife or a sweetheart learned of her man's involvement with a prostitute.

Then she sobered and asked softly, "You weren't really sure, were you?"

Raine knew what she was asking and answered with as much confidence as she could. "No, I wasn't sure just how—well you know Lance."

Then, changing the subject she found so painful, Raine looked once more at the scarlet garments and nodded in deference to the woman who knew Lance better than she. It was a bitter admission, but it was true. "If that's what he likes, that's what I'll wear."

"Determined to catch him, are you?" Tess asked unnecessarily, for every line of the younger woman's face was set in a sort of innocent faith. Then Tess let out a slow breath and asked an important question. "You thinking of marriage or will you be content just to—uh . . . Well, dammit," she blurted, "do you want to marry Lance or will you be satisfied with just going to bed with him?"

A slow smile lit Raine's face. "Why, I intend to marry him, of course. What else?"

A frown creased Tess's brow. "I don't think he's the marrying kind, honey. He doesn't talk much about himself, but from what little I've learned, he's got things on his mind that don't include marrying."

"Maybe I can change his mind," Raine suggested hopefully. "I've been told that I'm rather pretty, and if I dress more like you, maybe I can convince him that I'm the girl he's been waiting for.''

The expression of confident expectation that flooded Raine's face made Tess uneasy, for she knew in her heart that this child was no match for Lance Randall. Not the Lance Randall she knew, anyway. But she'd go slow. There was no need to frighten the girl or to goad her into hasty, ill-advised action that could only bring heartbreak.

''I'm not sure he's been waiting for *any* woman,'' Tess began softly, then dug a little deeper. ''You can't have known him long or I would have heard about you,'' she explained without malice, but the insinuation that Lance would have talked about her to a whore made Raine wince.

She braced herself and forced a cheerfulness she did not feel. ''You're right. I've only known him for a few days—not very long, but Tess, he's so good and so kind. I think I fell in love with him almost the very first moment I saw him.''

The older woman frowned in disbelief. This girl knew absolutely nothing of the man she said she loved. ''You sure? Do you have any idea what you're letting yourself in for? Lance is different, you know.''

Raine shook her head in denial. ''It's only that he's kinder, gentler than other men. And I'm quite sure. I love him. There's no question in my mind. He's the man I've dreamed of. Whether or not I'm the right woman for *him*, I don't know. I hope so, but in either case, I *must* try. If I don't, I shall wonder all my life whether or not I let my one true love escape me simply because I lacked the courage to reach out to him."

Smiling shyly, Raine confessed, "He's the first man I've ever wanted to love. You know, Tess, *really* love, the way married people do."

A tender, haunting chord from long ago touched Tess's heart. "You just be careful, honey. There's no man alive worth the torment they put us through!"

For a moment Raine pondered Tess's warning. "Maybe not," she agreed, and then smiled impishly, "but we surely do keep coming back for more."

Raine's eyes sparkled with happiness as the room once more echoed with Tess's laughter. "Come on, honey," the aging prostitute prompted. "Slip this on and we'll see how much we need to take in."

Happy to have the unsettling conversation behind her, Raine slipped out of her underwear and let the sensual silk gown slip over her. She shivered with delight as it touched the curves and hollows of her body. Forgetting all about her illness, she twisted this way and that so she could see every side in the mirror. Then she pouted her disappointment. She looked like a little girl dressed in her mother's clothes. The daringly thin straps of the gown were too long, allowing the bodice to hang too low, almost baring her breasts entirely. None of the lace panels were in the right place and not one portion of the daring garment hit her where it should. Even the bottom of the gown lay in folds on the floor.

Not willing to give up, Raine slipped into the robe, hitched it up and tied a sash around the whole thing. When she studied herself in the mirror again she almost cried in chargin.

"Oh, blast!" she swore, and flopped in disappointment and exhaustion onto the bed. Then she pushed herself to her feet. Resigned that she could not possibly wear these lovely things she had her heart set on, Raine untied the sash and removed the robe.

Lance walked into the bedroom. He stood for a moment taking in the ridiculous scene. He tried not to smile, but Raine saw the laughter twitch at the corners of his lips.

"Red is not your color," Lance commented easily, avoiding any mention of the fact that the style and size of the gown only made Raine look more like a child, something she was obviously trying to correct. "Besides, it's hardly appropriate for a sick bed. Better take it off."

"I can hardly do that while you're standing there ogling me," Raine complained.

Lance flashed her a brilliant smile. He pulled out the shapeless white flannel nightgown from Raine's valise. "If you'll hold up your arms, I'll slip this over your head, and I assure you, I shall not ogle."

Raine's eyes lowered so Lance would not see her chagrin. She knew what she looked like in Tess's gown. He didn't have to rub it in. Obediently, she raised her arms and shivered from fatigue and humiliation as yards of warm flannel shrouded her body. Then her exertions caught up with her and she swayed unsteadily on her feet.

Lance caught and steadied her. He turned to Tess. "How long has this been going on?" he asked in irritation.

Tess shrugged. "Not long. Only a few minutes. She needed a little something to take her mind off her troubles. Besides, she was looking for something you couldn't help but notice."

Lance flashed Tess a warning and then turned his attention to Raine, whose eyes glistened with unshed tears. She knew Tess and Lance were making fun of her, and all she had wanted to do was to make herself more alluring, more irresistible to Lance. And just the opposite had happened. She had looked like a fool.

Lance lowered her to the bed gently and pulled the covers up over her. "What *am* I going to do with you?" he asked as he smiled down into her eyes. Instantly, he knew he had blundered. He sounded like a doting father scolding a recalcitrant child. Quickly, he added the words that he knew would restore Raine's confidence in her womanhood. "Besides, I much prefer you in demure white—it suits a bride better, you know."

Neither noticed as Tess silently left the room, a look of pain on her face.

Raine's humiliation and budding anger were forgotten as a radiant smile broke over her face. She forgave Lance everything—including the fact that he had made her feel like a three-year-old when she was trying to be a provocative woman.

"A bride? Me?" she asked, dumbfounded by the suddenness of Lance's proposal. It was something she had wished for, hoped for, but had hardly dared to say out loud. It was too soon. How could Lance possibly know that she found him to be the most handsome of men?

"Yes, you," Lance confirmed, and Raine threw her arms around him. "Will you do me the honor of becoming my wife?" he asked with mock formality.

"Oh, Lance, yes! When?" she asked eagerly, and then eased herself back to the pillows, for she was very weary now, and she was uncertain. She could not believe that Lance wanted to marry her.

"Just as soon as you grow up, I guess," Lance teased.

"I'm trying," she responded in a muffled voice.

"I do appreciate that, my dear, especially since I am too old to live in a state of constant terror, wondering what you might do next. I have known you only a few days, and you have proved yourself to be a rather rash young woman who makes foolish, if not downright disastrous, decisions without a thought for the consequences of your actions.

"First, you trudge around all day and half the night in pouring rain, searching for a man. Second, you enter a glorified saloon and whorehouse alone and unprotected. Third," he continued relentlessly, ticking off her sins, "you stab a man in front of countless witnesses. Had the man died, you could have been hanged. Do you ever stop to think of the price you might have to pay one day if this continues?"

Raine felt deeply ashamed, for everything Lance said was true. "No," she answered contritely, making no effort to defend herself.

"And if that weren't enough," he continued, ignoring her misery, "you decide to get out of a sick bed to attend a funeral when any fool could see that the weather was turning foul. And you suffered for it. In fact, we all suffered for it.

"Finally," he finished in exasperation, "after we struggle to keep you alive, you no sooner open your eyes than you're indulging your every whim regardless of the consequences to you or to us. You stand around in a drafty room trying on a flimsy gown that is too large for you, a gown that leaves your chest entirely exposed, risking pneumonia at the very least."

Lance shook his head and his eyes flashed a mild reprimand Raine did not miss. "I can only hope you will make a serious effort to think a situation through instead of acting on childish impulse."

Then Lance stopped and smiled, for Raine's teeth were clenched and her eyes were closed tight. She was shutting him out. She had heard quite enough for one day, and rebellion was building.

Lance took her resisting hand in both of his and Raine opened her eyes. Defiance flashed up at him. To complete her show of resentment and independence, she tried to pull her hand away, but Lance simply ignored the feeble effort and smiled into the sullen face.

"Did you hear anything I've said?" he asked.

"Yes," Raine replied reluctantly, her eyes reproaching Lance for bullying her when she was too sick to defend herself.

Then her heart melted and all the resentment faded as Lance smiled and nodded his approval. "Good, for I shall have very little time to teach you to be a woman. You must manage that on your own, if you still want to marry me."

Gratitude flooded Raine's eyes. "I will," she promised, and thrilled to the touch of Lance's finger as it traced the outline of her lips. A surge of emotion flooded through her as he lowered his lips to hers.

There was no more rebellion, no defiance left in Raine as Lance slipped his arms under her and held her tightly to him. Again his lips brushed hers, then moved to her eyes before returning again, persuading—promising.

Raine shivered in delight, and the first tormenting sparks of passion began to stir. "Lance," she sobbed, throwing her arms around him as the sparks caught hold and flared into flame.

Quickly, Lance backed off. This was not the time. "I am sorry I had to be so harsh, but I do not think I could bear it if anything happened to you. Will you promise to take better care of yourself?" he asked tenderly, and Raine felt she would dissolve under those pale green eyes that were so gentle and so loving.

"I promise," she answered quite seriously, and for the moment, at least, she meant every word of it.

Lance's answering grin turned Raine's bones to liquid. Then he pulled the warm robe from Raine's valise and dropped it on the bed. "You sleep for a while and then we'll get you up for an hour or so if you're feeling well enough. I'll have the kitchen hold breakfast for a couple of hours."

Raine nodded. She was very tired, and she slept for almost three hours. When she awakened Lance was still there, and Tess was back.

"Feeling well enough to sit up for a spell?" Lance asked as she roused herself.

"Yes, I'm much better," Raine assured him. "Tess has taken very good care of me."

"Then I guess it's about time we give her a break," he said as he turned to Tess and suggested pointedly, "Why don't you go get some rest? Take your time. I'll stay for a couple of hours and if Raine's all right, if there's no recurrence of the fever, we can both stop playing nursemaid."

Glancing at Raine, he smiled. "All right with you?"

Raine frowned in disappointment. She wanted Lance to stay with her always. Then she sighed. There were so many things she wanted from him but since one of them was his approval, she agreed.

There was a knock at the door, and a waiter brought in a large tray of food, which he put on the small round table by the window. After fussing over the dishes for a few minutes, he turned to Lance. "Will that be all, sir?"

"That's it," Lance replied cheerfully, and flipped the young man a silver coin.

"Thank you, sir," the waiter replied, deftly plucking the coin from mid-air.

When he had gone Lance helped Raine to the table. She was still weak, but she made the short walk without difficulty. Lance sat across from her as she attacked the soft-boiled eggs and toast, washing it all down with sweetened tea. He smiled as she suddenly put down her spoon and remembered her manners. Blushing furiously, Raine proceeded at a much slower pace.

"Guess I would've done the same thing

if I hadn't eaten anything solid for a couple of days," Lance commented, and Raine lifted her head, startling Lance with the gratitude and love that glowed in her eyes.

And Tess, who had gathered her things as she prepared to leave the suite, also saw the defenseless light of first love in the girl's face. She drew in her breath and let it out slowly. There was nothing she could do. Lance had proposed to the girl. It was up to him to do right by her.

"Lance," she began hesitantly, and paused uncertainly when he turned toward her. "Never mind," Tess finished lamely as she studied the hardened features. "Let me know if I'm needed."

"Sure will," he replied in disinterested dismissal.

The fading beauty fought down the bitterness she could not entirely keep out of her voice. "Yeah, sure you will," she muttered, and left the room before she made an even bigger fool of herself.

But Raine understood at last. Tess was in love with Lance. The young woman's eyes widened in dismay at the discovery, and she lowered them as she settled her cup carefully on the saucer. She was stealing another woman's sweetheart.

Leaning back in her chair, lost in her troubled thoughts, Raine's practical nature reasserted itself. Tess might love Lance, but how deep were his feelings for her? It was time to find out.

"Tess is in love with you, you know." The softness of her voice and the unexpectedness of the words made Lance doubt that he had heard right.

"What? Tess?" He laughed derisively. "Hell no! Haven't you guessed what Tess is? She's obligin' to every man who has the right amount of gold in his pockets." His eyes twinkled in amusement at the thought of Tess being in love with anyone. She had more sense than that. A whore didn't fall in love with her customers; she just collected the money and kept them happy.

"Nevertheless, it's true," Raine stated quietly.

This time Lance did not laugh. The pale green eyes flicked in discomfort. Tess was a friend, and she was a woman he could talk to, a woman who had been through the wars just as he had. She understood what he didn't say as well as what he did. He frowned at the thought of losing her, for he valued her opinion. She was an endless source of useful information. She knew everyone in San Francisco who mattered, and she knew everything that was happening. But if Tess were in love with him, he had to end their friendship now.

"Damn," he muttered unhappily before meeting Raine's steady, open gaze. "You sure?"

She nodded and watched as regret washed over Lance's features. It was all the answer she needed. He did not love the prostitute who had been so good to her, who had tried to warn her of something she did not wish to hear.

Lance leaned back in the beautifully upholstered Queen Anne chair and studied the young woman in front of him. He had already dismissed Tess from his mind. There were more important things to think about.

"How old are you?" he asked.

Raine stared at him and wondered what her age had to do with anything, but she answered. "The day my father was killed was the day I turned seventeen."

Inwardly, Lance cringed. Seventeen! And he was thirty-two. He spread his large hand over the arm of his chair. Unconsciously, the fingers dug into the expensive cloth. "How old was your dad when he died?"

Raine frowned to hold back the tears. "He was thirty-seven. He was only nineteen when he and Mama were married. My mother was fifteen. I was born when she was sixteen. She died almost seven years ago." Raine hoped that Lance would not ask any more questions about her parents. It was too painful to talk about them, and she would surely start to cry if it continued.

Lance did not notice Raine's distress. Instead he did some fast mental calculations. Her mother would be but a year older than he was now had she lived. He was robbing the cradle, but if it would get him what he wanted he would do it without a twinge of conscience. Claire had been a year younger than Raine was now when he had lost her. It would be as though time had stood still and she was back with him, still young and still so very beautiful.

"And the rest of your family?" he probed.

Again Raine frowned. "I have no one. No one except a grandfather who wants nothing to do with me. He told Mama if she married my father, she would be dead as far as he was concerned. So I guess I'm alone."

"No aunts, no uncles?"

Raine shook her head and fought back the tears. "No."

That bit of information suited Lance just fine. It certainly would make things easier.

Once more, Lance studied Raine as she sat toying nervously with the twisted cord that tied the flannel robe securely around her body. A bit of lace from the demure neckline of her nightdress peeked out from the small V that was formed by the high-crossed lapels of the robe. Her feet were bare and tucked under her. The long hair fell in silken waves to the middle of her back. Her skin was taut over the high cheek bones, and the slanted Mediterranean eyes held his in a guileless, trusting gaze. The fact that she was infatuated with him was obvious, but Lance was not certain it was any more than that—a young girl smitten by her first love. The thought bothered him, and he blinked once as he pushed it from his mind.

Stretching his long legs, Lance began slowly. "Even though we've been acquainted only a few days, I feel I know you rather well."

Raine misinterpreted his meaning and blushed furiously. She guessed he certainly did know her, all right. From head to toe. "Yes," she answered quietly, choosing to say no more.

Lance shifted positions and crossed his legs. His boots were newly polished, the trousers fit perfectly and a fine silk vest, embroidered with small flowers of gold, complemented the expertly tailored jacket. The snowy-white shirt heightened the sun-darkened bronze of his skin as well as the pale green eyes that made Raine feel weak when she looked into them. She thought him altogether the most handsome of men—and the kindest. Her heart stopped beating as she waited for him to say what was on his mind, for she knew it concerned her.

Lance studied her through lowered lids. "Despite the fact that we have known each other for such a short time, you've said you would be willing to become my wife. Did you mean it, Raine?"

He braced himself for a refusal. Her whole face glowed with acceptance. "Yes, I meant it if you did."

To Lance's credit, he felt an acute sense

of guilt as he answered, "Yes, I meant it. Nothing would give me more satisfaction than to take you as my wife."

It was an oddly worded proposition of marriage, and Raine felt that something was missing, but she was too happy to explore her uneasiness. All she could think of was becoming Mrs. Lance Randall. The very thought made her giddy. She felt as though she had just conquered the world, and she got up from her chair and threw herself into Lance's lap as she put her arms around his neck, hugging him tightly.

"It's just like my mother and father," she sighed as her eyes misted. "For them, too, it was love at first sight. It's just the way I always knew it would be. One day I would look up and there would be my valiant knight. And here you are!" she gloated, her face radiant with happiness.

Lance would have been amused by the scene had he not understood that Raine was telling him her most private thoughts and hopes and dreams. She actually was still child enough to think of him as her knight, her protector. Lance had the grace to blush.

Then he smiled wryly. "This is all kind of new to me. I guess the first thing we have to do is get you an engagement ring. Make it official."

Struggling to be proper at such an important moment in her life, Raine answered primly. "That would be very nice. And then we can buy two wedding rings. One for you and one for me."

An indulgent smile brightened Lance's features. "Tryin' to put your brand on me?" he asked, and then stopped smiling when Raine looked at him through serious eyes.

"Yes," she admitted honestly. "I want everyone to know that you belong to me."

An eyebrow arched in doubt. "Hope you're not the jealous type."

"I don't know," Raine replied thoughtfully. "But I'm sure I won't be if you give me no cause."

For the first time since he had met this young woman, Lance paused to wonder if she were really the thoughtless, impulsive little creature he had assumed her to be. There was a certain purpose and logic to her thinking, despite the fact that she still reacted to situations with a childish lack of concern for the consequences. Could she be more than the sweet, haunting face that had gripped his heart from the beginning? Could she be more than the fascinating little girl who was the embodiment of childish innocence and of a love lost?

That she was unworldly and untutored in a great many things was obvious, yet her speech was soft and refined. Her grammar was that of the educated classes, but how could it be? By her own admission, she had lost her mother more than six years ago when she had been only eleven years old.

Since that time she had lived a harsh life in a mining camp, devoid of refinement, surrounded by rough adventurous men, most of them without the taming influence of women.

How had she survived all of that and yet remained a lady of obvious, if somewhat incomplete, breeding? He didn't understand a great deal concerning Raine Colter.

Then, for the first time, Lance felt compelled to warn her. "In my line of work I need a wife who trusts me completely. There will be times when I must carry out certain assignments that I cannot discuss with you. There will also be times when I will be gone for days or even months at a stretch. Do you understand what I'm telling you?"

For a long moment uncertain eyes searched Lance's face. "I'm not sure," Raine admitted at last. "I think you're telling me that no matter what happens, I must trust you. I must never be jealous, and I must never pry."

Lance's smile was bittersweet. "That's part of it. And for now it's enough. Think you can handle it?"

"I'll try," Raine promised earnestly. "I will do my very best to trust you always. And," she added, smiling mischievously, "to mind my own business."

Lance nodded. He was sure she would try, but there would be times when he would stretch that trust to the breaking point.

For some time after that they talked

about little things. Raine told Lance about her early life on a farm in Pennsylvania, and he gave her some hint of the wealth and power his family possessed. When it was time for him to go, Raine clung to him and forgot all about the unbecoming gown and robe. "Come back soon," she pleaded.

Lance leaned down, stirring the smoldering embers once more with a kiss that drew a deep and disturbing response from Raine. "I love you," she whispered, and did not think it strange when Lance simply patted her absently.

"See you tomorrow, Muffin," he replied easily, and walked from the bedroom.

As Lance closed the door to her suite behind him, Raine settled back in the chair and smiled dreamily. "Just like Mama and Papa," she purred. "Love at first sight." Then she stretched, feeling the happiness flow to every part of her. It was just like a fairytale and she was the princess.

6

When Lance entered Raine's suite at midmorning on the following day she was up and dressed. Her cold had improved, her lungs were clear and she was regaining her usual excessive energy.

"Looks like you're feelin' a lot better," Lance commented as he automatically put his hand to Raine's forehead to check for any return of the dreaded fever.

"Yes," Raine answered, smiling brightly, "I'm feeling much better, but I don't think I have ever, in my entire life, had a cold like that."

"It was a little more than a cold," Lance corrected. "You were a pretty sick pup. But then," he teased, "lots of things go wrong once you're past your prime."

Raine laughed with him and then remembered her manners. "Won't you be
seated? If you like, I'll have some tea or coffee
sent up."

"Nothin' for me, thanks," Lance responded as he settled himself in the large
armchair that sat in the sunny path of the
window.

The rains had gone. They would be
back, but until then, the citizens of San
Francisco enjoyed the sun as it broke
through the gloom that had hung over them
for days, dulling the mind as well as the
spirit.

Raine's spirits, too, were high as the sun
streamed into the room. She stared fascinated as its rays touched Lance's hair,
which flashed brilliant sparks of gold fire.
She drew in her breath, mesmerized by the
beauty of the man as the sun warmed the
bronzed skin and outlined the hard, masculine mouth and the lean line of the jaw. And
it seemed to her that his brow must have
been sculpted by the hand of a skilled artist
as the silhouette of long bronze lashes
shaded the pale green eyes, which Raine
suddenly realized were watching her with
an expression of amusement.

The heat of acute embarrassment
seared her cheeks. She had been mooning
over him like some schoolgirl, but she
couldn't help it. Never had she seen a man
so handsome. Her heart stuttered, and she
lowered her head so Lance Randall would

not see the longing in her eyes.

But it was already too late. Lance's features underwent a subtle change as he read the hero worship and adoration blazing out at him with an intensity he had never before experienced. And certainly not with Claire.

"Damn," he cursed silently, and took a deep breath to control the emotions that threatened to break his resolve. He did not *want* to wait until they were married. He wanted her *now*, this very minute. It would be different from the last time. This time she would know.

But he wasn't ready. Before he could take her to bed again, very special preparations must be made, for Raine must never suspect she was anything other than the virgin she had been when he first took her. They must both wait until the marriage vows had been spoken.

The silence seemed to crackle around them, making each one acutely aware of the other's presence, and Raine felt the growing tension in her body. The passion and the desire that gathered like storm clouds in Lance's eyes reached out to her, churning her need for him to a fearsome storm.

As the electricity of unbearable anticipation sparked through her, she concentrated every fiber of her mind and body on Lance. Then she could endure no more. She loved him. She needed him. The demon that drove her was new and strange, yet there was a haunting familiarity in the yearning she was struggling desperately to deny, which defied and conquered her upbringing with all its taboos and rules and forbidden thoughts.

With her eyes fixed on his, Raine went to Lance. He stood and took her in his arms. His mouth received hers as she arched her body on tiptoe. He curled his taller, larger frame to accommodate hers and held her tight as the mutual need and desire flowed through them in a silent invocation, urging them on. The pulsing rhythm of their bodies became one, and Raine pressed deeper. She barely heard the whisper which drifted like the soft mist of morning through her mind, the whisper which assured her that this time it would be better.

Ignoring the frightening thought that was gone before her mind could grasp it, Raine slipped her hands under Lance's suit coat. Her fingers touched and teased as they moved over the thin cloth of his shirt. She breathed in the smell of him and revelled in the feel of him. And the heat of his body penetrated to the secret core of her being.

Lance moaned as his grip tightened around her, and he fought against the touch of the temptress. His muscles stiffened as he struggled for control. He wanted her as he had not wanted any woman for fourteen years, but he could not have her. Not now. He could not risk it.

"Lance," Raine sobbed as she felt him hesitate. "Love me—please."

"I can't," he replied in a voice that was husky with emotion. "Don't you understand? I can't take you until we're married."

Stepping back but keeping his hands on her arms, Lance stared full into eyes that reflected pain and confusion. He cursed himself and he cursed Claire. "When we're married," he promised softly.

Raine shuddered with need and unfulfilled desire. "I'm not sure I can survive your honor," she stated bitterly, for she could not understand how a love such as hers could ever be wrong or wicked. What difference did it make? Now or days from now? "When?" she asked, breathing deeply.

"Three days," Lance promised. "Just long enough for me to announce our engagement, get a license and make it legal."

Raine closed her eyes and shivered as the throbbing in her body refused to cease. She clenched her teeth and tensed against it. "I'm not sure I'll last that long," she replied in a voice tight with the agony of her struggle.

"I'm sorry," Lance apologized, and put his hands to Raine's face and tenderly tilted it to his. "I should never have allowed this to start." He tried to smile, but the result was a poor imitation, and Raine understood that he, too, was suffering.

"I don't know why it's so important to

wait until we're married," she said slowly, for she was quite certain that Lance was not restrained by convention. He cared as little for the opinion of others as she. "But if that's what you insist upon, then I will do my best to resist temptation."

The impish light in her eyes coaxed the soft sound of laughter from Lance. "Until then," he suggested, "shall we occupy ourselves with choosing our rings? And then there's the matter of a trousseau," he reminded her. "Three days is not a lot of time."

"Sometimes three days can be an eternity," Raine corrected, and then went on to concentrate on other things. "I can get Tess to help me with the trousseau," she continued unenthusiastically, for the truth was that Raine had no women friends in San Francisco.

"And guests?" Lance asked.

"Well, there's Bart and Zeke, of course. And Tess. The only friend my father and I had in San Francisco is Jake Finch. He owns a saloon down by the waterfront. I'll ask him. And I should like to invite Dr. and Mrs. Redding. I wish I could have my father's best friend to give me away, but he lives too far away, I'm afraid. He wouldn't even receive the message in three days' time, much less get here.

"And his name?"

"Tom—Tom Morley," Raine replied as

she smiled unconsciously. "He and my father became friends on the trip to California, but Tom had a grant for land located higher in the Sierras. Our camp was located several days of hard riding away. I'm not even sure exactly where it is."

"The high Sierras takes in a lot of territory," Lance said, stating the obvious. "Surely, if he and your father were such good friends, there must be better directions than that around."

Raine frowned as she tried to remember. "Papa had a map. It's probably somewhere in his papers. I haven't looked at any of his things yet."

She thought for a moment and then shook her head. "No, even if I could find the map, it would still take Tom too long to get here, even if he were willing to leave his claim unguarded."

"We could always postpone the wedding for a few days," Lance suggested. "We could wait for Mr. Morley."

"Oh, no!" Raine protested. "I'm going to have enough trouble waiting for three days as it is. I certainly don't intend to wait any longer—for anybody!"

Lance laughed out loud and hugged Raine to him with a fierce possessiveness that surprised even him. "Relieved to hear it," he said. "I'm not any too anxious to wait longer than three days myself." Then he suggested that Raine might want to inform her grandfather of her marriage since he was her only living relative.

"I will not!" she replied bitterly. "He made my mother cry. I hate him!"

Not at all pleased by Raine's reaction to a situation Lance felt sure was more complicated than she knew, he shrugged almost indifferently and once more let her have her way. "It's your decision."

"Yes, it is!" she snapped in a tone that caused Lance to narrow his eyes. The next moment however, Raine apologized. "I'm sorry. That was very mean of me. I'm taking it out on you when you're only trying to be helpful. Forgive me?"

Lance looked at that repentant face and smiled. She was playing him like a harp but, strangely, he did not mind, for she truly was sorry. Not to forgive her was unthinkable. He tipped her face up to his. "You're forgiven," he said. "Now, shall we find a suitable engagement ring for my bride-to-be?"

It was a question that embarrassed Raine. "I would much rather be surprised by *your* choice."

Lance shrugged. "We'll do it any way you want, of course." But he was disappointed. He had wanted Raine to look over the stones and mountings and choose something she would treasure for as long as she lived. He had wanted her to share in the choice, but apparently she was not interested enough to do so. Lance did not understand the importance Raine attached to accepting with pleasure and with love whatever he cared to offer her—just as her mother had done before her.

Raine was sensitive to Lance's moods, and she knew instantly that he was unhappy with her. She felt the sting of tears and blinked them back. Somehow she had failed him. Somehow she had not been equal to his expectations.

Turning aside so he would not see her hurt, she caught sight of herself in the mirror. Her image only reinforced the sudden feeling of doubt. What did Lance see in her? She looked childish and hopelessly provincial in her home-made blouse and skirt. And Lance, who was dressed impeccably himself must be embarrassed by her unfashionable wardrobe. "I must do something about my clothes," she stated matter-of-factly, staring at her image in the mirror. The unexpected change in conversation threw Lance off balance.

"And my hair," she added with distaste, glaring at the reflection of the tousled mane that made her look younger than she was. "It's terrible!" she declared flatly. Surely there were many knowledgeable, sophisticated woman who would jump at the chance to marry Lance. Why had he chosen her? It didn't make sense, and despite the fact that her girlish dreams conjured up a handsome prince who would love her instantly, Raine had always known that such dreams didn't really come true. She shivered with uncertainty and turned to Lance.

"Why are you marrying me?" she asked, all her uncertainty showing on her face.

Lance blinked. She had caught him flat-footed. She was becoming suspicious of this whirlwind courtship. He was at a loss for words, but one thing he knew. He could not tell her the truth. Not now, or he'd lose her.

"Would you mind explaining what you're talking about?" His soft tones did not betray the fear he felt about the question she had asked. He needed time to think.

"Look at me," Raine said, shaking her head in despair. "Just look at me. What in the world do you see that could possibly have won your heart?"

Lance relaxed. A slow-breaking smile spread over his face. It was just a case of pre-marriage nerves. She needed reassuring. Pale green eyes laughed into hers. "You gotta ask?" he inquired, raising one brow, studying her in a way that made her blush.

"Seems to me you got a whole lot a man like me could feel mighty affectionate about."

Despite her desire to believe him with all her heart, Raine spoke what she thought was the truth. "You could get that anywhere, and I imagine you have."

An odd expression appeared on Lance's

face. His eyes blinked once and then he spoke with a quiet intensity. "Do you want me, Raine? The way I want you?"

It seemed an oddly worded question to Raine, but she knew that her answer would be very important to her future, and despite the sudden apprehension that had temporarily caused her to doubt him, she answered truthfully. "Yes," she admitted, still not knowing why the question was not quite the right one. "You know I do. You know I love you with all my heart. How can you not know? Or do you seriously believe that I go around throwing myself at every man I meet?"

A flicker of unconscious warning glinted in Lance's eyes. "Never crossed my mind," he answered easily before the warning was stated plainly. "And it better never happen. Bein' made a fool of by a woman is not somethin' I have much patience with. Now, if you're ready, shall we go?"

Raine nodded. Lance loved her. He wanted to marry her, and that was all that really mattered. But she could not fully rid herself of the nagging fear that something was not right.

She frowned as she draped the plain shawl around her shoulders, picked up her drawstring purse and walked from her suite to the hall. She turned Lance's words over again in her mind and tried to convince herself that she was being foolish. But she couldn't. Something was wrong; she just didn't know what. The vague uneasiness that had so disturbed her a few minutes ago was still there. She was nervous and didn't know why.

She had felt it since her first night aboard Lance's ship, but she had never quite been able to put her finger on it.

Her thoughts filled her mind as she walked down the stairs of the plush hotel. It was only when she got to the lobby and noticed the stylishly dressed women as they came and went that her thoughts turned once more to her own unhappy appearance. Nothing she owned would be suitable to wear when she married the handsome man at her side.

And, again, she was puzzled. For the life of her she did not understand why Lance wanted to marry *her* when he could obviously have his pick of women who possessed all the social graces, women who were well educated and spoke French.

She smiled ruefully. The only French she knew was what she had been able to pick up from the French miners who had stopped by her father's cabin for fresh baked pie and a cup of coffee. Even at that, half of what she knew could not be repeated in polite society.

A sigh of futility escaped Raine's lips, and Lance stopped in the middle of the street and turned her to him. His eyes, too,

were clouded with inner doubts. "Havin'
second thoughts?" he asked, giving her this
one last chance to back out.

Raine looked up at him. The fear she felt
at the thought of losing him made all her
doubts and concerns suddenly unimpor-
tant. "Only if you are," she answered reluctantly. And it was the truth. If Lance did not
love her, it would be better for them to part
now. She knew in her heart that she would
never stop loving him, but that was a pain
she would just have to endure. She could not
marry a man who did not love her, no matter
how much she loved him.

The easy smile that lit Lance Randall's
face, the warmth that filled his eyes, eased
Raine's heart. "Not hardly," he drawled,
and Raine thought them the most beautiful
two words in the English language.

Ignoring the people on the sidewalk and
the horses that came close to running them
down, Raine impulsively threw her arms
around Lance's waist, hugging him tightly.
"Me neither," she said, imitating his drawl.

Then, as though to seal the bargain, as
though to announce to all the curious pass-
ersby that this was his woman, Lance
leaned down and touched his lips to Raine's.
"Mighty glad to hear it," he teased, and then
put his arms around her waist as they continued down the street.

As they proceeded to the jewelry shop
Lance had in mind, Raine enjoyed the sun
that warmed her shoulders. She snuggled

deeper into the shawl and held her joy close.
The all-pervading chill that had invaded her
body when she had been so ill was gone. In
its place was the warmth of perfect happiness on this gorgeous, sunlit day.

They strolled leisurely, Raine's arm
tucked comfortably in Lance's, until they
came to the most expensive jewelry store in
San Francisco. The overhead bell tinkled
discreetly as they walked into the shop and
took seats on chairs upholstered in blue
velvet.

A clerk approached and made a very
shrewd judgment as to the price range of the
jewelry the obviously wealthy gentleman
would be interested in. The woman, who
was totally out of fashion, hardly mattered.
It was the expensively dressed gentleman
who would be paying the bill.

"May I help you, sir?" he asked in a
practiced voice that contained just the right
amount of subservience as he bowed slightly
with just the right touch of deference.

"We want to see somethin' in an engagement ring. For the little lady here,"
Lance added with a hint of amusement in
his voice, for he had read the clerk's dismissal of Raine. "What we buy will be up to the
lady."

Immediately, the clerk changed tactics.
"Would mademoiselle be interested in any
particular stone? Diamonds, perhaps, or
emeralds to match mademoiselle's eyes?"

Raine lowered her head to hide the smile

she was trying to suppress. Not even the unwanted task of choosing her own engagement ring dismayed her any longer, for Lance had assessed the situation and had chosen this means of sharing his power with her. He, too, had seen the clerk dismiss her presence as being of little consequence, and Lance was giving her the chance for sweet revenge if she cared to exercise it.

The expression in Raine's eyes when she could at last look up was all the confirmation Lance needed. He had done the right thing.

"I should like to see something in a diamond. A solitaire mounting, I think. Something large enough to satisfy the expectations of those who attach importance to such things, but not so large as to be gauche," she explained in a tone that implied that she spoke from experience.

Lance relaxed, leaned back in the Louis XIV chair and watched through eyes that danced with laughter. Not once did Raine ask for his opinion. She put her trust in her innate good taste and chose a ring somewhat over two carats, a flawless blue-white that reflected the light from a thousand facets. It was a breath-taking choice.

When Lance took the ring from the salesman he took Raine's left hand in his and slipped the ring on her third finger. "A promise made; a promise to be kept," he said solemnly.

Then they turned their attention to wedding rings and chose plain gold bands that would mark them as man and wife. The clerk accepted a bank draft and watched with increased interest as his two patrons walked from the shop into the bright sunny day. The young woman was really quite lovely, he decided, once one managed to get past the unfashionable clothing.

7

Every waking moment that remained before the wedding took place was spent tearing apart and remaking several expensive gowns Tess had given her. Three expert seamstresses were kept busy as bows were removed and layer upon layer of precious lace was carefully salvaged. Fine silks and satins were recut in styles more suited to Raine's diminutive figure.

As she admired the last ensemble to be finished, Raine could not help but smile her pleasure. She had gotten the dresses for nothing, and the fee she had paid to the seamstresses who had done such a fine job would barely have been enough to purchase even one of the gowns Tess had given her, for fashionable clothing could be prohibitively expensive in San Francisco, especially for items that had to be shipped around the Horn.

Critical eyes studied the three new outfits, noting each detail. The garnet silk glowed softly. Its wide skirt with an open front showed the black petticoat underneath. A short, tight jacket with sleeves that ended just below the elbows was trimmed in the same black silk.

The suit was beautifully tailored and was of the finest quality, but Raine had not forgotten Lance's dislike of the garish red color of the scarlet nightgown. Nor had she forgotten the hidden smiles. It was an experience she did not wish to repeat, and she wondered if he would like this deeper shade of red, a softer, more subdued shade. She released a pent-up breath as she fervently hoped so, for the lovely garnet was one of her favorite colors.

But the real prize was the dress Raine intended to wear when she and Lance spoke their vows. It was of pale green satin with a beautiful cascade of golden silk flowers flowing a little off center down the front of the full skirt. The hem was lifted in graceful scallops at even intervals by other golden flowers, allowing layers of gold lace to peek from beneath. Finishing it off was a matching garland of tiny gold flowers interspersed with green leaves for her hair. She was quite certain Lance would approve of this outfit.

Holding up her hand, turning it this way
and that, Raine admired her engagement
ring and felt that the world could surely hold
no greater happiness for her. She was almost afraid to be so happy, for no one deserved such joy as she felt the night before
her wedding.

Tess would be there, of course. And Zeke
and Bart, but that was all, for Dr. and Mrs.
Redding had made other plans that could
not be changed on such short notice, and
Jake Finch had politely but firmly declined
her invitation. It would be a disappointingly
small wedding, but Raine was determined to
wear the gown that would have been more
appropriate at a much grander affair. She
knew that she would be married only this
once, and she would make it as festive as she
could. And there would be pictures. Lance
had insisted on it, so she would always have
something to remind her of her great joy and
of her great love for the man she was about
to marry.

Sleep did not come easily that night.
Excitement kept Raine awake as all the
lovely visions of what the future held floated
through her mind, even into the early hours
of the morning.

Finally she drifted into a contented
sleep, her mind totally at peace. She would
be happy with her handsome knight forever
and ever. The smile that touched her lips
reflected her dreams.

* * *

The wedding was to be at 10:30 that morning, and Tess had arrived resplendent in feathers and bows to assist the younger woman. Tess sighed as she helped Raine into underclothing that would mold her figure to every line and curve of the green satin that highlighted the green of her eyes. The deeply curving neckline was adorned only by a gold locket that had belonged to Raine's mother. The final touch was the garland of flowers, which Tess arranged skillfully in the gleaming mass of upswept hair.

"Oh, Tess," she cried happily, and hugged the only female friend she had in San Francisco.

"Easy, honey," Tess interrupted good naturedly. "You'll get that dress all wrinkled. You shouldn't even sit down until the wedding's over. Of course," she added practically, "I don't see how you're going to ride in a carriage without sitting."

Raine smiled at the woman who had been so kind and generous, the woman who still loved Lance but was doing such a courageous job of hiding it. Then, slipping into a new woolen cape trimmed with fur, the one real extravagance Raine had allowed herself, she nodded to Tess. "I'm ready," she declared with absolute confidence.

Accompanied by Tess, Raine left her suite, descended the stairs and stepped into the waiting carriage. Within minutes she and Tess were in front of the parsonage where Lance was waiting for her.

His eyes smiled into hers as he helped her from the carriage and offered his arm as they proceeded up the stairs, across the front porch and into the beautifully decorated parlor where the ceremony would take place.

Flowers were everywhere, and Raine's eyes glowed with love as she looked into Lance's face. He had guessed what a disappointment the small affair would be for her and had done his best to make it a beautiful occasion. Only the presence of her parents could have made it any more perfect.

Unclasping Raine's cape with a quiet possessiveness that everyone present noted, Lance removed it and stood back to admire the effect of green satin as it glowed with a soft patina in the light of the lamps.

"Mighty pretty," he said, but his eyes said much more, and Raine's face was radiant with happiness. She had pleased him and he thought her beautiful. Nothing else mattered.

Zeke, the oldest of the three men, acted as best man, and Tess was maid of honor. Lance had ordered a lovely nosegay of bright yellow flowers decorated with lace and ribbon. Raine smiled as she realized that Tess had helped him with the color.

Raine promised to love, honor and obey. Lance vowed to love, protect and share all his worldly goods. Rings were exchanged and papers were signed. Raine was now legally Mrs. Lance Randall. Her eyes were luminous as she looked up at her husband. There was not a doubt in her mind that the two of them would live in a world of bliss forever and ever.

Lance in his turn breathed a sigh of relief. His tracks would soon be covered. Raine need never know that he had taken her as she was fighting her way from the grip of fever and delirium. Maybe, just maybe, it could now be put behind him. He could bury it deep where he had buried all the other miseries of his life. She loved him with all the passion that little body could hold. She would be what Claire never was.

Leaning down to kiss his wife, Lance touched her face gently. Then he led the small wedding party to a photographer's studio where they posed for pictures in every possible grouping. First there was the entire party. Then the groom and best man. After that, the images of the three men were captured. Then Raine and Lance posed together, and finally Raine and Tess were immortalized by the process introduced by Louis Daguerre more than a decade before.

Posing was an exhausting and sometimes exasperating experience, and the entire wedding party was overjoyed when it was finally done. They needed no prompting to return to the Parker House, where a midday feast awaited them in a private dining room.

For his wedding meal Lance had spared no expense. There were cold-water lobsters, smoked salmon, caviar, cheeses, and fruits of all kinds, which supplemented the main meal of steak and potatoes. Dessert was an impressive array of marzipan, pies and miniature French pastries, and everything was washed down with champagne.

But Lance's appetite was dulled by quiet anticipation. Raine did no more than nibble at the fruit and cheese. She was anxious to escape the toasts and the jokes. Finally Lance tapped his glass with a spoon and made the last toast. He stood and raised his glass. "To my bride," he said, turning toward Raine. "To Raine Colter Randall. May whatever fates control our destinies grant her long life and happiness."

"To Raine," came the echoing chorus as Lance fixed his gaze on his wife and asked the silent question only she understood, and she nodded in acquiesence.

"Now if you folks will excuse us, we'll be lookin' for a little privacy," Lance drawled with an expression of serene innocence on his face as he put down his glass.

Raine accepted the hand he offered her, and she held it tightly for several long seconds, feeling warm and safe in its strength. Then she rose from her chair to go with her husband. She had committed herself to Lance even before they had been married, but now that committment was irrevocable. The depths of her love and devotion to the tall, muscular man glowed in her eyes.

A rush of tenderness and gratitude played havoc with Lance's composure. A sudden stinging in his eyes announced the presence of uncharacteristic tears. He put his hands to each side of Raine's face and bent his head so only she could hear. "Thank you for marrying me. It's probably one of the few right things I've ever done. Thank you, Muffin," he repeated softly, and touched his lips to hers in a gentle, lingering kiss.

Raine felt only a deep and abiding faith in the man she loved. She would trust him with her life and with her future for now and forever. She had never been more certain of anything than she was of the rightness of this marriage.

Lance and Raine excused themselves from the celebration, but the rest of the wedding party stayed to drink and eat and raise many toasts to the new bride and groom. The revelry lasted into the evening hours, when Bart and Zeke escorted Tess back to her place of employment. Bart smiled with knowing eyes as he returned to the ship alone, leaving Zeke in Tess's capable hands.

While their guests had been celebrating with fine wines and food, Raine and Lance had hearts and minds only for each other. Raine thrilled to her husband's touch as he unfastened each hook and pushed away each obscuring article of clothing. He was in no hurry and his hands were gentle. His kisses were tender and reassuring, and Raine responded to the love and gentleness.

She shivered in anticipation as the last barrier between her and her husband was discarded. Then Lance removed his own clothing in full view of his wife. His movements were natural and unselfconscious, and to Raine he was the most beautiful of men. She could not take her eyes off him, and studied him as she would a marvelously worked statue, for to her Lance was, indeed, a work of art. Each muscle that rippled under the smooth golden skin was accentuated by every fluid motion of his body. And when Lance came to her and held her close she needed no enticing. She was ready for him even as she felt his need for her grow hard against her loins.

When Lance eased them both to the bed they lay quiet for a moment and then began the slow exploration, a ritual as old as time. Raine's fingers teased and encouraged, while Lance's hands stroked the firm young body, which responded to each touch. His lips brushed across the curves and hollows of her body, and Raine arched in yearning. She had waited so long and now she wanted the fullness, the completeness that only Lance could give her. She was not afraid nor was she shy. "Love me," she whispered, and Lance nodded.

Turning her on her side with her back to a small bedside table, he eased slowly between her legs and adjusted her body to his, showing her the right position. Raine needed no other tutoring. Her body had a knowledge all its own as she pressed against the hardened pulsing of Lance's desire.

Slowly, applying only the lightest pressure, Lance penetrated and then stopped. Raine moaned and tried to move forward, to drive him deeper into her body, but Lance held her still. His hands gripped her with thumbs pressing high against her thighs, forcing Raine to wait, helpless as the pulsing rhythm of his body sparked and twitched through them both, building their need for each other to an unbearable pitch.

Then his hand slid around to her bottom, slowly but inexorably increasing the pressure as the hard fullness of him gradually filled every inch of her until Raine was totally consumed by him. She moaned and twisted under the torment of insatiable need, squeezing Lance tight between her legs, pleading with every move of her body, but Lance waited. It was not time. He allowed Raine to search with small, desperate movements. When he heard her breathing turn into soft moans and felt the pressure of her hands on his buttocks increase even as her nails scratched, Lance eased her legs higher and held her until she gave a quick, sharp cry of rapture. Then he helped her find release even as his own body broke free of the shackles of self-imposed restraint.

When the driving need eased Lance and
Raine lay joined for an instant until his
spent body slipped from hers. It was then
that Lance reached to the night table. Holding his wife so she could not see, he eased a
small vial from the drawer. Then he dripped
a little of its contents on himself and on
Raine. His stroking hand smeared the contents over their thighs, and Raine suspected
nothing.

Tapping Raine lightly on her bare bottom, he smiled and said, ''Guess we'd better
get cleaned up.'' He was anxious now for her
to see the results of their lovemaking.

When Raine roused herself from a bed
still warm with the heat of passion she
frowned. She had forgotten that her blood
would be spilled on their first night. She
glanced at her husband, who was stretched
out comfortably with one arm thrown over
his eyes. Then she blushed. He, too, had
blood smeared over his private parts. Quickly, she retreated behind the screen that hid
the washstand from view and rubbed the
blood from her thighs.

While she was taking care of her own
needs, Lance lay relaxed, awaiting her
return. He smiled and kissed her lightly
before rising and disappearing behind the
screen, where he washed the blood of a
butchered calf from his body. His eyes
gleamed in satisfaction, for Raine suspected
nothing. He blew out a cleansing breath. It

had worked. She had not guessed. It was over.

Not long after Lance had returned to bed, he laughed and pulled her to him. Guiding her hand to his enlarged organ, he waited, and Raine snuggled close, trying to capture the hardness of him, trying to move so she could know once more the agonizing joy that had filled her only moments before.

But Lance had other ideas. Without warning, he turned her on her back and, before Raine could protest, he had her imprisoned between powerful, muscular thighs. Then he began to tease. He played and he touched. He caught soft, tender flesh between his teeth, and Raine held her breath for fear of being hurt, something that amused Lance and at the same time roused a great sense of protectiveness in him.

When he could stand no more Lance obeyed the unsubtle pressure of his wife's hands on his back. He came to her with a roughness that made Raine frown, but the frown quickly changed into a long series of sobs as she pleaded with him to help her. Finally she writhed and twisted her way to the summit of ecstacy. When she squirmed in desperation, trying to impale herself even further on the spear of Lance's manhood, her husband shifted her position slightly and joined her as the dam of passion broke, drowning them in the waters of a love at flood tide.

Lance shuddered and lay still. His heart raced and pounded. It had been a long time since he had made love to anyone so fiercely and completely or with such terrible need. And never had he been loved so thoroughly in return. Raine had given him all the love she possessed, and it was a great deal more than he had ever been offered before.

As he held her comforting warmth close to him, Raine whispered, "I love you."

With his black humor surfacing, Lance drawled in sardonic tones, "Seems to me we'd be in quite a fix if you didn't."

Raine was disappointed, but she would have to be satisfied. There were some men who just couldn't bring themselves to say the words out loud, but Lance showed her in every *other* way that he loved her.

Sighing in resignation, she turned over and drifted to sleep until, just before daylight, she awoke with a very definite need pulsing through her. She turned and watched as Lance slept peacefully beside her. The small smile that danced at the corners of her mouth was wicked as she thought how mean it would be to awaken him so soon.

Then a soft, musical giggle slipped from her as she leaned over and began to touch Lance's ear with the lightest brush of her lips. She moved on to his closed eyes and down to his mouth, and still there was no response.

Raine was about to give up when Lance

frightened her out of her wits by turning on her so suddenly he made her jump. Then laughing and pulling her to him roughly, he locked her legs between his own so she could not move.

"Lookin' for trouble?" he asked playfully.

Raine purred like a kitten. "I don't think it's trouble." Then, encouraged by the gleam in her husband's eyes, Raine continued her assault.

She felt as bold as brass as she nuzzled and nibbled all the sensitive areas where Lance had touched her. She advanced from his ears to lips to chest and still did not stop. When she had progressed past his navel, nipping the hard, tight flesh with her small white teeth, Lance drew up his legs as the shock of arousal coursed through him.

"Oh Lord," he moaned, "I'm not goin' to live out the year."

"Want me to stop?" Raine asked, feigning an innocence and a concern she did not feel even as her hand slipped between his legs and fondled the twin jewels that guarded his erect staff of desire.

"No," he whispered hoarsely, and proceeded to take her with a roughness that only spurred Raine's desire. He rode her until she cried out and then he ended it, bringing her gently out of her torment and assuaging his own.

When it was over, when her heart pounded from the effort she had expended,

Raine still ached for Lance, and a twinge of fear shot through her. Was she one of those women she had heard the miners joke about, a woman who was never content? Even when Lance had fulfilled her completely, even when she was exhausted from responding to him, even then she needed him.

She caught her lower lip between her teeth and shivered. If she *were* one of those women whom no man could satiate, what would she do, for nothing would drive Lance away quicker than a woman he could never hope to satisfy.

Lance saw the frown and the look of distress. "Somethin' on your mind?"

She wasn't sure she should tell him, but after a brief silence Raine decided she must be honest no matter what the cost. "I always want more," she mumbled in embarrassment. "Even when I'm so exhausted from making love that I couldn't possibly do it again, I want more. Oh, Lance," she sobbed, deeply afraid, "what's wrong with me?"

He looked into that troubled face, reading the pain and confusion. She trusted him and looked to him for the answer, but it was an answer he wasn't going to give.

"Some people just need more lovin' than others," he answered quietly, and soothed away her frown with gentle hands. "Maybe you're one of them."

A rakish smile chased her fears. "Anyway, I got plenty to give and lots of ways to give it. So don't fret. Besides," he added on a more practical note, "when the first baby comes, I'll probably have to hogtie you to get you into bed with me. Once you suffer the consequences, maybe you won't be so eager to keep comin' back for more."

"I can only hope!" Raine laughed as Lance's large hand, which could have done some damage, landed in gentle rebuke on her bare bottom.

"Don't try it," he growled playfully, and then sent her into a fit of giggling and begging for mercy as he nibbled and nuzzled every sensitive spot on her body. This time Lance aroused *her*. If she wanted more, she was going to get it. All she could handle and then some. He smiled as he drew her close. She had definitely married the right man.

When it was over Lance was exhausted. His body was drained and he loved it. He loved having a woman want him so very much that she begged him to give her all he was capable of giving. And it was real. There was no pretense. He had had enough of that in the past to know the difference.

Then his eyes clouded with guilt as he studied the face of the woman who lay sleeping in his arms. He knew only too well what was wrong. It was not lovemaking Raine needed. It was *love*. His love.

The physical act satisfied her only for the moment. There was a deeper yearning, a yearning no amount of bedding could ever banish. What Raine sought from him he had not given, and somewhere deep in that young mind she knew it, and she hungered for it.

Lance frowned against the pain. He had cheated her. He had robbed her of the thing she needed most, a deep and abiding love. He had no right to do it. Claire was gone. He could not bring her back. Neither could the child who lay dreaming in his arms.

8

For two weeks Raine lived in her world of make-believe. Her turreted castle was the opulent suite in which she lived, and her handsome prince was Lance. She smiled when she thought of him, and already she missed him terribly. He'd had important business to attend to this morning and though he had only been gone for three hours, she was lonesome.

At a loss for anything to do to keep herself occupied, Raine decided to walk to a bookstore where she might purchase the volume about which she had heard several heated discussions. It seemed that a woman named Stowe had caused quite a stir last year with something called *Uncle Tom's*

Cabin, and she had been anxious to purchase a copy.

Throwing on her cape, Raine walked down the stairs and out onto the sidewalk. The wind was coming in from the ocean and it almost took her breath away. It was cold and damp, and the sky was so dark, mid-day seemed more like the coming of night. Everything had an eerie feeling to it. It was one of those days that sent a shiver of apprehension down Raine's spine. She pulled her cape tighter around her and continued on her errand.

Not more than two blocks from the hotel, Raine stopped abruptly. She stared in disbelief at the figures across the street who scurried like dried leaves before the wind. There was no mistaking the man. It was Lance. And the person he hugged to him, the person he protected from the blustering wind was a woman.

For an instant slashing pain immobilized Raine. Then she stepped back into a recessed doorway; for some odd reason she felt guilty. She was spying on her husband. And then bitterness replaced guilt. Her resolve hardened and her conscience turned the other way. She had to know.

Squinting against the wind, Raine looked again and, at that moment, the woman turned her laughing face up to Lance. An involuntary moan of distress pushed past the lump of fear in Raine's throat. There was no doubt what the woman was. She was almost a carbon copy of Tess, only she was ten years younger.

The rouged cheeks and lips, the darkened areas around the eyes that made them seem larger and more inviting, told the story. And to make it worse, she was very attractive in her paints and powders.

Raine shook the fear away and looked for a safe spot to cross the street that separated her from Lance. The rains had turned the public thoroughfares into little more than mud pits that sometimes seemed to have no bottom. Still, she had to admit, things had improved a great deal since she and her father had first seen the raw tent city called San Francisco. Now, at least, there were sidewalks in some parts of town, and a few of the streets in the more fashionable neighborhoods had been improved. But the rats were still there. Raine shivered as she thought of the hordes that infested the streets near the water, especially at night. But there were more than rats to be afraid of in Sydney Town.

Shaking the old anxieties from her, Raine found sure footing where boards, barrel tops and any other item that could be spared formed an uncertain bridge across the mud. Carefully, Raine made her way to the other side, where she stood still, watching as Lance escorted the young woman through the doorway of the same jewelry shop where they had bought their wedding rings. Somehow this fact made it even less bearable, and Raine fought back tears. Then she became angry, so angry that she dared face Lance and his latest whore.

Entering the store, Raine did not care that the tinkling of the overhead bell caused Lance to turn in her direction. The quickly covered expression of guilt on his face told her all she needed to know. Her temper flared, but she managed to remember her mother's dictum and, outwardly, at least, she was calm.

Her husband almost knocked over his chair in his haste to stand. Raine asked pointedly, "Aren't you going to introduce me?"

With just the barest hint of amusement in his eyes, Lance replied in his most maddening tone of casual indifference, "Guess you two should get to know each other at that. Alice, may I present my wife, Raine?"

The reversed order of introduction was a deliberate slight and Raine knew it. It was one of the many things her mother had drummed into her at an early age. You presented the person of lesser rank to the person of higher rank, never the other way around. And Lance had presented *her* to this Alice creature. And he had *dared* use her first name!

A temper Raine had struggled against all her life erupted. With eyes blazing, she turned on her husband. "How dare you present me to this whore, and by my first name. Really, your lack of breeding is obvious—both from your deplorable manners and from the company you keep."

The coldness that frosted Lance's pale eyes frightened Raine, and she fell silent. She couldn't think of anything more to say. "My manners aren't always what they should be, my dear, but then neither are yours. I would appreciate it if you would allow me to get on with my business. Surely you must have something better to do than spy on your husband."

Nothing in this loathesome situation enraged Raine more than the sly smirk on the face of Lance's newest conquest, and she couldn't decide whom to hit first. Then she settled on her husband.

Before Lance could react the full force of her gloved hand caught him across the face. It was a stinging blow, but Raine didn't care. Neither did she waste any time assessing its effectiveness.

No sooner had her hand cleared the first target than she delivered a blow to the shocked face of Alice. The beautifully coiffed prostitute made the mistake of trying to fight back, but Raine had not spent the last six years of her life in a rough mining camp without learning the rudiments of self-defense. She did not waste time pulling hair or scratching the eyes from the face of the whore for whom she felt a bitter hatred. Instead, she landed a vicious blow to the face of her enemy. The woman went down like a rock as Raine was lifted bodily from her feet by her husband.

"Damn," Lance hissed in a tone that warned Raine that she had gone too far. But she was too furious to care what Lance thought.

"Put me down!" she ordered imperiously as she kicked and squirmed to break the crushing hold, but Lance just shifted her weight under his arm and carried her to the front door, where he shoved her out of the shop.

"Go home," he commanded in a deceptively quiet voice. "Stay there until I have a chance to talk to you." Then he shut the door in Raine's face, leaving her fuming on the sidewalk. She turned defiantly on her heel and walked in a direction that did not lead to the hotel.

Lance could feel the anger rise in him. She was defying him. He had given her an order and she was now in open rebellion. His temper seethed just beneath the surface. Outwardly, however, he was calm. Opening the door, he called her name against the wind as Raine half walked and half ran from him.

But she did not hear Lance as the wind pushed his voice back to him. Nor did she hear him close the distance between them with long, angry strides, but she did feel the iron grip of his fingers digging into her arm as he spun her around to face him.

"Where do you think you're going?" he asked almost casually, one eyebrow raised quizzically.

And Raine, who really knew very little about her husband, made the mistake of defying him a second time. "I don't know! Anywhere I please! Now let go of me," she demanded.

"Not likely," Lance drawled in that aggravating way of his. "And since you can't seem to get there on your own, I'll see you home myself."

"Don't you think you'd better get back to your whore?" Raine asked in icy tones of barely concealed contempt.

Lance blinked, and his eyes narrowed under the strain of his wife's outrageous behavior. He took a deep breath and answered calmly, "I'll do that all right—*after* I get you off the street." His eyes were cold and unrelenting as they locked with hers. "You can either go under your own steam or I can help you along."

It was a threat Raine did not ignore. Besides, the fight had just about gone out of her. Only the pain remained. "I'll walk, thank you," she answered primly.

"Wise decision," Lance remarked cryptically, and then guided his wife in the proper direction.

When they reached the boards Raine had used to cross the street Lance picked her up and carried her to the other side, where he stood her on her feet. "Now git!" he commanded, and gave her a smart slap on the rump just as he would a stubborn horse who needed a little encouragement to get moving.

Then, in a voice that gave little hint of the anger that still boiled just beneath the surface, Lance gave his last order. "I'll be home this evening. You wait for me, you understand?"

A small muscle along the side of Raine's jaw twitched at the command. Her eyes flashed angry fire. She clenched her teeth to hold back the flood of words that would destroy their marriage forever. She was not yet sure what she was going to do, and until she was, she would remain silent. "Yes, I understand," she replied, and then said no more.

Lance read her uncertainty. A flicker of regret showed in his usually expressionless eyes. "Be there," he warned. "You won't like it if I have to come looking for you."

Defiance was written all over Raine's upturned face. "Don't you threaten me, Lance Randall. If I decide to run, *you'll* never find me," she warned, and stalked away.

Lance stared after her until she entered the wide front door of the hotel. Not once had she looked back. It was not like her. Then he grinned. She had quite a temper, and she'd fight if she had to. "Hell," he moaned as he suddenly remembered Alice Rafferty, who had been knocked to the floor by Raine's vicious attack.

Hurrying back to the shop, he entered to find Alice glaring at him from the overstuffed chair to which she had been helped by the clerk. Her hat was comically askew, and Lance could barely repress a smile as he asked, "You all right?"

With a sullen pout, Alice snarled, "Yeah, I'm all right. Better than your wife is right now. At least I don't have to wonder where my husband is or who he's in bed with the way she does." The smile on Alice's face reflected her satisfaction, for she knew that it was Raine Randall who had been hurt the most.

Lance shrugged in seeming indifference. "You pick out what you want?"

"Yeah," Alice replied, realizing that she could probably ask for and get a much more valuable piece than she could have coaxed out of Lance before his wife had made such a fearful scene. "That brooch," she said, pointing to a dazzling diamond and sapphire sunburst that Lance knew would cost him a small fortune.

"On one condition," Lance warned.

"And what's that?" Alice asked suspiciously.

"That you keep my wife's outburst of temper to yourself."

Alice Rafferty raised her eyebrows and then shrugged her shoulders. "Sure. Why not?"

Lance nodded to the clerk. "We'll take it."

"Yes sir," the clerk answered respectfully. "A marvelous choice, if I may say."

"And a marvelous price to go with it, I suppose," Lance drawled in wry humor, for he was indeed paying a much higher price than he had intended. And if he couldn't assure his wife that he had not intentionally humiliated her, he would eventually pay a far greater price.

"But of course, sir," the clerk replied cheerfully. "Shall I wrap the brooch or will the lady wear it?"

"I'll wear it," Alice interposed before Lance could reply. The clerk made quite a show of pinning the stunning brooch on the prostitute who had wangled such an expensive present from her admirer.

After he had escorted Alice back to her place of employment Lance walked around to the door of the pleasure palace, which opened onto a dining area. Crossing the room, he headed for a raised area where he could see everything without being too conspicuous himself, for his table was shielded by several potted ferns, which provided a degree of privacy.

Easing his large frame onto the gilt and crimson chair, Lance gazed from one group of men to another as he perused the room.

There were men he recognized as steady patrons, and as he fixed each face in his mind, Zeke and Bart strolled in the front door.

Standing to attract their attention, Lance motioned for them to join him, and when they sat with their backs protected Lance shared the information he had gotten at such a high price from Alice Rafferty.

"The Clary brothers went north. Into Washington Territory. Not south as we had thought. We'll head out as soon as we can get our gear together. Zeke, you get the ship ready to sail by tomorrow, and if any of the crew gives you trouble, you know what to do."

"Sure do," Zeke answered casually. "They'll be aboard if I have to hogtie 'em, every man-jack of 'em. But what about Raine? Who's gonna look out for her? Hell, Lance, she's all alone here."

"I don't think we have to worry about her. She seems capable of takin' care of herself," Lance answered and then smiled as the last of his annoyance dissipated. "Shoulda seen the haymaker she landed on Alice today."

Bart's normally tanned face paled and his vivid blue eyes shot sparks of anger at his friend. "She saw you with Alice?"

"Afraid so," Lance admitted ruefully. "Kicked up quite a fuss about it too. I told her to go on to the hotel and wait for me, but I'm not too anxious to face a woman who's probably bawling her eyes out. She was pretty upset. She'd have to be to create the kind of scene she did.''

Zeke's eyes locked with his friend's. "I don't think Miss Raine is the bawlin' type. Not for very long, at least," he warned, and for the first time in years he was furious with the man who had been as close to him as a brother. "I'd watch my step if I were you. That is," he added seriously, "if you want to keep her."

Though his body remained in its loose, languid pose and his face was relaxed, Lance felt a twinge of fear. Then he brushed it aside. "Hell," he muttered, "don't see as how I can lose her. She loves me enough to believe anything I tell her. Besides," he added sharply, "she's my wife. She'll do what I tell her, and she'll believe what I want her to believe."

Bart shook his head doubtfully. "I wouldn't count on it, Lance. That little lady has a lot of pride. If I were you, I'd flat-out tell her the truth about Alice Rafferty. I wouldn't let this go any farther."

Annoyed by the unsolicited advice he was getting, Lance's temper flared. "She's *my* wife," he muttered. "Suppose you leave this to me."

"Glad to!" Bart answered with the greatest degree of disgust he could muster.

Lance was about to pick up the gauntlet when the waiter arrived with the large

tassled menus. Without glancing at his,
Lance ordered dinner, but Zeke and Bart
delayed, deliberately taking more time than
necessary to decide upon their choice. When
they thought Lance had been irritated
enough they ordered the same meal he had
requested, the same meal they always had.

Lance was thoughtful. It was one thing
to be annoyed with Raine, but it was quite
another to let her think the worst just to
garner a sweet drop of revenge for her behavior. *And her lack of trust*, he thought
bitterly. But Raine had a temper and he'd
better step easy.

He tried to convince himself that everything would be all right. Raine would understand once he explained. She would forgive
him for being seen in public with a whore—
and buying her an expensive piece of jewelry
at that. Just maybe things would be all right
between them. Maybe Raine loved him
enough to forgive the insult.

Picking at a meal he didn't find appetiz-
ing, Lance lingered over coffee, a lot more
worried than he had been just an hour ago.
Then he decided there was no point in putting it off. He had to face Raine sooner or
later. "Think I'll head on back to the hotel.
I'll meet you aboard ship in the morning."

The brothers nodded, stood and walked
through the dining room. They did not look
back at Lance as he paid the bill.

Sighing in acceptance of the rebuff,

Lance glanced around the room out of habit. There seemed to be no source of danger lurking in any of the corners. Most of the people here were regulars, but that didn't always mean much. As often as not, the man who was after someone's hide would be sure to be seen at many of the places his victim frequented. A false sense of security would be built up, and soon he'd drop his guard. That's when it would come. He had played that game himself. Again his eyes took in the room, only this time he noticed the bulge of guns that had been poorly concealed under suit coats, and he kept his eyes on them until he had eased out the door.

His thoughts were on Raine as he walked home, and he felt a sharp pang of guilt for the heartache he had caused her. Nobody needed to tell him how much she loved him. As far as she was concerned, he was her whole life. He should have been much more discreet with Alice Rafferty. Escorting her through the streets of San Francisco in broad daylight had been an insult to his wife. He had treated Raine with less consideration than he showed to the whores who worked in the pleasure palace he had just left.

Lance smiled as he thought of the word Raine had once used. "Chivalry," he said quietly. Being married put quite a strain on getting the job done, the job he had been sent here to do regardless of the cost.

Lance breathed deeply and his mind returned once more to his mission. He wondered how he was going to tell Raine that he had to leave her after only two weeks of marriage. A short, bitter laugh jerked from his lips. It wasn't going to be easy.

By the time he reached the hotel, Lance had made up his mind. He had no choice. He would explain about Alice and tell Raine why his dealings with her had been necessary.

He felt more confident as he stood in front of their door, inserting the key in the lock. Everything would be all right. If Raine loved him enough, she would understand that Alice Rafferty had been no more than a source of information and that the piece of jewelry had been her price for that information.

Easing the door open, Lance stepped in. The day had turned darker and the drapes had been drawn. Only one lamp burned low, its feeble light driving back the shadows just far enough to allow Lance to see the small figure sitting calmly in the high Queen Anne chair. A slight movement gave notice that Raine was aware of his presence.

Raine's thoughts during her time of waiting had been ones of confusion and uncertainty, but finally she had decided to put off any decision until she heard what her husband had to say. He must tell her the truth. There could be no lies between them, no matter how bitter the truth might be. And there could be no more knives twisting in her heart.

"You all right, Muffin?" Lance asked as he made his way toward the chair.

"No," Raine answered truthfully, "I'm not all right."

Lance stopped short and stared through the dim light. Raine's back was straight. Her hands were folded quietly in her lap. She was tense—waiting, waiting for something.

With despair written on his face, Lance continued toward his wife. "I'm sorry, Raine. I didn't mean for you to see me with Alice."

She stared at him in disbelief. "And if I hadn't caught you with Alice, everything would have been all right as far as you're concerned," she said ominously.

"That's not the way I meant it. Damn," Lance cursed in chagrin, "I should have just bought her something. I should have taken it to her instead of parading her through town the way I did. I sure didn't mean to hurt you."

Raine blinked and looked at him through eyes filled with pain. "That was the least of it, Lance, though God knows that part of it was cruel enough. I'm not going to enjoy every whore in San Francisco pointing her finger at me, laughing at me. Lance," she sobbed before regaining her composure, "how could you do it? How could you?"

Then, putting her hand to her eyes, she

paused before she had the courage to continue. She was not sure she wanted to know the answer to her question. She was afraid to know it. "What I must know, Lance, is whether or not you have been sleeping with prostitutes since I married you."

The pain in Raine's eyes was too much for Lance to bear. She was still a child. How could she know that he would no more betray her than he would his own particular code of honor? She had known him for less than a month. And from what she had seen, she had every right to feel betrayed. All these thoughts and more flashed through Lance's mind as he studied the desolation on his wife's face.

Lance took the first step. He gathered Raine in his arms and held her close to him as he explained. "No," he said, the sound of his voice muffled by her hair, "no, Muffin, I haven't slept with any other woman since I met you—prostitute or not." Then he laughed. "Where would I get the energy?"

Raine dared to look up at him. She could hardly believe her ears. Lance had not betrayed her. "But why?" she began, and Lance put a finger to her lips.

"Alice Rafferty had information I needed to do the job I was sent here to do. Her price was jewelry, but the price went up when you went into a jealous frenzy and knocked her to the floor. I was hopin' to get away a lot cheaper than I did," he concluded with wry humor.

A shamefaced, nervous smile touched Raine's mouth. "I'm sorry," she said as she lowered her gaze.

"I've told you before we married that you would have to trust me," Lance said. "Now, can we forget it?"

"Yes," Raine assured him, and took his hand in hers. "I love you, Lance. With all my heart. I could never bear to share you with others. I would sooner give you up than have your love for me diminish."

Lance put his arms around her and felt her heart racing. He had terrified her. He let out a long sigh and tilted Raine's face to his. "I have to act on Alice's information right away. We've already lost too much time. I'll be sailing on the morning tide, and I don't know when I'll be back," he said as gently as he could. "Will you be all right here by yourself? We can always get Tess to stay with you if you're afraid to be alone."

Raine tried not to let her disappointment show, but she could hardly help it. She wanted to plead with Lance not to go. If she did, however, he would be very disappointed in her, and despite her anguish and fear, she still very much wanted to please her husband. And she knew that she must not ask questions. Lance had warned her, and she knew that the time would come when her promises would be tested.

"Be careful, my darling," she pleaded, and Lance smiled down at her. She wasn't going to cry or cling to him. She was going to let him do his job without a scene, and he loved her all the more for it.

Then he decided that she had to know what it was about. It was not fair to keep her in the dark, to let her think all kinds of terrible things and worry herself to death. "Sit down," he said quietly, and took a seat opposite her. "In the summer of fifty-two a wagonload of gold was on its way to San Francisco from my father's mine. It was waylaid, and as much gold as the holdup men could carry away with them was stolen. The driver and the guard recognized the thieves. Zeke and Bart and I were sent here to find them and, if possible, to recover the gold. We've been here for months trying to pick up any kind of lead, and finally Alice Rafferty was able to provide one. The Clary brothers, according to her, went north to Washington Territory. I don't know if we'll have much luck since so much time has gone by, but we have to try.

"Now," he continued with an inviting gleam in his eyes, "how about giving your husband a proper send-off? It might help to keep me out of trouble."

Raine laughed with him. She deserved the mild rebuke for having so little faith in Lance, and she knew she had hurt him by suspecting him of betraying her. So ashamed of herself that she could not look into her husband's eyes, Raine slipped from her chair and knelt at his feet and lay her head on his knees. "Please forgive me, Lance. I was so jealous I couldn't bear it."

"I know, Muffin," he said softly as he put his hand on her head. "But you must trust me. You must not doubt. Promise?"

"I promise," she answered, and put her arms around Lance's neck as he picked her up and carried her to their bed.

9

Early the next morning Lance boarded his ship in time to catch the ebbing tide. With any luck at all he would be entering the Columbia River within the week. But once under sail time dragged, and Lance spent much of each day isolated in his cabin, where his thoughts invariably turned to Raine. He recalled almost every moment they had spent together, and he smiled as he remembered the first night he had made love to her.

Then he frowned at the thought. Until now, he had not considered the possibility that it was Raine he had loved that terrible night. Was it really Claire who had inflamed his passions and tormented his soul? He didn't know anymore. All he knew was that he missed Raine's loving arms and the luminous eyes that reflected her love for him. He also knew that he was miserable away from her.

Zeke and Bart had a pretty good idea of what was bothering their friend and they did not intrude upon his melancholy. Instead, they accepted his desire for solitude as well as his taciturn demeanor the few times he sought out their company.

Despite their tact and the fact that Zeke and Bart tried to divert Lance's attention to other matters, he continued to chafe under his monastic state, something that had seldom troubled him before he had met Raine. It was something neither Zeke nor Bart ever alluded to, for they thought they must be mistaken. Needing a woman on a regular basis was something they couldn't afford— not with the kind of work they did. Besides, Lance was the one among them who needed a bed partner the least. Then a smile of understanding touched Zeke's lips. It certainly hadn't taken Miss Raine long to spoil her husband.

Fortunately, Lance had little time to brood, for their ship made good time and they turned into the Columbia River sooner than they'd expected. The captain navigated the river as far as he dared with a ship that size, and when he anchored Lance and his friends disembarked, hoping that their crew would still be there when they returned.

Once ashore, the three men arranged

for the purchase of sturdy horses, which were examined thoroughly for any weaknesses that might mean the difference between living and dying. They bought food and extra clothing designed for the colder weather they would encounter as they moved inland.

Finally, and only as a precaution against the worst possible eventuality, they purchased snowshoes, for if they were caught in mountain country when the real blizzards of winter hit, they would never make it through the deep drifts without them. The horses, of course, would be destroyed, for they could not be abandoned to suffer from the bitter cold as they struggled and fought the deep drifts only to find themselves hopelessly trapped, unable to save themselves from creeping death.

The only good part about it was that once they hit Snake River country their task would almost be done, for it was in this region that Alice Rafferty had assured Lance he would find the Clary brothers. Lance hoped she was right, for they had only a short time before the winter snows closed the passes. And if that happened, they would have to return to San Francisco, where they would wait for spring before continuing their hunt, since Lance had no intention of deliberately risking his own life or the lives of his friends.

Even if the weather cooperated, there was yet another concern. Wars between the

Indians and the white settlers still continued. There had been massacres on both
sides. Red man and white man alike were
determined to exterminate each other, and
Lance didn't like the thought of getting
caught in the middle.

Unconsciously, his hand went to his
throat and touched the necklace that had
been in his family for generations. It was
made of bear teeth and claws. From the
center hung the finely carved head of a
mountain lion. For a hundred years it had
provided safe passage through hostile territory for the Randall family, and Lance hoped
it would this time as well. But he wasn't
sure. Some of the younger braves had broken with tribal leaders and were attacking
white settlements without warning. They
also attacked travelers along the lonely and
desolate trails. He might never even have the
chance to show the totem that he counted
on to keep him and his men safe.

While Lance proceeded on his mission
with more than usual caution, Raine sat
alone and forlorn in her suite. She was
exceedingly bored and had almost read herself blind. Now she sat at the dressing table
staring sullenly at her image in the mirror.
Then she smiled happily as she thought of
Tess. Tess could help her.

Throwing on a cloak to protect herself
from the chill of late December, Raine
litterally skipped down the steps and

through the lobby of the hotel. Once out on the street, she breathed deeply of the invigorating air. She felt better already, for just the prospect of pleasing Lance exhilarated her.

It was painfully obvious to Raine that Lance was attracted to women like Tess and Alice. She knew that he admired the stylishness of those daring women who dressed in such extravagant gowns and wore all sorts of rouges and powders, and she was determined to be just as alluring and provocative as they were. It was going to be great fun learning their secrets, for Raine was convinced that such women surely knew more than she could even imagine. And who better to teach her than Tess—Tess whose hair was always perfect, whose makeup was so alluring and whose eye sparked with interest when she glanced in the direction of a wealthy man.

But first there was an even more important errand to complete. She was going to face Alice Rafferty, for Raine had not yet forgotten the sly smirk on the whore's face. Now it was her turn.

Upon reaching the side door of the fancy establishment in which both Alice and Tess worked, Raine did not hesitate. She hungered and thirsted for revenge.

She pushed open the door and entered an imposing reception room, which was beautifully and expensively furnished.

Raine stood quite still, taking in every detail of the warm and inviting room with its cozy groupings of settees and chairs, the cheery fire in the ornate fireplace and the walls, which boasted one oil painting after another.

As her eyes took in each work of art, Raine could not help but smile, for each scene was much like the one before it. In one degree of nudity or another, voluptuous ladies with coquettish eyes smiled vapidly into hers. Often there was no more than a gracefully flowing ribbon or a strategically held flower to lend some semblance of respectability to the portraits, and only then did Raine *really* begin to understand.

It was not necessary for her to face Alice Rafferty. It was not necessary for her to demean the woman who was no more a threat to her than the paintings on the wall.

But fate would not allow Raine to escape undetected, for at that precise moment Alice appeared on the stairs and gaped in surprise. Then her mood turned surly. "If you came to make any more trouble, I'll have you thrown out," she whined. Raine's smile was cherubic.

"Why, Miss Alice," she cooed, "whatever put such a silly notion in your head? I merely came to inquire after your health. I'm very much afraid I should have come sooner, but I *have* been dreadfully busy. However, now that my husband is away on business, I find that I have more than enough idle time to be able to spare a few minutes for you. It really was a nasty thing I did—hitting you so terribly hard, I mean.''

Alice Rafferty heard the contempt that dripped from Raine's every word, and she understood the insult. Nevertheless, she had been in her business long enough to know when to bow out gracefully in the face of certain defeat. She laughed as cynical eyes admitted Raine's victory. ''It's quite all right, Mrs. Randall. As you can see, there was no permanent damage done. Besides, Lance paid me more than an adequate amount for the pain I suffered. I've been hurt a lot worse and gotten a lot less out of it.''

Suddenly Raine was very ashamed of herself. She had no right to be such a nasty snob. Instead, she should be grateful for her own good fortune. She had been raised by loving parents, and she was married to the most wonderful man in the world. And what did she really know about either Alice or Tess? Exactly nothing, and here she was, acting as though they weren't good enough to iron her petticoats.

''I am very pleased my husband compensated you, Miss Rafferty,'' Raine replied graciously. ''And now, if you will excuse me, I really must talk to Tess.''

Alice eyed Raine with idle curiosity. ''Only payin' customers allowed upstairs, Mrs. Randall. If you wait here, I'll get Tess.''

Without waiting for a reply, Alice retraced her way to the second story. Within minutes she returned.

"Tess says she'll meet you at your hotel," Alice stated blandly, not choosing to tell Raine what else Tess had said.

"Thank you," Raine replied, and turned to leave.

Alice Rafferty watched as the beautiful wife of Lance Randall opened the door and stepped out onto the sidewalk. She knew that the woman had come here for more than she had accomplished. She had come to flaunt her victory, yet she had not done so. Oh, she had started out snippy enough, but then something had changed her mind. *Well,* Alice thought, *maybe Tess was right. Maybe Mrs. Randall is a decent enough sort if you meet her under the right circumstances.* Then Alice smiled. There *were* no right circumstances for a wife and a whore to meet.

She shrugged and turned toward the door that led to the gaming room. She wondered if someday she might find a good man who would not hold her past against her. Soft, bitter laughter trailed after her as she sauntered into the room where her day's work would begin.

Happy that she had not been quite as vengeful as she had intended, Raine proceeded to her hotel. But her happiness dissipated as her thoughts returned to Lance.

She missed him terribly, but she understood that she must make the best of it. He had told her from the beginning that he might be gone for long periods of time, and he expected her to wait patiently. She was trying, but it was so difficult. She was so lonely.

Smiling politely at the doorman, Raine entered her hotel and went directly to her suite. Within a half hour, Tess knocked at the door.

Raine smiled up at the taller woman. "Thank you for coming, Tess. Please—come in."

Looking about her surreptitiously to be sure no one was watching, Tess entered swiftly and closed the door behind her. "Good Lord, Raine, don't you know better than to come to the pleasure palace? What if somebody saw you and word got back to Lance?"

Raine frowned. "But why should he mind? *He* goes there. Besides, he's out of town."

Tess blew out an exasperated breath. "Out of town doesn't mean a thing. There are always people who take a lot of pleasure from making other folks miserable. Can't wait to cause trouble. Besides," Tess continued, looking straight into Raine's upturned face, "Lance doesn't come to the pleasure palace anymore. Zeke and Bart, they still come, but not Lance."

Tears of gratitude stung Raine's eyes.

Tess had been under no obligation to tell her that Lance was being faithful to her, that he no longer patronized the pleasure palace or the whores who worked there. Her voice was soft and polite when she replied. "Thank you, Tess. Won't you have a seat? Shall I ring for tea?"

"No," Tess replied. "I really shouldn't have come. Just tell me why you wanted to see me."

Raine sat in her usual chair and Tess took the opposite one. "I know how much Lance is attracted to women like you and Alice—women who dress so beautifully and who know all the secrets of attracting a man. I want you to teach me, Tess. I want Lance to think me as glamorous and as beautiful as you, but I don't know how. Will you help me?"

Even under the skillfully applied make-up, Raine could see Tess lose the natural color from her face. "Good God!" Tess whispered hoarsely. "Have you lost your mind? Lance'll wring both our necks. What's gotten into you?"

"I just want Lance to look at me the way he looked at you," Raine replied honestly.

"Oh, no you don't, honey!" Tess answered emphatically. "Hell, he *married* you. Must have liked what he saw. Why go change it now? And as I understand it, he fell in love with you when you looked worse than a drowned cat."

Once more her doubts and anxieties surfaced. Raine lowered her eyes. "Yes, and that is one of the things I don't understand. He told me himself he never mixes in other people's troubles, yet he risked a great deal for me, a stranger. And I know what I must have looked like coming in from the rain, soaked to the skin, hair matted to my skull. It had to be dreadful. Yet Lance chose me. I just don't understand why. You can see for yourself that I'm not very good with hairstyles, and I certainly know nothing of makeup. Yet out of all the beautiful, sophisticated women in San Francisco, he chose me.

"It happened so fast. I hardly had time to think. But I love him and will do anything to please him, to have him look at me and see a desirable, exciting woman, not just a pretty little girl. I want it so much."

Tess blinked back her surprise. Lance had never told her. Raine really didn't know why Lance had married her so quickly. She didn't know that he had taken her while she lay delirious with fever. She didn't know that he had married her before she might find herself pregnant and guess what had happened. Yet it had been obvious to Tess and to anyone else who had seen Lance touch Raine and care for her so tenderly.

Tess frowned. If Raine had been as pure and innocent as Lance had once inferred, then she would have guessed what had happened when she and Lance got married. She had to know that she was no longer a virgin. How could she not know?

A sly smile touched Tess's lips. She didn't know how, but in one way or another Lance had taken care of that problem too. She shook her head in admiration. Lance Randall could cheat the devil and get away with it. Then she sobered. This little girl was no match for him. Not yet, and she could only guess at how much it had cost Raine to come to a prostitute for help—a prostitute who had once serviced the man who was now her husband.

"Men!" she spat, and then got down to business.

"Sure, honey," she said good-naturedly, "I'll teach you a few of the tricks, but nothing too fancy, you understand. Just a little something that'll gild the lily, so to speak. Though to tell the truth, I don't think you need it."

Raine hardly dared believe that Tess was willing to help her. She smiled in delight. "Thank you. Thank you, Tess. And I'll pay you, of course. You just tell me how much."

Shrewd violet eyes studied Raine. "You've got money?"

Raine laughed in delight. "I've got *tons* of money. Daddy struck it rich, and almost everything he ever dug out of the earth or panned from the creek is in a New York bank. The gold we brought with us in November is still in the assay office. It's a sizable amount. And then there's the bank draft that the others in the camp sent me when they learned of daddy's death. They paid me what they thought his claim was worth. All in all, I suppose I'm really rather wealthy.''

''In that case,'' the ever practical Tess replied, ''you can pay me an ounce of gold for every hour I work with you. Is that satisfactory?''

A guilty smile touched Raine's lips. ''Yes, that's most satisfactory, but I should warn you, I'm really a rather fast learner. You won't make much that way.''

Contagious laughter rolled from Tess. ''Hell, the money almost doesn't matter. This is going to be interesting. But if Lance comes after me, I'm going to tell him that you cried and begged 'til I just didn't have the heart to refuse you.''

Raine's musical laughter filled the room. ''I was prepared to do something very much like that,'' she admitted, and both women smiled in understanding.

''And Tess,'' Raine added, ''my appearance isn't all I want to change. I want you to tell me about making love. The special little things you do, the things that keep men coming back even though they're married and have loving wives.''

Tess raised her eyebrows and stared, dumbfounded. ''Don't you think you should let your husband teach you those things?'' she finally managed to ask.

"I would like to surprise him," Raine replied, and Tess could see the eager expectation in the girl's eyes.

"You'll surprise him, all right," the prostitute muttered unhappily, and then stood. "Shall we get started, Mrs. Randall?"

"The hair first," Raine requested as she led the way into her bedroom. Tess brushed and combed and smoothed with professional ease. Carefully, Raine watched as Tess created the upswept style she had done for the wedding. Then Tess tore it apart and combed and brushed again until the hair could be done up in a marvelous soft coil that covered the back of her head. And always Tess pulled out a few wisps here and there to soften the style.

"Have you got a curling iron?" Tess asked, and Raine shook her head.

"How about lip rouge or kohl?"

Again Raine shook her head, and Tess shrugged. "Well, I suppose you can use mine until we see what suits you," she offered, and Raine smiled into the mirror at Tess's reflection.

"Thank you, Tess. Other than you and Jake Finch, I really don't have any friends in San Francisco, and I'm very grateful for all your help."

Tess's face showed her deep disapproval. "You know Jake Finch?"

"Quite well," Raine admitted as she turned to try to see just exactly how Tess had twisted the hair so she would be able to do the same thing.

"Lance know that?"

"I mentioned it. I asked Jake to come to our wedding, but he refused."

"Thank God for small favors," Tess muttered in relief, but she was surprised that Raine would know someone like Jake Finch, who had been one of the Sydney Ducks, that band of Australian thugs who robbed and killed along the waterfront. Only Jake had gotten out. He had seen almost immediately that the real money could be easily plucked from the pockets of the miners, so he had opened the infamous saloon the Aces Up—a place where men could drink and gamble and whore their gold away. And if they didn't have gold enough, Jake managed to have some captain who needed seamen drag them away for a price. It was a mean, hard business, and Jake had made a fortune from it. The fact that Raine knew the man disturbed Tess deeply.

"How do you know him?" she asked bluntly.

"Why shouldn't I know him?" Raine asked in return. "He has always been very kind to Papa and me. In fact, Jake was the one who introduced us to Chinese food, and Papa and I would often stop by for an early supper of rice and pork and every fresh vegetable the cook could lay his hands on. We didn't see much fresh fruit or vegetables in the digs, but we made up for it at Jake's." Raine laughed. Then she sobered. "Papa and Jake would sit and talk for an hour or more. They became good friends, and Jake was always very kind to me."

"Hmm," Tess sneered. "Friendly as a crocodile."

"You don't like him." It was a statement, and Tess gave Raine a disgusted look.

"Can't think of anybody who does," Tess answered evasively. "I've been negotiating with him to sell me his saloon when he goes back to Australia, which is something he says he's going to do, but so far the price is so high, I can only afford about half of it. Besides, I wouldn't pay the price he's asking anyway. Highway robbery. That's what it is. But if he wants to sell it enough, he'll come down."

Finally Tess stood back and admired her handiwork. Raine's beauty was accentuated by the style she now wore, a style that lifted the hair from the sides of her face and swept it in graceful waves to a loosely formed coil at the back of her head. It was perfect, and Raine smiled with pleasure.

"I really do look older, don't I?" she asked, as pleased as she could be.

"Indeed you do," Tess answered with good humor. "All of eighteen, at least."

Raine laughed with her as she thought of how pleased Lance would be when her transformation was complete. She could hardly wait.

10

Christmas came and went. January blended into February, and still Lance had not returned. Raine tried to hide her mounting anxiety, for she had not received a single communication from her husband since he had left San Francisco on the last day of November.

Tess's daily visits had long since ceased, and Raine felt the full burden of her isolation and loneliness, for none of the *nice* families of San Francisco would associate with her, or at least none of them went out of their way to invite her to any event and no one spoke to her on the street.

At first Raine was puzzled, for she frequently bumped into these society women as she shopped for one thing or another, and no one did more than nod her head briefly in recognition. Some of the women ignored her completely when she smiled at them.

Finally Raine asked Tess and learned the truth. The Randalls were powerful and they used that power to take what they wanted. The family was feared and hated, and all anyone wanted to do was to stay out of harm's way. No one would befriend her, because she was married to a Randall who might at any time turn covetous eyes on their profitable businesses.

"They're afraid," Tess explained. "They're afraid of Lance."

Raine jerked her head up sharply and looked at Tess with fury in her eyes. "What do you mean, they're afraid of Lance? He's the kindest, dearest person in this blasted town."

Tess smiled at the strongest expletive Raine ever used. "To you maybe," she said, and then decided that Raine should know just a little more of the truth.

"Do you have any idea what Lance intends to do with the Clary brothers once he tracks them down?"

Raine's face went blank. She had no idea what Tess was leading up to. "I suppose he intends to turn them over to the law."

"Not likely," Tess answered grimly. "From everything I've heard, and I hear plenty in my business, those brothers are as good as dead once they're caught."

"I don't believe you," Raine replied in icy tones, and Tess just shrugged.

"Believe what you want, but that's another reason the *good* people of San Francisco won't have anything to do with you or Lance. It seems there's some question about who that mine and that gold really belong to."

"Then why . . ." Raine began, but stopped in mid-sentence. Her eyes clouded with confusion and she frowned as she shook her head in denial. "No, Lance isn't like that." She was quick to defend him, but she wasn't sure. "Are you certain, Tess?"

"Afraid so, honey. There's no doubt about it. The family's reputation is not too good. Not among honest people, anyway."

"I don't care about the family," Raine almost sobbed. "I mean Lance. Are you sure about Lance?"

Tess saw the anguish in Raine's eyes, and she backed off. "Well, not for *certain* sure, but that's the talk."

"Ohhh," Raine sighed weakly, and she closed her eyes before the tears of relief could escape. "Thank God. I knew they were wrong about Lance. He wouldn't kill two men because they stole a little gold. All he wants is for them to give it back," she explained, convincing herself of the truth of her words even as she spoke them. "Yes," she started with confidence, "that's all Lance wants."

"Might be," Tess agreed easily. "Folks around here are always ready to believe the worst, I guess."

"Yes," Raine said bitterly. "Well, if we aren't good enough for them and they have to make up all those horrid stories about Lance, then I shall ignore them completely. You can believe me that there won't be any more contributions to the Fireman's Fund or to anything else. And if they *dare* ask me, they're going to get an earful!"

Sympathy for this young woman dulled Tess's eyes. Raine really didn't know anything about Lance. She didn't know that he was the one in the Randall family who saw to it that *no one* ever escaped unpunished. She sighed.

"Don't blame you one bit," Tess agreed heartily, but she knew better. Still, she didn't want Raine to hear a lot of talk that would only disturb her. The further away she stayed from all the *nice* people, the better. Lance could tell her what he wanted. It was up to him.

Suddenly Tess's face brightened as she thought of much happier news to share with Raine. "Have you heard? Jake's finally done it. He's leaving for Australia at the end of the week, and he's come down in his price so that I can almost afford the Aces Up."

"No!" Raine exclaimed in surprise. "Jake's really going back home? I hadn't heard."

"Yes," Tess confirmed happily. "That'll be one less Sydney Duck swimming in our bay."

Frowning, Raine defended Jake. "He's my friend, Tess. He was kind to me all the years Papa and I have been coming to San Francisco for the winter. And Papa thought the world of him. When is he leaving?"

Tess wanted to warn Raine again about Jake Finch, but she shrugged it off. Apparently Raine knew a different man than she did. "He's sailing on the *Southern Cross* Saturday morning. Why?"

"Why?" Raine asked, not believing Tess would have to ask. "Because I must say good-bye to him, of course. I couldn't think of letting him go without wishing him God's speed."

Tess groaned. "Hell, you can't go there by yourself. You let me know when you're going and I'll go with you. All right?"

Smiling gratefully at the woman who would soon be her only friend in town, Raine nodded. "We can go Friday night if you aren't busy, and Tess, I would consider it an honor to advance you whatever amount you need to close the sale on Jake's saloon."

Gratitude softened the prostitute's usually cynical eyes. "Thanks, honey. I just might have to take you up on it. But I'm good for it. You'll get it back, every penny."

Merry laughter spilled from Raine's lips. "If you're half as good in bed as you tell me you are, I have no doubt that I'll be paid back in no time at all."

Tess didn't smile. She shook her head slowly. "No more of that for me. I'm going to be like the Duchess from now on. I'll just run the place."

No one needed to tell Raine who the Duchess was. She was perhaps the wealthiest woman in town, and all her money came from the pleasure palace.

Raine couldn't resist teasing Tess just a little. "Not even for Zeke?" she asked coyly.

Tess grinned. "Well, maybe I might make *one* exception," she drawled, and laughed in a manner that could only be described as lewd. Raine enjoyed it all. Tess had become a good friend. She wished her luck. Zeke was a good man, and Tess deserved a good man.

Then the two women turned their conversation to Friday night. It was agreed that Tess would call for Raine at the hotel in a closed carriage. It was something Tess had always insisted on, that her presence at this hotel be kept as secret as possible. She had always come in the morning before guests were up and she left quietly by the back stairs, heavily veiled. She wanted no one to know that a whore was a frequent guest of the woman who resided in the Presidential suite. It wasn't fit. Tess felt a twinge of guilt. The talk had started already. Somehow, somebody knew about the visits, knew about her friendship with Raine.

Now she had to be doubly careful. Lance would hear the talk when he got back, and he wouldn't be pleased. She twitched her lips in disgust. It wouldn't do Raine much good either, and she didn't want the young woman to be hurt. No more than was inevitable when she woke up to the truth about her husband.

When everything had been settled Tess headed for Jake's saloon. She had a draft signed by Raine in her purse. That, along with the money she had already saved up over the years, would be enough. It was a proud moment when Tess plunked down the money and received a deed of purchase. She was sole owner of the Aces Up, a saloon, gaming house and whorehouse, a place of business that would now be called the Cherokee Rose, which was the name of a small tavern in the hills from which she had come.

While Tess savored her victory, Raine searched the town over for just the right present to give to Jake as a remembrance. She knew all the taboos that regulated a woman's choice when it came to giving a man a present—a man who was not her husband or brother or father. And she decided to ignore all of them.

Once more Raine returned to the shop where she and Lance had purchased their rings, and she found just the thing for Jake. It was an ornately decorated watch depicting a ship under full sail, and beneath the ship were waves done by a skilled hand. When the watch was opened it played a tune. Raine decided no other present would do. This was the one for Jake. It would be something for him to remember her and her father by. Her father would be pleased. She paid the sizable sum and carried the beautifully wrapped gift back to her hotel.

Then Raine proceeded to dress with care. She brushed and combed and swirled her hair high on her head and she tucked an artificial flower under one of the curls so that it peeped out just enough to be noticed. Then she made up her face with the skill that had come from many hours of practice. And since Jake's saloon was just a trifle dark under the stairs where he had his private table, Raine applied more lip rouge and eye color than she ordinarily did. When she studied the results she was extraordinarily pleased. Placing a towel carefully over her head and face, Raine slid into her finest party dress.

When she was done she admired herself in the mirror, and she was grateful that Tess had taught her so much. Raine was thrilled as she stared into the reflection of her own eyes. She was looking at an absolutely gorgeous woman.

Then she glanced at the dainty cloisonné clock on her dresser. She must hurry. Tess was already waiting for her a short distance from the entrance of the hotel. Clutching her fur-lined cape, Raine threw it around her shoulders and arranged the hood carefully so that her face was partially hidden from view, just as Tess had instructed. Then she raced down the stairs, holding Jake's present tightly.

Joining Tess in the carriage, Raine settled back comfortably. "I won't stay long," she promised, for Raine understood that Tess did not approve of this trip. In fact, Tess would disapprove just as much when the Aces Up became the Cherokee Rose. *And that will be tomorrow,* Raine thought happily.

As she entered the saloon, Raine remembered all the times she and her father had come here. The same smell of stale beer hung in the air, and there was the dense cloud of smoke from cigars that had always annoyed her. The music was as loud as ever and the roulette wheel provided a rhythmic background noise of its own.

Raine's eyes sparkled with happy memories as they searched out Jake. And there he was, just as she knew he would be at this hour. He sat in the shadows of the balcony and watched everything that was going on.

Raine picked up her skirts and walked across the room to greet her friend. But Jake saw her coming and stood hastily. His face told her that she was not welcome. Then his eyes slid to Tess. "What the hell you doin' bringin' her here?"

Tess shrugged. "She told me she came here lots of times with her father."

"Yeah," Jake growled. "With her

father. Not with some bloody whore who don't have good sense," he growled. "And it was durin' the *day,* it was. Practically nothin' goin' on at that time. Bloody hell, do you think ol' Emmett would bring his tyke here at night?" he asked accusingly.

Raine was distressed. Tess was taking the blame, which was not hers. "Please, Jake," she pleaded softly, "don't blame Tess. It was my fault, really. I insisted. Forgive me?" she cajoled, and Jake relented.

"I came to say good-bye before you sail. And I came to give you something so that you will always remember Papa and me."

Jake was almost embarrassed as he took the present from Raine's hand. He had always been very fond of the little golden-haired girl who had allowed him to think of other things rather than the murky business in which he was involved. "Thank ya, luv," he said as he unwrapped the gift, then stood absolutely still as he took in the beauty of the present she had picked for him. "Lord love a duck," he sputtered as he realized what a special gift this was. He opened the case and listened to the gay melody; his eyes glistened with tears.

"God love ya, Raine, darlin'. You and your dad were very special to me and I'll remember you forever. Now, if you don't mind, you should be leavin'. This is no place for ya, luv. Not without your dad."

But Raine had no intention of being shooed away like some child. She smiled sweetly, removed her cape, and sat in the chair opposite Jake's. Tess sighed and rolled her eyes, but she sat as well.

"Now, Jake Finch," Raine said cheerfully, "we'll have one farewell toast and then I'll let you throw me out. Fair enough?"

Jake grinned his pleasure. "Aye, mate," he responded with good humor as he fell into the mood of friendship and good cheer that Raine had brought with her. Then he snapped his fingers for service.

When the glasses and bottle of wine arrived, Jake filled all three. Tess raised hers along with the others.

"I wish you a safe journey home and a long and happy life," Raine offered, and then sipped a drop of wine from her glass.

When it was done, Raine walked to the other side of the table, leaned down to press a farewell kiss on Jake's cheek and then gave him a hug. Instinctively, Jake put his arms around Raine and returned the awkward hug, for while Raine was standing, Jake was sitting, and he wasn't quite sure where to put his arms. He had an odd sensation that they were being closely scrutinized, and he wanted to do nothing to harm Raine's reputation. A sudden hush filled the room, confirming his hunch. Jake looked up quickly to see what was wrong.

"You would do me a courtesy, Mr. Finch, by taking your hands off my wife." The voice was as soft as a panther's hiss of warning, and there was the same deadly menace beneath.

Upon hearing her husband's voice Raine straightened. Her face was aglow with happiness as she turned toward him. Before Lance could do or say any more, she rushed to his side and threw her arms around his neck.

"Lance! Oh, my darling!" she cried, and then stopped as Lance forced her arms down and stared at her through eyes filled with fury.

"I don't want to hear one word out of you. Not one word," he commanded quietly, and Raine shivered under the tone of his voice and stepped back hesitantly. She knew what he was thinking. She could not help but know as Lance stared at her in total disapproval. His eyes missed nothing. Not the cape she had bought for their wedding, not the revealing party dress and not the makeup she wore.

"There's a carriage waiting outside," he said quietly. "Get in and wait for me. We'll discuss this when we get home."

Raine's eyes flashed in anger, but she knew that if she did not obey quickly, there would be a terrible scene; she had already spotted Zeke and Bart as they had positioned themselves, ready for any trouble. It was obvious that Lance did not want a public row. Neither did she, so she gave in quietly.

"Yes, Lance," she replied. "I'm going."

Her eyes were downcast as she picked up her cape and walked across the room, which seemed to have no end. Finally, to her profound relief, the door was at hand. She opened it and walked out into the brisk night air. Tears of humiliation clouded her eyes as she climbed into the waiting cab. Seconds later Lance emerged, closely followed by Zeke and Bart, who headed toward the docks.

As soon as her husband had settled himself beside her, Raine tried to explain, but he cut her off. "I said we'll settle this when we get home."

When the carriage stopped in front of their hotel Lance assisted Raine from the cab. Keeping a tight grip on her arm, he propelled her through the lobby, up the stairs and into their suite. He did not let go until he had marched her forcibly into their bedroom, where he splashed water in the basin and pushed Raine's face into it. When she was thoroughly soaked and came up sputtering for breath Lance took a towel and rubbed her face until Raine whimpered in pain. At the sound of her discomfort, Lance relented. He threw the towel down and held both of Raine's arms in a grip that made her wince. His eyes glittered.

"Have you *become* a whore or do you just *look* like one?"

Raine stared at him dumbfounded, and her knees went weak. Lance had to support her. There, in Jake's saloon, it had been obvious that Lance had been enraged with her presence and her appearance, but that he should question her fidelity had never occurred to her. She drew in a painful breath. Lance did not trust her.

Collecting herself, Raine spoke slowly and deliberately. Nothing mattered but regaining her husband's trust. "I'm sorry if I've displeased you. All I wanted to do was to be more beautiful in your eyes, to look more like Tess and Alice. I wanted to be as provocative as they. But I have not become a whore. I have been faithful to you, Lance. I always shall be.

"The only reason I went to Jake's saloon tonight was to give him a going-away present. He sails for Australia tomorrow, and I wanted him to have something to remember us by."

Lance blinked his confusion. He remembered that Jake had been on Raine's guest list for their wedding, but that the man had wisely declined. "Us?"

"Papa and me," Raine explained. "Jake and Papa were good friends. We often went to his place for lunch, and they would talk for hours. Then we would go back to our hotel across the square or walk down to the docks to watch the boats come and go. I was saying good-bye to a friend, and I don't care how high or how low a station in life he occupies."

Lance twitched his lips under the reprimand. "And Tess?"

"Tess insisted that she go with me, for she knew I could not go unchaperoned."

"Some chaperone," Lance mumbled, but secretly he was pleased. Raine was *not* like Claire; she had not been unfaithful. The terror in his heart subsided and then was gone.

A guilty expression that he could not control spread across Lance's face and made him feel like a schoolboy. It was most difficult for him to apologize, but he tried. "I'm sorry. I saw you go into Jake's saloon and I couldn't believe it. Do you know how it looked? You and Tess going into a whorehouse?"

Raine smiled smugly. "The same as it looked when I saw you with Alice Rafferty, I suspect."

Despite his discomfort, Lance grinned. "Guess we're even."

Raine sighed. "I certainly hope so. Can we kiss and make up?"

"We can do a lot more than that," Lance suggested with a wicked glint in his eyes. He removed his coat and then his wife's cape and dropped them to the floor. "Do you forgive me, Raine?"

"Of course I forgive you," she assured him tenderly. "I love you. I shall always forgive you."

With supreme gentleness, a gentleness that had always surprised Raine, Lance undressed her and then removed his own clothing. When he came to her in their bed all the emptiness of the past months closed in on him, and he clung to her with a budding faith in her and in himself.

His lips touched hers and his body pressed hard against her. Raine's arms encircled him as his mouth demanded more and she responded. Her lips touched his chest, and Lance could feel the lingering warmth of them even as they moved on to torment another part of him.

He shuddered as he felt her tongue touch and savor the taste of him as she went slowly down his length. It was not until her fingers touched his aroused organ that he understood what she meant to do.

"God," he whispered, and drew in a sharp breath. "I want it. Lord only knows how much, but that's a whore's work, Muffin. It's not for you." Then his eyes narrowed devilishly. "Of course, there are a few *other* things we can do if you wish."

"I can hardly wait," Raine replied, her eyes slanting mischievously, and then they both laughed and put all the doubt and all the tension behind them.

They made love slowly, savoring every moment. They had been apart for so long that neither wished to hurry. Lance could not seem to get enough of his wife. He could not love her enough and he could not hold her close enough.

His hands touched and caressed; his

mouth moved and claimed her once again.
And his lovemaking never failed to thrill
Raine and rouse her to the heights of pas-
sion. Tonight was no different.

She pressed against him. She held him
close. Her need and her urgings caused already enflamed passions to leap and flare in
fiery explosions, and Lance gave her the love
she so desperately needed from him.

When it was over and they had rested
Lance began to teach Raine some of the
positions that had caused her to blush when
Tess had first described them to her. She
squealed in alarm when her husband came
at her from unexpected directions, and she
squirmed in ecstacy as she learned to mount
the man who responded just as fiercely as
she, the man who helped and supported and
loved her.

Then Raine asked Lance to say the
words he never had. "Please, just this once. I
need so desperately to hear you say it."

Lance pressed her cheek to his bare
chest. "Do you hear my heart racing, Muffin?" he asked tenderly.

"Yes," she whispered. "But you must
tell me. What is it saying?"

"It says that I love you."

Raine smiled and was content. He had
told her at last, and she was sure no woman
had ever had a lover like Lance. She sighed
and closed her eyes. She would tell him
about Tess some other time. She barely
heard Lance when he spoke.

"Never leave me, Muffin," he said in a voice that sounded very far away.

"Not ever," she promised, and that was her last thought before falling into a contented sleep.

11

The next day dawned bright and clear. It was one of those glorious mornings that sometimes blessed the city of San Francisco at that time of year. The rains had stopped. The wind blew soft and warm, and the snow that had encroached from the hills was gone from the countryside. Only the peaks of the distant heights still bore a thinning mantle of white.

Raine stretched lazily and smiled with contentment. Her happiness was complete. Then a small frown creased her brow. She could not understand why Lance had been afraid—afraid that she had been unfaithful to him, that she had found comfort in another man's arms while he was gone. The thought that he had not completely trusted her still hurt and confused her. She had never given him reason to doubt her love for him and she never would.

Then her mind went over the events that had occurred in Jake's saloon. Lance had come for her. He had brought Zeke and Bart with him and had been prepared to fight all of Sydney Town to bring her home.

Lance glanced at her and laughed. "You look as smug as a cat in the cream."

"I'm *feeling* smug," Raine admitted brightly. "You're home and you love me. You said so!" she declared with supreme confidence.

"And you?" Lance asked with a trace of doubt in his mind, for his suspicions about Raine had been totally unfounded. Jake Finch had told him as much after Raine had left the saloon, but he had not believed it until Raine had told him herself.

Raine traced the line of his lips with her finger, and her eyes met his. "I love you more than words can say. I love you now; I shall love you forever. Nothing—nothing will ever diminish that love."

The simple words and the love that shone in his wife's eyes comforted Lance. He studied the lovely creature who lay warm and content beside him. The sun that streamed in the window touched her face. Her fine-grained skin was as smooth as a baby's and Lance marveled at the highlights that flashed and danced in her golden hair.

She was a beauty, and she did not need

the paints and powders that Tess had taught her to apply with an expert hand, but if that was what she wanted, she would have it. Many of the great beauties enhanced their looks with such things. It was not just the whore or the actress who understood the advantage of strategically placed rouges and eye colors. Even Kathleen, his brother's wife, accentuated her natural good looks with a touch of lip rouge and eye color.

He smiled as he continued to examine his wife's face. She would have to apply it with a light hand, however, or the good women of San Francisco would consider her to be as brazen as any actress who ever trod the boards. And they would be just as jealous of Raine as they were of the bold and charming women who made their living on the stage.

As he continued to stare in fascination, Raine blushed. She was not accustomed to this kind of close scrutiny and was uncomfortable under her husband's intense gaze.

Then Lance grinned, and Raine squealed as he flicked the sheet from the bed, leaned over and kissed the tip of each breast, teasing with tongue and lips until the nipples were hard and erect. He laughed with the sheer joy of being alive, and he grabbed Raine to him. Her body stiffened under the sudden attack, but she relaxed immediately as her husband began to arouse her with desire and anticipation in his every movement.

They came to each other with one heart and one mind as they shared their mutual arousal. And once Lance found it necessary to slap Raine's hand. "No," he said sternly, and Raine giggled in delight. She wasn't the only one who could be surprised, for Tess had been a thorough teacher.

The boldness of his wife's response inflamed Lance's desire, and he took her immediately. He moved, turned and manipulated her body to suit himself, and when the soft sounds of passion seeped from Raine's throat Lance brought them both to the precipice and held tight as they crashed down the other side, oblivious to all except each other.

When it was done they lay still, each holding the other until the wild beating of their hearts calmed. Lance was first to break the silence. "You all right?" he asked only because he remembered the need that had once gnawed at his wife even after they had made love.

Raine stretched against him. "I have never been so content." She marveled at the truth of her words, for she was satisfied both in mind and body. No longer was she seeking something she could not find. Lance loved her. He had said it at last. She had always known it deep down in her heart but had hungered to hear it from his lips. And now that need had been fulfilled.

Turning on her back, Raine looked up at the ornate ceiling. Her mind drifted for a few minutes as she pondered all the things Tess had told her. She wondered if Lance would tell her the truth.

"Did you find the men you were looking for?"

Lance frowned his displeasure as a world that had grown wearisome intruded upon him. "No. We traveled every inch of the area, but they were gone. We found one man who had seen them. He said they had headed south. That's all. Just south.

"Hell," Lance continued, in despair of ever completing his assignment, "that covers a lot of ground, and it doesn't make sense unless they aim to follow the Snake all the way to the Oregon Trail, which means they could be headin' for the Continental Divide and back east. Or they could drop down to Nevada in the Utah Territory and head for Donner Pass, which would bring them back into California. We just don't know. But we went as far as we could before turnin' back. Even then the passes were closing behind us every step of the way. We barely made it out," he admitted. "Guess we're not done with it yet."

Raine was satisfied; Lance was telling her the truth. "Why do you do it? I know something about mountains in winter. They're treacherous. You could have died in a thousand ways and never have been found. Why do you take such chances?"

Lance rearranged his pillow and sat up. He stared into space and thought about the

question. "It suited me once. Guess I didn't
have anything better to do when I first got
into this business. Anyway, Pop depends on
me to get on with whatever needs doin'."

"Including killing?" Raine questioned
cautiously, hoping that Lance would deny
the gossip Tess had relayed. But he didn't.

"The family prefers to think of it as a
sorely needed lesson. We only go after those
who commit some crime against us."

Raine made a few mental calculations.
"How long have you been after the Clary
brothers?"

"Since we learned what they had done
in late summer of fifty-two."

"Over a year," Raine mused aloud.
"And how much did they steal?"

Lance's eyes narrowed. He knew exactly
where she was going with her questions,
and she was right. He had already spent an
enormous sum on this assignment, and he
was no nearer to an end than he was the
first day he had set foot in San Francisco.
"As much as they could carry. Now that's
the end of it. I don't want to hear any more
about it."

"Very well." Raine sighed unhappily
and for the first time wondered if Tess might
have been right. Her thoughts began to circle the question. Lance had to repeat what
he was saying.

"Did you hear me, Raine? I asked who
you've been talking to."

"Just Tess. I asked her to teach me

about the latest hairstyles and a few other things. We talked about a great deal, including the latest gossip concerning you and your family."

"We take a little gettin' used to, I guess."

Suddenly Raine was weary of talking about theft and revenge, and she certainly had no intention of telling Lance what else Tess had said—that she was being snubbed because people were afraid of Lance and his family. She suspected she didn't really care. No matter what his life was like away from her, he was the kindest, dearest husband any woman could have.

A bittersweet smile touched her lips as her finger explored the dimple in Lance's chin. A man with such a fierce reputation should not have a dimple.

Lance leaned down and put his lips to her. "Afraid you'll have to wait awhile," he said gently, misreading her actions.

"I'll wait," she promised, "for as long as I must."

Lance knew that Raine was telling him more than the words actually said. He had work to do. He had to start all over again. He closed his eyes in weary despair.

Then he shrugged. This pleasant interlude with Raine must end. Once again, he had to beat the bushes for some word of William and Robert Clary. "Afraid I'll have to leave you for a while. I told Zeke and Bart I'd meet them this morning as soon as I'd dealt with you. They're probably wondering

what's takin' so long to tame one little girl."
The insinuating grin softened the words, but
Raine could not help but wonder if he had
really said any such thing and thought not.

However, the implication of his words
was not lost on her. She slanted a glance in
his direction. "You intended to take me back
all along. No matter what I had done," she
gloated. "You did, didn't you? And you even
had a carriage waiting. Just for me."

Lance felt rather foolish. She had seen
through him so easily. His eyes met hers,
unguarded. "Yes," he admitted, and slid out
of bed.

With a ridiculously smug expression on
her face, Raine retrieved the sheet, covered
herself and snuggled contentedly into her
pillow. She watched Lance as he moved
about the room—washing, shaving and
dressing. It was not until he was almost
ready to leave that she asked the question.

"How did you know I was at Jake's? I
had only just arrived when you came after
me."

"We had just gotten off the ship and
were going for a decent meal when I saw you
enter Jake's saloon. I'd know that cape of
yours anywhere. And nobody could ever mistake Tess. Besides," he added, grinning,
"you were standing under a streetlight. By
the way," he added quietly, "you've seen
enough of Tess for a while." He waited until
Raine nodded her compliance, for he had
been disturbed by some of the things she

had done last night, things she had never
known about until she had studied with
Tess. He wasn't too sure he wanted to know
what else Tess had taught her.

After Lance had kissed her good-bye
and left their rooms Raine roused herself
and prepared for another day, only this time
Lance would be nearby. A vague shadow
drifted across her happy thoughts, making
her shiver.

Then, just as swiftly as it had come, it
was gone. The distant fear, the half-
remembered nightmare receded once more
to the deepest recesses of her brain.

Shrugging off the uncomfortable feeling,
Raine brushed and arranged her hair in the
becoming twist Tess had shown her. She
pulled a few shorter strands loose and let
them fall in wispy curls, then smiled at
herself in the mirror, and the happy image
smiled back.

As she sat studying herself through ob-
jective eyes, Raine made her decision, but
this time she would be more careful. Reaching into one of the drawers, she removed
several small jars and proceeded to apply
just the faintest blush to lips and cheeks.
After that Raine highlighted her eyes. It was
so skillfully done, only those who looked
carefully would see the difference. Others
would only know that there was a heightened radiance in her appearance.

Deciding that she had done as much as

she could, Raine put on her fur-lined cape
and stepped confidently through the door of
her suite and into the hall. As she proceeded
down the steps and across the lobby, she
took spiteful pleasure in the envious glances
cast her way by some of the worthy matrons
who had congregated on the chairs and
settees. She was quite certain that the gossip would begin to hum the moment she set
her foot out the door, and she smiled coyly at
one man who was daring enough to tip his
hat in a silent salute.

Following the routine she had estab-
lished while Lance was away, Raine walked
to the various shops she patronized. This
time she was looking for something for her
husband, something that would always remind him of her love, but nothing was right.
She couldn't find anything that satisfied
her, and so she walked back toward the
hotel in disappointment. She would try
again tomorrow, but before she had walked
two blocks Lance came hurrying across the
street.

"Eaten yet?" he asked hopefully.

"No," Raine replied, "but I am getting
hungry. Where shall we go?"

"How about the St. Francis?" Lance
asked. "Their food is good. At least it will get
you away from the dining room at our hotel."

Raine agreed, and they walked arm in
arm to the hotel, which had as fine a dining
room as any to be found in San Francisco.

Lance escorted his wife to a table and removed her cape, draped it over one chair and then seated Raine in another.

When he had taken his own chair Lance smiled at his wife. "You're looking especially pretty this morning."

Raine slanted a mischievous look his way. "I have on a little makeup," she confessed.

"I know," Lance replied, and his eyes smiled their approval before he turned his attention to the menu the waiter handed him.

"Well," he commented after studying it briefly. "I'm as hungry as a bear. Missed my supper last night and my breakfast this morning. Think I'll have steak and eggs with fried potatoes and coffee. How about you?"

"I think I'll have a bowl of hot oatmeal with cream. And I'd like to have toast and hot tea to go with it."

Lance did not show his surprise that Raine had ordered a grain usually reserved for horses. Instead, he looked at the waiter and asked if the cook had oatmeal on hand. When assured that the St. Francis did, indeed, serve hot oatmeal Lance placed the order, then sat back in his chair and studied his wife. He had had a brief conversation with Tess that had disturbed him deeply. It seemed that Raine was paying for the sins of his family, and he wasn't quite sure what to do about it.

"Is something wrong?" Raine asked, breaking the long silence.

"Had a little talk with Tess this morning, and she tells me some of the folks around here aren't too polite. You want me to do something about it?"

The horror Raine felt at the mere mention of such a thing showed in her face. "No, Lance, no. Please don't make an issue of it. I wouldn't want that kind of friendship anyway. I'm fine, really. As long as I have you, I don't need anyone else."

Lance nodded and changed the topic. "I saw a poster advertising a minstrel show tonight. Want to go?"

A happy smile brightened Raine's face. "I'd love it," she replied eagerly, and that eagerness told Lance more than he wanted to know about the isolation and loneliness Raine had endured while he had been chasing two inconsequential crooks up one mountain and down another. The chase had to end soon. Raine deserved a full-time husband, not just some part-time lover who hopped into her bed anytime he happened to be in the area. Then it struck him. There were many charity balls and plays at which he and Raine would be seen. There would be casual conversations with a few of the more wealthy and influential men. What was the old saw about catching more flies with honey than vinegar? He might have to change his tactics, but Raine would never again be snubbed. They might never be invited into the homes of the inner circle, but his wife would be treated with respect.

As the days passed, Lance saw to it that he was seen frequently with his wife on his arm. He smiled charmingly at the ladies who passed them on the streets and stepped in front of them, thereby blocking their way until he had spoken a few words of greeting. "May I take this opportunity to introduce my wife," he said on numerous occasions, and Raine could not suppress her smile. Lance was giving them back everything they had thrown at her and more. He was forcing them to acknowledge her. But Raine was not interested in them, and she made that perfectly clear when she refused several invitations delivered to her suite by servants who worked for some of the wealthiest families. Lance was very proud of her. She would not accept any courtesy from those who had treated her so cruelly. She would not sell her friendship.

Gradually, as the days grew warmer, some of the younger women dared defy the clearly implied orders of those matrons who controlled the social world through their husbands' wealth and station. To her joy, Raine began to be included in their gatherings.

Then there were the days when Lance and Raine, accompanied by Bart, Tess and Zeke would ride up to the Mission Road and sit under the trees, enjoying a picnic lunch. Sometimes they would linger to watch the sun setting in the west, and they would marvel as the brilliant reflections flashed off the water. Raine would find herself unbelievably happy and content as she leaned back, supported by Lance's strong arms. And she smiled when she saw the rising affection between Zeke and Tess.

They were probably the happiest six weeks of Raine's life, and she stored the memories in her heart. Her love for Lance grew, as did his love for her. It was something both of them marvelled at, for neither had ever realized that their passion and love could be contained in so small a thing as the human heart.

During the day they touched often, and during the night they lay content in the aftermath of love making. Then, on a sunny pleasant day in April, came the message that shattered Raine's dream of a normal future with her husband. She had known it would come, for his mission was not complete. The very reason for his being here in San Francisco was to find two men who had robbed the Randall family of some of their wealth, and Lance had yet to find those men.

The note was from Alice Slattery. Raine took it from Lance's hand when he offered it to her. Alice had further news about the Clary brothers. One of her customers had seen them at Frenchmen's Creek less than two weeks ago.

Raine stared at the letter, trying to hide her disappointment. Then she handed it back to him. "When will you be leaving?" she asked in what she hoped was a normal tone of voice.

"As soon as I can get ready," he answered with no enthusiasm. Then he looked into Raine's unhappy face. "I'm sorry, Muffin, but the sooner I can get this over with, the sooner we can get on with our lives. Just be patient a little while longer."

She nodded in understanding, but in her heart Raine was terribly disappointed. She would have to endure endless weeks alone in this city. Oh, there would be Tess, but she was busy with the Cherokee Rose, and Zeke was spending much of his time there helping her. Then there were a few young ladies who had befriended her, but they couldn't make up for Lance's absence. Well, she just wouldn't wait here again for weeks and weeks. She had something else on her mind, but she was not about to tell Lance, for he would most certainly forbid it. So Raine kept her plans to herself even as she helped Lance get ready for the journey that would take him to the mining camp known as Frenchmen's Creek.

Within days after Lance's departure, Raine visited the general store, where she purchased sturdy blue denims and several shirts that she took with her back to her hotel. The rest of her order would be picked up tomorrow morning before she boarded the steamer that would take her up the Sacramento River. From there she would proceed into the mountains in her search for Tom Morley. She still regretted the fact that he had not been able to attend her wedding, and was determined to tell him of her marriage and her father's death. That was the excuse Raine used to assuage her conscience, for she knew that Lance would have forbidden this trip if he had known about it.

Raine's feelings of guilt lasted only for a moment. She was overjoyed to be leaving San Francisco, to get back to the hills and valleys she knew so well. And she would find Tom, even if the map in her father's belongings proved to be somewhat vague.

The next morning Raine collected the two horses she had bought, loaded one with supplies and threw a saddle over the other. Then she headed for the landing where the steamer would be waiting for passengers and cargo going upriver. She saw to the comfort of her animals and then retired to her quarters just long enough to have the porters store her supplies inside her cabin.

After locking her door from the outside Raine proceeded along the deck to the stern of the ship, where she stood for several minutes, watching the stern wheel of the riverboat churn and spray the water in a fine mist. She smelled the air and smiled with an inner fulfillment. She had not realized just how badly she needed to get away from San Francisco with its noise and muddy streets and its people who scurried through those streets like so many lemmings intent upon their own destruction.

With a sigh of longing for the mountains and the valleys that had been her home for almost seven years, Raine turned and walked back to her cabin. She must take another look at the crude map Tom Morley had drawn for her father.

12

Sitting astride her horse, Raine put a hand above her eyes to shade them from the rising sun that shot its rays toward her as it rose above the peaks to the east. As the red ball of fire washed the sky in scarlet, Raine felt a familiar tug at her heart. She breathed deeply of the clean, pure air that sometimes made her lightheaded with joy. She laughed out loud as the swaying trees that towered over her hummed their lonesome song to the wind.

"Papa," she said softly, and felt his presence in the trees and in the wind. It was a bittersweet time for Raine, and finally, with an aching throat and tears in her eyes, she faced the truth and let her father go. His body might be buried in San Francisco, but he was here. Somehow that certainty gave Raine a great deal of comfort, and her eyes sought out the distant peaks, which were still white with snow. The high country was fighting off the last vestige of a mild winter. The snow had a soft look about it, and there was a mist just beginning to rise from its surface. Soon it would obscure the peaks from view.

Turning her horse northeast, with her second horse trailing behind on the end of a lead rope, Raine heeled the animal into a cautious trot. They were entering gold country, and the dangers were many and real. The trails between camps were lonesome places, and even the hardened miners traveled in twos and threes for mutual protection.

Stopping just long enough to find her battered old hat in her valise, Raine tucked her hair under so her silhouette would resemble that of a man. The miners she had first met in these hills had been an honest lot, but later, as the word of gold had spread, a more dangerous breed of men moved in. These were the ones honest men feared. And these were the men she hoped to avoid.

Standing in her stirrups, Raine scanned the horizon, getting her bearings by the sun and the mountains to the east. Cutting across country on an angle, she urged her horses up inclines where soil and rocks gave way under their scrambling hooves. She cut across cold mountain streams running fresh with melting snow, allowing her animals to drink and graze along the bank where fresh, succulent greens revived them into new effort.

When nightfall came Raine traveled by moonlight as it cast its eerie light through the swaying branches of the trees and scattered it in dancing patterns across the rock- and moss-covered earth. She was alert to every sound, and her eyes strained as she searched for any sign of danger. Several times she patted her pistol and the rifle that was tied behind the saddle. At times like these they could be a great comfort.

When morning of the second day spread its light on the trail in front of her Raine stopped to scan the surrounding area. She should be almost on top of the hidden pass Tom had written about to her father.

Pulling the map from her pocket, Raine studied it and then concentrated on the rock formation that ran along the trail to her left. She compared it to the sketch at the bottom of the map. This had to be it, but where was the pass?

Urging her horse forward, Raine studied every fold and convolution of the high, barren rock formation that edged the narrow trail. She could find nothing. Then she eased her horse around the huge verticle bulge. There, behind the deceptive formation, was a narrow opening.

Cautiously, Raine squeezed her two animals through the almost invisible fissure in the otherwise solid surface. Entering the narrow pass, she began to move forward, always alert for any sound or sign of danger, for if anything should go wrong, she would have to move forward. There was no room for the horses to turn in this cramped space.

As she inched forward, Raine felt the walls close in on her. Pressing on and winding her way through for about a quarter mile, she began to feel increasingly uneasy. She could see no end to this narrow, serpentine pass. Heeling her horse more forcefully, she finally emerged from the dark trail into the sun. Before her spread a valley just coming green. It wasn't much of a valley, perhaps forty acres at most, but what it lacked in size it made up for in beauty.

It was shaped like a shallow bowl. The peaks of the mountains that surrounded it were little more than pointed hills from this perspective. Except for the east; to the east were high, rocky hills where a thunderous waterfall splashed and tore its way over the protruding shelves of rock to the swift-running creek below.

Raine turned in her saddle. She was looking for the place where the creek exited the valley, and soon saw that it disappeared in a hissing, swirling malestrom of foam and water into another fissure. From there it ran underground, and Raine could not imagine where it surfaced, if, indeed, it did. She shook her head in wonder at the way nature had hidden this little paradise.

Her gaze swept the entire valley again, and she smiled with pleasure. The earliest wildflowers were beginning to bloom. Soon the entire meadow would be filled with the blues and yellows and russets of their blossoms. The creek swirled and frothed its way over gravel and rock. The scene was captivating, and Raine sat her horse for several minutes just breathing in the fragrance of new grass, allowing her eyes to feast upon the panorama that had opened up in front of her so unexpectedly.

But she did not sit there dreaming for long. She heard a shot and felt bits of shattered rock spitting at her. The horses, too, were pelted by the small pieces of stone, which hit them like bird shot. They reared and plunged in terror, and Raine had all she could handle to stay in the saddle while bringing them under control. No sooner had she done so than another shot rang out. This time Raine leaned low in the saddle and spurred her horse forward, for her animals did not understand being bitten by the rock behind them.

Once clear of the high rock formation Raine dismounted and waved her hat. "Haloo the house. Tom! Tom Morley. It's me. Raine Colter," she shouted, and then waited.

She stood there exposed, her arms out

from her sides. She did nothing to make the old man nervous, and then the answer came. "Raine? That really you?"

"It's me, Tom," she shouted toward the sound of the voice she recognized.

"Why, gal, you come right on up. Where's your father?"

Not wishing to shout herself hoarse, Raine left the question unanswered as she walked toward the small cabin whose chimney was cold. Briefly, Raine wondered about it, for the days were still chilly and the nights were near freezing. There should be a cookfire, at least, and the cabin needed heat.

A few feet in front of the door Raine decided to stop. She waited until the occupant of the house could get a good look at her. Then the door swung open and the old man came out. He had changed little in six years. A little more stooped, perhaps. A little slower of step, but he was still the dear friend she remembered.

"Dang!" Tom exclaimed. "It sure enough is little Raine all growed up."

"Yes, and I'm a married woman now, Tom," Raine blurted out, unable to contain her happy news.

An expression of pleasure crossed Tom's face; then he looked back down the path. "Where's your pa?" he asked again.

"Papa's dead," Raine answered unsteadily. It was still difficult for her to say the words.

"No." The old man sighed in futile denial, and the joy went out of him. "I am truly sorry to hear such a thing. He was a good man—better than most. I was sure hopin' to see him afore my time run out."

Slipping her arm under Tom Morley's, Raine ended the conversation and walked into the cabin with him. The one room that made up his shelter was cold and dark and damp. "Why no fire?" she questioned.

"Injuns, dang 'em!" Tom cursed. "All through these hills. Almost run into a small war party when I started out for supplies, but I seen 'em afore they seen me. Missed me by that much," he said, holding thumb and forefinger about half an inch apart. "Like to scared old Ginger to death."

"Which way they come from?" Raine asked, not particularly concerned about Tom's old mule, Ginger.

"They was travelin' south. Comin' along the trail from the north. Bold as brass. Had their war paint on. Ain't seen 'em since."

"How long ago?" Raine's question was short, but they both understood its significance.

"Let's see," he mumbled, counting back in his mind. "This here is April. Musta been two weeks ago. Last week in March. Yep. Just about two weeks ago. All wrapped up in blankets and skins. Bitter cold on that trail, but they just kept a'comin'."

"And you haven't seen them since?" Raine asked, wondering why they would have headed south where they were sure to run into a whole string of mining camps guarded by well-armed men.

"Nope," the old man confirmed.

"How many were there?"

Tom scratched at his beard. "Oh, mebbee six, seven. Like I said, it was a small party. If'n they hadn't had their paint on, I wouldn't a given it another thought, but they was painted up worse'n a gal in a San Francisco whorehouse."

Suddenly Tom blushed. "Beg pardon, Raine, honey. Sure have forgotten my manners. Now, yer gonna visit with me a while, ain't ya?"

"Of course," she answered, laughing. "Why else would I trail all the way up here? I've just got to be sure I get back to San Francisco before my husband does."

Tom wasn't the kind of man to pry into someone else's business. It was enough to know that he would have Raine's company for a time. "Glad to hear it," he said simply.

"Wouldn't know it by the welcome you gave me," Raine teased. "Did you miss me on purpose, or is your eyesight going?"

"Eyesight's as good as your'n," he snapped. "Now don't go gettin' insultin' less ya wanna sleep in the woodshed!"

Laughing softly in the face of the old man's pride, Raine realized that six years of living alone had done nothing to improve the prickly nature she remembered. "Just as ornery as ever, I see," she teased, and then laid some dry straw in the fireplace. Over that she put a few twigs and then stood slightly larger sticks, teepee fashion, enclosing the tinder.

"What ya doin', dang it all?" Tom demanded irritably. "I just told you about them Injuns!"

"Well," Raine drawled, laughter once more dancing in her eyes, "I figured you could take care of at least four of 'em, and I sure can take care of the other three."

Tom grinned sheepishly and relaxed. It was a pure pleasure for him just to have company, and he had taken to this little gal the minute he had laid eyes on her. Not afraid of him, she wasn't, not then and not now. The woman growed had just as much gumption as that spindly-legged little girl he remembered so vividly.

Content just to watch her as she started an almost smokeless fire, Tom sat back in his wooden rocker, lit his pipe and let his mind drift back to the days when trapping had been good and the beaver plentiful. Those had been grand days. A mountain man he had been. Had a cabin and a squaw of his own. Good woman she was too. He nodded as he remembered. But then the beaver had gone and his woman had died, so he had returned east, but he no longer fit in. Cities had grown. People were everywhere. And then he had heard about the gold.

The smoke wreathed above his head as he smiled and puffed on his pipe. And he had panned more than his share of it. "Yep," he thought contentedly, "best move I ever made."

While Tom was dreaming of other hills and other times, Raine searched for supplies, but they were meager and of poor quality. "This all you got?" she asked as she sliced down a little bacon and put it in the pan.

"Got a little corn meal in the sack. That's about all I need. But we're runnin' short, all right. Been waitin' till I was sure them Injuns is gone afore headin' down the trail to get more."

"Watch the bacon while I unload my supplies." Raine said, and then was gone. When she had unsaddled her riding horse and unloaded the other one, Raine turned the animals out to graze, and they drifted down toward the creek where the lush new growth was thick and green.

Mixing up a fast corn bread, Raine put it in the ashes of the fire and let it bake. Then she pulled out a small bag of raisins and put them in a bowl on the table. There would be no coffee or tea until Raine was sure a bigger fire would not endanger her life and Tom's.

When the thin layer of cornbread batter had baked through Raine put the hot pan on the table next to the frying pan that contained the bacon grease. The bread and bacon were served from tin plates. A mug of water each completed the meal.

Tom grunted in satisfaction as he sopped the bread in the pan of grease. "Sure good to have somethin' hot to eat," he commented casually, but Raine understood that the old man had been living in fear for two weeks or more.

He had not dared light a cookfire for fear of giving his location away. She shook her head in concern. He was no match for a young brave, much less six or seven, and he knew it. So he had watched and waited in the dark cabin, and he had shivered through the cold nights.

She watched as he devoured the raisins and ran his finger around the skillet to collect every last drop of grease. And she understood. Tom had been frightened and he had not yet worked up the courage to go after sorely needed supplies. Raine was happy she had come well supplied with food of her own.

When the valley was dark Raine walked outside and looked up at the starlit sky. Her eyes scanned the rim of the mountains and saw only the silhouettes of their shapes outlined brightly in the moonlight that bathed the whole valley. Nothing moved except the horses and the mule. Raine returned to the cabin and slept under blankets with her saddle as her pillow. Her rifle and pistol were by her side.

In the morning she and Tom scouted the trail to the south and to the north for a distance of at least three miles in each direction and saw nothing over which to become alarmed. Wherever the Indians had gone, they were not within close proximity to the cabin.

For a week Raine and Tom Morley visited and enjoyed each other's company. At last Tom broached the subject that was on Raine's mind. "Guess I'm gettin' a mite old to spend any more winters in this valley. I reckon I'll find me a place in Sacramento before the passes close up again."

Raine nodded. "Sounds like a good idea."

The old man smiled and decided to spring his big surprise. He walked to the back wall and went down on his knees, prying at a floorboard with his Bowie knife. When the plank lifted Tom got his fingers under it and pulled it up. Then he pulled up the one next to it. "Lookee here, Raine, gal," he urged with a sly smile on his face.

When Raine lifted a lantern so she could see into the dark space the light played over numerous tins and makeshift leather bags. Tom picked one up and spilled its contents. Pure nuggets of gold poured onto the floor. "Got gold under every inch of this cabin," Tom gloated. "Struck it rich. Pure gold comin' down from those hills. The waterfall brings it down into my creek. Nuggets as big as my fist to the size you see here. Never seen nothin' like it," he ended in awe. "Still, it ain't doin' me much good here, but I'm afraid to move it for fear of being robbed or killed."

"I can take some of it out with me, if you

like," Raine suggested. "Of course, there's only so much my horse will be able to carry, but we can put it in the assay office for safe-keeping. In fact, why don't you come with me? It's an easy two-day ride, and we can make it in less if you're in a hurry."

"Just might do that," Tom mused. Ol' Ginger could carry a few pounds as well. "Yessir, might just do that."

Raine smiled indulgently. Tom would be leaving this valley as soon as he got his gold out. It was something he wouldn't admit, but he was getting too old to defend his home. It was clear to Raine that if powerful men like Sutter and Fremont hadn't been able to stop the gold-seeking horde from overrunning their lands, neither could one lone old man.

When the matter was settled Tom Morley slept easy. He would get his gold out of this valley and then he would settle in a comfortable home near Sacramento. He and Ginger would live out the rest of their years in peace and comfort.

He and Raine were discussing his plans at breakfast the next morning when the air was suddenly rent by an ear-splitting scream of terror. Raine grabbed her rifle and squatted by the window. At first she saw nothing. Then her eyes caught movement on the northern rim. A man—no, two men— were scrambling into view from the other side of the mountain. Then she saw what had caused the scream as an armed Indian riding a pony also came into view as he ascended the steep northern slope.

Advancing at an arrogantly slow pace, the brave sat his pony with pride and confidence. He carried a lance and a rifle. As he approached the two men who were trying desperately to get to the other side of the mountain ahead of him, he thrust the lance into the back of one of the men, and even from across the valley the sound of a grown man in pain was carried on the wind to Raine's ears.

She waited impatiently and with growing anger. To the Indian it was a game, a cruel and painful game, but to Raine it was unforgiveable. If you must kill, then it should be quick and clean. She hated the torture that seemed to give the red man so much pleasure.

Again the lance was thrust at the defenseless man as his companion attempted to interfere in a useless gesture. Raine could only guess what these men had already endured. Still, she waited.

Finally, when she was satisfied that the Indian was alone, she went to the door, opened it and aimed her rifle carefully. It was good. She was sure of herself. From here she could get a clean shot at the Indian, who continued to use his lance to prod the men to the edge of the precipice.

Taking a deep breath and holding it, Raine squinted along the barrel of the rifle. She judged her distance and increased the angle of trajectory. Squeezing the trigger with a smooth, steady pressure, Raine fired. The brave was dead before he heard the shot that had killed him.

A split second later the two men who had been pursued stopped and stared in disbelief as they heard the shot and then watched as the Indian slid from his pony. The frightened animal snorted and pranced nervously until one of the men reached for the reins and calmed him down. Then both men stared down into the valley and spotted the cabin.

But Raine was waiting to see what the echoing sound of the shot would bring, and when she was sure there were no other pursuers, she stepped out of the cabin and signaled for the men to come down. Only as they came into full view did she see that they were without clothing.

Turning to reenter the cabin, Raine picked up two pairs of Tom's pants and two of his shirts. She put them a few feet from the door and then returned to the cabin. It was not long before the knock came and two men sought permission to enter.

Holding her pistol level, Raine stepped back. "Come in, but don't sit. I want to know who you are and what you're doing here. Then maybe you can rest awhile."

Obediently, the men closed the door and leaned against it. "Name's Robert Clary, ma'am," said the taller one. "This here's my brother Bill."

"Clary!" Raine exclaimed. That was the name of the two brothers Lance had been tracking! Were these the thieves?

"Yes'm. We were on our way to Sacramento when them renegade Injuns jumped us. Put in some mighty hard time, Missus. Seems them Injuns like to hear a man scream, and they know all kinds of ways to make him do just that," he said, and Raine could see the hatred well up in his eyes. "Sure as God lets me live, I'm gonna pay 'em back. Every last stinkin' one of 'em."

"Sit down," Raine said at last. Her mind was racing, but she decided to bide her time. "You hungry?"

William Clary, the shorter man spoke up. "Lord, ma'am, we're starvin'. Been tied up for two days. No water, no food. Just a bunch of heathen savages figurin' out what they could do to us next. Lucky for us they got their hands on three other whites. Kind of took their minds off us. In fact, that's how we escaped. They were so busy with Randall and his men that we were able to slip away during the night unnoticed. Only one buck even bothered to track us when they discovered we had escaped."

By the way, Missus, we put the pony around back. Wouldn't want him wandering back to camp without his rider. That would bring the whole mess of 'em down on us. But the both of them will be missed. And they'll be tracked to the top of that ridge. My advice is to get outta here quick."

Little of what William had said after he spoke the name Randall penetrated Raine's mind. She felt fear invade her body, a helpless fear, for Lance could already be dead. Then she breathed deeply to bring her racing heart under control. She must think. She had to help Lance, and these men she had saved were not friends.

As she rekindled the fire and prepared more food, Raine's mind raced. By the time she put dishes of bacon and warmed-up leftover beans in front of the men, she knew what she was going to do.

"We have some dried-apple pie to go along with the bacon," she said casually. "Coffee will be ready in a few minutes."

"Don't know how we'll ever thank you, Missus. You sure enough saved our hides or what's left of them," Robert Clary exclaimed sincerely.

"There's only one way you can repay me," Raine stated. "You and your brother must help us to wipe out that bunch of murdering savages now. And I'd much rather surprise *them* than have them surprise *us*. What do you say?"

"You mean go back?" William inquired thoughtfully. "But with what? An old man, a young woman and two unarmed men who are hurtin' bad?"

Raine held up her hand to silence him. "We have an old man who can cut a man in two with that buffalo gun of his. And your lives were saved by a woman who can handle a rifle or a pistol. And Tom will be happy to lend one of you his Bowie knife.

"So to sum it up gentlemen, we have three guns, a Bowie knife, two horses, one Indian pony and a mule. But this won't be a fair fight, not if I can help it. This is going to be an ambush, and we shoot from the dark to kill. Now, what will we be up against?"

Robert Clary scooped the last spoonful of cold beans from his dish. "About a dozen redskins, half of 'em with rifles, the rest with hatchets, knives and spears. And they know how to use 'em, Missus."

Then he frowned as he watched Raine cut two generous slices of dried-apple pie and pour two steaming mugs of coffee. She had saved their lives by risking her own, for the Indians would track their missing brother right to her front door, and they would find the body of the man she had killed. Either she had to run or she had to kill all those red bastards before they killed her. The idea of killing the Indians who had tortured them appealed to Robert.

He nodded. "Like I said, we owe ya, and as soon as Bill here can sit a horse, we'll give it a try."

"No," Raine replied emphatically. "We must go now. Tomorrow will be too late."

Robert looked at his brother, who nodded. "She's right, Bob. By tomorrow they'll be lookin' for the Injun she killed. And once they find him, they'll come lookin' for us wherever we go. If I can get something to wrap around my ribs so's I can stop the bleeding, I think I can make it. We sure as hell can't run out on her.''

"Guess that about settles it, ma'am," Robert agreed.

Raine nodded, and searched through Tom's ragbag for something suitable to tear into strips and bind up the wounds that had been inflicted on these two men. As she wrapped and cleaned the wounds, Raine asked, "How far is it?"

"About four miles by the trail and then a mile into a pine thicket. We'll have to go part of the way on foot."

Rubbing some ointment into a painful burn, Raine nodded. "We can wrap some of these rags around your feet to ease the pain, and we can muffle the horses' hooves when the time comes."

When she had done the best she could to ease the men's wounds Raine handed her pistol to Robert. Automatically, he checked the chamber. It was empty, and he understood. The woman wasn't about to take any chances. She didn't trust them. "You are gonna give me bullets, ain't ya, Missus?"

"Yes," Raine replied. "When a shot will bring a dozen Indians down on us you'll get the bullets."

Robert smiled at her. "Can't say as how I wouldn't do the same myself. Under the circumstances."

Then Raine gathered those things she might need to ease the pain of her husband

and his two companions. If they were still alive, they would have to be transported to Sacramento, where they could receive medical attention. Packing several home remedies that Tom had into her valise, Raine gathered up the blankets and filled a flask with water.

The easy part was over. Now came the nervous hours of waiting. When the sun began to descend in the western sky Raine paced the cabin until finally the golden glow of sunset spread over the valley for a few brief minutes and then was gone.

Giving William the Bowie knife, Raine lugged her saddle out the door and whistled for her two horses. "Robert, you take the pony. William, you'll have to ride my pack horse bareback. Can you manage?"

"No problem, Missus," William replied confidently. And when Raine looked at Bob he nodded.

"We'll be all right, ma'am. The Indians hadn't really gotten started on us with their worst when they got their hands on Randall and his men."

The Clary brothers were put in the lead. Raine followed and Tom Morley rode rear guard. They traveled as the night grew darker and when they approached the place where they would leave the horses Raine stopped and sniffed the air.

She smelled smoke. They were downwind of the Indian encampment. Nothing could have been better. The others were also

ering their animals to bushes and trees.

Steeling herself for what she might find,
Raine watched the backs of the Clary brothers as they moved cautiously on foot. For
now, she needed them, but when the Indians were dead they would be expendable. If
they tried to hurt Lance, they would be
killed. She and Tom would manage somehow.

Raine clenched her teeth each time William Clary grunted with pain as he made his
way over the rough terrain. Finally it was
time to tell them. "William, Robert," she
hissed, and the two men stopped dead in
their tracks.

They turned and waited for Raine to
speak. "Lance Randall is my husband," she
whispered, and watched the stunned expressions on their faces. "He's not to be
harmed. If you try, I'll kill you."

It was all the warning the Clary brothers
needed. "Wasn't plannin' on killin' anybody
except them Injuns," William growled.
"Randall's our enemy, all right, but nobody
deserves to die like that. When it's over you
just give us a head start, Missus."

Raine nodded her agreement and then
waved the men on, but regardless of what
they had said she would be keeping a very
close eye on them. She felt in her pocket for
the cartridges. A few minutes more and she
would have to give them to Robert Clary. She
drew in a deep breath of uncertainty. For

now she would go along with them. She would not change her plans. Not unless one of the Clary brothers made a very stupid move.

When the stench at the outter edges of the encampment became strong Raine and the three men flattened themselves on the ground and sought out advantageous positions. Raine passed the cartridges to Robert as William eased further along. The soft sound of moccasined feet had caught his attention. Raine watched as the moonlit night silhouetted William's every move. One arm crushed the Indian's windpipe, and the free hand shoved the Bowie knife up and under the ribs. Silently, the dead brave was lowered to the ground.

The group's anxiety increased, for if one guard had been positioned, there could be more. From her position behind a fallen tree Raine peered from left to right. She even turned to make sure no one was behind her. Satisfied, she fixed her full attention on the camp. There was still movement. Not all the Indians had settled down for the night.

The low-burning fire gave enough light for Raine to count the men in their blankets. There were ten. The one William had killed was eleven. Then Raine saw the missing man as he walked from the opposite side of the camp.

But where was Lance? Her eyes strained to penetrate the shadows, and she saw them. Three men were strung up like butch-

ered beef. They were in deep shadow, and
Raine could not make out their identities.

She winced as she watched the men
hang, suspended from the branches of trees,
their feet not touching the ground. It was a
painful position. Their arms were raised
over their heads, and there was no way for
them to ease their agony. Raine felt the
quick tears sting her eyes, and she blinked
them back. So far, she had done exactly as
her mother had admonished. She had stayed
calm. She had not given way to hysteria. Her
mind was functioning clearly.

Checking once more to be sure that the
four of them could do the job quickly and
efficiently, Raine's attention was drawn
again to the one Indian still moving about.
He glanced over at the prisoners, picked up
a firebrand and sauntered in their direction. Lifting one head, he held up the red-hot
stick which flared into flame in the soft
night breeze, and Raine swallowed a cry
of terror as she saw that he had chosen
Lance.

Slowly, the Indian moved the torch closer to her husband's face. He intended to
burn him. He would set his hair afire and
leave nothing but a blackened, shriveled
scalp behind. Raine had heard all the horrible stories.

Slowly, she raised her rifle and took
deadly aim at the Indian's head. She must be
careful not to hit Lance. Her finger moved
even as the torch's flame touched Lance's

face. The shot roared through the stillness of the night, and the Indian dropped to the ground, falling on top of the torch he had intended to use on Lance.

Raine felt no remorse. The camp was aroused. Men scrambled for safety they were never to find. Sharp cries of alarm mingled with the sound of gunfire. Calmly, Raine spread eight bullets on top of the log. She placed them in a neat row and loaded again.

An Indian who came charging directly in front of her was the next to feel the impact of one of her bullets. Once more she loaded and was aware of the thunderous roar of Tom's rifle at her left. The distinctive sound of her pistol chattered from her right. Within minutes it was over. It had been clean and quick just as she had planned.

"Help me get them down," Raine cried to Tom as she rushed to the three men hanging from the trees, and Tom cursed in chagrin.

"Ain't got my blasted knife. That Willie feller there has got it."

"Step back, Missus, we'll get it done," William said as he reached up and cut the rope that held Lance. Robert Clary eased his fall to the ground. Then the other two men were released, and all the while Raine kept her rifle ready to kill the first man who harmed any of them.

Quickly, Raine examined the three men, and it was obvious that Lance was the most seriously wounded. Bart and Zeke were wob-

bly and in pain but they could stand, and as
soon as they got their legs firmly under them
they scrambled to the pile that contained
their clothing.

Hastily pulling on their pants, they collected their weapons as well as the guns that
had belonged to the Indians. Then they cut
their horses out from the others and saddled
all three.

Only then did William and Robert Clary
seek their own weapons and clothing. They
both knew how nervous Mrs. Randall was,
and how fearful she was for her husband's
safety. They left their weapons in plain view
by the dying camp fire as they retreated
behind the trees to change into their own
clothing. William had to leave his boots off. It
was too painful to even try to put his feet into
them. The soft rags he wore were more
soothing to his burned feet.

As Tom kept his rifle pointed at them,
Raine bent over her unconscious husband.
She put her ear to his chest and frowned.
The heartbeat was weak and thready. Something more than the burns and bruises and
the slashes across his body was wrong.
Then her exploring fingers found the problem. He had been shot, and the bullet was
still buried deep in his flesh.

"Get some clothes on him," she said to
Zeke, "and then get a litter built. We're
going to carry him to Sacramento, where he
can get proper medical treatment."

There was no point in protesting or in

telling Raine what she had probably already guessed. It was a toss-up if Lance would make it to Sacramento.

While Bart and Zeke followed orders, Raine turned to the Clary brothers. "Thank you for helping me. I shall tell my husband of your efforts on his behalf," she continued, ignoring the half-guilty expressions on their faces. "Meanwhile, why don't you go round up the Indian ponies and take them with you? You ought to be able to get something for them, enough to help you travel a long distance from California. Do I make myself clear?"

The two men grinned. "Yes'm. Neither you nor Mr. Randall will ever see or hear of the Clary boys again." Robert hesitated. "We wanna thank ya, ma'am. For everything. We won't be breakin' our word. It's been a pleasure knowin' ya, Missus," he finished awkwardly, and then the two men set about their task of rounding up all the ponies, saddling their own horses and leading the string out of the encampment. Raine was too concerned with Lance to see them turn in their saddles one last time. Then they set off at a brisk trot, and Tom Morley lowered his rifle, walked over to the camp fire and picked up his Bowie knife from where William had left it. His clothing had been neatly folded and left with the knife. He stroked his beard. There was something wrong between Raine's husband and the two men who had just left. He wondered why she hadn't told him of the bad blood that existed between these men.

Tom shrugged and decided once again that it was none of his business. As he passed Raine, he explained that he was going back to his cabin to load Ginger with as much gold as she could carry. "I'll meet ya in Sacramento, Raine, gal. Now you hurry and git there. That man of yours needs help."

Raine nodded. "You be careful, Tom."

"Sure will, Raine, honey," he promised, and he slipped noiselessly into the forest, which stood between him and the trail.

By this time the litter had been thrown together and Lance had been strapped in. Bart and Zeke lifted the litter between the two horses and Raine secured the ropes.

Lance was carried high so he would not be bumped over the uneven terrain, and sometimes the going was much slower than Raine liked. But she was patient as she set a steady course across country. Every few hours she stopped to bathe his burned body and face with cold water from the mountain streams, but nothing seemed to draw the fire of fever from him.

Tears fell despite her best efforts to contain them, and Raine wiped them away angrily. Then she remounted and continued leading the small party, careful not to take any trail that would cause the two horses who supported her husband's weight between them to lurch or stumble. By noon of the next day they saw Sacramento spread out before them.

Moving carefully down the trail that led into town, Raine and her small group proceeded along the main street in search of medical care for the unconscious man strapped to the litter. Remembering the horror of her father's death at the hands of an incompetent, Raine dismounted and walked into a large and noisy saloon.

She ignored the comments and rude stares of the patrons, who quieted down immediately as Zeke walked through the door and stood at her side. "I need a doctor. A *good* one," she emphasized. "Who's the best in town?"

One man spoke up. "Ol' Doc Pritchett, I guess. Lives down the street a piece. Can't miss the house. Only one with a big front porch. Got his sign by the door."

Raine nodded her thanks and left the saloon. She remounted and led the way to the rough plank house with the large front porch.

Zeke and Bart, who needed medical attention themselves, carried the litter inside. Shivering with fear and fatigue, Raine led the way through the front hall. A woman in a crisp, clean bib apron bustled in and took one look at Lance as he lay helpless and almost drained of life. Without hesitation she led them into the surgery.

Dr. Pritchett helped Zeke and Bart put

the litter on the operating table. Briefly he poked and pried the bloody, tortured body. Then he inserted a probe deep into the wound that had all but killed Lance.

"Bullet's still in there," he mumbled. "That's why the fever." Then he turned to the others. "Gonna die of lead poisoning if we don't get it out." He waited for instructions, and Raine gave them.

"Go ahead. Do what you have to, but we'll be sitting right over there," she said, indicating several chairs on the other side of the room, "and we'll be watching every move you make, doctor."

Dr. Pritchett directed an odd look her way, but he understood the seriousness of her words when Zeke drew his gun and let it rest easily in his lap while his finger remained on the trigger. "Believe me, madam, I shall do my very best."

"You'd better," Raine warned in her soft, refined voice, but her meaning was plain to the doctor.

The woman Raine had assumed was the doctor's wife stepped up to the operating table. Raine, Zeke and Bart perched like owls watching every move the doctor made. But Dr. Pritchett was a fine surgeon. He was swift and skilled. Within minutes the bullet was out and Lance was bandaged.

He had not stirred through the painful process and for that, at least, Raine was grateful. He had suffered so much already.

She wasn't sure she could bear to see him in anymore pain. Then she sighed. She would bear what she had to.

"Well," the doctor said, "guess that does it for now. But I think he ought to stay here for a while so I can keep an eye on him. You his wife?" he asked, turning to Raine.

"Yes," she answered and waited.

"Well then, either you or one of your friends can stay if you like. Might make you feel better, and you can keep him cooled down as well. It's entirely up to you, of course."

"I'll stay with him," Raine answered. "Besides, these men need some looking after themselves."

"After they get this man in the next room I'll take a look at them. Indians got to them too?"

"Yes," Raine stated. "All three were tortured."

The doctor nodded his head in understanding and motioned for Zeke and Bart to move Lance from the table. The woman who had assisted during the operation opened the door to a room that contained two beds. She showed the two men how to move Lance from the litter to the bed, and when he was settled Raine insisted that both Zeke and Bart have the doctor look them over.

When she was alone in the room with her husband Raine poured water into the basin and began to bathe the heat from his body. She was as gentle as she could be with the areas that had been cut and burned, and hot tears spilled onto Lance's body as she cared for him with exquisite tenderness. Then she covered him with a sheet and sat by his bedside.

Before long, Zeke and Bart entered the room. "Doc says we'll live," Zeke joked, and then stared at his friend who lay so still and white. "Damn, he looks like hell," he said, trying to control the emotions that threatened to betray him. "Lost so much blood," he mumbled, and then looked at Raine.

"I got so many questions to ask you, but they'll have to wait. Doc says Bart and I can leave anytime. Gave us some ointment to put on the bad spots. He says there's a boarding-house close by where Bart and I can put up until Lance is better. Want us to get a room for you?"

Raine smiled gratefully. Zeke would no more think of Lance dying than she would. He would make plans just as though her husband's life weren't hanging by a thread. The smell of death was strong in the room. Once more a tremor ran through her body, but she brought it under control and thought of Zeke and his brother.

"You'll find money in my saddle bags. Use what you need. And yes," she said quietly as she laid her hand over her husband's, "get us a room, too, but it will be a few days before we can move him."

"Hell, we got money, Miss Raine. Injuns never bothered it. Guess when they had done us in they would have used it to buy guns, but you came too quick. How'd ya know?" Bart asked.

"Later, Bart," she replied wearily. "We'll have plenty of time to talk later."

"Yes'm," he replied, and the two brothers walked quietly from the room.

Raine sat with Lance and continued to draw the heat from his fevered body, and she wet his lips frequently. It was only when Dr. Pritchett came in several hours later to check on his patient that she paused in her efforts. Moving from Lance's side, she watched as the doctor felt for his pulse. When he found it he frowned in concentration and puckered his lips.

"A little stronger, maybe. Can't be sure. If he can hold on until his body can begin to repair itself and replace the terrible amount of blood he's lost, he just might make it, but I can't guarantee a thing. You understand?"

"Yes, doctor," Raine answered quietly. "You did all that anyone could. Thank you."

Dr. Pritchett patted Raine's arm. "I'll have my wife bring in a pot of coffee. Can we get you anything else?"

"Coffee's fine, thank you," Raine replied, and took her seat by Lance's side as Dr. Pritchett walked out of the room.

She held his hand in hers and her thoughts drifted back to the time when she had been so ill. She smiled as she remembered how Lance had cared for her, how concerned he had been and how kind he had been to a stranger.

Napping occasionally, Raine kept her vigil through the night. She applied cooling cloths to her husband's body. She rubbed the ointment into his wounds, and each time she touched him she spoke of little things they had done together. Frequently her fingers brushed his forehead, and once she bent her head to his to press a gentle kiss on his lips, and when the first light of day crept softly into the room Raine knew. His breathing was close to normal. The fever had gone, and she no longer smelled death. Lance would live.

13

The breeze of early morning caressed Raine's cheek. She breathed deeply and smelled the mixed odors of the town and the river as she leaned on the railing of the front porch. As tired as she was, she could not resist a small smile as she saw Tom Morley, all safe and sound, come plodding slowly down the street with his mule Ginger. They raised a small cloud of dust behind them as they approached.

When Tom was only a few feet from the bottom of the steps he stopped and doffed his old weather-beaten hat. "Mornin', Raine. How's the mister?"

"I think the worst is over, but he's still in bad shape," Raine answered, and then changed the subject. "Got some of your gold out, I see."

"Sure did. And now that them Injuns is dead, I reckon I'll go back in a few days and bring out some more. Before anybody catches on to what I'm doin' and follows me."

Raine nodded in agreement. "The sooner you get it done, the better. But if you can wait a few days, Zeke and Bart might escort you there and back. Be a little safer than going by yourself."

"Might just do that," Tom replied, thinking it over. "And if you won't be a'needin' him any time soon, Maybe I can borry your extra horse."

"You're welcome to him. We certainly won't be going anywhere for weeks. Not on horseback, anyway. I'm fairly certain Lance is on the mend, but he has a long recuperation ahead. We all took rooms at the boardinghouse back the way you came. Why don't you get yourself settled in as well?"

"Guess I'll do that," Tom replied gratefully, for Raine was just about the last friend he had anywhere and it would be nice to have her company a spell longer.

Watching Tom and Ginger as they retraced weary steps, Raine waited until Tom entered the boardinghouse with his leather bags of gold weighing him down. Then she went inside to resume her vigil.

Lance had not yet recovered consciousness, but she sat by his side, holding his hand, talking to him. Her eyes were fixed on his face when Lance opened his.

He was confused. He didn't understand, but he was grateful. "Raine, honey," he whispered weakly. "How?"

But Raine put her finger to his lips. "We'll talk later, when you're stronger. Meanwhile try to swallow a little of this tonic. The doctor says it will build up your blood."

As Raine held the tonic to his lips, Lance sipped and grimaced. It was as bitter as sin, and he could taste the pulverized iron. "Lord," he complained, and grunted at the horrible taste, but he drank it.

Lance looked up at his wife and the love shone from his eyes. "Thought I'd never see you again, Muffin. Glad I was wrong," he said as his voice trailed off, for despite his intense desire to stay awake, his eyes closed and he drifted into a normal sleep. Raine leaned over him and kissed him. Then she sat for a while longer watching the even breathing of the man she loved with all her heart, the man she had come very close to losing.

When Zeke and Bart came in Raine gathered her strength and answered their questions. How had she gotten here? Where were the Clary brothers? And didn't she think she ought to get some rest?

"We'll stay with Lance so's you can get

some sleep," Zeke suggested, but Raine shook her head.

"Just a little longer," she insisted. "I thought I had lost him," she added softly, and wiped the tears from her eyes.

"Yeah, we know all right," Zeke responded. "They gave Lance the worst of it. He was the only one of us who managed to get off a shot. Killed one of 'em and that sure as hell made the rest of 'em mad as hornets.

"He was shot out of his saddle. They dragged him the rest of the way. At least we could follow on foot as best we could. But Lance never stood a chance from the beginning. He drifted in and out and when he was conscious they caused him a lot of pain. I don't think any of us will ever forget it. It's a good thing you came when you did."

"If it hadn't been for the Clary brothers, I wouldn't even have known that you and Lance had been captured," Raine commented thoughtfully, understanding for the first time the full scope of her husband's work and the danger that went with it.

"Yeah," Bart agreed, knowing he would have no more part in chasing men who had helped save his life, "it's a good thing the Clarys came your way, and it's a good thing you were there, Miss Raine. God's will or somethin'."

The sound of familiar voices penetrated Lance's mind, and he stirred. Raine put her finger to her lips to stop the conversation, and motioned the men to follow her out of the room. "I'm going to the boardinghouse now to bathe and get a little sleep. Did Tom get settled all right?"

"Sure did," Zeke replied, smiling as he recalled the conversation in which Tom had sung Raine's praises and spelled out the exact details of how she had managed to get Bob and Bill Clary to go back to the Indian encampment with her and how she had waited 'til the last minute to tell them who she was. And how they hadn't dared harm them or Lance because she had them covered every minute of the time.

Bart laughed. "Took him half an hour to stop talkin'. Didn't think he'd ever quit, but he finally wore himself out and went to bed. The old man's right fond of you, Miss Raine."

"Yes," Raine replied, "we're kind of fond of each other. Now, if you'll promise to take turns sitting with Lance, I'll feel more easy about leaving him for a while. And," she added, smiling into their eyes, "I am so very happy to see that you are well enough to get about."

"Not near as happy as we are," Zeke drawled with just a trace of his dry humor surfacing.

When Raine had introduced herself to Mrs. Bradley, owner of the boardinghouse, the woman smiled with delight. "Come with me," she said as she bustled through the parlor and unlocked a door that led to a ground-floor bedroom. "Your men explained that your husband had been severely wounded by those heathen savages, and we thought it would be good to give you the room on the first floor. So's to make it easier on your man, you understand. No stairs to climb."

"That's very kind of you, Mrs. Bradley. And would you happen to have a tub? I'm so tired, all I want to do is get a bath and crawl into bed."

"Bless your heart," the older woman replied, "the tub's off the kitchen. Nice and private and not so far to carry the hot water. We'll have it ready in twenty minutes. And don't you worry about such things as soap or towels. That all comes with the bath."

"I can't thank you enough," Raine answered gratefully. "I'll just shake out my robe and slippers while the water's heating. See you in twenty minutes," she confirmed, and smiled as she closed the door in polite dismissal.

As soon as she was alone, Raine put her valise on the bed and took out a warm nightgown and her robe. Then she placed her slippers and her valise on the floor and began to undress. When she had slipped her gown over her head Raine sat at a battered and scarred dressing table, brushing her hair. She was almost too weary to complete the task, but as she hung her head down between her knees to finish the back, her energy level increased a little. When the knock came at her door and Mrs. Bradley announced that the water was good and warm Raine followed the cheerful and obliging woman through the parlor, into the hall and through the kitchen to a small room barely large enough to accommodate the round wooden tub. Raine tested the water with her fingers and sighed with pleasure.

"Thank you, Mrs. Bradley. When I'm through here I'm going straight to bed. I would appreciate it if you would not disturb me unless it's important."

Mrs. Bradley nodded her understanding, smiled at the young woman and closed the door as she left. Raine turned the key in the lock, disrobed and stepped up on the small stool, then into the tub of pleasantly warm water.

She leaned back and relaxed for the first time in three days. Lance was going to be all right. Tom was safe, and Zeke and Bart would heal completely in a few more days. She could ask for no more.

As she began to doze, the water cooled. Raine roused herself, lathered quickly and then rinsed off. She knelt and put her head under the water, soaping it down, scrubbing her scalp vigorously. After drying off, she wrapped the towel around her head, put on her gown and robe and slippers. When she emerged from the room Mrs. Bradley looked up from the wood stove and smiled.

"Feelin' better?"

"Yes, thanks," Raine replied, and made

her way back to her room. Briefly, she wondered where Tom was, but thought no more about it. The minute she put her head on the pillow she was asleep.

It was growing dark when Raine awakened refreshed and renewed. She was ready to face whatever she must, but she was certain that the worst was over.

Frowning as she pulled the rest of her clothes out of her valise, Raine spread the scanty wardrobe on the bed. Other than underwear, hose and an extra change of shirt and denims, there was one skirt and blouse suitable for town wear.

She shrugged her problem away. It would have to do until she returned to San Francisco, where the expensive wardrobe she had begun to assemble waited for her. She could certainly use one or two of those things now.

Dressed in boots, a skirt that hit just above her ankles and a white high-collared blouse, Raine ventured into the parlor and almost bumped into Mrs. Bradley.

"I'm so glad you're awake, Mrs. Randall. Won't you join us for supper? Your friends are already at the table."

"Yes, thank you, Mrs. Bradley. I am rather hungry."

"Won't you call me Anna?" the older woman requested. "Almost everyone does."

"I shall be happy to," Raine answered, and then smiled at her friends, who looked her way as she entered the dining room.

"Saved ya a place next to me," Tom called out. "Sit down, gal. You ain't et nothin' in days. Got a mighty tasty stew here. Anna's a fine cook."

All the pressure and fears of the past few days were gone, and Raine laughed merrily. "I'm sure she is, Tom. Better than bacon and beans any day."

Two regular boarders sat at the table and listened discreetly. They were enthralled as the men who accompanied this woman spoke of Indians and capture and rescue. They talked through the main course and through pie and coffee. The young man who worked in the assay office could not stop looking at Raine, whose eyes glowed in the lamplight and whose face was radiant with happiness.

Finally Raine could sit no longer. She needed to get back to Lance. "Fine supper, Anna. And now, if you folks will excuse me, I'll be getting back to my husband." Raine would not leave Lance unattended until he was able to do for himself.

"He was still sleepin' when we left to have supper," Zeke offered. "Sure should be wakin' up soon."

"Yes, I think you're right," Raine responded happily, and hurried out of the house and down the street to Lance.

As she entered Dr. Pritchett's house, Mrs. Pritchett smiled encouragingly. "He's starting to rouse. Won't be long now and he'll be awake."

Raine's eyes shone as she hurried to her husband's room. Mrs. Pritchett was right. Lance was stirring. He moaned and stretched and grunted in pain, but he was coming out of it.

She sat by his bed and waited. Finally Lance opened his eyes, and Raine felt her heart stop beating as she looked into them. She leaned down and kissed him lightly.

"Hello, my darling," she said softly, and smiled her happiness.

"Muffin," Lance said, and his voice was a little stronger. He took her hand in his. "Tell me what happened. How did I get here? Are Zeke and Bart all right? Where are they?"

"Yes, my love," Raine said, answering the most important question first. "Zeke and Bart are just fine. Their injuries weren't that serious. Painful, but not life-threatening. In fact, they're at the boarding-house, where we also have a room, eating pie and drinking coffee."

Lance almost managed a smile. "And the rest?" he questioned, his strength ebbing swiftly.

"Hush, my darling," Raine whispered. "Save your strength. I'll talk and you listen. All right?"

Lance nodded and closed his eyes. As much as he wanted to, he couldn't keep them open. He listened to Raine's voice and was comforted by the sound of it. Every now and then he managed to pick up the thread of her narrative, but it didn't matter. Nothing mattered except that he had been spared to see her once more.

Raine sat by Lance's bed for hours as he drifted in and out of sleep. It was almost as though he had been drugged, but when she questioned Dr. Pritchett about it he said that he had given Lance no more than the tonic she, herself, had administered. "Drugs won't help him. What he needs is to eat and build up his blood. You see to it that he takes that tonic."

And Raine did. Each time Lance roused she put the cup to his lips, and he sipped the vile concoction without complaint. Finally he said he was hungry.

Not many days after he had eaten his first meal, Lance insisted on getting dressed and sitting up in a chair. He waved away any help Zeke tried to give him and wobbled unsteadily on his feet as he tried to stand without support. He was irritable, and snapped when Zeke again tried to give him a hand.

"I'm capable of puttin' my own pants on," he carped. "If I can get out of this damned night shirt, that is."

"Lord a'mighty, Lance, will you quit your bellyachin'? It's all you've done for the last two days. You *must* be gettin' better," Zeke growled back.

There wasn't much Lance could say in reply. Zeke was right, so he satisfied himself with glaring at his best friend. "Tell me again how Raine got us out of there. She told me once, but I was half asleep and don't remember too much."

"Well, now," Zeke began, relishing the task, "she came sneakin' up in the night and the first thing I knew, one of the redskin lookouts got himself knifed right behind me."

Zeke smiled innocently into Lance's disgruntled eyes. His friend did not like being beholden to an enemy. "William Clary was the one who managed that. All I could do to keep from cheerin'. Then all hell broke loose. Old Tom, Raine and Bob Clary opened fire. Not a shot wasted, I can tell ya. In less than two minutes it was all over. And there we were," he admitted, blushing at the thought, "naked as three jay birds, hangin' there helpless. I tell ya, Lance, you were mighty lucky you were unconscious. It was truly a humiliatin' experience," Zeke concluded, shaking his head in chagrin.

Lance muttered something unintelligible and sat down while he tried to lift one leg in order to put his pants on; his foot clomped heavily to the floor. He didn't have the strength to put one foot after the other into his pantlegs.

As someone who never asked for help and saw it as a sign of weakness, Lance was totally frustrated. He let out a growl and threw the pants on the floor. But Zeke said nothing. He just stood with his arms folded across his chest and waited. Finally Lance looked up and admitted that he needed some assistance.

"Just hold the damned pants so I can get my foot in," he said gruffly.

Zeke Hubbard smiled and picked up the offending garment from the floor, bunched the waist down to the crotch and slipped the trousers over Lance's legs. "Think you can manage from here?" he asked with not a trace of the smugness he felt evident in his face or voice, for at last Lance had been forced to rely on someone else. For the first time in his adult life he had lost control of a situation and been vulnerable. He was alive today only because someone had come to his rescue. And Zeke knew exactly how he felt. It was a truly shattering experience for a man with Lance's pride.

Ignoring the remark, Lance managed to stand and pull his pants up to his waist. Then he removed the detested night shirt, which always rode up, leaving his rear end hanging out. And he muttered under his breath as he remembered the humiliation of the bed pan and the sponge baths Mrs. Pritchett had insisted on. He had been as helpless as an infant when, despite his pro-tests, she had chatted away as though she hadn't heard a word he had said but had continued her ministrations, washing, dry-ing, turning him over so he wouldn't get bed sores and generally handling him as though he had been no more than a mindless slab of beef.

Lance moaned as he realized that Raine must have felt the same way when he had ignored her wishes and handled her in much the same way. There had been times —not many, thank God—when, despite her struggles, he had simply moved her body to suit his purpose. There had been times when he had insisted on positions that had embarrassed her, and he had ignored her feelings.

"Damn!" Lance cursed, and buried his face in his hands to hide the rising color of shame and regret.

"You all right?" Zeke asked anxiously, suspecting that Lance was trying to do too much too soon.

"Yeah, I'm about as good as I'm gonna be for a while," Lance answered irritably, and then shrugged into his shirt. "Help me with these boots, will ya?"

Then he stood, swaying a little before his legs went out from under him and he sat down hard on the bed. Lance sat there for a few minutes, coming to terms with his weakness. "Better get a carriage, Zeke. I'm not gonna make it on foot."

"Be right back," Zeke replied cheerfully, and hurried out the door.

Lance sat and waited for his friend to return. There was nothing else he could do. Finally he resigned himself to the situation and accepted Zeke's help to the carriage with as much grace as he could muster.

"Raine's gonna be mighty surprised to see ya," Zeke commented casually. "She was plannin' on comin' to visit ya a little later this mornin'."

"Yeah," Lance agreed, "*mighty* surprised, but I'm not goin' to argue about it. I can't stand it in that little room one more day. Besides," he added with a glint of triumph in his eyes, "I'd rather spend my nights with Raine than alone in a sick bed."

"Can't blame ya for that," Zeke quipped, and then helped his friend from the carriage.

Before Lance got his feet on the ground, Raine was at his side. Her eyes gleamed with happiness. Lance had been getting testy over the past few days, and she had known it would only be a matter of time before he insisted on joining her at the boardinghouse. She lifted his hand and put it to her cheek. "Welcome home, my darling. Such as it is." She laughed and led the way to the private outside entrance at the rear of the house. She pretended not to notice when Lance sagged a time or two, and Zeke had all he could do to support his friend's dead weight.

Opening the door, Raine indicated a large overstuffed chair and Zeke eased Lance into it. "You'd better get his boots off," she said to Zeke. "I'm not sure I can manage." And Lance cast his wife a sidelong glance.

"You managed to save my neck. You managed to shoot up the whole damned Indian camp and you managed to get me to Sacramento. Now you don't think you can manage a pair of boots?"

Raine smiled sweetly. She was not about to argue the matter. "I prefer that Zeke help you. It would make it much easier for me. Do you really mind so very much?"

"No, I guess not," he relented, and felt just a little ashamed of himself. Everyone had been kind and helpful. Everyone had tried to make him comfortable and do what was best for him, and Lance resented it. He knew he shouldn't, but he did just the same.

Then he looked around the room he had barely noticed. It was bright and airy, with two windows and a back door. The brisk April breeze was blowing the curtains, bringing the freshness of spring with it. Lance sighed and leaned back in the chair. He did not protest when Raine draped a blanket over his legs. Rather, he touched her face with his fingers and smiled his thanks.

"When we goin' home, Muffin?"

"Very soon," she promised. "Just as soon as you can walk unassisted." She put her hands to either side of his face and kissed him lightly. "And that, I imagine," she said cheerfully, "should be in a few days."

The trip to San Francisco was lazy and uneventful. The paddlewheeler churned its way downriver, and Lance spent time in the sun and was soothed by the restless waters. He sighed in regret. He had wasted so many years of his life running from the truth, a truth that had been too much to face at the time. He smiled as he envisioned Raine faced with three grown men as naked as the day they were born. But she had done what she had to do, even to the point of using his enemies to help her.

Lance frowned. He was caught in a dilemma. He had been sent out to do a job and he hadn't done it. Now he didn't see how he could justify continuing the pursuit. How in God's name could he square killing the men who had helped save his life? Raine had assured him that no one would ever hear of the Clary brothers again. He hoped that was true, but he would not lie to his father. He would have to tell him the truth, and Jarrett Randall was not going to like it.

Unconsciously, Lance's hand went to his belt, and he loosened it. The burns had not completely healed, but they would. Raine had gotten there in time. She had come before they had put the fire to his feet. She had come before he had been set aflame.

Well, almost, he thought as he rubbed the eyebrows that had been badly singed but were growing back. His eyes narrowed as he thought of what would have happened if Raine and Tom and the Clary brothers hadn't come when they did.

Then Lance turned and walked back to his cabin. He was grateful that Raine was no longer hovering over him. Without saying a word, she had decided that he was well enough to look after himself, and she let him do it. Lance was exceptionally pleased with her. No man could have a more loving wife. She had risked her life for him, and though he never wanted it to happen again, he was full of pride. She had great courage and she loved him enough to face a bunch of murdering Indians to save him. Lance smiled, smug in the knowledge that he had married a woman like no other. She was quite something. Claire could not hold a candle to her.

14

By the end of the first week in May Lance had almost fully recovered. His body would be scarred, but not badly. Considering what he had been through, the damage was remarkably slight. Except for the bullet wound. That would leave an ugly scar that would be with him for the rest of his life. Still, he felt himself to be a fortunate man, and his spirits were high.

On his first excursion out of the hotel, Lance headed Raine for the jewelry store. He needed to buy her something beautiful and dazzling to match her provocative beauty. He had no idea what it would be; he only knew that he would know it when he saw it.

Entering the shop and smiling at the pleasant tinkling of the overhead bell, Lance guided Raine to one of the chairs. After she had been seated he turned to the clerk. "I am looking for something out of the ordinary. Something very special for my wife. Let me see the finest piece you have in the store."

Without hesitation, the clerk went through the curtained doorway that led to the back room. He picked up a large jewel case and returned to the showroom. Almost reverently, he placed the case on the countertop and opened it.

Raine gasped in wonder, and Lance smiled in delight. It was perfect. There could not be another like it. He lifted the brilliant empress-style necklace from its resting place and walked with it to the window. He held the necklace up, and the diamonds threw back a blinding light as they reflected the sun from thousands of facets. Each stone was a triumph of the diamond cutter's art. "I'll take it," Lance said without asking the price. "Do you have paper and pen so I might write a draft on my bank account?"

"Indeed, sir, and may I say you have made an exquisite choice. This piece is from the collection of the Czarina herself. The war in the Crimea, you know. We have the honor of representing her."

Lance nodded and returned to the counter, where he accepted paper and pen and wrote out the sum the clerk indicated. Then, turning to Raine, he dared at last to indicate the depths of his love for her. "This does not do justice to you, and it can only express the very smallest part of my love for you, but I hope that each time you wear it you will remember that love which is as timeless and as enduring as the stones it contains. Will you accept it and with it all my devotion?"

Tears filled Raine's eyes, and she dabbed them away with her handkerchief. She did not care who was watching as she rose and embraced her husband. "I shall accept your gift with great joy, my darling. And, always, I shall remember the love that is the greater part of the gift. Thank you," Raine concluded simply.

Lance finally understood. It was not the gift that mattered to Raine. It was the love that was given with it that was the most important thing. A simple gold locket would have been treasured just as highly as the priceless piece he had just purchased.

Tilting his wife's face to his, Lance said, "Will you wear it for me tonight? I thought perhaps you might enjoy seeing what Tess has done with the Cherokee Rose. Zeke can talk of nothing else since we've returned to San Francisco."

Raine's eyes opened a little wider. "The Cherokee Rose?" she questioned hesitantly, wondering at Lance's sudden change in attitude.

"You won't recognize the place," Lance assured her, "and you'll need to dress in your very finest gown to blend in with the other customers."

Raine looked into her husband's face, which was as full of joy and mischief as a small boy's. She decided to ask no questions, for it was obvious he wanted to surprise her. "I shall dress as grandly as though I were going to a ball at Queen Victoria's court," she replied seriously, and they both smiled at this shared bit of intrigue. "And," Raine added, "your gift will put to shame even my finest gown."

"But not the woman who wears the gown," Lance added sincerely. He tucked the jewel case under his arm and escorted his wife back to the hotel. He was tiring and needed to rest before the night's activities began.

The moment the carriage stopped in front of the Cherokee Rose Raine began to have some understanding of the changes that had been made by Tess. The dismal front of the building had been transformed into a lovely well-lit lobby. Everything had been painted a fresh pink that was highlighted by vases of brilliant red roses. When they entered the main part of the building Raine stopped and gaped in amazement. The dingy, smelly saloon had disappeared. In its place was a brilliant, beautiful room of white and pink and gilt. There were lovely chandeliers and romantic, candlelit tables.

Snowy linens emphasized the silver table-
ware and the single red rose on each table.
As Raine stood gaping in wonder, the band
began to play. Lance removed the cape from
his wife's shoulders and handed it to an
attendant. Then he bowed.

"May I have this dance?" he asked, and
his eyes glowed softly with love and happiness.

"Why, sir," Raine cooed, "it would be
my absolute pleasure." She managed to execute the deep curtsy her mother had taught
her as a child.

With expert grace Lance led Raine on to
the dance floor, taking her most carefully in
his arms. His gloved hand rested ever so
lightly at the back of her waist, and Raine
floated across the room in her elegant gown
of green satin. The empress necklace graced
her bare neck and caught every eye. There
were audible gasps of wonder as the light
from the chandeliers danced across the diamonds and gleamed from their gold setting.
But Raine noticed none of it. She was filled
with joy by this gesture of love from her
husband. The celebration was for her.

Then as polite applause sounded and
other dancers took the floor, Lance guided
Raine to their table. It was in a very private
setting under the gallery, but the area was
no longer dark and foreboding. Soft candle-
light glowed from the wall behind her, and
the wall itself had been painted white with

gilt trim. The chairs had seats of crimson velvet and the portions that were wood were also painted white with gilt trim. Large green ferns graced the corners. Raine could hardly believe that this place had once been Jake's saloon, with sawdust and tobacco juice on the floor and horrible spittoons placed at strategic locations along the floor by the bar.

As Lance seated Raine, Tess approached the table. Zeke was at her side. "Welcome to the Cherokee Rose," Tess said with pride, and then turned to Lance. "Enjoy your evening, and if there's anything we can do to be of service, please let us know."

With that short welcome, Tess was gone. Raine was confused. "Why didn't you ask her to join us?" she asked, and Lance smiled. His wife was, in some ways, extremely capable and shrewd. But in other ways she was hopelessly out of her depth.

"Tess would not want to tarnish your reputation. She knows that everyone present is quite aware of what she once did for a living, and she wants none of that to rub off on you."

Raine looked at Lance as though he had suddenly gone quite mad. "But she's my friend. I don't *care* what the others think."

Lance changed the subject. "For a little girl who grew up in a mining camp, you dance extraordinarily well."

A soft smile touched Raine's face as her

thoughts drifted back in time. "Yes, my father taught me. Whenever it was too bad to work outside, we would amuse ourselves inside with all kinds of games. But the thing Papa loved most was dancing. He would whistle or hum or sing some lovely song and we would dance away for hours. He was very good at it."

"Then by all means, we shall have to do more of it, but first I think we should greet our guests."

"Guests?" Raine asked, and only then understood the extent to which Lance had gone. She looked around at the tables that were closest to hers and smiled. Somehow Lance had managed to persuade Tom to attend. He had come all the way from Sacramento, and he looked grand in new clothes, with his hair and beard trimmed.

Then Raine looked a little further along the semi-circle of tables that spread out in front of her. Dr. and Mrs. Redding had come. Bart was there. So were four other couples. Raine smiled and inclined her head to each woman who had dared befriend her in the past.

"How did you manage?" she asked in wonder.

"Had a lot of help," Lance admitted as he took her hand in his.

"But this place," Raine began in amazement. "How on earth could Tess afford to do all of this?"

"It's not just Tess, now," Lance explained as he glanced over at the waiters who were serving the champagne. "Zeke's money is in it too. He's worked with me a long time, and over the years he's saved most of the generous salary my father paid him. Of course, in our business we have very little time to spend much, so he had a sizable sum to invest."

"And the upstairs?" Raine asked fearfully.

Lance could barely suppress a smile. "Tess changed her mind. No more whores and their cribs," he answered softly so no one else would hear. "The upstairs is now a very fancy gambling casino. Quite profitable, I understand."

"So Zeke is settled in a very good business. Will he be going with you on any more—errands for your father?"

"He'll be there when I need him, just as I would be for him," Lance answered with confidence.

"I'm glad," Raine said quietly.

"Not half as glad as I am," Lance replied seriously, for there was no one he'd rather have guarding his back than Zeke Hubbard.

"Shall we say hello to our guests before the meal is served?" Lance asked, anxious to have the wonderful things he had planned for Raine begin.

She smiled and nodded. As she greeted each guest, Raine's heart was filled with

happiness. Lance had done so much——just
for her.

The party lasted into the early morning
hours. Champagne flowed; the orchestra
played, and guests dined on the finest foods
available. Even though it was a rather small
party, it was a grand one. It was one Raine
would never forget.

Another week of lazy living passed before Lance returned to the docks the first
time to check on his ship. While Raine
waited for him to return, she sat poring over
each page of fashion magazines that she
knew by heart. Her thoughts drifted back to
the night of the party. She thought of Tom,
who had managed to get his gold out of the
valley with help from Bart and Zeke. And
she thought of Tess, who had come so far.

The corners of Raine's eyes crinkled
with pleasure. There had been some rather
heavy-handed hints that Zeke and Tess
might be forming a partnership in more
than business. She hoped so, for she had
never seen either one of them look as happy
as they did when they were together.

All manner of happy memories crowded
Raine's mind, and she looked up smiling
when Lance returned. But the smile slid
from her face at once. A stranger would see
nothing alarming, but Raine had learned to
read every flicker of his eye, every twitch of
his hand. There was nothing about her husband she had not studied and memorized,

and his distress was immediately obvious to her.

The outline of his lips was white, standing out starkly against his skin. The pale green eyes were shaded by lashes that attempted to hide them from scrutiny. Something was terribly wrong.

Her voice was little more than a fearful whisper. "What is it?"

"There was a message for me at the desk. I must return to Maryland at once," Lance stated in a voice that was under tight control.

Raine stood and waited for the rest. It came with a reaction that shook her to the very core of her being.

Quiet tears began their descent from eyes that had been hardened to every perversion and cruelty the world had to offer. Eyes that could look upon any horror with all the unfeeling speculation of a scientist observing the death throes of some insect, filled and spilled out their grief.

The words when they finally came were hard and uncompromising. "My mother is dying. The message was sent from Baltimore weeks ago. For all I know she could be dead already."

From somewhere deep within, Raine found the courage to speak into the face of the despair that almost incapacitated Lance Randall. "Or she might have already recovered," she offered tentatively, hoping against hope that she did not sound like some insensitive boor who had no idea of what the man in front of her was suffering.

Her husband's contorted face told her she had missed the mark. "No! You don't understand. It's cholera!"

There were two kinds of cholera, and Raine did not need to ask which this was. She shivered with apprehension at the word that could be a death sentence. Deadly cholera was almost always fatal. The second kind rarely was. And Raine knew the former well, indeed. The wretched, dehumanizing agony of it would never be erased from her mind, for her own mother had died of it.

Nothing she and her father had been able to do had stopped the horror of those symptoms. The diarrhea, the vomiting, the inability of the victim to control his bodily functions all stood out as clearly in her mind as though they were happening still.

"I'll go with you," Raine stated, and began to throw a few of Lance's things into her traveling bag. Then she changed into a heavy skirt, a fresh blouse and boots. She stuffed several changes of underwear in with her husband's things as well as a nightdress. A few more items would complete her wardrobe, for there was no time to worry about the niceties of fashion. They would be traveling fast and light. They would make do with what they could carry themselves.

"How are we going?" Raine asked, for Lance had managed to collect himself and could now begin to make arrangements for the fastest means of travel.

"By steamer to the isthmus. My father will have one of our ships waiting for us on the Atlantic side."

Raine understood. There was no time to sail around the Horn. Nor was there time to take the arduous southern land route. It would have to be across the isthmus. But tickets for the steamers were often difficult to get. Men were arriving in San Francisco every day, but just as many, broke and disillusioned, were returning home. A few were leaving richer than when they had arrived.

The steamer would be the fastest, but if worse came to worse, Lance could always press his own sailing vessel into service one more time. However, it was in bad shape. The hull had not been scraped or caulked since he had left Maryland. It had been pushed to its limits on its latest voyage, and half his crew had deserted for the gold fields.

Raine realized that her husband had taken all these things into consideration before making his decision. There was no need to waste time going over them. "Shall I come with you or do you want me to wait here until you have the tickets?"

"Wait here," Lance said as he thought of what he might do in order to get the tickets he needed.

When he had gone, Raine looked around, checking to see if she had forgotten anything they would absolutely need on their trip. Satisfied that she had stuffed everything necessary into her small valise, she waited. The minutes dragged on endlessly, or so it seemed. Actually, only a half hour passed before Lance returned, triumphantly waving their tickets. "We'll be leaving in half an hour. Let's get moving."

"What about Zeke and Bart? Will they be going?"

"If they have to step over my dead body to get there," Lance confirmed grimly.

Without wasting any more time, he picked up the traveling bag and escorted his wife to the lobby, where he paid an additional six months' rent, then drove the carriage he had waiting straight to the docks. Bart and Zeke were already there, and Raine could not help but notice that their faces were as grim as her husband's.

Shortly after they had found their quarters the last of the warning blasts reverberated through the ship. Lance and Raine left their cabin and went out on deck, watching while lines were cast off fore and aft.

Slowly, the unwieldy sternwheeler backed out of its berth and shuddered as it was coaxed from reverse to forward; but once in the current of the bay it swung like some suddenly freed bird, found its head and glided gracefully with paddlewheel propelling it toward the open sea.

From their position on the lower deck, Lance and Raine could hear the captain in the wheelhouse above shouting orders through a tube that connected to the boiler room below. Heavy smoke poured from the stack as fires were stoked and pressure was increased.

Not knowing what lay ahead, Raine watched the receding shoreline until even the heights above the city were lost. She shivered from more than the cold sea air, and Lance put his arm around her. He, too, was fearful of what he would find when they finally arrived at Promise Kept Manor, the house four generations of his family had called home.

Unconsciously, he held his wife closer to him as his eyes stared at the open water that stretched behind them, water disturbed only by the frothy wake of the wheel. Then he turned and led Raine to their cabin, the cabin for which he had shamelessly bribed the ticket agent, for it was the very best the steamer had to offer.

And if the room were a trifle small, there was an elegant salon where many uneventful daylight hours could be spent in conversation. There was also a bar with a bartender who was adept in preparing all the latest alcoholic concoctions. For others who preferred to while away their time with games of chance, there were card tables and men who were waiting for just such an opportunity. But Lance was interested in only one thing and that was getting to his mother's side while she still lived—if, indeed, she did.

Anxiety about his mother was heightened by the fact that Lance was uncertain how his family would react to Raine. He could not warn everyone. Someone would be sure to blurt out the truth. His days were restless and his nights all but sleepless. Raine lay silent by his side and felt him toss and turn until, at last, he would rise, get dressed and walk out onto the deck.

The sea air, the wind and the spray always comforted Lance, for he was a man born to the sea, and it was something he understood. Ever changing, always the same, the sea rolled and swelled, buffeting the pitiful creations of man upon its breast. Lance submerged himself in the ancient rhythm and accepted his fate as well as that of his mother. Yet he was desperate to tell her once more that he loved her. If only they could make better time!

Even as the thought touched his mind, Lance rejected it, for there were shoals and rocks that lay in wait for the unwary sailor. And they were approaching a particularly treacherous stretch where arms of jagged rocks reached out into the sea to entrap any so careless as not to obey the pounding and hissing of the water as it beat upon the great boulders. It was a place of death, a graveyard for many fine ships. Lance was more than a little relieved when he felt the ship veer further to starboard to avoid the churning waters that roiled and thundered amid the rocks.

There was always the danger of an exploding boiler. Such events were common, reported almost daily in one or another of the San Francisco papers. The sea was never safe, and Lance had learned long ago to respect it and never let down his guard while sailing it.

Breathing deeply of the sea air, Lance felt better. His mind was clear and he was prepared. Deciding that he might be able to sleep after all, he returned to his cabin, where his wife lay awake, waiting for him. She never spoke. She never told him that she slept no more than he, but he could feel the tension in her body as it lay unnaturally still while he tossed and turned. She knew what he was going through, and why not? She, herself, had already lost both mother and father.

Lance undressed and eased himself into bed next to Raine, but he let her know that her nightly vigils had not gone unnoticed. His hand searched for hers and squeezed it tight. Raine returned the pressure and lay still. She would make no move toward him until he was ready. Lance smiled, breathed out a long sigh of exhaustion and fell asleep still holding on to his wife's hand.

Raine did not move. She lay very still, listening to the even, quiet breathing of her husband, who finally was able to rest his weary body and mind.

15

It was not yet dawn when their steamer nosed into Panama Bay. Even though their journey was only half complete, Raine breathed a sigh of relief. For a short time, at least, they would be on dry land, and she could hardly believe her eyes when she saw for herself how much conditions had improved since she and her father had made the crossing almost seven years ago.

In fact, Raine could not take her eyes away from the new railroad that would whisk them within a few miles of the Caribbean itself. There would be no more frightening swamps, jungle or other impossible terrain. There would be no more burying men who had dropped like flies from tropical diseases that had struck without warning. And there would be no more fighting off insects that had delighted in tormenting the hapless travelers who had traversed this land with her and her father.

How she had ever survived Raine did not know. If it had not been for her father, who had kept her covered with netting to protect her from the torment of stinging biting insects and who had carried her over and through the worst of it, she would *not* have survived. And when her father had tired, Tom Morley, the old man her father had befriended, took on the burden of keeping her safe.

As Raine stood on the small platform waiting for Zeke to purchase tickets, she stared admiringly at the train they would soon board. Unlike most other things in this wretched land, it was new and sleek and it *worked.*

When it was time to board Raine eagerly mounted the stool and then the steps and followed Lance to their seats. "I can't believe it," she commented for at least the third time as she craned her neck to catch glimpses of familiar scenery as they sped along at the dizzying rate of twenty miles an hour.

"When Papa and I crossed it was terrible," she said, more to herself than to Lance, and then was silent as she remembered in minutest detail the torture they had suffered and the misery-filled days they had endured just to cross this narrow stretch of land.

Now, in less than one full day, she would be gazing upon the blue waters of the Caribbean. They would cross this narrow waist of land that effectively blocked shipping, forcing ocean-going vessels to sail thousands of miles to the south and then around the Horn.

"I just cannot believe it!" she said again, and Lance laughed in understanding.

He, too, had crossed this strip of land when conditions had been far more severe and dangerous than they were now. "One day it might be different," he mused. "There are canals in many countries including our own that carry cargo from one navigable waterway to another. Why not here? Surely this fifty mile stretch of land can be no more difficult to ditch than the Chesapeake and Ohio Canal, which is one hundred eighty-four miles long and contains seventy-four locks. It's a magnificent job of engineering that has opened up navigation from Georgetown to Cumberland," he commented, as though Raine surely must know the two towns in Maryland to which he referred.

But Raine had little knowledge of the geography of the United States or of any other place for that matter. In general she knew where the states and territories were located, but she knew almost nothing of the terrain. "Perhaps one day I might be able to see it," she said hopefully, knowing that it would not be any time soon, for this was not a pleasure trip they were taking. Lance's mother could already be dead, for very few ever recovered from *deadly* cholera.

"How long will it take us to get to your home once we've reached the Caribbean?" she asked in growing concern.

Lance sighed his impatience. "The message I received said the *Victoria* will be waiting for us. It's propeller-driven and is the fastest thing we own. With the kind of speed she can give us, we should be home within the week."

Raine did not really understand all the differences involved between a paddle-wheeler and a propeller-driven ship, but she had seen enough of the former along the Sacramento River and in San Francisco to know that they were dangerous beasts. Any improvement was welcome.

For the rest of the train ride Raine took her cue from Lance. If he did not speak, neither did she, and when he directed a comment to her, she tried to give the answer he wanted.

Long, weary hours dragged by as the train fought the mountains. Finally it came to the end of track. From here they would have to travel the remaining few miles by a horse-drawn conveyance. However, the road from track's end to their destination was a good one, much better than anything she had traveled on before.

Following Lance, who carried their one

bag, Raine climbed aboard the horse-drawn coach that would carry them to the Caribbean. The eighteen miles where track still had to be laid proved to be a fairly easy ride, and when they reached port Lance hustled her off in the direction of the docks, where he left her in the company of Zeke and Bart while he walked to the end of one long pier and signaled. He was spotted at once by a lookout stationed aboard the *Victoria.*

Within minutes, a boat was lowered over the side and two stalwart seamen rowed directly for the man they had been sent to meet. "Any word," Lance asked brusquely, even as he swung Raine into the boat that would carry them outside the harbor where the *Victoria* rode at anchor.

"Your mother's still alive, sir. At least she was when your brother, Garron, last sent word. He is anxious for you to get home. He asks that you make all deliberate speed," the man added as he and his companion bent their backs to the oars.

Lance drew in a deep, steadying breath. If Garron was getting nervous, then it was serious, much more so than his father's panicky note betrayed, for where his mother's health was concerned his father was easily spooked.

"I'm a little anxious to get home myself," he answered almost casually, and Raine looked in awe at the calm facade her husband was presenting to the others. He simply refused to let his fear show.

Raine's mind was soon occupied by other fears. She clung to anything handy as the choppy waters tossed the small boat about roughly. She hated deep water, and almost cried out in fear as the boat leaned precariously to one side. Her knuckles turned white as she gripped the seat in an effort to keep herself from sliding overboard.

It was then that Lance put his arms around her and held her steady. "Scared?" he asked, smiling down into eyes that were wide with terror.

"Yes," Raine croaked, "I can't swim very well."

"You mean there's *somethin'* Tess didn't get around to teaching you?" he teased, and laughed softly as his lips brushed hers.

Raine held tightly to her husband and the fear left her eyes. She was grateful to him for not making her look foolish in front of the others. "A couple of things, I think," she answered with false bravado. "Guess she thought you could teach me the rest yourself."

For the first time since he had gotten the message from his father Lance put his own fear aside. Purring laughter insinuated more than the words said. "Anytime you're ready, Muffin. Anytime."

Zeke and Bart glanced at each other and smiled discreetly as they understood the implication of the conversation they had overheard. Nothing could make them happier than having Lance behave like a loving husband. And Zeke's smile broadened as he thought of Tess.

Then they turned their attention to the ship that loomed before them. It was a discreetly armed merchantman of massive proportions whose main deck was riding high above the water, indicating that the vessel that had been designed to hold thousands of tons of cargo was empty.

Raine, too, stared at the largest ship she had ever seen. She almost tumbled backward as she craned her neck to see to the top of the hull, which looked impossibly far away. How would they ever get aboard?

Even as she studied the problem in growing dismay, lines were dropped and made fast. Before she had time to understand the significance of what had happened, the boat began to rise. Her eyes widened, and she held tighter to Lance's arm as they and the boat were lifted toward the deck.

Even as fearful as she was, however, Raine could not help but notice the tiny objects moving about as she looked landward. They were people and horses and wagons, and how small and insignificant they looked from her vantage point.

Her attention soon returned to the task at hand as the boat was swung over the deck and lowered into place. The men helped her over the side, and Raine was never so grateful as to be standing on the deck of a ship.

The deep water she feared was far below her, and so were the sharks. Barring any great mishap, they were going to get to Maryland alive, and Raine swore then and there she was going to learn to swim instead of being dependent upon the ridiculous paddling about she had been satisfied with until now.

"We'll be bunkin' in the owner's quarters," Lance told her as he took the valise she still clutched in her hand and proceeded to a nearby stairway that led below.

When Raine saw the steep steps she was supposed to descend she again doubted her adequacy. This was not a stairway. It was more of a ladder with rails that confronted her. But she was tired of being the only one who needed help. It was becoming an embarrassment. So she gathered her skirt around herself and cautiously maneuvered the steep incline of the narrow treads, deathly afraid that her heel might catch on the back edge, pitching her forward. A smug smile of triumph lightened her features when she stepped off the last tread and put her feet on solid planking.

Lance's eyes smiled in approval, and he led her down a corridor that reflected the warm glow of polished wood. There was carpet underfoot and bright brass lamps overhead, and when Lance opened the door to their quarters it was almost as though they were entering a world apart from the rest of the ship.

Raine stood spellbound, a look of wonder on her face as Lance asked with pride, "Like it?"

"Oh, yes. It's beautiful," Raine breathed in astonishment as she took in every detail of the magnificent room she had entered. "I've never seen anything so grand. Not even the rooms at our hotel."

Chairs and settees covered in finest velvets and trimmed in gilded wood were scattered in casual groupings. Heavy rugs covered the floor and where they did not, the planking shimmered in the light that streamed from chandeliers and wall sconces. Heavy velvet drapes trimmed in gold fringe were thrown open to allow the balmy sea breezes to flow through the room. Beautifully tooled books were safely shelved behind glass doors that were reinforced by panels of open woodwork. Colorful oils brightened walls that had been paneled in pale green.

But the thing that intrigued Raine most was the fierce-looking head of a snarling mountain lion that had been woven in the center rug. Expert hands had crafted the realistic pattern with threads ranging from palest to darkest gold with touches of black. It was beautiful, and at the same time there was something ominous and fearsome in the sharp teeth, the narrowed eyes and the curled-back lip.

"It's the same design as the one on the

flag that flies from your ship in San Francisco and from this ship," Raine commented. "What does it mean?"

"It's a symbol," Lance explained. "Wherever that symbol appears there you will find a Randall or a Randall possession. My great-grandfather designed it in honor of his wife, and flew it above every ship in his fleet."

Raine saw the change in her husband's expression when he talked of his great-grandparents. "You must have loved them very much."

"I never knew them," Lance replied almost sadly. "I wish I had. It was my grandfather who brought them to life for me. Marcus and Victoria Randall. This ship is named for her. And even though Grandfather was an old man in his nineties when he died, his love for his parents never dimmed. He passed that love on to us. He made them real. You'll see their pictures when we get home."

"You were very lucky to have such a wonderful grandfather," Raine responded wistfully.

"Very lucky, indeed," Lance confirmed. "He was a fine old gentleman whose stories I never tired of hearing. Yes, he was a rare one," Lance murmured as his eyes smiled in remembrance.

"How I envy you." Raine sighed. "I've always wished I had grandparents to love."

There was an odd expression on Lance's

face when he asked the question. "Are you quite sure your mother's father will not receive you? After all, it seems rather childish to carry on a family feud for so long, especially when you have no other blood kin."

Raine slanted a look full of hatred in Lance's direction, but her words made it clear that the hate she felt was directed toward her grandfather, not her husband. "This particular feud will be carried on until the day one of us dies. The year before she died my mother wrote to my grandfather, pleading with him to acknowledge me. He didn't even have the decency to write himself. The coward had his attorney answer for him, telling my mother that as far as he was concerned, she was dead; therefore, he had neither daughter nor granddaughter."

Lance was shaken. He had not imagined that his wife could be capable of the hatred that glinted in her eyes, the hatred that was intensified by her words. Then, as suddenly as the rage had come, it was gone.

"Wait," Raine exclaimed as happily as though the previous conversation had never taken place, "I have a picture of my mother."

Rummaging in the valise, Raine pulled out a small package carefully wrapped in a silk scarf. Opening the tiny bundle, Raine lovingly spread its contents. "There," she exclaimed, picking up one piece at a time. "This bracelet belonged to my mother, and this is her wedding ring. Papa gave her this brooch on their first wedding anniversary. I had already been born by then," she added.

Laying aside a gold locket with loving hands, Raine picked up the watch Lance had seen once before. She pressed it to her cheek and held it there for a moment. Then she pushed a small lever and the watch sprung open. It was something Lance had not bothered to do when Emmett Colter's personal effects had been returned by the mortician.

Raine smiled as she looked at something on the inside of the watch. "Here," she said, holding it out so Lance might see, "this is my mother."

Almost afraid to look, Lance forced himself to meet the smiling eyes of the woman in the portrait. The beautiful face was exactly as he knew it would be. The emerald eyes and the hair that was a half shade lighter than Raine's accentuated the beauty of the woman who was Raine's mother.

Lance blinked and a muscle in his jaw twitched as he clenched his teeth. Claire and Raine's mother could have been sisters. The resemblance was so strong as to be undeniable.

"What does your grandfather look like?" he asked, not daring to hope that the man might also be green-eyed and blond.

Raine shrugged. "Mother had a small portrait of him, and, if I remember correctly, he had black hair, or maybe it was brown, and a fair complexion. I think his eyes were brown. I haven't seen the picture in so many years, I really can't be sure."

But Lance was sure. The resemblance was too great to be coincidental. "And your grandmother? What did she look like?"

A bright smile brought happy lights to Raine's eyes. "My mother said that she was very beautiful. Everyone had told her that my grandmother was the most beautiful belle in all Philadelphia. Of course, Mama could not remember very much herself, because Grandmother went away when Mama was very small."

"You have no pictures of your grandmother?"

"No. Apparently when my grandmother left my grandfather destroyed them all. I think he loved Grandmother so much he couldn't bear to look at her picture once she had run away with another man. That's what Mother said, anyway."

"Yes, of course," Lance agreed absently, but he was almost certain that there was a great deal more to the story of his wife's grandmother than Raine suspected.

However, for the present, Lance kept his suspicions to himself—suspicions that might eventually explain the uncanny resemblance of both Raine and her mother to the Randall family. It might also provide another clue to the disappearance of Jay Randall almost thirty years ago.

Again Lance stared into the face that

had haunted him from the beginning. He closed his eyes as he allowed the suffering to wash over him. Raine had not yet guessed just how much anguish she had brought back into his life, but the past must not touch her. She was innocent. It was Claire who was guilty. It was Claire he sometimes cursed from the depths of his torment.

One day he must tell Raine the truth. He must tell her about Claire and a rape and a vial of calf's blood. And when he did, then what?

16

As the *Victoria* steamed its way north-ward, Raine's isolation became almost complete. The closer they came to their destination, the more Lance withdrew from her. She almost never saw him, and even when she went on deck to search him out he found some excuse to literally ignore her.

Stunned by this unexpected treatment, Raine's troubled mind went over the unhappy situation again and again. For some reason she knew nothing of, Lance was avoiding her. It was almost as though he wished she hadn't come on this trip. But why? What had she done this time?

For long hours she concentrated on the problem, and then gave up. She did not know what was troubling her husband. All she could do was wait. If Lance chose to avoid her, then there was little she could do. She would give him all the privacy he seemed to crave. She would not throw herself at his feet begging forgiveness for some offense she had unknowingly committed. His solitude would remain inviolate until he chose to break it. Nor would she further humiliate herself by turning to him when he slipped into their bed at night, long after he thought her asleep, only to be rejected.

If it had not been for Zeke and Bart, Raine's spirits would have sunk to even lower depths. But those two kind men saw what was happening and took Raine under their wing.

Even when she did not wish to go topside they managed to coax her out of her splendid prison. And, frequently, they would join her for lunch, regaling her with stories of their childhood. Raine found herself laughing at the antics of the two brothers who had included Lance in all their boyhood adventures.

Zeke, particularly, was a master storyteller who kept Raine happily distracted for hours at a time. As the days passed a strong bond of companionship formed between Raine and the two men. The three of them were rarely seen apart, and Lance's self-imposed isolation became more complete as his friends ignored him and his mood.

There were times, however, when Zeke and Bart would glance his way with puzzled expressions on their faces. It was almost as though they had suddenly discovered a serious flaw in Lance's character and were showing their displeasure by putting some distance between him and themselves. In fact, they had taken sides, and Lance knew it.

Raine pondered this latest development, and her heart went out to the lonely man she had married, the man who did not or could not trust her enough to confide in her. Then she admitted that she had done precious little to earn that trust.

Since the first time Lance had laid eyes on her she had been nothing but a source of embarrassment and irritation for him. She had been violently jealous. She had openly quarreled with him and had physically attacked him and the woman she had mistakenly assumed to be his mistress. Then she had gone to the Aces Up, a saloon that no decent woman would ever enter. She had transformed herself into the painted woman she had thought he wanted. She had even learned a few whore's tricks to practice in bed. And through it all Lance had put up with her. He had endured her vile behavior and her insulting suspicions. No wonder he didn't trust her. How could he?

A chill went through Raine's heart as she realized how difficult it must have been for him to tolerate her childish actions and the vulgar, unladylike image she had adopted. Then a pathetic moan of regret seeped from Raine's lips as she realized the great disappointment she must be to the man she loved with all her heart. Her mother had taught her better. Why hadn't she listened?

Determined never to make those mistakes again, Raine waited patiently until Lance settled the matter in his own mind. However, Zeke was not so tolerant. He had a long talk with his friend and gradually came to understand Lance's troubled mind. Once again Claire Randall would be the cause of great unhappiness.

"You gotta tell her," Zeke said, feeling miserable. "You should have told her in the beginning. It's what Bart and I were afraid of. It's gonna break her heart to learn you married her because she looks like Claire!"

"I know," Lance answered, his voice heavy with regret. "How do I tell her? She might never forgive me. I don't think I could stand it."

Zeke shook his head in commiseration. He didn't know the solution, but he did know that Raine's entire life was wrapped up in her husband. "Jesus," he hissed in sorrow.

Lance continued to pace. "I know her. This will be more than she can bear," he predicted. Then he turned his back to his friend until he regained his composure. "I can't handle it now, Zeke. I've done nothing for days but think about it, and there's just no way I can deal with it. I can only hope

Raine doesn't find out about Claire before I have a chance to tell her myself. It must come from me, though God knows I'd rather die than hurt her like this."

He paused. "After I know about Mother. I'll tell her then."

"Yeah," Zeke replied, and heaved a disconsolate, sigh. "Guess we better warn everybody not to mention her likeness to Claire. That's about all we can do, I guess."

"That's about the size of it," Lance replied, and fought down the deep remorse only he fully understood, for he had not told Zeke of his rape of Raine when she had been desperately ill with fever, nor would he ever tell anyone—except the victim. "But how am I going to protect her? Everybody knew Claire. Somebody's sure to let something slip. God, but I wish I had never let her come on this trip."

Zeke smiled a sad little smile. "You had no choice. You couldn't run out on her again, not when you just got back. I don't think she'd put up with it again."

"Why should she?" Lance asked softly, expecting no answer. Then his eyes locked with Zeke's. "Do you think we ever get a second chance in life?"

"Seems to me ya already got your second chance. Guess it all depends on what you do with it," he said compassionately.

Lance nodded in agreement. "Yeah, you're right. I got as much as any man can expect. I never thought I'd ever love another

woman, but I love Raine. At first I was
convinced that I loved her only because she
looks so much like Claire. Then I realized my
love for her had nothing to do with Claire.''

Lance was distraught. ''I compounded
one sin with another, and I don't know how
I'm going to undo it.''

Zeke looked at his friend through world-
weary eyes. ''Seems to me the truth is
what's needed now.''

''Yeah,'' Lance agreed sadly. ''I know.
It's facing the consequences that scares the
hell out of me.''

Then he made up his mind. He could not
continue to think about the problem night
after night. It would be resolved, but not
now, not until he could think more clearly.
For the time being, his own problems must
wait.

As the ship passed from warm, subtrop-
ical waters and steamed into the colder cur-
rents of the north, Lance made peace with
himself and with Raine. No matter what the
future held, they were together now, and he
gave her all the love he had. Too happy to ask
questions, Raine basked in the warmth of
that love even as the wind turned chilly. Her
joy was complete as she lay safe in her
husband's arms.

As the ship approached Cape Charles,
lightning and thunder crackled and echoed
around them. Drenching rain whipped the
deck, forcing everyone below. When it

cleared the sun came out to reflect brilliantly from the water, and the air was warm and
muggy, but the wind picked up and blew
away the oppressive dampness.

Sails, fore and aft, were raised to help
the boilers, and the ship literally skimmed
over the surface of the sea. Raine and Lance
walked the decks in high spirits. The combi-
nation of salt air and freshening wind
exhilerated them both.

Any attempt to hold her hair in place
was futile, so Raine allowed the mass of
golden curls to blow where they pleased. She
glanced up at Lance, who had lost the dark,
foreboding look and now resembled nothing
so much as a cheerful seaman who was once
again in his own realm.

Lance was at ease as he paced the distance from bow to stern, enjoying the free-
dom he always felt when at sea. Raine did
her best to keep up with the long-legged
stride, but she soon found herself double-
stepping in order to stay alongside. It was
not until she tugged at Lance's sleeve that
he understood the problem.

His mind had been on his mother and on
the amount of time it was taking to reach
home. Yet he knew they could do no better.

He smiled down at Raine, and his pace
slowed. Her breathing came easier, and the
breeze evaporated the perspiration from her
face. She looked up gratefully at her husband's smiling face. "Thank you," she said
breathlessly.

Her gratitude for such a small thing touched Lance, and he breathed deeply to ease the ache in his heart. She asked for so little, and there were times when he gave her less than she needed. Putting his arm around her, he grunted playfully as he pulled her close. A smile brightened his face. "I keep forgetting what a feisty, determined little bundle you are."

"Not too feisty, I hope," Raine replied, blushing as she remembered the public brawl in which she had engaged with Alice Rafferty.

Lance laughed and turned his back to the wind, his body protecting his wife. He lowered his head to hers and touched her lips with a gentle, lingering kiss, and Raine clung to him. Her remorse for all her past transgressions overwhelmed her.

"Oh, my darling," she sobbed, thoroughly ashamed of herself, "I love you so much! I couldn't bear it if you hadn't forgiven me for all those horrid things I did."

Lance cupped her face in his hands. "One day when I need your forgiveness I'll ask you to remember those words."

Not understanding what Lance was really saying, Raine smiled her love. Her valiant knight was absolving her of all blame, something she could not allow him to do. "You have my promise, but I shall do much better in the future, you'll see," she said, and barely suppressed the moan of a martyr as pictures of dreary tea parties flashed through her mind. But she was determined to do anything, no matter how distasteful, if it would please her husband.

The soft, purring laughter she had not heard recently touched Raine's ears, and Lance's warm breath sent a shiver through her. "Shall we go below?" he asked as he lifted her head so he could see her face. His eyes flashed a wicked invitation.

It was a look Raine understood. She laughed up at him, her eyes reflecting the joy that surged through her and, arm in arm, they retraced their steps, stopping long enough to acknowledge Zeke's smile as he stepped aside so they could descend the stairway.

When they reached their quarters each turned to the other expectantly. After so many days of misery they were both content to be done with it, to put it behind them. Lance approached Raine and disrobed her with gentle hands.

She thrilled to the feathery touch that never failed to arouse her. Then Lance waited patiently as Raine fumbled with the impossible buttons on his shirt. Laughing good naturedly, he slipped out of the troublesome garment and finished undressing.

"I shall die of old age if I wait for you to complete the chore," he teased, but there was an impatience underlying his words, and Raine heard it.

Sinking to their bed, she lifted her arms to her husband, and Lance came to her. She made love *to* him and *with* him, and when it was over Lance took her again, quickly, hurriedly, as though she might slip away from him.

"I love you, Muffin," he said huskily, and Raine nodded in total contentment.

"It's all I've ever wanted, and it's all I'll ever need," she whispered in return. Then she lowered her eyes in shyness. "I shall always love you, my darling. I have never loved any man before you, and I shall love only you until I die."

Lance's eyes filled with pain. "When the day comes I'll remind you of your promise, and I shall ask you to honor it."

Raine frowned. She could not imagine why he doubted her, why he always alluded to some terrible day that was yet to come. Did he think there was anything he could do for which she would not forgive him? "I will honor it," she promised again, and then snuggled against him, absolutely secure in his love for her and in hers for him.

17

By the time the *Victoria* steamed her way up the Chesapeake Bay to Bodkin Point, located at the mouth of the Patapsco River, the sky began to warn of the storm that was blowing in from the sea. Dark clouds to the southeast gave an eerie cast to the sky, and there was an unnatural softness to the air. It was as though nature were holding its breath.

Clutching her light cape around her, Raine stood at the rail, peering through light that hurt her eyes. She concentrated on the tower that was located on the point, then turned to Lance, who was at her side. "What's he doing?" she asked as she watched a figure made small by distance.

"If you look closely, you will see that the watchman is hanging out a flag that is an exact duplicate of the one we are flying aboard the *Victoria*. Fourteen miles away, another man is watching through a glass from Telegraph Tower. It's a structure built atop a hill near the harbor. When the man there spies the Randall flag flying from this tower he, in turn, will fly our flag. A third man will be watching from the Exchange in Baltimore and·will notify the owner or his representative that one of his ships is approaching port."

Lance laughed. "My great-grandmother had a much simpler method. She used carrier pigeons, and when one of her ships approached the harbor the pigeons would be released. They'd fly straight to their coops and the message they carried would be relayed to the proper agent. Of course, that was before the days of the electric telegraph."

"Oh," Raine murmured, very curious as to why the pigeons were no longer being used, but she decided against asking. Instead, she nodded in appreciation of such cleverness. "I think I would have liked your great-grandmother."

A soft chuckle bubbled from Lance's throat. "Don't be too sure. Victoria Randall was almost more than her husband could handle, and she wouldn't hesitate to shoot anyone who was a threat to her. She's the one who really built the Randall fortune, and she passed that skill on to her children."

Then Lance frowned, and he looked to starboard. "There's a storm coming. Can you smell it?"

Raine turned windward and drew in a deep breath. "Yes, I can. It's just like home. The farm, I mean. There's something very special about the air just before a storm hits."

"I hope it holds off until we get home," Lance commented casually, but he was worried. It was early for hurricane season, but he could not deny the evil-looking sky off the stern.

His anxiety touched Raine. "How much longer before we reach port?" she asked.

"Too long, I'm afraid," Lance answered in resignation. "But storm or no storm, I've got to get home." Then he changed the subject. "I don't know about you, but I'm getting chilly, and since it will be hours before we reach port I suggest we go below for a while."

Agreeing, Raine turned to make her way to the stairs. As she did, a powerful wind that seemed to come from nowhere nearly knocked her off her feet. Lance grabbed her and planted his feet until she regained her balance, thus enabling them to proceed even as they fought against the first wave of the wretched weather that was yet to come. "Damn," Lance cursed as he realized that there was no hope of outracing this storm.

Once inside their quarters, Raine shed her cape and sprawled in one of the chairs, sighing her contentment. The dark mood that had, for a short time, taken Lance away from her had gone and had not returned. He was once again the man she had fallen in love with, the man who had cared for her so tenderly.

Smiling over at him, Raine's eyes glowed with the soft light of remembrance. He had helped her when she had most needed that help, and he loved her. For Raine this was more than enough.

Gradually drowsiness overtook her as it always did when she came in from out of a strong wind. Putting a hand to her mouth, she stifled a yawn, then shook her head to clear it as she forced her eyes to stay open.

"I think I'll take a short walk through the ship's corridors or I'll surely fall asleep, and I don't want to miss our entrance into the harbor."

Pushing aside one of the velvet drapes that covered a porthole, Lance shrugged his shoulders. "Might as well stay here and sleep," he suggested. "Looks like the storm is going to get there before we do. You won't be able to see much if the weather gets as bad as I think it will."

Raine heard the slight edge of anxiety in his voice and wished she could do something to help, but there was nothing anyone could do. Not knowing whether his mother still lived was probably the most difficult part of all, and it amazed Raine that Lance had been able to keep his emotions under such tight control.

Frowning as she remembered the torrential rains and the raging rivers of her childhood, Raine cast another glance at Lance, who had taken up a book and was trying to concentrate on it. He knew as well as she that they could be in for a most difficult time.

By now Raine's mood of happy contentment was gone. She felt the same apprehension and uncertainty that tortured Lance. The same fears crowded her mind, and all thought of personal comfort vanished as she realized that she had not thought of Amy Randall for several days. Or if she had, it had only been in passing, because she had been far too preoccupied with her own happiness.

Glancing toward her husband, she wondered if he had noticed. She hoped not, for she had been thoughtless and selfish—two qualities she did not admire.

Quietly, Raine stood and walked into the bedroom, where she gathered the few pieces of clothing that needed washing and busied herself rinsing them out in the wash basin. Lance needed time to himself and she would give it to him.

Presently the sound of the wind changed, and Raine rushed to look out. She drew her breath in sharply as she peered into the ominous blackness that was on top of them.

The disaster could not have been more complete as the *Victoria* inched its way through blinding sheets of rain. The captain sounded the horn every few seconds, hoping that it would be heard above the howling storm. Then he heard an answering call given by some other foolhardy soul who had also delayed too long in seeking safe harbor.

Almost immediately, Lance left the cabin to assist the captain in finding his way safely through the storm. Each man knew the river as well as he knew his own house. Bells sounding on buoys gave some indication of distance and place. Charts were constantly checked as time was calculated against speed, and both men prespired freely as the tension mounted.

Watching a seaman who was posted at the very tip of the prow, the captain followed the man's signals and eased slightly to port or to starboard, whichever way the sailor indicated, in an attempt to stay in the channel. Finally the bright lights of Fells Point could be discerned through the downpour. Lance heaved a sigh of relief and clasped the captain on the shoulder. "Nice piece of seamanship," he stated with sincerity.

The captain nodded. "Guess we'll make it, all right. Unless we run into some fool who's decided to drop anchor in the middle of the channel."

Lance laughed. "You mean as we were almost forced to do," he said over his shoulder as he headed below to hurry Raine along so there would be no delay starting out for Promise Kept Manor.

Once the steamer nudged the Randall dock, it was made fast by men who had been watching and waiting since the message had been relayed from Bodkin Point. Hustling Raine ashore, closely followed by Bart and Zeke, Lance's heart sank when he saw the conditions of the street, which were growing worse. A carriage could be used only as far as Charles Street was paved. After that they would surely be bogged down in mud.

He turned to the man who managed the warehouse and ordered two extra horses to be saddled and tied on to the back of the carriage. There were also to be two saddles thrown on top for the horses who were to pull the carriage.

Then he turned to Raine. "Can you make it when we have to abandon the carriage?"

"Yes," she answered simply and waited for his decision.

"It's going to be rough," Lance warned.

"I can make it," she stated flatly.

Not sure that he was doing the right thing, not at all sure that Raine could endure riding horseback in this raging storm, Lance looked to Zeke for his opinion, but the older man only shrugged. He wasn't sure, either, so he expressed no opinion. However, he was certain that Raine would travel for as long as she could. She would cling to her horse until she dropped from the saddle.

"If things get too bad," he offered, "I'll find shelter while you go on ahead."

But Lance hesitated. Zeke would look after her, but he did not want to leave Raine stranded somewhere in some barn or other outbuilding. Yet, he was worried about the affect this terrible dampness would have on her lungs, which he feared might have been weakened by her illness. And then Lance decided to put his trust in his wife. If she said she could do it, then she could. She would not be so foolish as to risk her life or to delay him when she knew that speed was of the utmost importance.

At that moment two saddled horses were tied onto the rear of the carriage and saddles for the other two already in harness were secured atop the carriage. Zeke offered to take the first turn in driving the vehicle as far as it would go.

Ignoring the torrential rain, he urged the horses forward into a distance-eating trot as he headed them toward Charles Street. The rain obscured the lovely homes that became more and more distant as they advanced past North Avenue. With each turn of the wheels the day grew darker. By four o'clock it was as dark as night.

To make matters worse, they had passed

the point where the gas streetlights had
guided them like beacons along the road,
and they had come to the end of the paved
surface. Zeke whistled and flicked the whip
to little avail. They were foundering in the
mud and the deep ruts made by farm wagons on their way to market. They could no
longer go by carriage.

Lance untied the two saddled horses
and boosted Raine up onto the back of the
large gelding. Then he mounted the second
horse and started out for Promise Kept Man-
or. Raine followed closely behind, hunched
against the rain and the wind. Zeke and Bart
would come just as soon as they got their
horses unhitched and saddled.

Keeping the fierce wind to his horse's
right flank, Lance literally inched his way
forward, watching for any light that might be
visible along the way. His eyes automatically
picked out the rain-obscured trees and
fences.

The horses were laboring now as mud
clung to their legs and seemed to pull them
back into the ooze. Lance had his hat pulled
low and his collar upturned. Raine's short
cape and hood were now thoroughly
drenched. The rain stung her face and she
leaned forward, bending low to the horse's
neck, which offered only limited protection.

After what seemed an eternity, after
fighting her increasingly reluctant horse for
miles to keep him advancing, Raine almost

wept with relief when she heard Lance shout the words she feared she might never hear. "Lights ahead! We're home!"

Stiff from the chill of wet clothes clinging to her, hands numb from fighting the reins, Raine urged her horse to the drive that loomed ahead. Men holding lanterns lighted the way up the long tree-lined approach to the Randall mansion.

As Raine rounded a curve in the drive, an apparition that sent a chill through her whole body came into view. Hazy, disembodied lights glowed eerily from what seemed like empty space. Men with oilskins flapped about like so many birds of prey, and Raine shivered from more than the rain and the chill of the day.

Then Raine laughed. What she thought to be eerie, disembodied lights were merely the bright lamps of the house shining from every window to guide the travelers to safety. The rain had obscured the lovely white marble home and only the lights had been visible, and all she had been able to see from a distance were the beacons set ablaze by a worried family.

Before Raine was able to dismount, a tall, well-built man who looked remarkably like Lance rushed from the house. The overhead light on the porch shone down on him, highlighting blond hair much the shade of her husband's.

Garron Randall did not have a chance to

speak before Lance blurted out the question.
"Mother?" he asked, all the tightly contained fear wrapped in that one word.

"Still alive," came the answer from the
brother who took the steps in one stride as
he hurried to Lance's side. "Have you seen
Sis?" he asked urgently, brushing aside further inquiry concerning their mother.

Lance understood the question and
froze in the act of dismounting. "My God,"
he whispered, "is Star on the road in this
storm?"

"We don't know," Garron replied. "We
got the message that Martim's ship was
coming upriver about twenty minutes before
we were told of your approach. You didn't see
them?"

"No, and we should have. Visibility was
still fair about the time you would have
gotten the message that we were coming up
the Patapsco. I don't understand it."

Turning to Raine, Lance issued orders
in a voice that said he would not tolerate any
argument. "Get inside. I've got to go back. If
my sister is caught out on the road, I've got
to go after her."

"I wouldn't advise it," Garron suggested
mildly, for he had to step easy where Lance
was concerned, especially if their little sister
might be in trouble. "They could be holed up
in town."

"Can't be!" Lance replied curtly. "One
of us would've seen Martim's ship. It wasn't

anywhere, I'm telling you. Not anywhere from Bodkin Point to our dock in the harbor."

"Then they have to be somewhere along the way," Garron concluded logically. "Neither Star nor Martim would jeopardize their baby's life by taking unnecessary risks."

Lance stared at his older brother. "She brought her baby?"

"According to their message, she, Martim and little Paul were all headed this way."

For a minute Lance weighed the situation in his mind, and then decided that Garron was right. "Yeah," he admitted, "Star wouldn't take any chances. Not with her baby on board. Neither would Martim. Probably pulled into some sheltered cove to wait out the storm. We damned near didn't make it ourselves, and we know that river like the backs of our hands."

Knowing his sister as he did and understanding the protective nature of her husband, Lance concluded that they were in no immediate danger. Somewhere, hidden in one of the many coves or creeks that lined the Patapsco River, Star and her baby were waiting for the weather to improve before continuing on. Martim would allow nothing else.

Relaxing at last, Lance dismounted and turned to Raine, who had not gone inside as she had been told to do. Instead, she sat in her saddle, waiting to see what he was going to do, and Lance had no doubt that she would have put up a fight if he had tried to retrace his steps, which had already been obliterated by the rain.

He lifted his arms to his wife and she slid into them as Lance swung her wet, numb body to the ground. His smile of pride and approval eased her physical pain, which had increased with each succeeding mile. "I keep forgettin' what a little fighter you are," he admitted as he handed her off to Garron. "Take care of her," was all he said before disappearing into the house.

Garron hurried Raine up the steps, through the open door and into a hall that dazzled Raine's already overtaxed senses. She caught only a glimpse of Lance as he disappeared from the gallery that led off the wide, winding staircase. She bent her head backward as the walls soared upward at least three more stories to a dome that was ablaze with the lanterns Lance had first spotted. Even though the small working windows that ran the full circumference of the base of the dome were made of the thickest glass Raine had ever seen, she could still make out the rivers of water that swirled down and around their outside surface. The beacons were now lighting someone else's way home, and Raine silently wished Lance's sister a safe journey.

As Raine brought her attention back to Garron Randall, she paused for a moment, aware that he was studying her minutely. It was the first time Garron had gotten a good look at the woman his brother had brought home, and as he helped her off with the dripping cape, he continued to stare in fascination. His face was expressionless as he took in every feature. The coloring was the same, and the shape of those eyes was a throwback to Victoria Randall. Slanted, almost like a wolf's.

There was no doubt in Garron's mind. The little girl Lance had dragged home with him was a Randall. Maybe the product of some indiscreet mating the family knew nothing about. Silently, he wondered where in the hell his brother had picked her up, and whose bastard she could be. Which one of the Randall men had sired this little consequence of wild oats?

Suddenly realizing that the woman was waiting for him to speak, Garron smiled his slow, lazy smile and addressed himself to the bedraggled waif. "You look as though you could use something hot to drink and some dry clothing as well. Is this all the luggage you brought with you?" he asked as he picked up the valise Lance had dropped in the hall. Raine nodded and walked with Garron as he took her arm and guided her toward the stairs.

"By the way," he added in a slightly amused tone, "I'm Lance's brother, Garron."

Raine heard the laughter in his voice and suspected that it was at her expense.

She knew that she could not make a very presentable appearance at the moment, but surely Garron Randall had enough sense to know what she and Lance had just been through. She could hardly resemble a picture in a fashion magazine after the difficult journey that had just been completed.

Refusing to be annoyed, refusing to be baited into anything less than courteous behavior, Raine stopped and looked up at her husband's brother. "How do you do, Garron. I am Raine, Lance's wife. And I'm afraid that we could not be slowed down by a huge retinue and all manner of luggage that it would entail. When Lance received the message about his mother our only thought was to get here as quickly as possible. We knew we would be traveling fast and light. We had no time for needless delay while porters were rounded up to tote our bags." She smiled in friendship as Garron's color heightened slightly. "So here we are," she said lightly, a touch of humor softening her words, "with very little other than the clothes on our backs."

Garron grinned down at the woman who had so charmingly put him in his place. Lance had not married a shrinking violet; that much was obvious. Raine Randall had spunk, but she also had breeding. "So Lance finally got married! Afraid we weren't told. Didn't quite know what the situation was." He grinned.

Raine laughed. "It's quite respectable, I assure you."

"Well, in that case," Garron quipped, "may I offer you my very best wishes and welcome you into the family?"

"Thank you, Garron," was all Raine felt it necessary to say as she followed him, but in truth, Garron Randall's curiosity was tormenting him. There were so many questions he wanted to ask, but now was not the time. Besides, it might be better to talk to Lance first.

Raine's resemblance to Claire Randall, however, troubled him deeply. It had been so long ago, but was it possible? "No, the girl's too young," he decided, and put the matter to rest for a few minutes as they turned onto the second-floor hall.

About halfway down the brightly lit corridor Garron opened a door. As Raine entered the room, she stood for a moment taking it all in—the huge feather bed covered with a dark green velvet spread, the stark white walls, decorated only by graceful vertical plaster scrolls done in gilt, the open drapes also of dark velvet and the pale green rug that covered every inch of the floor. It was a beautiful, sterile room, and once again Raine shivered from more than the cold.

Garron saw her discomfort and misread it. Instantly he was the solicitous host. "Please forgive me. I'm afraid that with all the long hours and uncertainty we've endured for so long, I've completely forgotten my manners. Do you have anything that might still be dry in this valise?" he asked as he held the traveling bag at arm's length.

Raine clenched her teeth to keep back the nasty answer she had in mind. Taking the bag from Garron's hand, she opened it and pulled out the few garments it contained. Everything was damp, and some things were downright wet. The rain had soaked through the carpet from which her bag was made and nothing was totally dry. Raine sighed in resignation and began spreading a few of the drier pieces over two chairs. The room was warm and with any luck her nightgown would be dry before she needed it. If not, she'd sleep without it as she had done many times in the past.

Garron watched, fascinated. Lance's wife was not the least upset about the condition of their clothing. It was obvious she had faced such minor calamities before. It was also obvious that she was used to taking care of herself. Requesting the services of a maid had not even entered her mind. He would not embarrass her by suggesting that this might be the time for a servant to take over.

At any rate, he was quite sure Raine would not expect to be turned over to hired help. Most certainly she *would* expect some suitable member of the family to offer assistance, just as she would have undoubtedly done in the much poorer household from which she had obviously come. "The arrogance of poverty," Garron thought in resignation, and then offered the only thing he could think of at the moment.

"My wife, Kathleen, is feeding our youngest, but if it is agreeable to you, she will help you sort things out as soon as she's free."

Raine's face brightened instantly. "You have children?"

Not letting his surprise show, Garron raised four fingers. "Been married five years and we have four children," he said with a twinkle in his eyes. "However, it's really not so bad as it seems. There's a set of twins. They run in Kathleen's family. Still," he admitted, laughing companionably, "I suspect we'd better slow down just a bit or we'll be like Grandfather Paul. He and his wife had eleven children. Eleven who survived, at any rate."

"It must be wonderful to come from a large family," Raine commented wistfully, and Garron could read the twinge of sadness in those emerald eyes.

"It has its drawbacks, I assure you," Garron admitted, thinking of Kathleen, who had been less than thrilled when he had insisted on trying for a fifth child while she was still nursing the fourth.

Now Garron gave his full attention to his brother's wife. The light cape she had worn had not kept any part of her dry. Every piece of clothing she wore was soaked through, and her boots would need a lot of work to keep them from drying as hard as a rock. Worse yet, she would probably catch pneumonia if she didn't get into dry clothing.

"Let me see if Kathleen is free, but I think we must find something for you to wear right away until your own things dry out."

"Thank you, I could certainly use a robe until my things dry. Is there an indoor clothesline I might use?" she asked as she frowned at the condition of the few articles of clothing that remained in the valise.

"Of course," Garron answered, and took the bundle of wet clothes from her hands. "We'll hang these in the basement where they will be out of the way. Now, is there anything more I can do before I fetch my wife?"

"No thank you, Garron. You've been most kind to a stranger, and I am sorry you were not notified that Lance and I were married."

Garron shrugged. "That's the way he does things. He's a very private person. He keeps his plans to himself, but his decisions are usually good ones."

Raine laughed. "Thank you again, but I suggest you do whatever you're going to do with those clothes in a hurry."

Garron returned the pleasant smile and

held the dripping bundle a little further away from himself. "Kathleen will be here in a few minutes," he promised as he left the room, closing the door softly behind him.

Sitting on the side of the bed, Raine tugged at her boots. They were wet through, and difficult to remove. She winced in pain as her heel slipped up, catching her instep in a painful position. Puffing with exertion, she tugged and tugged until the rest of her foot came free. By the time she had removed both boots she was exhausted.

As she stood, the clamminess of her skirt wrapped itself around her legs and Raine lost no time in getting out of it. Looking around for a place to hang it, she spotted a door that looked as though it might lead to a closet. Removing her wet woolen hose, Raine walked across the soft warm rug and sighed as the comforting surface soothed her cold, tingling feet.

Opening the door, Raine stared at the room that lay before her. It was much more than a closet. There were drawers and shelves filling every space that was not needed for rods that were jammed with men's clothing. All manner of hats were nestled neatly on the shelf above and boots filled the space below. Occupying the clothes rods were jackets and trousers and coats of all kinds. Then Raine's eyes lit up as she spotted the warm wool robe among all the other things.

Eagerly, she reached for it and put on the garment, which was far too big for her. Raine slipped out of her petticoat and pulled the robe up. Fastening it with the belt, she smiled in total contentment. It was the first time in hours she had had on dry clothes, and the warmth that encompassed her as she snuggled deeper into the garment relaxed tired, aching muscles. Even though she was now warm and snug, Raine yearned for a fireplace or even a stove where she might warm her back close to leaping flames or toast her hands, but this room, like the boat, offered none of those comforting things. Here she was surrounded by an invisible current of heat. There were no flames, no friendly embers, but neither were there unbearable hot spots where the front burned and the rear froze. But there were no mesmerizing flames that leapt and danced, flames that erased all the days' cares from the mind. Nor were there roasting chestnuts and popping corn, not in a house where all the heat came through pipes.

Shrugging off the sacrifices she must make for the sake of progress, Raine opened a few of the drawers that lined one side of this oversized closet. She smiled as she catalogued the hose, underwear and shirts. There was even a nightshirt. In one of the few empty drawers, Raine found an old miniature in an elegant silver frame that had grown dark from lack of care.

For an instant Raine felt the shock of disbelief as confusion held her immobile, for she was looking at a portrait of her mother. She frowned and shook her head. No. It was not Jennifer Raine Colter. Although there was a striking resemblance to her mother, it was not she. The chin was softer and less defined. The hair was a shade paler, but it was the eyes that were really different. Her mother's eyes had been warm and loving. There had been no hint of false coyness in them as there were in the eyes that peered up at her from an artful and studied sidelong glance.

Putting the miniature away, Raine closed the drawer, but she could not help but wonder who the girl in the picture was. Perhaps it was Lance's sister who had laughed at her from eyes that were false. *I hope not.* Raine sighed, for there was something about the girl that made her uneasy; there was definitely something about her that Raine did not like.

Still wondering about the resemblance to her mother and, for that matter, to herself, Raine removed the neatly folded nightshirt from another drawer and returned to the bedroom. She hung the wet garments she had just removed over chairs and over the brass frame of a gaslight fixture. It was the best she could do for now.

A soft knock at the door distracted her. "Come in," she called, and could not help but stare at the remarkably beautiful woman who entered the room. Behind her was a servant, who carried clothing and towels.

A warm smile of welcome put Raine instantly at ease and chased away the thoughts that had troubled her. "I'm Kathleen Randall, Garron's wife," the stranger said, and Raine smiled into eyes as blue as Garron's own.

Blurting out the first thought that came to her mind, Raine asked, "Are there no plain people in this family? Certainly there must be someone who is not a raving beauty or as handsome as Lance and Garron."

Kathleen's eyes twinkled in merriment as she took a towel from the servant and handed it to Raine. "Your hair is still quite wet. Perhaps you'd better wrap your head so you don't catch cold. And I must say, you, too, add to the good looks that run through the family."

Quite pleased with the compliment, Raine smiled her thanks and watched as Kathleen indicated with a subtle gesture that the maid was to put the clothing she was carrying on the bed. Bobbing a polite curtsy to Raine, she spread out all manner of skirts, petticoats, blouses and hose for Raine's use.

The materials, ribbons and laces transported Raine into a fairyland of princes and princesses. Immediately she felt pampered beyond measure. The fine silks and cottons, the matching skirts and blouses and the sheer nightdress with matching robe captured Raine's heart. "Oh my," was all she could manage as she continued to stare at some of the finest clothes she had ever seen. Everything was understated, yet it was perfect.

A soft smile graced Kathleen Randall's beautiful lips. "It is rather overwhelming, isn't it? I felt much the same way when I first came to this house as a bride." There was no polite pretense about misunderstanding Raine's feelings; there was no condescending lie, nor was there the faintest hint of superiority in Kathleen's honest words.

"Yes," Raine agreed softly. "It takes some getting used to, but I'm sure I'll manage." Then Raine looked into Kathleen's open face. "How is Mrs. Randall?"

Absolute joy shone from Kathleen's gentle eyes. "She's much better. I think just knowing that her family would soon be with her gave her the strength to fight. And the doctors attending her are really very good. Two of them are research scholars from the University of Maryland's College of Medicine. Father Randall would have only the best and the brightest."

Pausing for a moment, Kathleen looked around the room, which could certainly do with a woman's touch. "I suspect Lance should be here rather soon," she remarked, understanding only too well the anxiety

Raine felt at being thrown into the midst of strangers and then being left alone to fend for herself. "But you must be totally exhausted from your harrowing ride, and here I stand chattering away. Dinner will be served at eight if you care to join us," she added pleasantly, and then smiled her good-bye as she hustled the servant out, leaving Raine alone in the large bedroom.

Raine stared at the closed door for some time after Kathleen had gone. She was a beautiful woman whose silvery hair had glistened in the light. Her azure eyes had been warm and kind. Her figure was lean and lithe, and surely she could not have borne four children already. But most of all Raine admired her grace and poise.

As Raine stood with the towel in her hand, still contemplating all the points of Kathleen's breathtaking beauty and charm, there was a knock at the door and the same servant entered. "Pardon me, ma'am, but Miss Kathleen sent me back to show you where the necessaries are. If you'll come with me, miss," the maid added expectantly, and then trailed off.

Raine did not disappoint her. Obligingly, she followed the woman as she turned down the hall, where she opened a door to reveal things Raine had only heard about.

After demonstrating how to work the water closet and the tub the maid opened a cabinet whose shelves were piled high with towels and soaps as well as with creams and oils.

"Now, if there's anything else you'll be needin', please ring for me. Me name's Mary, miss, and if I can't get you what you want, you can rest assured the mister will manage it somehow."

" 'The mister'?" Raine asked.

Mary laughed. "That's what the servants call Mr. Jarrett Randall, master of the house."

"Yes," Raine replied, "I suppose there are quite a few *Mr.* Randalls."

"Indeed, yes, miss. There are five of them in this house, countin' the mister, himself, of course."

"I'm sure there's nothing I could possibly want that isn't already here," Raine replied. "And thank you, Mary, for helping me. I was feeling rather lost."

Dismissing Mary, Raine hurried back to the bedroom and collected an armful of clothing. Returning to the bathing room, she enjoyed the luxury of a hot bath. The soap smelled of jasmine, and Raine slipped lower in the tub, letting the tiredness flow from her body. Then she washed her hair, put it up in a towel and dressed. She felt much better.

When she arrived back at her room she found that several pairs of shoes had been placed by the bed in her absence, and she smiled gratefully as she understood that Kathleen had judged for herself what size would be appropriate. And she had been right. The shoes were only a trifle large; they would do nicely.

Raine felt like a new woman as she stood in front of a mirror and toweled her hair briskly. Then she brushed it, wishing she had a stove or fireplace to sit in front of while she combed it dry. But she made the best of her situation and toweled some more. Before long her hair began to fluff up. She looked almost normal as she arranged it in a large coil and pulled a few short ends out to form wispy bangs. Smiling, she decided that she would do.

"A penny for your thoughts," Lance said quietly as he stood just inside the open doorway, watching his wife.

Turning to look at him, Raine thought how typical it was that she had not heard him enter the room. Even here in his own home, Lance stepped with care. Somehow, some part of him never relaxed.

"I was just thinking that I am certainly going to be lost in the brilliance of Kathleen's beauty," Raine replied honestly.

Lance stared at her for a few seconds before realizing that she had not been fishing for a compliment. As usual, Raine had no idea just how lovely she was. "You'll do just fine," he said quietly, and then walked into the huge closet and selected his wardrobe.

"By God," Lance muttered as he brought his clothing into the bedroom, "when we build our house we're going to have a dressing and bathing room for every bedroom.''

Deciding that she had no wish to talk about water closets and tubs, Raine changed the subject. "I'm very happy for you, my darling. Kathleen tells me your mother is somewhat improved. Is she out of danger?"

A shadow of doubt crossed Lance's face. "We're not sure. It's true she's better, but whether there will be a full recovery we don't yet know. It's something not even the doctors can predict."

"But she *has* improved," Raine stated, refusing to let Lance dwell on the unhappy possibilities.

"Yeah," Lance admitted, feeling a little better himself. "Sorry I was so long, but Mother was asleep when I went to see her and I didn't have the heart to wake her up. I just sat holding her hand until she opened her eyes, but she's still so weak."

"Did she recognize you?" Raine asked anxiously, looking for some sign of hope, refusing to think the worst.

Lance directed a peculiar look her way. He knew exactly what she was doing. "Knew me right off. Guess I should be happy for that much, at least."

"It sounds hopeful," Raine said, and Lance grinned as he walked out of the bedroom carrying boots, hose and pants with him.

"Won't be long," he threw back over his

shoulder. "Got to get cleaned up before supper."

While Lance was busy Raine stepped into the hall and looked more closely at the priceless treasures that added to its beauty. Impressive oils painted by a master's hand graced the gallery. Wall sconces with their bright gas flames bathed the corridor in brilliant light. Her fingers caressed lovely woods and jades.

A particularly lovely porcelain caught her eye, and Raine picked it up to examine it more carefully. As she put it back in place, she wondered how these fragile treasures had survived the natural exuberance of small children.

That thought caused her to frown. She had neither seen nor heard any children in the time she had been here. Where were they? And, for that matter, where were Kathleen and Garron, for surely this corridor with its fine treasures was deserted except for Lance and herself.

Glancing around to make sure no one was watching, Raine gave in to her curiosity. Even though she knew it to be the height of rudeness, she eased open one door after another. No one. No one at all was in this wing of the house. Though each and every room was ready to receive guests, not a single person stirred in this part of the house.

Suddenly Raine felt very much alone. It

was so different from the cabin she and her father had shared, and it was not at all like the hotel in San Francisco, where one needed only to step out the door to be caught up in a swirl of excitement and activity. By comparison this house was as quiet as a tomb, and Raine didn't like it.

As she turned to walk back to her room, Lance emerged from his bath dressed in boots and pants. His upper body was bare, and Raine felt a familiar tingle of excitement rush through her. She stood staring at the man whose body resembled nothing so much as a priceless statue. The muscles that rippled under the smooth skin fascinated her. The leashed power she knew to be lurking under the bronze exterior with such deceptive calm thrilled her, and to her Lance was as beautiful as any ancient diety. How anyone could look so serene, so composed, yet be able to strike in the blink of an eye would always be a mystery to her. But the greatest wonder of all was that he loved her.

Finally realizing that Lance had stopped, Raine raised her eyes to meet his and what she saw in them caused her to blush. Once again he had caught her gawking like a schoolgirl, but she couldn't help it.

"Think you can wait until after supper?" he teased, and Raine's color flamed even brighter.

"I hope so," she answered truthfully, then lowered her eyes demurely so Lance could not read them. She really wasn't terribly hungry.

18

Just as the hall clock struck six Lance stretched himself awake and turned to Raine, who was still sleeping soundly. "Come on, Muffin," he coaxed as he touched his lips to hers. "I want to show you a little more of the house before breakfast. You've hardly had a chance to see more than the hallways," he joked, and laughed that soft purring sound that always caused Raine to be instantly alert.

"And bedrooms," she reminded him coyly as she stretched in contentment, releasing a long, straining sound of satisfaction.

Lance laughed again and hugged her to him. He was supremely happy. His mother was getting better, and he and Raine had made unrestrained love, each one giving and each one receiving. Here in his bachelor bed at Promise Kept Manor, it had been unbelievably good, and Raine had not only responded, she had demanded. And he had obliged her every whim.

"God, but I love you," he growled as he nuzzled her neck and felt his body about to burst with happiness. But then a shock of terror shot through him as he remembered the miniature of Claire. He had to find it before Raine did.

"Well, I have to get moving. Breakfast is at seven. If you want something to eat this morning, you'd better get up. Stragglers got to fend for themselves."

Raine frowned in indecision. Her mind clicked off the routine that had been spelled out to her last night at supper. Then she decided she had better get up and join the others for breakfast. Dinner would not be served until one-thirty in the afternoon. It was a long time from now till then.

As she threw off the coverlet and sheet, Lance entered the closet, where Raine heard him rummaging through drawers and slamming the door of the large, built-in chifferobe. Finally he reappeared carrying fresh clothes.

"Be back as soon as I shave," he explained, pulling on his trousers so as not to shock any servants who might be roaming the halls at this hour.

When he had gone Raine put on her

underclothing and pulled the lovely flowing
robe Kathleen had let her use over them.
Then she laid out one of the borrowed skirt
and blouse sets and combed and arranged
her hair in a becoming French twist.

By the time Lance returned she was
ready to wash her face and brush her teeth.
Then, rummaging in the bathroom closet,
she found some enchanting perfumes and a
pot of lip rouge. She also found a shade of eye
makeup that suited her far better than the
kohl Tess used. As she studied her new
image in the mirror, Raine perked up considerably. She looked exceptionally smart.

Returning to her room to finish dressing, Raine felt renewed and refreshed and
exceptionally hungry. She smiled at Lance,
who looked so handsome in a snowy white
shirt and a pale beige suit. The light bronze
of his skin and the pale green of his eyes
were accentuated by the soft, unobtrusive
shades he wore, and Raine stood quite still,
drinking in the beauty of the man she had
married. Then she slipped into the skirt and
blouse and thought that she didn't look so
bad either.

Her eyes were still warm with love as
she accepted Lance's arm and walked with
him into the now familiar hallway, across
the gallery and down the wide, winding
stairs. She smiled as she wondered how
many children had slid down the smooth
railing that felt so cool under her hand. But
there was no time for questions, for Lance

was already pointing to a picture of his mother and father on their wedding day. Raine stared in fascination at the man whose green eyes were the exact shade of her own, and then her gaze drifted to the woman who stood within the protecting circle of Jarrett Randall's arm. Amy Randall's azure eyes smiled back at her, and Raine knew from where the color of Garron's eyes had come. They were the same beautiful shade as his mother's.

"Almost forty years ago," Lance remarked quietly as he gazed at the portrait. His face had softened, and his voice reflected his love.

The next portrait was of the man Lance had spoken of with such respect and devotion, and Raine looked once again into the same emerald eyes that belonged to Jarrett Randall and to herself. She felt increasingly uneasy as she concentrated on Paul Andrew Chisholm Randall, with his bronze hair, which was highlighted by streaks of palest blond. The same deep waves that made her own hair almost impossible to manage curled through his heavy locks. But the thing that puzzled Raine the most was the fact that he wore a strange necklace that was entirely out of place with the elegant clothes he had on, a necklace she had seen in Lance's possession.

"It's the head of a mountain lion, isn't it?" she asked, and Lance confirmed her observation.

"It's a necklace that was given to my great-grandmother a hundred years ago by an Indian chief. It gives the wearer safe passage through Indian territory."

"So that's where it comes from," Raine murmured, more to herself than to her husband.

Lance heard and understood. "Yes," he answered. "My great-grandmother was known to the Indians as Le Cougar because of her coloring and her courage. The mountain cat was also the totem of their tribe. The symbol of the panther. It was hers."

Full of curiosity and feeling that she could pick out Lance's great-grandmother, Raine moved on until she came to a portrait that reached out and held her with its power. A dark-haired man, a fair-haired woman whose pale eyes went through Raine and a boy with golden hair were grouped in a masterful portrait that portrayed strength and love, both at the same time.

"Victoria," Raine whispered in awe as she squinted to see past the aura of danger and great power.

"How did you know?" Lance asked, looking at the portrait he had passed thousands of times while growing up in this house.

Once again Raine confounded him. "She is smiling but she is also on guard. Danger lurks in those eyes that are just like yours, and because I can read yours I can read hers as well. I should not wish to be her enemy." Then Raine laughed and told the truth. "Besides, she wears that same necklace wrapped around her wrist like some primitive warrior. She could be no one else."

Lance was pleased with Raine's description of his great-grandmother. It was the way he had always felt about her. Though she had been warm and loving with her five children, she had also been firm and quick to chastise when one of her young had strayed beyond the limits she had set.

"She was, indeed, like her namesake," Lance said softly, staring at the woman whose journals he had read many times over. "My grandfather was her first born," he commented, and then smiled broadly. "He was delivered in an Indian village only weeks after my great-grandparents were married."

"But—" Raine began, and then decided it would be best to keep her thoughts to herself.

Lance grinned. "Afraid so. The man who made love to her before their marriage pursued her from Virginia to the wilderness of their day. Apparently he finally wore her down. The journals aren't too clear on that point, but if you read them carefully, you will decide as I have that Marcus Randall finally won the game my great-grandmother had been playing since she first met him. And quite a game it was," Lance added with pride shining in his eyes. "They came near to destroying each other several times, but each time they survived and so did their love. I think this family shall never see their like again."

At that moment Garron and Kathleen appeared from another corridor, which led to the main dining room and then onto the terrace at the back of the house. Raine sighed in disappointment at the interruption. There were so many questions she wanted to ask about Victoria Randall. Lance's resemblance to her was uncanny. Both had the same golden coloring, the same shade of hair and the same pale eyes that could glow with love one minute and then turn cold with deadly menace the next. But it would have to wait.

Turning to Kathleen and Garron, Raine smiled her greeting as Lance spoke for them both. "Morning brother, Kathleen," he said pleasantly. "Have you seen Mother this morning?"

Garron returned his brother's smile and gave a helpless gesture with his hands. "You know Father. Won't let anybody in that room until Mother's been bathed and dressed in fresh nightclothes. We'll see her later."

"Will your father eat with us this morning?" Raine asked as she was guided toward a large morning room where breakfast would be served.

"Afraid not," Garron answered. "We

haven't seen much of Father since Mother's been sick. He won't leave her until he's convinced she's going to be all right.''

Garron paused as he suddenly realized that Raine had not yet met either of his parents. ''We'll introduce you after breakfast if Father feels Mother's well enough to receive company.''

''I'd be very pleased to meet them,'' Raine responded quietly, ''whenever they're ready.''

Then Raine gave her attention to the lovely room they were entering. Ivy climbed trellised windows on three sides, eliminating the need for any kind of drapes or shades, and Raine could not help but let out a soft sound of delight.

Scarlet geraniums bloomed from hanging pots and the wallpaper continued the theme of climbing ivy. Matching material covered the cushions that brightened the rattan furniture. The top of the large table was a round of thick glass that had been expertly fitted into its frame. A brilliant green rug dressed up the stone floor directly under the table. The rest of the floor was bare, warmed only by shades of rust and brown that streaked their way through the flat layer of stone. French doors led out onto the terrace, which was shaded by gracefully arched apple trees.

As she studied the lovely scene, Raine could almost smell the fragrance of the blossoms, and she could see the petals drifting to the ground covering the terrace in a sweet-smelling carpet of white. One day she would have a room like this in a home of her own.

As Lance seated her at the table, a servant entered with a steaming pot of coffee and filled the cups all around. Garron passed the cream and sugar as Kathleen invited Raine to join her at the sideboard, where warming dishes held a variety of food. Raine was overwhelmed by the choices that were offered since she had been almost too weary to notice what she had eaten at last night's supper. Now, however, she was alert, and she wished she could sample everything. Her early training curbed such a show of poor breeding and she settled for crisp bacon, a delicious apple-cinnamon crepe and something she simply could not resist —fresh figs.

Savoring each morsel, Raine watched the others as they picked and chose. She noticed that Kathleen was extremely frugal in her eating habits again this morning, just as she had been last evening. Raine sighed and wished she had taken some of the enticing rum rolls.

Just then the clicking sound of a telegraph key intruded upon Raine's thoughts. She looked up in time to see both Garron and Lance bolt for the door that led into the rest of the house. Less than a minute passed before she heard whatever message had come in over the wire being answered, but since she knew very little Mörse code she looked toward Kathleen.

"It's Star!" she exclaimed in delight as she put her finger to her lips so she could listen to the stacatto sounds that announced the safety of the youngest member of the Randall family.

"They're all right," Kathleen explained. "The ship's coming upriver. They'll be here in time for dinner." Then Kathleen excused herself and almost ran to the kitchen, where she gave orders for a huge meal to be served no later than two o'clock.

Returning to her guest, Kathleen explained. "This will be quite an occasion. Mother Randall hasn't seen Star for more than a year, and we're all so anxious to see her baby. She's named him Paul Lance Cabrall. Paul for his great-grandfather and Lance for your husband, of course.

"Everyone in the kitchen is so excited. I just know they're going to cook all her favorites, no matter what orders I give," she said, laughing happily. "Which means, of course, we shall all gain ten pounds while she's here."

Raine smiled in happy expectation. "I believe I saw a miniature of Star in Lance's room. Does she have blond hair and green eyes?"

Kathleen frowned and shook her head. "No, Star has blue eyes. Actually, they're a brilliant aquamarine. I suppose some artist could have tinted them green, but I don't see how. Once you've looked into those eyes, you never forget them."

Raine suggested that the miniature might be of some other member of the family. "But whoever it is," she concluded, "she is quite lovely. Now, you must tell me more about Star and her husband. I know so little about Lance's family. He never talks about any of you except for some small comment that tells me almost nothing at all."

"Lance says very little about anybody," Kathleen commented. "I think it's the kind of work he does. He never wants anyone to know too much about himself. He's very secretive, and if he tells you anything, it's usually only half true."

Kathleen paused for a moment, a frown of concentration on her face. "He's like quicksilver. Just when you think you have him trapped, he slips away. Yes," she mused, propping her chin on the heel of one hand, "of all the Randall boys Lance is the most elusive. He simply will not let you get to know him, and there are times when he's in and out of the house like some phantom. He comes unannounced and leaves so quietly, you don't realize he's gone until you miss him at meals. I know Mother Randall worries about him constantly. Maybe now that he's married he'll settle down, though," Kathleen added in wonder, "I don't know how you managed to catch him. He's hardly ever in one place long enough."

Raine hoped that Kathleen was right. Perhaps Lance would settle down now that he was married, but she said nothing for fear it might sound like a complaint. She listened as Kathleen filled her in on the rest of the family. And quite a fascinating family it was.

Raine drank in all that Kathleen revealed about Jarrett and Amy Randall and their five children. Gradually she came to understand that it was a family that was run almost like an army. Each son had an assignment and was expected to accomplish it flawlessly. Even Jesse, the youngest male in the family, was engaged in buying up coffee plantations in Brazil. "He and Star will probably be there indefinitely," Kathleen concluded as Lance and Garron returned.

"Have you taken care of arrangements for dinner?" Garron asked as he sat to resume his interrupted breakfast.

"Of course," Kathleen responded. "Cook has promised to have duck l'orange, that rice, peas and black mushroom dish that Star loves so much and apple pie."

"And ice cream," Lance added, eyes twinkling with delight. "I'll wager Star will not be here more than two hours before Charles starts filling her with ice cream."

Turning to Raine, he explained. "Charles is one of our chefs, and Star is the apple of his eye. Even as a little girl she'd rush into the kitchen to hug and kiss him for making one of her favorite dishes. What the rest of the family did or didn't like hardly mattered. Many meals were planned around whatever it was that Star craved on that particular day.''

Garron laughed as he remembered one particularly outrageous incident. "Have you ever had apple pie, baked apples and apple fritters all at the same meal?" he asked Raine, who smiled while shaking her head as she remained silent, for she wanted to say nothing that would cause this happy peek into her husband's family to end.

"Well, we have!" Garron responded, his eyes sparkling with remembrance. "And there was no point in arguing with Charles, either. Whatever Star wanted, she got. I'm afraid she's been terribly spoiled, but she's the only girl in the family and the baby to boot. I suppose there's no help for it."

"Well," Lance drawled, barely able to hide a smug expression, "her husband isn't much better. Spoils her every bit as much as we ever did."

Kathleen came to her sister-in-law's defense. "Perhaps Star likes to get her way, just as we all do, but I hardly think she's as bad as you make her sound. Why, there isn't a thing she wouldn't do for you if she could. And you ought to be ashamed, Lance Randall. You know very well she almost died trying to save your worthless hide! Really! The way you talk about her is disgraceful. Why, Raine will probably expect some horrid little monster to come prancing through the door!"

Both Garron and Lance laughed at Kathleen's impassioned defense of their little sister, who needed no defending, for they both loved her and had also been guilty of spoiling her. But it hardly mattered, for Star had turned out to be a loving, courageous woman who would make any sacrifice for her family.

"Now, now," Garron warned playfully. "Watch that Irish temper of yours, me darlin' or sure'n I'll have ta send ya back to your poor ol' mither."

A slight twitching of Kathleen's lips gave way to a broad smile. Her beautiful blue eyes sparkled at some private joke between Garron and herself. "Sure'n she'd ship me back first chance she got. There'll be no dumpin' used goods and a brood of young ones at her door, me bucko."

Lance struggled to hold back the laughter that tugged at the corners of his mouth, and he looked at his brother, whose own expression was none too respectful, for he resembled nothing so much as a prideful, self-satisfied cat who had just dragged home a particularly difficult kill. "Guess I'll be showin' Raine a little more of the house," he commented diplomatically. "Mind if we stop by the nursery to see the kids?"

"Thought you'd never ask," Garron drawled.

Raine studied her brother-in-law carefully. She had seen several sides to Garron Randall since last night, and she strongly suspected that she had yet to discover the man he really was. She also wondered just how well she knew the man she had married, who talked so very little of himself or of anyone else.

By the time Star and her family, accompanied by her brother, Jesse, were blown through the door by a brisk wind, Raine had seen the main portions of the house and had met Kathleen's four adorable children. She had also seen the wedding portrait of Star and her husband, Martim Cabrall, a very wealthy nobleman in his native Brazil. The miniature had not been of Star.

Unceremoniously, Star shed her wraps, handed her baby to her husband and hugged her brothers one at a time before greeting Kathleen. Then she turned and ran for the stairs. No one in the family thought it the least unusual that she had left her husband standing there, just as Lance had left Raine the night before.

Blinking back quick tears, Raine suddenly realized that this family was closed to outsiders, even to the husband and wives of the three children who were married. She would never truly be a Randall, no more than Martim Cabral could ever be. Kathleen, however, was a different story. Somehow, she would belong. Perhaps it was just that she had lived in this house for five years and had borne four children here. And perhaps it was the fact that she was married to the eldest Randall son, the one who would inherit this house and everything in it when Jarrett and Amy Randall were gone. It would be Kathleen who would then become matriarch of the Baltimore branch of the Randall clan.

Raine found herself quite content. She did not want to live in a house with more than a hundred rooms. She did not want to live in a house where there were always servants underfoot. And she most definitely did not care to live in a house that contained not one comforting fireplace. The Randalls could have their cold white marble and their brilliant gold trim. She would take the gentle warmth of wood and stone and the comfort of a rocking chair by the fire. That would be her palace, and her kingdom would be her husband and children.

Then she looked at the baby who was being freed from his warm outer clothing and blankets. She smiled as she saw the lovely face capped by rich brown ringlets of hair and long lashes that would be the envy of the girls he was yet to meet. His eyes were the color of a soft gray fog.

Still smiling, she made a clucking sound with her tongue and was rewarded with the cheerful gurgling of a baby not more than six months old. When Martim handed her his child Raine held him tenderly, bending her head to his, rubbing his nose with the tip of her own as curious fingers curled in her upswept hair.

Lance came to her rescue as Raine laughed helplessly. Gently opening the baby's fingers, he disentangled the tiny hand from his wife's hair and then took his nephew from her arms. "Time for you to visit your cousins in the nursery, young man," he said, but he looked to Martim for approval before taking the child anywhere.

"Yes," the Brazilian agreed. "In fact, it would be good if he could sleep a little. It was a difficult trip—for all of us."

"It was good of you to come," Lance responded sincerely. "Thank God Mother's much better now, and all our worry was for nothing. I guess we can relax a little since the worst seems to be over.

"By the way," Lance said, pulling Raine closer to him, "this is my wife, Raine." Then, feeling it unnecessary to say anymore, Lance left the room carrying his nephew. The child would be put in the care of the nursemaid and her helper.

Martim managed to cover his surprise. He smiled at Raine and bent his head in recognition. "I am honored, senhora. And when did this happy union take place?" he inquired.

"Last November," Raine answered, immediately at ease with Star's husband.

"Ah, then you are still a bride," Martim responded gallantly, white teeth flashing in his tanned face. "I am in time to offer a toast to your great happiness. That is," he said, lifting his shoulders in a slight shrug, "if the men who are hauling the rest of our luggage manage to survive the road that surely must be a foot deep with mud. They are bringing not only our clothes but the champagne I bottle as well."

Kathleen interrupted long enough to invite everyone into the company parlor, and Martim strolled easily at Raine's side. "A most formidable family," he whispered, and smiled comfortingly, and Raine laughed up into the dark eyes that sparkled with mischief.

"Yes," she replied. "They seem to be very wealthy and powerful."

Martim nodded in agreement and remained at her side for many minutes, speaking softly and giving her much of his attention. He shrugged when he learned that she hoped to live in California. "I fear that my business does not take me that way; however, I feel sure my wife shall find some excuse to make it quite necessary for us to pay a visit whenever you are gracious enough to invite us. Star and Lance are exceptionally close, as you may know."

"I'm afraid I really know very little about the family," Raine admitted, and then hid her smile behind her hand as Martim

Cabral raised his eyes to heaven and flared his nostrils in an unmistakable gesture.

"I fear you have much to learn, senhora. But then, like us, you and Lance will live thousands of miles away. That does help," he concluded softly but with a definite note of thanksgiving in his voice.

Before Raine had a chance to question this strange remark, a servant entered the room and curtsied. "The mistress asks that Miss Raine and Mr. Martim come to her room if it is convenient. She is most anxious to greet you and welcome you to Promise Kept Manor," the young woman intoned as though the little speech had been memorized.

"Ah," Martim purred in satisfaction, "Miss Amy is feeling much better. Will you allow me to escort you, Raine?"

No one needed to ask her twice. She was most anxious to meet Lance's parents. Taking the arm Martim so graciously offered, Raine followed after the maid, who led the way up the stairs, turned left and walked to the end of the corridor before knocking softly on the door.

No sooner had the servant rapped than Star flung the door open. Her eyes danced with happiness. "Please, come in. Mama is so distressed that she must greet you under these circumstances, but she simply could not wait another minute to see you."

It was obvious that Star had brought

with her a lightness of spirit and a gay optimism that pervaded the sick room. Amy Randall smiled and extended her hands to her visitors.

Martim, gallant as always, raised one fragile hand to his lips. "Senhora," he murmured, "I am so thankful to see that you are recovering from your illness. Star was so worried. I thought surely I must bury her beside you if things had gone wrong."

"No, Martim. You must never let Star grieve for me. I have had a good life. She must be happy with you and your little son, who I hope to see soon."

Then, having made the obligatory speech, Amy turned her attention to Raine, who had approached the bed and was waiting quietly. "My dear child." Amy sighed; weariness was written on her face and could be heard in her voice. "Come, sit beside me. Let me look at you."

Happy to fulfill the older woman's request, Raine went to the bed and took Amy's hand in hers. She held the delicate, cool fingers lightly in her own warm, strong ones. Looking deep into those azure eyes, Raine studied them for awkward seconds. But when she spoke Amy understood. Raine had been looking for death and had not found it.

"I am pleased to see you so well, Mrs. Randall. I have dealt with cholera before, and you will be one of the lucky ones. You've beaten it," she declared with utmost confidence, and Amy acknowledged the truth.

"Yes, I believe I have." Then she sighed in exhaustion and let her hand drop to her side. But Raine was satisfied. She had always been able to see death. There was something in the eyes of all dying creatures that was the same—a certain look, a dullness, an opacity that lacked light or depth that foretold what was to come. Whatever it was, Raine had always recognized it. But it was not in Amy Randall's eyes. Neither was there the smell of death in the room.

"I know how exhausting your struggle has been and I shall not add to your burden. Perhaps tomorrow, when you shall be much stronger, you will permit me to come again."

Amy relaxed against her pillows and breathed deeply. She felt the promised strength returning, and as she gazed deeply into the eyes that were the same as her husband's, she felt a power in them that she was helpless to resist. If Raine said that she would be stronger, then it was a fact, for the child possessed a sight that was granted to only a few.

A faint smile touched Amy's face as she studied the young woman who sat so calmly at her side. Indeed, Lance had been correct. She did resemble Claire. There was a definite similarity, but there was also a great difference, for Raine possessed an inner tranquility that set her apart from Claire

Randall. Amy welcomed the warm, comforting presence of Lance's wife.

"Yes, my child. You must come tomorrow. I shall be much better then."

Just as Raine stood and Martim bowed his farewell, Jarrett Randall strolled into the bedroom from an adjoining one. He had overheard the entire conversation, and he, too, studied Raine, but from a different perspective.

Lance had prepared him for Raine's striking resemblance to Claire, but there was much more to the girl than just that resemblance. There was something gentle and loving and very reassuring about her. He thought Lance had made a wise choice, this time. He smiled and bowed slightly in Raine's direction. "Welcome to our family, Raine Randall."

Raine returned the smile, but she was disturbed. "It's rather like looking into a mirror, isn't it?"

Jarrett Randall knew instantly what she was talking about. "Yes. I noticed it immediately. You look very much like a Randall born," he answered casually, but he was extremely curious about Raine's bloodline and said so. "Do you think it possible that we might somehow be related?"

It was out in the open now, the very thing Raine had been turning over and over in her mind. "I don't know," she answered honestly. "Perhaps what little I know of my family history could be of help to you. One of these days," she added pleasantly, "when you are not quite so busy."

Jarrett smiled and nodded, then he turned his attention to Lance, who had entered the room quietly. "Your wife and I were just discussing the possibility of some common ancestor in our background, but there will be time for that later. Meanwhile, please tell Charles that I shall be joining the family for dinner this afternoon."

It was a dismissal, and everyone recognized it as such. Martim took Star's hand in his and waited patiently until she kissed her mother good-bye another two or three times. Finally he applied a steady yet gentle pressure to her wrist, and Raine watched in fascination as the woman who possessed such a dazzling, brilliant beauty obeyed her husband's silent command. Then she, too, took her leave as Lance lingered for a brief moment and eased his mother forward so he could embrace the fragile body and hold his mother safe.

"See ya tomorrow, Mother."

"Lance," Amy said weakly, and raised her hand to touch his cheek. "You must tell her about Claire. She might not understand if she hears the truth from strangers."

Lance closed his eyes and breathed deeply. When he opened them Amy Randall saw the pain he was unable to hide from her.

"Soon," he promised, and the mother felt the terrible ache in her son's heart and suddenly realized that there was more to her son's despair than she knew.

19

For two days the weather remained overcast. There were occasional rainstorms as the wind howled its unseasonable lament. Great sheets of water poured down the windowpanes. A small creek that Raine could see from her window had surged above its banks and flooded part of the valley through which it flowed.

During those two days the young women of the household occupied themselves with rummaging through the laden shelves in the sewing room. Patterns were chosen and fitted, and at the end of the two days three skilled seamstresses had increased Raine's personal wordrobe to the point where she was able to return most of the clothing Kathleen had so graciously lent her. Within a few more days everything could be returned.

When not occupied with fashion the three women spent time in the third-floor nursery playing with the children while the weary nursemaid and her helper retreated to the kitchen to sip hot tea and join in the household gossip.

Between times each one took turns visiting and running errands for an improving patient who began to take charge of her household once more. However, she accomplished it with discretion and kindness, leaving many of the decisions in Kathleen's capable hands.

On the fifth day after their arrival Raine was delighted to see a bright sun rising in the eastern sky, and she leapt at Jarrett Randall's offer to have the horses harnessed to an open buggy so Lance might give her a tour of the estate. Lance, who was also anxious to escape the house, agreed immediately. He and Raine put on light sweaters and settled themselves in the buggy, which was waiting at a side door. They were both eager for an exhilarating ride through the fresh spring air that had been scrubbed clean by the rains.

Lance clucked and the horses stepped out smartly, obeying his gentle touch on the reins. He guided them through the maze of paths that crisscrossed the estate, and Raine began to notice the various occupations being carried on. This was more than a rich man's estate, more than a well-run farm. It was a diversified commercial venture giving employment to hundreds of people who were never seen from the doors or windows of the manor house. Skillful terracing and groves of tall spruce shut the two separate worlds away from each other.

Besides the usual farm activities, there was a mill located by the side of a fast-running creek. When Raine asked about it she was informed that it was a textile mill that produced thousands upon thousands of yards of fine cotton cloth. Further along there was a general store, where the people who worked for Jarrett Randall were able to purchase everyday necessities.

Once they passed the textile mill it seemed as though they rode for miles before approaching a series of low buildings constructed of thick concrete walls, totally isolated from any other activity.

"Gunpowder," Lance replied in answer to Raine's question. "We leave plenty of space in case of an accident," and Raine could understand why.

As they sat for a few minutes watching the activity going on outside the thick walls of each building, barrel after barrel of black powder was loaded onto wagons or a railroad car that waited on a rail spur a short distance away.

When Lance clucked the horses on the scenery became more familiar. Fine thoroughbreds romped in the meadow. Whiteface cattle grazed contentedly in a shaded pasture. A family of pigs rooted hopefully in an abandoned turnip patch, and further down the road Raine heard the unmistakable ring of a smithy's hammer on the anvil.

Everywhere along the back roads fruit trees spread their fragrant branches, and Lance explained that anyone was permitted to harvest whatever he could use as each variety came into season. "Helps stop the kids from poaching from the family orchard," he explained as he drew rein at the top of a gentle knoll that looked out over the rolling land of the estate.

From this vantage point Raine could see much more than had been visible from the narrow tree-lined lanes they had just traveled. "It's beautiful," she said, and sat spellbound, watching the women tending the fires under large washtubs as they took advantage of this increasingly beautiful day. Small children who had been too long cooped up ran and frolicked, and Raine watched as they raced the wind with all the heedless joy of childhood. The scene brought back happy memories, and Lance watched each passing expression that played across her face.

"A penny for your thoughts," he offered as he put an arm around her and drew her closer to him.

Raine leaned against him easily as she continued to watch the panorama spread below. "I guess that's why Grandfather didn't want Mama to marry Papa," she said, the words catching Lance by surprise.

"Because he was a farmer?"

"Yes," Raine answered sadly. "I suppose Grandfather really didn't know much about farms, but Papa had a very good one," she defended. "We had three families helping work it, and the women helped Mama in the house. It wasn't some little grubby place where Mama had to get out and help plant potatoes or something like that," she finished angrily.

Lance decided not to pursue the matter, which never failed to enrage his wife. Still, he knew the time was near when he must insist that she confront her grandfather. There simply had to be a connection between Lawrence Raine and the Randall family somewhere, for Raine's mother was as much a Randall as he.

Clucking the horses forward, Lance guided them down a lane dominated by a large white clapboard house that had obviously been added to over the years. As soon as he stopped, the door opened and Zeke and Bart Hubbard stepped out onto the large front porch.

"Got time to come in for a cup of coffee?" Zeke inquired.

"Just about," Lance answered as he checked his pocket watch. "Gettin' on to dinner time so we can't stay long. How's your mother?"

"Same as usual," Bart answered, smiling good naturedly. "Still knocks us around some when we don't step fast enough to suit her."

"Well, you boys be on your best behavior now, so she can meet Raine," Lance joked. "I wouldn't want to get clipped because I was in the way when she's swingin' at one of you fellas," he drawled, and the three men broke into laughter over some private joke that Raine could only guess at.

Helping his wife from the buggy and carrying her over the muddy spots, Lance put her down on the front porch. They followed the two brothers into the front hall, where Raine breathed deeply of the smells that were familiar from her childhood. The distinctive odor of scrubbing soap and wax assailed her nostrils. She looked around and felt instantly at home.

Glass panels on each side of the front door let in what little natural light reached them from a northern exposure, but the brightly burning lamps with their brass reflectors bouncing back the cheerful light more than made up for it. The front stairs were on her right and proceeded up to a landing that turned the steps at a right angle as they continued to the second floor. The simple balustrade was entirely functional, and the railing showed the wear of many hands. Thick wooden treads were swaybacked, indicating generations of use. It was all familiar and comforting to Raine, who had grown up in a large farmhouse very much like this one, a home of distinctive smells and sounds and memories.

From somewhere in the back of the house, the tantalizing aroma of something being baked with cinnamon wafted its way into the hall. Not far behind came a tall, raw-boned woman with bright red hair and cheerful blue eyes.

"So," she said in her normal roaring tone, "this is the lass you've been wantin' me to meet, is it? Well, come along, child, don't just stand there gapin'. Me kitchen is where I do me entertainin'. Except for the parish priest, of course. Him I keep in the parlor!"

Raine could not control a giggle, but she was not the only one whose face reflected genuine amusement as they all followed Maureen Hubbard, mother of seven strapping sons, into the warmth and cheer of the kitchen. It was here that Raine found her roaring fireplace, but there was also a most modern stove with steaming and warming chambers. It was the kind of large, complicated monster her mother would have loved.

Maureen's eyes reflected pride as she noticed Lance's young bride eyeing her stove with envy. "The mister, himself, toted that evil beast all the way from Baltimore. Wouldn't hear of it bein' bumped and banged by some uncarin' lout. Took him and the boys days to set it up and ventilate it proper."

"It's a marvel," Raine commented, ignoring the woman's natural habit of demeaning whatever she might own so she wouldn't appear prideful. The farmers who had been her neighbors in Pennsylvania had been much the same, but Raine knew that Mrs. Hubbard was near to bursting with the pride she would not admit to.

"Come, child, sit here by the fire. Nothin' like a cheerful blaze to lift the heart, I always say."

Accepting the invitation, Raine sat in the plain wooden rocker and began to push off with one foot to get it going. From the corner of her eye she saw Lance and Bart take seats around the kitchen table as Zeke poured steaming coffee into large, heavy mugs.

Cupping the mug offered to her in both hands, Raine tested the dark liquid cautiously. It was still scalding, so she put it on a small table beside the rocking chair and waited for it to cool.

"It'll be just right by the time me cinnamon cake's ready to eat," Mrs. Hubbard stated with certainty as she rose from her chair, walked to the oven and removed four large pans of aromatic cake.

Returning to her guests, Maureen Hubbard took her time as she examined every detail of the young woman Lance had married. Her two boys were right. She looked a lot like Claire, but not exactly. There was no brooding look in the clear-eyed young woman, and there was no spitefulness. Besides,

Claire's hair had been a shade lighter and her skin paler. The face was not exactly the same and most certainly the character was different. The girl who sat rocking contentedly in her chair was a far cry from the Claire Randall she had known. Pursing her lips, she decided that Raine would make Lance a fine wife if he would put the past behind him. If not, he was creating his own tragedy.

Maureen thought about it briefly and then continued talking to Raine. "Sure'n it's a pleasure to see that one married at last," she stated bluntly as her head jerked toward Lance. "Thought it would never happen after so many years," she continued, and then abruptly changed the subject.

"But that's neither here nor there. You must tell me all about yourself and leave nothin' out, mind. Tryin' to get anything out of me boys is like pumpin' a dry well."

Again the soft, musical sound of Raine's laughter drifted over to the men seated at the table, and their eyes turned gentle. "When ya gonna tell Miss Raine about Claire?" Zeke asked almost belligerently.

Lance shook his head. "As soon as I can find the right opening. Mother's been after me too. Father, of course, is curious as hell over the family resemblance. Wants me to do some diggin' into her mother's side of the family."

"Why?" Bart asked, just to make sure he already knew the answer.

"Have you ever seen the picture of Raine's mother, the one Emmett Colter carried in his watch?"

"No."

"Maybe you ought to have a look at it. The spittin' image of Claire, and her mother is from Philadelphia."

Zeke's eyes widened in shock. "Jay!"

Lance nodded in confirmation. "Yep. Can't think of anybody else it could've been."

"I'll be damned," the older man whispered, casting a furtive glance toward the two women who sat in animated conversation, not the least interested in what the men were talking about.

Raine, in the meantime, was much too involved in her own story to pay the slightest attention to anything else. She had just told Mrs. Hubbard how she and Lance had met and about their whirlwind courtship.

"That fast, was it?" Maureen asked in an Irish brogue that was still heavy even after almost forty years in the United States. "Sure'n he was afraid someone would steal you away right from under his nose."

Delighted laughter crept to the corners of the room, and Lance stirred himself. Standing, he made his apologies. "Afraid we'll have to be getting back, Mrs. Hubbard. It was good to see you again.

"Come on, Muffin," he urged as he handed Raine the sweater she had discarded a happy forty minutes ago.

Watching as the buggy pulled away, Maureen Hubbard looked to her oldest son. "Well, Zeke, what do ya think?"

"I don't know, Mama. Raine loves him, there's no doubtin' that. She risked her life for him. She knew what could be waitin' for her if those Indians got their hands on her, but she came anyway. But what she's goin' to do when she finds out why Lance married her so fast is anybody's guess. I'll tell ya one thing, though, in all the years I've known Lance, I've never seen him as scared as he is now."

"And well he might be," she murmured, her eyes narrowing suspiciously. "Sure now and there's got to be more to it than just her resemblance to an old sweetheart. There's somethin' else troublin' Lance. Somethin' he's havin' great difficulty dealin' with.

"Ah, well," she sighed, "at least Raine has assured me that Tess is a fine woman. Says she looks a lot like me. Tall and very striking with her red hair and violet eyes."

A soft smile crinkled the corners of Zeke's eyes. Raine had kept his secret. There was no reason for his mother to know of Tess's past occupation, and Raine had not told her. "Yeah, I guess she does at that," Zeke answered, smiling happily at his mother.

At the same time Zeke and Maureen Hubbard were discussing the problems of the couple who had just left Lance was

reining in the horses at the back of the
house, which sat high above them. Under
the beautifully railed terrace and the immac-
ulately groomed lawn there was a series of
doors built into the hillside.

Lance escorted her through one of the
doors, and Raine found herself in a part of
the house she had not yet seen. She was
captivated by the maze of underground tunnels that led to various rooms, including
servants' quarters, a summer kitchen, a
wine cellar that lay behind a thick barred
door and a root cellar.

Ventilation shafts brought in fresh air,
and lanterns of polished brass illuminated
the high, arched brick tunnels. The expertly
laid brick walks sloped almost imperceptibly
toward strategically placed drains.

As she followed Lance through the laby-
rinth, Raine knew that she was seeing only
a small part of the underground fortress she
had never dreamed was here, and she was
sorry when the floor sloped up and Lance
opened another heavy door leading into a
small accounting room in the main part of
the house.

Walking from there into the huge kitch-
en and then to the family dining room where
dinner would be served, Lance removed his
own sweater and took Raine's from her.
There was no time to wash and primp, for
the rest of the family had already gathered at
the table.

"Sorry we're late," Lance apologized to everyone in general. "Had a little difficulty in getting away from Mrs. Hubbard."

Knowing smiles touched the faces of the family members, for they knew how easy it was to sit in Maureen Hubbard's kitchen while she rocked and spun tales of home and the little people and so many other things that had enthralled the Randall children as they were growing up.

"She's a grand woman," Jarrett volunteered. "She and your mother came to this place about the same time. Old Josh Hubbard brought Maureen home with him when he went to Ireland to buy a fine mare we'd both had our eyes on. He was so taken with his strapping Irish lass that he almost forgot about the mare."

"Oh, Papa," Star admonished, but her eyes sparkled and Jarrett Randall was almost content.

"I wish Damon would get here," he remarked casually, but his eyes revealed his troubled thoughts.

"I'm surprised we beat him home," Lance agreed. "Still, he's got quite a way to come, especially if he chooses an overland route. Of course, there's always the possibility he's snowed in someplace. The Rockies aren't too hospitable in winter. Zeke, Bart and I had trouble enough gettin' out of the Cascades a few months back, but I wouldn't worry. Damon's as good as they come. He'll make it."

"Yes, I suppose you're right," Jarrett agreed, but everyone at the table knew he was fretting about his third born. "Still, I'd like to have him home."

Lance looked full into his father's eyes. "I'm sure he'd rather *be* home," he stated bluntly.

The two men understood each other perfectly. "And now that you're married, I suppose you'll be wanting to settle down as well," Jarrett suggested easily.

"It's what I'm planning," Lance replied quietly. "Raine wants to settle in California, and I kinda like that part of the country myself."

Before Jarrett Randall had a chance to reply, Jesse spoke up. "Me, too, Father. Everything in Brazil is running smoothly, and if there's any problem, sis and Martim can take care of it. I'm not needed there anymore, and I'd rather be home as well. Hell, Father, all us boys would."

Jarrett leaned back in his chair and looked around the table. His family was breaking up. Lance had told him in private about his near escape from death and his decision to end the manhunt that had nearly caused it. Jesse was discontented in an alien land, and Damon was tired of the endless hardships of surveying and mapping hostile country.

A tender smile touched his face as his gaze lingered on his baby, his little girl who was now a married woman and a mother.

Star's eyes met her father's and there was no one at the table who did not see the love that flowed between them.

Raine looked away. There was a great deal of love between Jarrett and Star Randall Cabral, just as there had been between her and her own father. The memory of it brought tears to her eyes, and Lance, who understood the pain that was still fresh, put his hand over hers. He was going to hurt her even more.

Then, so suddenly that Raine jumped, Jarrett Randall pushed back his chair, knocking it over as he lunged for the doorway that separated the family dining room from the kitchen. His face reflected fear. Every eye followed him. Kathleen gasped and clutched at Garron's sleeve. Lance cursed and Jesse sat, unable to move, for there, framed in the doorway, was Amy Randall, leaning heavily on the arm of her very frightened maid.

"What can you be thinking?" Jarrett asked brusquely as he swept his wife up into his arms and carried her to the nearest chair. "My God, Amy, haven't we been through enough? Whatever possessed you?"

Amy Randall heard the fear in her husband's voice and interrupted. "Jarrett, my dear, I cannot bear one more day of being cooped up in my bedroom. I will not be kept there."

Amy Randall's voice was so mild, her pale face so angelic that Raine almost missed the steely resolve in every inch of her. Jarrett Randall, who had lived with her for almost forty years, recognized it and backed down.

"Well, if you insist," he said grudgingly. "But you'd better not have a relapse," he threatened, and everyone smiled. Everyone except Amy, who put a small, gentle hand to her husband's face.

"I won't, my darling, I promise." Then she looked around at her family. "Would someone be so kind as to cut me a slice of beef? I've had quite enough mush and broth, thank you."

As a plate was passed to her with a small portion of paper-thin roast beef and a few vegetables, Amy sipped a hot cup of coffee. Her eyes lingered on each child and she, too, fretted over Damon. Shy, quiet Damon, who had somehow been lost in the shadows of his two older brothers.

But not Star. Star had always had more than her share of stubborn determination and had always fought for her share of attention, but never had she shined more brilliantly than she did now in her role of wife and mother.

Then there was Lance, whose usually noncommittal face had softened and come alive since he had returned home with his bride. By some miracle he had found another woman to love, and Amy did not question it. She only breathed a silent prayer of thanks that it had happened at last. Now if only Raine had the strength to endure the past and the wisdom to see just how deeply she was loved, it would all work out. It must for the sake of her most deeply wounded child.

She smiled into the azure eyes of Jesse, who was so much like her. No matter what happened he would land on his feet. And everyone liked Jesse. He was a favorite everywhere he went. Then her gaze drifted to her firstborn. Garron and Kathleen would one day take Jarrett's place—and hers. If only she could live to see Jesse and Damon happily married and settled in a life of their own.

A circle in a circle in a circle, she thought idly, and then began to yawn. Her hand flew to her mouth to hide the unmannerly lapse, and Jarrett smiled into the eyes of cerulean blue.

"Would you like to go back to your room now?"

"Yes, my darling." Amy sighed wearily. She had been too ambitious in her hopes, but it had been a lovely visit.

Jarrett Randall, who was over seventy years old, was still strong and straight. As easily as though he were lifting a feather, he picked his wife out of her chair and carried her to the back stairs in the kitchen, which led to the hall outside their second-story suite. He would not be back until Amy had drifted off to sleep.

No one at the table was anxious to break

the mood of quiet contentment, the snug, safe feeling Raine had always imagined a butterfly felt curled up in its cocoon. Her gaze lingered on each of the Randall children present, and for at least the tenth time she wished she, too, might have had brothers and sisters.

Finally the group bestirred itself, and each member of the family went his own way. Star slipped her hand under Martim's arm as they took the long way to her parents' suite. When she tapped on the door it was opened by Amy's maid. Looking past her, Star saw her father, who sat in a chair at his wife's bedside, holding her hand as she drifted off to sleep. Jarrett put a warning finger to his lips, and Star smiled her love to him and retreated.

"Shall we pay Paul a visit?" she asked, and then laughed softly in delight as Martim's dark eyes flashed another, much different message to her.

"Paul can wait," he suggested and guided his wife toward their bedroom.

Lance, Jesse and Garron went into the small accounting room. Sitting at the large desk, Garron opened the latest ledger and went over the affairs of the estate in meticulous detail.

Lance and Jesse looked at each other and rolled their eyes in an expression of helpless exasperation, for Garron would insist that they know, down to the last penny, what monies had been spent and what profits had been made. As usual, the well-run estate had earned a great deal, but Jesse and Lance both dreaded the hours it would take Garron to present the usual annual report on all of the other family holdings, which would eventually be divided into five equal shares. All except the house and grounds. They would always be retained by the first-born son and his family. It had been their father's burden and one day it would be Garron's. Not one of the other Randall children begrudged him any part of it. He had been trained since childhood to manage family finances, and he was well suited to the task.

Lance smiled as his mind drifted while Garron droned on. He was the second of Jarrett Randall's children to leave the magnificent home the workers and townspeople called White Hall. Promise Kept Manor had always been too much of a mouthful, so they had rechristened it to suit themselves. His baby sister had been first, and now he was leaving the nest as well.

About time, he thought derisively. *Hell, I should've done it years ago.* Then he mentally corrected himself. He hadn't known Raine years ago. It would not have been right years ago.

Even while her husband was thinking of her, Raine left quietly by a side door. She walked quickly along the road that led to the large white clapboard house. Her knock was answered by Zeke, who invited her inside, but Raine refused. "Do you think we might sit on the porch a while? I'd like to talk to you privately."

"Sure, Raine. What's on your mind?" he asked as he seated himself in the rocker next to hers.

"I saw an unusual necklace in Lance's possessions before he set out on his last trip, the one to Frenchmen's Creek. But it wasn't on him when we took him to Sacramento, and I've not seen it since. I understand it was a family heirloom, and I've seen it in several of the family portraits. What happened to it?"

Zeke released a pent-up breath. He had been afraid of what Raine was going to ask him, but her question was a safe one. It had nothing to do with Claire or with Lance's past. "It's gone. When Lance was captured it was ripped from his neck and thrown in the fire. To the Indians who caught us it was a symbol of a betrayal by their own kind. They hate all white men, and a symbol of friendship and protection given to a white man by another Indian enraged them, and they took it out on Lance."

Raine's heart skipped a beat as even now the terror of her husband's ordeal flashed through her mind. He had been bound and helpless, and he had suffered grievously at the hands of the men she and Tom and the Clary brothers had killed.

"I have been searching for something very special to give to Lance as a token of my love for him, and I think you have helped me. Tom Morley has been a mountain man most of his life. It would be no problem for him to duplicate it. Do you think a new amulet would please Lance? It wouldn't be the original, of course, but it would look just like it, and it could be kept in the family for future generations."

"I think it's somethin' he'd appreciate, all right. He feels mighty bad about bein' the one to lose it. I think he'd be most pleased that you thought of it."

Raine was overjoyed that she had at last found something to give to her husband. It was difficult to find something he would enjoy, for he seemed to have everything he wanted already. Then Raine smiled a small, secret smile. She wasn't sure yet, but there might be something else she would be giving her husband about nine months from now.

That evening as she lay in bed, waiting for Lance to join her, Raine asked him about the miniature. Lance's breathing came with difficulty as his mind raced. He decided to answer almost truthfully.

"It's a portrait of Claire Randall, a cousin. I think she was rather sweet on me a long time ago. Gave me the miniature as a remembrance," he said as he slipped into bed, took his wife in his arms and proceeded to give her something else to think about.

And Raine forgot all about the miniature as she moved within the circle of her husband's embrace. She loved Lance and he loved her. Nothing else could ever matter.

When the passion was done, when they had savored it all Lance was at peace with himself. The dark, crippling pain of a too-long remembered betrayal had eased its way from his heart, and he wondered just when it had happened.

He watched his wife sleeping at his side, so trusting, so loving, and he felt his heart swell with love for her. But he shivered under the chill of fear. There was a great deal he must tell Raine. He could only hope she loved him enough to forgive his transgression, one made more terrible by lies and half truths, a transgression that still weighed heavily in his heart and mind.

20

Two days later Amy Randall, having fully recovered from her attempt to rejoin her family for meals, sat on the sunny terrace wrapped in a shawl. It was a mild day in early June. Nevertheless, Jarrett insisted that his wife protect herself from the pleasant breeze.

Rays from the sun settled warmly into every corner of the gracefully balustraded terrace. Roses bloomed as far as the eye could see, filling the surrounding gardens with a profusion of red and pink blossoms.

Beautiful azaleas that had grown tall in this protected location rivaled the roses for brilliant color, and Raine watched in fascination as a hummingbird examined each blossom that would be gone before long. Even now the busy honey bee had stirred and was touching every bloom, no matter how large or small. Not a single grain of pollen was overlooked, and Raine almost laughed out loud as she watched a greedy bumblebee with overloaded pollen sacs lifting off clumsily from one blossom, struggling to reach her nest, where she would safely deposit her treasure. Finally, unable to lift straight up, the heavy-bodied creature managed to veer sideways and thus gain some altitude.

Amy Randall's eyes were troubled as she studied the younger woman who was so interested in the insect that had struggled valiantly only to be whisked away by an errant breeze. The color had returned to Amy's cheeks and the fear was gone from her husband's eyes, but Jarrett still insisted that she stay warmly dressed in spite of the gentle sun that touched every creature and blade of grass with its healing balm. Jarrett knew better than to trust the early spring sun. Just as life was stirring, just as buds swelled full with promise, the cruel hand of winter frequently returned to kill all that it touched. His Amy must be kept safe for as long as there was breath in his body.

Turning her face up to the sun, Raine closed her eyes and let her mind drift. She thought of how she had raced the deer as they had sprinted across the open meadow to the comparative safety of the shadowy wood beyond. And she remembered the charming chipmunk with its gaily striped back and the nose that was never still. Her lips parted slightly as the beauty of the mocking bird's warning thrilled her heart. It was so much like the place she had once called home.

Then all was still as every expectant ear strained to confirm the first distant sound of drumming hooves. The message had come over the telegraph line that Damon was on his way, and the rider approaching the front of the house could be none other than he.

Within seconds their expectations were fulfilled as Damon came rushing through the open doors leading to the terrace. His face was alight with joy. No one else mattered to him as he made straight for his mother and picked her up bodily, swinging her around as he held her securely in his arms before settling her comfortably back in her chair.

"I got the good news the minute my foot touched the docks of Baltimore," he exclaimed, happiness shining from his face. Then, kissing his mother lightly on the cheek, he turned to greet the rest of the growing family.

"Father!" he exclaimed, and hugged his father to him.

Jarrett Randall seemed a bit uncomfortable with his son's unrestrained greeting, but he accepted the breathless entry as part of the exuberance of youth. Then Damon laughed out loud as he headed for his little sister, who came running across the terrace to throw herself into his arms. Star hugged him fiercely. Her brother lifted her from her feet and swung her through the air in a most undignified manner, but Star didn't care. The moment he put her down she grabbed his arm and tugged him to where her husband waited to greet Jarrett Randall's middle child.

"We were most concerned about you," Martim said after Damon had all but pumped his arm from his shoulder.

"Got snowed in with the rest of the surveying crew," Damon offered as though that explained everything, and in a way Martim supposed it did.

"We are most pleased to see you, Damon. Most pleased," the more subdued Brazilian answered, genuinely relieved that his wife's brother had survived the perils of the wild and treacherous mountains that lay to the west.

A wide grin acknowledged Martim's remarks even as Damon turned to greet his three brothers. Lance held out his hand to forestall his brother's enthusiasm, and Star made a disapproving sound.

"Oh, don't be such a sour apple," she scolded as Lance effectively contained his brother's euphoric outburst.

"Don't scold," Amy admonished quietly from her chair. "Garron and Lance are Randalls, my dear. You three younger children are Santees. Each line has its own fine qualities, but the Randalls are more reserved. They love just as deeply," Amy continued as she turned away from Star to look at Raine, "and they are hurt just as easily. More so, perhaps, since they have a somewhat dark and brooding side to their natures."

Raine knew that Amy Randall was telling her something important, for the woman's eyes bored into her as though to burn the words in her brain forever. She would remember them, for she was quite certain there would come a time when they would have some very special meaning for her.

Damon took advantage of the lull in conversation. "Lord, but I'm famished. Haven't had anything to eat since last night. "Karl!" he shouted unnecessarily, for the well-trained servant was hovering just out of sight, waiting to be of service.

"Yes, Mr. Damon," he answered in his most disapproving tone, for Karl was a firm believer that one of quality and breeding must never shout.

"Have cook fix me something to eat, something that will stick to my ribs."

"By all means, sir," Karl sniffed in an open display of disappointment in the young man he had personally instructed in proper decorum. "I believe you always implied that oatmeal was quite sticking, sir."

"You bring me oatmeal and you'll eat it," Damon threatened, but his eyes were laughing with his old mentor, who bowed and left the room to get the man a large steak and plenty of fried potatoes, all of which would be washed down by a pot of hot coffee.

When Karl had gone Damon turned confused eyes to the woman who looked so much like Claire. Before he had a chance to ask the question that was on the tip of his tongue, Lance stepped forward. "She belongs to me," he stated, grinning. "Raine, honey, this is my brother Damon. Now you've met us all. Don't know if that's good or bad," he drawled lazily.

Still not sure of the situation, Damon cast a hasty glance at Raine's left hand. And there it was, a wedding ring. His smile was almost shy. "Welcome, Miss Raine. You sure make a mighty pretty addition to the family. I'd be pleased if you'd keep me company while I have my meal out here on the terrace. It's such a beautiful day, and I'm not used to being cooped up in a house. Where I've been there aren't any. Besides, it will give us a chance to get to know each other a little."

His smile was bright and friendly, and Raine settled herself at the small garden table. Within minutes Damon had learned more about her than the rest of the family had learned in a week, for Damon had a way of drawing people out and of sharing confidences. He had put Raine at ease in the very first seconds after his arrival, and he had won her trust at that same time. Now, learning all about her was child's play.

"So your father was good with animals," he encouraged, sensing that there was a great deal more Raine would like to say about her parents.

She laughed and replied, "Yes, some of the farmers called him a horse doctor because he was so good at treating animals with all sorts of ailments."

"And your mother? You say she was from Philadelphia?"

"Yes, she met my father there."

Damon's eyes smiled. "Raine—that's a family name, isn't it? Any relation to the Raines of Philadelphia?" Then he laughed out loud. "We like to think we know all the influential families. Sure would be a feather in your cap if you came from one of them."

"Well," she responded somewhat belligerently, "I certainly don't see why it would be anything special, but my grandfather is Lawrence Raine. He's quite wealthy, I believe, but I have no interest in him. He's not a very nice person."

Damon backed off and changed the subject, but Amy Randall, who was sitting nearby, probed a little deeper. "Perhaps these hard feelings can be smoothed over,'' she suggested kindly, but Raine shook her head.

"No! I'll never forgive him! He didn't even come to see my mother when she lay dying, crying out for him. No! I never want to see him! Never!''

Damon put his hand over Raine's. "Please forgive me. I did not mean to bring up a subject that is so unpleasant for you. Sometimes, though, it's better to talk about it, to get it out of your system.''

"No,'' Raine muttered stubbornly. "I don't want to talk about him. I despise him!''

Without warning, a picture formed in Amy Randall's mind. All the old gossip came rushing back—stories about Jay and a young belle of Philadelphia. Jay had gone to that city and then had disappeared. No trace of him had ever been found. And Raine had, indeed, been created in his image. It was all there. Now it had to be proved.

She glanced up at Lance, hoping he would deny her thoughts, but he simply nodded his head, for he understood that the whole ugly possibility had occurred to his mother just as it had to him and his father. Raine was their first lead and they would follow it.

Even before he spoke, Lance knew he was asking for trouble. "Well, Muffin, I think you and I should go to Philadelphia and listen to his side of the story. There are always two sides, you know. Besides,

Damon's right. It's best to get it out of your system. Tell him what you think. Might make you feel better.''

"I will not!'' Raine muttered defiantly.

For an instant Lance was stunned. Raine was confronting him in public, and it wasn't the first time. Just to look into her face was to see raw rebellion, and Lance smiled. He had seen this kind of mutiny before. His little sister had been the same way whenever someone tried to force her into doing something she did not want to do. It had always been the old fable of the sun and the wind and the traveler who clutched his cape to him that had determined his behavior with her. It had always worked with Star, and it would work with Raine as well.

"Aren't you the least bit curious?'' he asked in astonishment. "Surely you've noticed your resemblance to us. And the picture of your mother. You must have wondered at her likeness to the miniature you asked me about. Or did you think they were one and the same? Which I assure you they were not.''

Raine cast a slanted glance at her husband. He was bringing up the very thing that had bothered her since she had gotten here. The miniature of the woman Lance had called Claire looked just like her mother. Claire and Jennifer Raine Colter could easily have passed for sisters. Was there really a connection? "I don't know," she answered uncertainly.

"Well, only you can decide, of course. But I'm so curious myself that I shall probably go to Philadelphia without you if you're absolutely set on staying here."

Raine glared at Lance, and it was all he could do to keep an innocent expression on his face. "I'll think about it," she muttered grudgingly, but inwardly she was burning with curiosity.

"Well, don't take too long because this little journey might clear up a family mystery of our own," Lance remarked casually, and then turned his attention to his half-finished glass of lemonade.

"What mystery?" she asked, trying not to sound too interested.

"Ah," Lance sighed mysteriously. "I must let my father tell you about that. I was very young when it happened and know few of the particulars."

Motioning for his father to join them, Lance sat back and listened as Jarrett Randall retold the story of Jay Randall, who had disappeared twenty-nine years ago from the city of Philadelphia. "He had broken with his family, had left his wife and young daughter, whose name was Claire. He also left a series of legal papers that turned over his estate to his wife. In other words, he did not intend to come back. However, he kept his sizable account in a London bank and took a large amount of cash with him, so he certainly did intend to lead a rather gracious life somewhere. And knowing Jay as I did, he would not lead that life alone. There was undoubtedly a woman involved."

Raine stared into the emerald eyes that matched her own. Jarrett Randall could almost hear her brain racing. "And you think that my close resemblance to the family might take you a step closer to your cousin?"

"Think about it, Raine. Jay arrived in Philadelphia. That much is known. Your mother was born in Philadelphia, and she is the spitting image of Claire, Jay's daughter. Your grandfather has disowned her. Why? Because she chose to marry a farmer, and a rather well-to-do farmer from what you tell us? I think not. What is it we don't know, Raine? Lance and I both believe that we must pursue the investigation, that we must trace your line back to the only possibility we can see. Your grandmother, La Belle Raine."

Jarrett held his hand up to silence Raine's protest. "Yes, I've made inquiries. Of course I have. From the very first day I saw you I knew you were a Randall. But how? How is it I knew nothing about you? It is not like our family to desert their own, and Jay would not have left his wife and child except for someone he loved even more. Who?" Jarrett smiled. "Again, could it have been your grandmother, the woman who gave birth to a child who is the twin of Jay's daughter?"

"And the London bank account?" she asked as her mind considered the unthinkable.

"Never touched," Jarrett confirmed. "Not until years later, when the courts awarded it to Jay's wife."

"He's an evil man," Raine warned.

"Then you and Lance must be cautious in your approach."

By this time Raine could barely contain her curiosity or her hatred. She understood all the possibilities. They had been spelled out in detail. A trip she had been quite determined not to make was now something she could not be stopped from doing.

"I believe I shall start packing," she announced primly as she stood to take her leave, but that night when they were preparing for bed Raine turned to Lance and stared at him through speculative eyes. "Don't think for one minute that I'm unaware of the way you and your father manipulated me. I allowed you to do it."

Lance smiled his sweetest. "Then, my angel, it isn't so underhanded, is it? I mean, if you *knew* we were trying our best to get you to agree, we didn't really manipulate you into doing anything against your will."

"Maybe," Raine answered absently, for her mind was already on Lawrence Raine and the city of Philadelphia. Then, quite suddenly, an air of foreboding closed in around her and she shivered as she sought shelter in her husband's arms.

"Promise me that you won't let anything happen to you," she demanded urgently as her eyes sought his.

"Not to either one of us. Never," Lance promised, and then scooped her up and carried her to their bed, where he reassured her with more than words.

21

Standing in front of the large house that took up half a city block, Raine tilted her head back, holding firmly to her hat so she might see to the top of the home that soared four stories above the ground. It was not so large as Promise Kept Manor, nor was it nearly so grand, but it made clear to all who cared enough to think about it that a man of wealth inhabited this mansion.

Certainly there had to be at least forty rooms behind the cold granite walls of the house that was shaped much like a large square box. Only the ornamentation at the front relieved the stark symmetry. At the back there was a balcony visible above the fence that enclosed the rear yard. Trees were beginning to drop their blossoms. The air that blew inland from the Delaware River was fresh and warm. Spring was touching this area of Pennsylvania with a fragrant promise Raine remembered well.

The noise of traffic at this busy intersection reminded Raine of the times her father had taken her to the market, which was located near this very street. Not once had he mentioned that her grandfather lived almost within shouting distance. Her eyes narrowed as she thought of the old man who lived inside those cold walls, and she understood why her father had remained silent.

For the first time Raine understood that her father had also suffered. He had shared his wife's pain and sorrow, for it was he who had caused it. It was he who had so boldly defied Lawrence Raine. It was he who had eloped with the man's only child, if, indeed, her mother had been his natural daughter. And Raine's eyes glinted coldly as she thought of how much that evil old man had to answer for, especially if what she suspected proved to be true. Still studying the outside of the forbidding house, still lost in her own thoughts, Raine did not notice when Lance touched her elbow and gently urged her toward the barren, railless steps that led to the front door.

The first flat, cheerless rap of the brass knocker against its plate brought Raine's thoughts back to the present. Now, despite her dislike for the man she had never seen,

Raine could not help but wonder what he looked like, for she could barely remember the picture she had seen so long ago.

A rush of dank, chilling air hit Raine as the wide front door swung open and a rather decrepit manservant in faded livery stood blocking the way. Raine almost laughed, for even she could have pushed past the old man whose stooped shoulders and thin, wispy hair gave an accurate indication of his advanced age.

"Mr. Lawrence Raine," Lance said firmly. "Mr. and Mrs. Lance Randall to see him."

The old man's face turned even whiter than his natural pasty complexion. "Randall?" he asked in a voice that betrayed uncertainty and fear.

Lance watched with the sensitivity of a serpent testing the air. He missed nothing. Not the fear, not the hesitation and not the tremor that had passed through the old man at the mention of the name Randall. He had been right. This house would provide the answer, and he meant to get it.

Neither his eyes nor his face gave any clue to his thoughts as Lance answered the servant's question. "Yes. Randall. Now if you would be so good as to announce us to the master of the house," he continued unctuously, "we should be most grateful."

From somewhere out of the darkness a disembodied voice spoke casually. "Show them in, Vernon."

"Yes, sir," the old man responded almost testily as he stepped to one side, beckoning the visitors into the reception hall.

Lance and Raine stepped across the threshold, their eyes automatically following in the direction Vernon's hand indicated vaguely. "If you will follow me," he said, and then led them through the wide, dim corridor that divided the house in two.

The servant's pace was slow and painful to watch. Raine felt a twinge of sympathy tug at her, for it was obvious the old man should have been pensioned off years ago, and spiteful thoughts about her grandfather's penuriousness flitted comfortingly through her mind, for anything that might confirm her judgment of the man she hated was welcome.

Then Vernon led them to a room that was in total darkness except for an antiquated oil lamp whose wick was turned low. An audible gasp greeted their entrance into the musty room whose drapes were drawn tight against the fresh beauty of spring. Then the lamp flared, and a man who might be in his late sixties stared at Raine through eyes as brown and warm as the earth itself. His hair was an uncertain mixture of gray and what was once brown. The smoothness and fairness of his complexion startled Raine. The man was nothing like what she had imagined.

"You say the name is Randall?" he asked, turning to Lance. "I know the name.

However, it is a large family. Which branch are you?''

Lance smiled in satisfaction. Lawrence Raine knew more than just the name. He also understood that it was a large clan with members gathered in more than one city. He had to admire Lawrence Raine. The man was as smooth as a peeled onion, and he wasn't easily spooked.

''It's all one family, Mr. Raine,'' Lance answered easily, his eyes never leaving the man's face. ''My *branch*, as you call it, lives in Baltimore. My father is Jarrett Randall. Perhaps you've heard of him?''

Soft laughter touched Raine's ears, and she watched in wonder as Lawrence Raine's eyes lost their warmth and turned cold as he shifted positions in his chair. Then, focusing his expressionless eyes on Raine, he spoke in a quiet, almost friendly voice. ''And you, my dear, you are also a Randall?''

''Only by marriage,'' Raine answered, and felt a chill run through her as the old man laughed again, only this time there was nothing but evil to be heard in that soft sound. The coldness in Lawrence Raine's eyes turned to hatred. But Raine did not flinch. She stood her ground as her own eyes reflected his hatred back to him.

Her voice was thick with contempt. ''Then you recognize me?''

''Yes,'' he answered, almost relieved that it had come at last. ''How could I fail to recognize you? You were created in your mother's image. She's dead, I understand," he concluded without a trace of emotion.

It was then that Raine's considerable temper flared. "Yes, she's dead, you dreadful old man. She died still loving you. But I don't love you. I detest you and wouldn't be here if my husband hadn't insisted."

A smile of acceptance touched Lance's face, but not his eyes. Raine had given the game away, of course. There could be no doubt now as to why a Randall married to a Raine was here. Of course the old man knew that he had put two and two together.

He stared at Lawrence Raine, who still held a mask before his face, but both men understood. Raine was only of peripheral importance in the matter her husband had come to settle.

Lawrence Raine picked up a small silver bell and rang for a servant. This time a middle-aged woman responded. "Yes, Mr. Raine?"

"Some tea and sandwiches, Mattie. And a little of that spice cake we had for supper last night," he added as though there was nothing more pressing on his mind than seeing to the comfort of his guests. "And Mattie," he added in an off-hand manner, "bring the tray to the main parlor."

The maid's eyes widened in shock. "The upstairs parlor, sir?"

"Of course. It's time we opened it up again for guests, wouldn't you say?"

"Whatever you say, sir," the maid mumbled, and hurried away to do as she had been ordered.

Waiting until she had disappeared into the deeper recesses of the house, Lawrence Raine stood and motioned for his granddaughter and her husband to accompany him even as he reached into the matchbox and removed a half dozen matches. "You are very much the image of your mother, my dear," he repeated as he studied Raine through impersonal eyes. "A variation on a theme, of course, but much like her all the same. Come, we shall have our tea in one of LaBelle's favorite rooms," he remarked almost gaily as he walked crisply toward the stairs.

Following along her grandfather, Raine was too preoccupied to appreciate the magnificence of the house. To her, the wide staircase was just another obstacle to be surmounted, and the old-fashioned chandelier hanging from the ceiling was simply a way of dispelling the gloom that permeated this darkened home.

She watched absently as her grandfather lowered the chandelier by means of a heavy silken cord that ran through a series of brass rings up the wall and across the ceiling, where it supported the weight of the elegant creation of brass and crystal. Striking one of the matches he had brought with him, Lawrence Raine lit one candle after another until six brightly burning candles illuminated the upper hall, whose opulence was in startling contrast to the stark exterior of the house.

As the chandelier was pulled back and fastened in place, a blaze of light was thrown into every corner and splashed back at them from the strategically placed mirrors that boasted ornate frames. Fine old woods gleamed in the reflected light. Velvets glowed warmly, and gold threads that had been worked through the damask upholstery winked back a softer light. A rug of deep red warmed the hard, cold marble beneath it.

A bittersweet smile touched Lawrence Raine's lips as he led them into an even more richly furnished parlor. "These were my wife's favorite rooms. Come, let me show you her portrait. It was done soon after we were married."

The smile turned cunning, but it was hidden by the comparative darkness of the room. Once more the old man lowered and lit a chandelier. Then he walked to the far end of the room and put another match to the candles in the silver candelabra that graced a fine old piano constructed of gleaming mahogany. Instinctively, Raine's gaze lifted to the space above, which was covered by drapes of blue velvet. As Lawrence Raine opened the drapes, Raine stared, fascinated, at the portrait behind them.

"My grandmother?" she asked softly as she drank in the beauty of the woman she had never known.

"Yes. Quite a beauty at the time," Lawrence remarked idly.

"Yes," Raine agreed. "Mama told me about her. She said she was only three when her mother, LaBelle, left and was never heard from again."

Lawrence Raine folded his arms across his chest and leaned against the piano. It was a pose of languid unconcern, but his eyes betrayed him as he really looked at the portrait for the first time since they had entered the parlor. "Yes," he answered, his eyes glittering his hatred. "She left with her lover. Of course, I could hardly tell your mother the ins and outs of such a sordid story. Besides, she was much too young to understand."

It was time for Raine to ask the question that her grandfather was quite prepared to answer, and she did not disappoint him. "But where did she go? Surely my grandmother would have kept in touch with her only child. I can't believe she would do otherwise."

"Nor can I," Lawrence answered smoothly. "Which is why I am quite convinced that LaBelle and her lover perished at sea. Otherwise there would have been some news of her and of the man who seduced her and stole her from her family."

"And the man's name?" Lance asked quietly.

Lawrence Raine's soft laughter sent a chill through Raine like fingernails on a chalkboard. "Why, I believe he must have been some relative of yours. If I recall, his name, too, was Randall."

"It was," Lance agreed in casual tones. "His name was Jay Randall. He was my father's cousin. His home was in Virginia. In fact, his wife still lives there."

"And his daughter?" Lawrence inquired, his voice betraying the strong emotions that lay just under the composed surface.

"Dead," Lance answered in a tone devoid of all feeling. "She died fourteen years ago."

A malevolent joy glinted in the older man's eyes. "Then they're both dead! Both of Jay Randall's children are dead!"

Without being asked, Lance sat down. He looked as though he might be ill. "You'd better start from the beginning, old man."

"But of course," Raine's grandfather gloated, and then fell silent until Mattie came to where they were sitting and began to arrange the items she had brought on the silver tray.

Carefully placing napkins, cups and saucers along with all the other accouterments of tea, including the requested spice cake, the servant began to pour. "Get out, get out!" Lawrence snapped irritably. "My granddaughter can pour."

Then he turned to Raine and asked sarcastically, "You do know how to serve tea?"

"We will neither eat nor drink in this house," Lance stated firmly, interrupting Raine as her hand automatically reached for the pot of freshly brewed tea.

Delighted laughter echoed through the room. "Do you really think I might poison you?" the old man asked with poorly disguised glee.

"Isn't that how you killed Jay Randall?" Lance inquired easily, his voice steady with the certainty of his conviction.

The old man's face collapsed in disappointment. "Do you really think Jay Randall would have accepted anything from my hand? No, no. The only thing he wanted from me was my wife."

Lance sighed as all the old gossip rushed back to fill his mind. Nothing definite. Never anything definite. "You were about to start from the beginning, I believe."

"Of course," Lawrence agreed again. "Well, let's see how it all began," he mused as he removed a pipe from his pocket and puffed great clouds of vile smoke into the air as he lit it.

Settling into a comfortably upholstered chair, he stared into space as though trying to decide on a starting point. Raine seated herself in a chair near Lance, prepared to listen.

The story that followed was a revelation to Lance, for little by little the missing details were filled in. All anyone had really known was that Jay Randall had fallen in

love with a woman he had met in Philadelphia. Her name had never been mentioned
by Jay. Then something had happened and
the romance had ended. Not quite a year
later Jay had taken a wife. It had been a
loveless marriage, but it had produced one
child. And then, a few years later, Jay had
left his wife and had gone to Philadelphia,
where he vanished. Now the only person
who knew what had happened was filling in
the rest.

"My wife, it seems, fell in love with Jay
Randall while she was betrothed to me. She
did the honorable thing, of course, and
broke our engagement, but she never would
tell me why. I could only guess at the truth,
but I knew nothing for sure.

"Then, several months after she had
broken our engagement, she changed her
mind once more and said she would marry
me after all. I didn't know what to make of
it," he said quietly as his eyes sought out the
portrait.

"She was so lovely." He sighed in sorrow. "But only on the outside. However," he
said sitting up straighter, bringing his mind
back to the present, "I asked no questions,
for I had never stopped loving her. Then,"
Lawrence said bitterly, "six months after
our marriage a daughter was born to us. Any
fool could see that it was a full-term infant
and that could only mean one thing. My wife
had slept with another man before we were
married. She had married me knowing she

was carrying another man's child." The calmness of his voice was betrayed by the hatred that glittered from his brown eyes.

"Naturally I accepted the child as my own. I allowed all of Philadelphia to believe that I had fathered a child before my wedding night, and I did this to protect LaBelle *and* her child."

"You did it to keep from looking like a fool," Lance corrected with no vindictiveness.

Lawrence Raine glared at the man who spoke the truth with such cruel finality. "Perhaps, but it would have been all right for several years later my wife conceived. This time the child was mine."

Lawrence Raine's face, which had been so briefly touched by triumph, contorted in pain and rage and humiliation. "Then he came back! The bastard came back! He came back for my wife and his daughter, your mother!" he spat at Raine, who could only look at him in stunned silence. Yet, at the same time, there was profound relief. The man she despised was no kin to her.

"Go on," she said calmly. "Tell us the rest."

Ah, but my dear, there is no rest," Lawrence replied smoothly, and then proceeded to repeat the same story he had told years ago. "I simply would not let him have your mother. Naturally when my wife chose to desert her husband and child to run away with her lover there was precious little I could do about it. But I could and did prevent them from taking the child I had raised as my own for three years."

"You're lying," Raine stated quietly. Her eyes met his and held steady. And once again Lawrence Raine saw Jay Randall in those eyes.

"And you, Raine Colter, are being most impertinent."

"No," Lance interrupted, agreeing with his wife. "You *are* lying. I know nothing about your wife, sir, but I do know that Jay Randall would never have left any child of his in your hands. He would have killed you first. I also doubt that you allowed your wife to leave you quite as easily as you say—not when she was carrying your child."

A sad smile touched Lance's mouth. "You're an evil man, sir. Perhaps that's why I understand you so well."

Lance Randall was big and blond, like Jay, but there the resemblance ended. Jay had been outgoing—even gullible. The adversary who challenged him now trusted no one. If provoked, he would kill. The game suddenly became much more interesting.

"I assure you, Mr. Randall, my wife and her lover left the child with me after I threatened to have the law on their heads if they didn't. After that I have no idea what happened to them. Presumably they sailed for parts unknown."

Lance stared at Lawrence Raine, his pale green eyes cold and disbelieving. "Jay

Randall was my father's cousin. He had considerable holdings in Virginia, including an estate of 1500 acres. He had a wife and child to whom he deeded all his properties in this country. So you see, Mr. Raine, Jay Randall did not come to Philadelphia on the spur of the moment. Something brought him here. Something that he knew would forever end the life he was leading in Virginia. After he disappeared my father had him traced as far as Philadelphia. There the trail ended. Until now no one knew what had happened to him."

Lawrence Raine smiled vacuously. "And just what did happen, sir?"

"You killed them. Both of them. And then you explained your wife's disappearance with the same story you just told us. But how did you manage it?" Lance asked, totally perplexed, for Jay Randall had been an expert with gun and sword. And, like all the Randall men, he had been tall and powerfully built.

"You simply will not be convinced," Lawrence stated sadly. "I can tell you little more. They left this house almost thirty years ago. I have neither seen nor heard from them since. I assume they went down in one of those terrible storms the North Atlantic is subject to."

Totally ignoring the man's disclaimer, Lance stared at him thoughtfully. "Why didn't you kill the child as well?"

The question hit the mark, and the light

of madness became visible in Lawrence Raine's eyes. He could no longer control the urge to throw his triumph into the face of the woman who was the last of Jay Randall's line. "I might have eventually," he remarked calmly. "But to get rid of her so soon after her mother's disappearance would have a-roused a great deal of suspicion. Truthfully, I had forgotten all about Jennifer until it was too late. Yes, you're right. I should have buried her with her mother. It was a serious mistake."

"Your unborn child was not so fortu-nate," Lance stated casually.

"No, no," the older man sobbed in pain and confusion. "She made me do it. It was all her fault. LaBelle did it. She was going to run away with that bastard, and she was carrying my child. I could not allow it. I could not!" he cried out in anguish, and Raine felt the first twinge of pity.

"Lance," she whispered, and clutched her husband's hand. "What shall we do?"

"We shall settle this once and for all," he answered coldly, and Lawrence Raine nodded.

Lifting the portrait of his wife from the wall, he removed a key attached to the back of it. "I'm glad it's over," he said wearily. "Come with me."

Leading Lance and Raine down the stairs and through the house to a door that led to the cellar, Lawrence began to descend the narrow stone steps. Every few feet he stopped to light one of the wall candles, whose flames flickered in the drafty staircase.

When he reached the bottom he removed a lantern from a shelf and lit it. Then he walked to the far end of the basement, where a heavy door marked the presence of some sort of closet.

With the key he had removed from LaBelle's portrait, he unlocked the door and swung it open. "You will find what you're looking for in there."

Lance smiled at the older man's foolishness. "By all means, sir, after you."

Cunning laughter echoed eerily in the cavernous arched cellar as Lawrence Raine stepped inside. "Come, come," he urged. "There's nothing to fear from the dead."

Hesitantly, and with suspicion pricking at him, Lance took a step forward, but he knew something was wrong. The devious old man had some sort of trap waiting for him, for how else could he have killed Jay Randall except through treachery?

"You stay here," he ordered, and Raine nodded in obedience.

With the very next step, Lance understood, for the floor was no longer brick; it was wood. At the very instant of understanding, Lawrence Raine pulled a chain, and the floor gave way under Lance's feet. He fell into total darkness as the trap door swung up and closed over him.

He grunted as the wind was knocked out

of him when he landed some fifteen feet or more below the surface. He sat up and rubbed his back, for he had landed on something hard, something that had made a sound he recognized. Feeling around, he fingered a pile of bones. He had found Jay and LaBelle.

"Damn," he cursed softly, and tried to climb the slick walls of his circular prison. It had to be an old well, but it was too wide across to allow a man to brace his arms and legs against opposite sides and thus make his way up. Besides, the trap door was another obstacle; but one way or another he would get out. He had to. Raine was up there with that madman who had killed her real grandparents. "Damn," he cursed again as he swept the bones away with his foot, but this time his voice was unsteady with fear—fear for his wife.

As Lawrence Raine scrambled from the small room, slamming and locking the door behind him, Raine charged. She slammed him against the heavy door with a force that stunned him and almost knocked the wind from her own body as well. Then she picked up the lantern that Lawrence Raine had dropped and swung it at his head, knocking him unconscious. Frantic fingers forced open the hand that still clutched the key.

Hastily, Raine tore it free, and fumbled as she tried to unlock the door. Taking a deep breath, she steadied herself. She was of absolutely no use to her husband unless she acted as he would act—calmly and logically. There was no time for nerves, not with Lance's life at stake.

Finally the door opened, and Raine retrieved the lantern, relit it with one of the matches Lawrence still carried in his jacket pocket and stepped gingerly into the room, which smelled of death and decay.

Everything had happened so fast, Raine had to stop to think about it. She had seen Lance fall, but before and after he had been swallowed by the earth she had heard the rattling of a chain. Moving the lantern so its light would touch every inch of the space where the old man had stood, Raine saw it: a rusty chain. She released it, and the trap door swung down almost beneath her feet.

Quickly she pressed herself flat against the wall until she could recover her balance. Then she extended the lantern out over the blackness of the hole. Holding on tightly to the iron ring that was embedded in the wall, Raine peered down into the pit and almost cried in relief.

Lance was standing with the knife he was never without in his hand. Like a wounded tiger, he was ready to fight until all life had gone from his body.

He grinned. "Well, are you going to stand there all day? Throw me a rope or something. It'll take me hours to carve steps in this damned brick."

Putting the lantern at the edge of the hole so Lance would not be in darkness,

Raine hurried to carry out his request. She raced for the stairs, plucked a candle from its holder and began her search. She found an old fishing net and some heavy cord, but she couldn't find any rope.

A slight sound from Lawrence Raine brought with it a sense of urgency. She could not let him regain consciousness unless he were restrained in some manner. So, grabbing the net and the twine, she raced back to the spot where the man was beginning to move.

Bending over him, Raine wrapped the twine around his wrists and then took a few turns around his ankles. It would probably hold until she could get Lance out of that hole.

Only a few minutes had passed but to Raine it seemed an eternity as she struggled to tie one end of the net securely through the iron ring that guided the chain. Then, dropping the other end of the net into the pit, she watched as it stopped just a few inches above Lance's head. She waited nervously as Lance made his way up the swinging net. Finally he hauled himself out and stood next to his wife.

"Well," Raine drawled in an exact imitation of Lance, "that's one problem solved."

Lance laughed, and then hurried her from the room. His smile broadened as he saw Lawrence Raine struggling against the heavy twine that bound him hand and foot.

"Couldn't have done better myself," he

remarked casually, which was, as Raine knew, the highest compliment he could pay anyone.

"Now, sir," he continued as he faced the man, who was fuming with rage, "would you care to tell my wife what happened to her real grandparents?"

"I killed them!" he screamed. "I killed them both. LaBelle sent a message to Jay Randall telling him that I was a cruel husband and she could not endure it any longer. And it was true. Before I knew she was carrying my child I took out my rage on her. I just couldn't seem to forgive her until I knew about my own baby, and then she betrayed me again."

He roused himself from painful memories and continued. "When your cousin arrived he demanded to see his Claire. Told me to my face that he was taking her and his child away, and that he had already settled matters with his wife, and once they walked out the door I would never see either of them again. He had no right. He had no right."

Lawrence Raine suddenly looked much older, but he continued. "When he started up the stairs for LaBelle I shot him. My wife heard the shot, of course, and came running. When she saw Jay lying dead on the steps she fainted and tumbled down the staircase. She broke her neck. She was dead."

"His *Claire*?" Raine asked, all the uneasiness the name stirred in her rushing back to confuse her once again. "I thought your wife's name was LaBelle."

"Yes, it was. Claire LaBelle Bennett, but everyone had called her LaBelle since childhood. Only Jay Randall called her by her first name. And he had the temerity to name his legitimate daughter after my wife! How dare he?" Lawrence cried out in anger. Then he sneered. "His bastard daughter, your mother, was named for my mother. LaBelle insisted on it."

He laughed the laughter of the demented as the irony of the situation struck him. "But she paid. They both paid. And my unborn child paid," he sobbed, as his eyes glazed over with the terrible memories of years gone by. "I put their bodies in the old cistern. You know the rest."

Lance watched his wife and saw her strange reaction each time the name Claire had been spoken. It confused and worried her. She remembered it dimly, and she would put it all together some day. She had been coming out of her fever when he had called her Claire, and the memory was working its way forward. He was going to have to explain soon.

Bending down, Lance cut the twine that bound Lawrence Raine. He had found out what he had come here to learn. Raine Colter resembled Claire Randall because they were aunt and niece. Raine's mother had been half sister to his Claire. They resembled each other so strongly because they both had inherited the features of their father's blood. Jay Randall had sired both Claire Randall and Jennifer Raine. Raine Colter Randall was Jay's grandchild.

"Come on, Muffin. We know all we have to know. We'll book passage for home."

"No," she said softly. "He's going to pay for what he did. I'm going to the authorities. I shall see him hang!"

"No," Lance responded sadly. "It's over. What more can anyone do to him now? It would only create a terrible scandal. Jay's wife is still alive, and her wounds have never healed. This might very well kill her."

Raine thought about it for an instant and decided that Lance was right. But there was something she had to know, something that had not yet been made clear. Turning to the man she had thought of as her grandfather for seventeen years, she asked, "Why did my grandmother ever marry you? If she loved Jay, if she was carrying his child, why did she marry you?"

Lawrence Raine was silent for a moment as he reached back in time. Then he told the story as he had pieced it together. "Apparently LaBelle's lover was to return to Philadelphia a month after they last parted. Unfortunately for all of us, he fell ill with fever. When he did not arrive at the appointed time LaBelle was growing frantic, for she was pregnant; she was carrying his child.

"She wrote a letter that was not answered. Apparently Jay Randall had no one to take care of his correspondence while he lay ill, and thus LaBelle thought she had been jilted. Her pride was deeply wounded and she sent another note to his home. This time she ordered him not to come to Philadelphia, for she had changed her mind again and was to be married to me in the near future. Neither note mentioned her pregnancy. LaBelle was much too proud to get him back that way. Jay never knew until the third note was sent, which told him everything, the note in which LaBelle begged him to help her escape this house. And of course he came. The rest you know."

Raine closed her eyes against the tragedy. Then she turned to Lance. "You're right. The past is done. There's nothing more to be accomplished here."

Lance nodded and picked up the lantern. He escorted Raine to the steps, put down the lantern and took her in his arms. "I'm sorry, Muffin, sorry that you never knew your true grandparents."

Raine frowned and then told the truth. "Well, Jay Randall would have been an improvement over Lawrence Raine, but I don't think I would have liked him very much. He seemed to think of what he wanted regardless of the consequences. Your father should have talked to him the way you talked to me in San Francisco," she said, smiling up at him. "Do you remember?"

Lance chuckled. "I'll never forget it. And if I remember correctly, you didn't think much of it at the time."

"No," Raine admitted. "I didn't like it at all."

"Yeah, I noticed," Lance said in good humor, and then escorted his wife to the top of the stairs and out of the house.

Raine breathed deeply of the warm air blowing in from the Delaware River. Her hatred for the old man was eased somewhat by the fact that he was not her grandfather, nor was he her mother's father. Raine shivered when she thought of what could have happened to her mother if she had stayed in that house. She, too, might have disappeared.

It was then that Lance smelled the smoke and looked back to see the flames shooting from the windows of the second story of the Raine mansion. Raine, too, turned to look, and she took a deep breath as she realized what had happened. Lawrence Raine had endured enough. He intended to burn down the house that had brought him nothing but tragedy, and he intended to perish with it.

There was nothing anyone could do. It was too late; Raine stood unable to move as the clanging of the horse-drawn fire engine grew louder. She saw the man she had hated for so long appear briefly at the window of the room that held the portrait of the beautiful LaBelle Bennett Raine, that weak, wavering woman two men had loved. Then, in a roaring wall of flame, he was gone.

She held tightly to Lance, who supported her as they walked away. Slowly tears spilled from her eyes. It had been such a senseless tragedy, and now it was over. At last she understood. She looked like the Randalls because she was a Randall. She was Claire Randall's niece, and the thought troubled her.

22

Raine paid a visit to her mother's grave, which was located in a small churchyard not far from the Raine mansion. Lance stood back as his wife knelt and told her mother everything. He did not try to comfort her as the tears flowed, for the tears were healing and he wanted above all else not to see her suffer anymore.

When she was through, when she had made peace with herself, Raine stood and dried her eyes. "Can we go home?" she asked, her eyes pleading with Lance, and Lance understood. She meant home to San Francisco, to California.

"Yes, my darling, we're going home. We'll stop to tell the family what we found out about Jay, and then we'll start for home."

The look of gratitude in Raine's eyes told Lance a great deal. He knew she was not comfortable in Promise Kept Manor, just as she would never have been at home in the Raine mansion. When she said home she meant the hills and rivers and trees of California. She had said her last good-bye to her mother. If she could help it, she would never come this way again.

They stayed one last night in Philadelphia before they boarded the ship that would take them back to Maryland. It was a comfortable old sailing vessel, devoid of boilers and steam. The flapping of the sails and the chanting of seamen as they worked in unison were their lullabys and their morning call. The ship's bells were their songs of joy and the wind was their master.

It was a time of healing and a time of love as the ungainly old merchantman lumbered its way downriver. Lance put chairs out on the deck, and the two of them sat in silence as the scenery drifted by. And Lance thought about his own life, which had been almost ruined years ago by a woman much like the one who had destroyed Jay Randall and Lawrence Raine—a weak woman who did not have the faith or the courage to hold tightly to the man she loved in time of adversity.

Lance smiled cynically. Somehow he doubted if Claire had ever been capable of truly loving anyone but herself. He did not know about LaBelle Raine. Only two men knew that answer, and both were dead.

He glanced at his wife and reached for her hand. "Shall we go below?"

Raine smiled her answer, but before Lance had a chance to take her arm, she leaned against him and held him close. When she was ready he escorted her below.

As she undressed, Lance watched with troubled eyes. The same blood that ran in Claire's veins also ran in his wife's. She was Jay Randall's grandchild. And Lance was afraid. The thought that she was the granddaughter of LaBelle frightened him even more.

He was not sure. He loved Raine with all his heart, but could he trust her? Would she, too, betray him?

Removing the last of his clothing, Lance slipped under the blanket. He watched as Raine hung her things from the pegs provided for that purpose. Then his heart skipped a beat as she turned around and he saw the expression of need in her eyes. He smiled up at her and held out his hand. Raine slid in beside him and touched the face she loved. "Hold me for a few minutes," she requested, and Lance obliged. He thought his heart would surely burst as she snuggled up to him and told him again of her love. It was something Lance never tired of hearing.

His hands touched her gently and

moved slowly. He was patient and waited. If Raine was not ready, he would not pursue it.

But Raine was ready; she wanted the comforting closeness of her husband. As he touched her in sensitive places, she shivered with delight, and she retaliated with teasing of her own.

Lance laughed in pleasure, and his lips and tongue played; his fingers sought out the essence of her, and Raine responded as she always had.

Her heart beat faster, and the pulsing low in her body became an insistent, demanding beat that only Lance could calm. She whispered against his lips, "Now." She was ready; she needed to be one with her husband.

Lance took her slowly and gently. There was no demand; there was no frantic need. There were just the slow, rhythmic motions of love.

Raine moaned her pleasure and moved with her husband. It was as though time had stopped and might never begin again. They were completely lost in each other, enjoying the sensual feel of each other's bodies, lost in wave after wave of mounting pleasure. And then it came, the tide that neither of them was able to resist. Lance held Raine tight as his love spilled from him, as he eased the woman he loved to fulfillment. Together they suffered torturous ecstacy and then lay still in total contentment. The deeply emotional experience left Lance drained and exhausted. He was helpless under Raine's touch. He loved her. There was no defense against it.

"Later?" she asked shyly as love glowed in her eyes.

Lance grinned. "Later," he promised, and that later was not long in coming.

Within hours Lance awoke, the need strong in him. This time there was nothing gentle in his approach. He shifted Raine's position and pulled her hard against him. Her nakedness inflamed his desire. Nor did Raine need to be encouraged. She had been waiting with increasing impatience as Lance had slept, and now she sought her release from torment. She did not want to wait. She did not want to tease. She needed him now, and she guided the hard, seeking core of his desire into her woman's softness. Lance hesitated only long enough to allow the full measure of passion to build. His body jerked in the soft, sensual confines of its prison. He drew in his breath with the short, sharp sounds of need that threatened to burst its bonds.

A soft groan marked the instant of his surrender, and he eased deeper into his wife's body. He could feel the pulsing tip of his manhood flick against the innermost part of her. Then, pulling her hard onto him, impaling her completely, Lance moved with short, desperate strokes until Raine found her own release. Only then did he allow the shackles of self-restraint to burst under the surging, irrestible raging of unleashed passion.

Raine held him to her even as she felt him slipping from her body. Her heart beat against his, and she did not want to let him go. Not ever.

Lance went cold with fear. It was back. The old hunger, the desperate need were back. Even now Raine was sensing an evil she could not see. He would tell her when they arrived home.

His arms tightened around her; he clung to her as though she might slip from his grasp. "Lord, but I love you!" he whispered hoarsely.

"And I you," she answered, snuggling closer.

For the rest of the night Lance thought only of what Raine would do when he told her the truth. Evil pictures filled his mind. His heart pounded as he realized that he might lose her. It was something he did not want to believe. She wasn't like Claire. Where Claire had played cruel, childish games, Raine had come to him with love. Never had she lied to him, never had she deceived him. She was open and honest. She was warm and forgiving. Gradually Lance calmed, and he dozed until Raine stirred. "Hungry?" he asked.

"Starving!" came the unambiguous reply, and Lance laughed.

"You stay here. I'll have breakfast

brought to our cabin. Want anything special?"

Raine thought a minute. "Oranges. See if they have any oranges. I have an absolute craving for them. And milk. See if they have any. I could drink a gallon!"

Lance glanced at Raine with an odd expression on his face. She didn't especially like oranges, and she rarely drank milk except in her coffee. Now, suddenly, she must have both. He pursed his lips and his eyes smiled, but he said nothing. Ships almost always carried some kind of citrus fruit or, at the very least, they had jugs of lime juice. Perhaps he could work out something with the cook to satisfy Raine's cravings.

As soon as her husband had left the cabin, Raine hopped out of bed and took a sponge bath. She sang softly to herself as she washed off and then rinsed. Drying herself briskly with a towel, she got dressed and then brushed her teeth. She felt wonderful. She had never felt better or more optimistic. She grinned at nothing until Lance returned with their food. And, sure enough, he had gotten three oranges for her.

Immediately Raine cut off the stem end of one orange and put it to her mouth. She had a marvelous time sucking the sweet liquid into her mouth and then letting it run down her throat. Then she tore the orange apart and pulled the pulp away from the skin with her small, sharp teeth. She munched and chewed her way through all three oranges. Then she sat back and sighed in contentment.

Lance watched the whole ritual with a grin on his face. He hoped what he suspected was true, but he would let Raine tell him. Just as soon as she realized it herself. "Here," he said, and offered her a napkin. "Your chin could use a cleaning."

Raine smiled brightly and accepted the napkin, dipped it in her glass of water and wiped her mouth and chin. Then she put the napkin down and poured herself a glass of milk. She drank it down in one breath.

Lance winced. She was going to be sick as a pup if she kept this up. He took her wrist in his hand. "Better give your stomach a chance to handle what you've already put in it."

She heaved another sigh of contentment and agreed. "All right. I'm full anyway, but, oh my, that was so good."

Lance ate his bread and cheese and finished up the coffee before suggesting that they take a walk on deck. "It's a glorious day, and the exercise will do you good." He laughed quietly to himself as he realized that he was already taking care of his wife and the child he suspected she had conceived.

Raine was more than eager to go topside. She was bursting with energy and could barely stand still. She wanted to break the restraints of propriety and pick up her skirts and run with the wind. She wanted to

skip and dance. Instead, she settled for a
brisk walk around the deck. Raine smiled as
Lance assisted her around the many impedi-
ments that cluttered the deck of a sailing
vessel. She could only hope that what she
suspected was true. She wouldn't tell Lance
until she knew for sure.

As they walked, Raine asked a great
many questions about the barrels and the
coils of rope and the different shapes and
sizes of the sails. Lance answered each
question in turn. In fact, he was delighted to
have her show an interest in a trade in
which he and his brothers excelled.

"Our family has sailed the seas for over
a hundred years," he concluded. "In fact,
every boy born to the Randall clan spends a
few of his growing years aboard ship. And
we're not given any special treatment, I
might add." He tilted Raine's face up. His
eyes were serious. "If we have a son, I'll
expect him to learn the trade as well. You
can be quite sure that Star will see to it that
little Paul gets his sea legs under him before
he's a man grown."

"And if we have a daughter?"

Lance laughed. "If she's anything like
my little sister, I'll have little to say in the
matter. Lord," he continued, "I hope she
won't give me the trouble Star gave Father."

A wistful smile touched Raine's lips.
"Your sister is a very lucky woman. She has
a beautiful son and a husband who absolutely adores her. It's so sad when I see

Martim looking at her with all his love shining in his eyes, and Star never seems to notice."

Lance grinned wickedly. "She notices, all right, and you can bet she thanks him properly when they're alone."

An impish smile flashed as Raine prompted. "You mean the way I do?"

Laughter rolled across the decks of the vessel, and even the busy deck hands smiled at the contagious sound. Lance answered as seriously as he could. "Yes, the way you do, my love, just the way you do."

The next afternoon Lance and Raine disembarked and rode in a comfortable coach toward Promise Kept Manor. Raine could not help but reflect on how different it was from the first time she had traveled these roads. Now they would make only one more journey: back to Baltimore. From there, they would head for California. She could barely wait.

But Lance had a more immediate problem on his mind. "How much do you want to tell the family?" As far as he was concerned, they should know everything about Lawrence Raine and the whole untidy mess, but it was up to Raine.

"I'm sure they will want to know the whole story. After all, it's their family too."

Her openness was one of the things that had always delighted Lance. From the very beginning she had been honest and had held nothing back from him. Not her love, not her trust and, on a few occasions, not her temper.

Leaning down, he whispered, "Remind me to tell you how much I love you."

With an impish gleam in her eyes, Raine replied, "Would tonight be too soon?"

Laughing in great good spirits, Lance held her close and pressed an enthusiastic kiss on her lips. His heart was lighter than it had been in years. His mood was cheerful, and the cynicism with which he greeted the world had, for the moment, disappeared. "Not too soon at all." He kissed her again and felt the urgency build. "Damn," he whispered, and moved away from his wife, putting a little distance between them.

Raine laughed and looked at him through knowing eyes. "Tonight will come soon enough. If I know your father, he'll be at you all through supper, dragging out every last detail of our trip."

"Might be," Lance acknowledged reluctantly, but he hoped his father would choose a more private time to hear their story.

Just then the coach pulled up in front of the house, and Lance helped Raine to the ground. Karl, who was always alert to the family's comings and goings, was there to take their luggage, and before Lance had a chance to close the carriage door, his cousin, Maryann Porter, emerged onto the columned portico.

"Lance, darling," she cried in genuine

pleasure, and rushed toward him, her arms extended for an embrace. But Lance caught her hands in his and held her at arm's length.

"Maryann, how nice to see you again. Your family come with you?"

"But of course, you ninny," she replied, and shook her head in chagrin. "And when are you going to allow your family to hug you once again the way we did before that awful Claire spoiled everything?"

Then her face collapsed and her eyes widened as she realized that she had mentioned a forbidden subject. She had just been warned not to mention Claire under any circumstances, and, as usual, she hadn't been able to keep her mouth shut. She jerked her head toward Raine, who only stared at her, for there was that name again. It tugged at her mind and brought a chill of fear with it.

"Claire?" she asked hesitantly. "Do you mean Jay Randall's daughter?"

A wave of relief washed over Maryann. Lance had apparently told his bride everything. "Oh, my dear," she said to Raine, "I am so sorry to have brought up what must be a painful subject. Please forgive me, but I promise I shall never mention it again."

The small frown on Raine's face was an eloquent message to the older woman. "Oh Lord," she moaned, and turned penitent eyes to her cousin. "Lance. Lance," she said, anguish contorting her face. "I thought she knew. Oh God, Lance, forgive me."

Pale green eyes frosted over with fear and rage. Every muscle in his body was taut. His fingers twitched in their eagerness to strangle the life out of Maryann. "May I suggest that you let the entire matter drop, cousin? Besides, Raine knows that Claire was Jay's daughter. She also knows a few other things I believe our family would be interested in."

To Maryann Porter, who had known Lance all her life, the message was clear. He was laying down a false trail to confuse his wife, and she had better follow it or he would never speak to her again as long as he lived.

Glaring reproachfully at Lance, Maryann's voice was bitter. "I'm sure there's a great deal we'd all like to know, cousin."

The casual tones were back as Lance replied, "Then shall we join the others?"

Looking at Lance in deep disappointment, Maryann shrugged and tagged along behind as they stepped up to the portico and entered the spacious portal, where they gave their outer garments to a waiting servant. "Everybody's in the game room," Maryann announced, and then stalked on ahead.

As they entered, the men stood, and one who was a stranger to Raine approached. "Lance, old man, so good to see you again," he exclaimed cheerfully, and pumped

Lance's hand with enthusiasm. "And this, I suppose," he continued, turning to Raine, "is the fabulous young woman about whom I have heard so much. In case you haven't guessed," he continued pleasantly, "I'm Tom Porter, Maryann's husband."

Raine inclined her head to acknowledge him. "Honored, sir," she replied politely, but it was obvious that her mind was elsewhere. An automatic smile was fixed on Raine's face as she went through the obligatory motions of greeting, and when it was done she found a chair a little away from the others and mentally withdrew from their company. She was deeply disturbed, a fact that was obvious to everyone in the room.

Amy broke the awkward silence. "You're back so soon, my dear. I hope things went well."

Lance broke in. "At least we learned why Raine looks so much like a Randall. It's because she *is* a Randall. She's Jay's granddaughter."

Absolute silence fell over the room. All eyes were turned toward Lance, who looked at his father. When Jarrett nodded Lance told the story of his visit to the Raine mansion.

"And Lawrence Raine?" Jarrett asked grimly before Lance had a chance to finish his narrative.

"Dead. Dead by his own hand. Set the house ablaze and went down in the flames."

"So" Jarrett sighed. "It's over," he commented before turning to his daughter-in-law. "Well now, young lady. It seems that you are twice a Randall, by birth and by marriage. Despite the tragedy, we couldn't be more pleased. And I am deucedly relieved that your uncanny likeness to our family has finally been explained!"

Once again Lance interrupted before Raine had a chance to answer. "Hate to change the subject, Father, but Raine and I will be leaving for California as soon as I can make the arrangements."

Amy's frail hands trembled. "Must you leave so soon?"

"Afraid so, Mother. I want to get back. I've got a house to build and a family to raise. And like all the Randall men, I'm a mite slow in gettin' to it."

Jarrett laughed. "Took me quite a while, too, but I'm glad I waited for exactly the right woman. Seems you've done the same thing, son. And it's time you stopped running around risking your life. You're a married man now, and we should consider a more settled occupation for you. How does agent for our growing western trade sound to you?"

Fully gratified, a slow smile spread over Lance's face. His father had not referred to the time he had spent in the hands of hostile Indians, nor would the old man ever mention it to his wife or other children, but it weighed heavy on his mind. His second-born son was ready now to take over the reins of part of the Randall empire. No longer would he be the hired killer for the Randall clan.

Lance knew all these things that were going through his father's mind, and his eyes met those of Jarrett Randall. "Zeke'll be goin' back with me. He's got a woman he's gonna marry, and he's got part of a business in San Francisco. Sure you can do without us?"

A wistful expression touched Jarrett's face. "I want nothing more than for you to be settled and happy. I won't be able to replace you. You're one of a kind. We both know that, but it's time, son. It's time for you to take your rightful place and put the past behind you where it belongs."

"Yeah, pop, it's more than time," he answered, and then obeyed the chimes that rang for the evening meal.

All through supper Raine was quiet. She spoke only when someone directed a question to her, for her mind was troubled, and the name *Claire* kept floating in and out of her thoughts. She tried to push it back. She didn't want to remember. She had never wanted to remember.

After what seemed like hours Raine and Lance finally retired to their room, but when Lance tried to soothe her obvious fears, Raine moved away from him. Her eyes were full of confusion as she looked into his. She sat in a chair and stared at her hands, which were folded in her lap.

When she spoke her voice was so low

that Lance had to strain to hear. "When you came to my rescue in the pleasure palace, you spoke the name Claire. And then there was that first night aboard your ship. It wasn't a dream or a hallucination brought on by fever, was it?"

Lance gripped the bedpost. His face lost its natural bronze coloring. His eyes frosted over with fear. It was time. It was time to tell Raine the truth. All of it. And he would rather die than hurt her as she was going to be hurt.

Then there was the uncertainty. What would Raine do once she knew the truth? He had asked her so many times to remember her promises, to forgive him when the time came, to remember that he loved her. Would she honor those promises? Would she forgive him? He didn't know, and the fear was so heavy within him, Lance began to perspire.

Raine saw the hesitation on her husband's face and asked the question she dreaded most. "When I was sick with fever you—you—made love to me," she finished, determined not to use the detested word rape.

Lance was grateful to her, grateful that she was cushioning the blow to his pride, grateful that she was not shaming him more than she must. "Yes, I made love to you. I was asleep, and I dreamed of Claire, but I made love to *you*. I didn't understand it then, and perhaps I don't really understand

it now, but it was and is you I love. I spoke
Claire's name, but I don't love her. You look
so much like her. The close resemblance
brought back so many memories I thought I
had buried. But one look at you and it all
came undone. Once more I dreamed of a
time fourteen years ago, a terrible time.''

Lance felt the tears threaten what little
dignity he had left, but he would not make
excuses for himself. He would say the words
that could destroy his marriage. ''I dreamed
of a time when I held Claire in my arms, and
then I took you.''

The tears flowed down Raine's face. She
fought valiantly to contain them, but there
was not enough strength in all the world to
stop them. And so she waited until she could
speak past the painful lump in her throat.
''Tell me,'' she said, struggling to push the
words from her mouth.

''About Claire? Yes, of course, you must
know. You must know what only I and Claire
knew.

''She was my cousin, as you know. She
was Jay Randall's legitimate daughter. I
found out too late that at the age of sixteen
she was quite an experienced young lady. It
seems that she was pregnant with another
man's child, but he did not choose to help
her. So she came to me, and as much as I
hate to admit it, I was not too well versed in
what to expect when taking a woman to bed.
I look back now and cannot believe that I
was so ignorant. God, I could have spared

myself so much pain had I understood the situation better.

"To make a long story short, we made love. We were together almost constantly that one summer, and then she asked me if I could marry a woman who was carrying another man's child. Oh, she made it sound as if she were telling me about a friend of hers, but she was really talking about herself. At any rate, I said no, I could not, that I didn't want another man's child to raise. I wanted my own."

Lance sighed as the pain of long-held guilt swept over him. "She went to a doctor in Baltimore. And she had an abortion. It was not successful and she died. Because of me, she died."

"And you married me because I looked like her," Raine stated, struggling against the pain and the humiliation.

"No," Lance said bluntly. "I married you because I took your innocence. You came to me a virgin, and you came to me with love. I could not and would not turn you out after that. Yet I did not want you to know what I had done to you." He smiled as his thoughts drifted back to the little girl who had come to him even as the fever began to break. "And you made it so easy for me. Your trust and your love wrapped around me like twin vines that I could never break. I didn't want to break them."

"And when did you know that it was I you loved?" Raine asked, hoping against hope that he would give her the answer she needed.

"Almost immediately, I think, though I didn't know it. I have loved you from the beginning, from the very first time you came to me. But I was so ashamed that I covered one crime with another."

Raine stared at him. "Yes. How did you manage to give me back my virginity?"

Lance blushed. "I used blood from a steer. I never wanted you to know."

Raine looked Lance straight in the eye. "And all this time you were afraid that I would be unfaithful to you, when in reality it was you who betrayed me."

Lance clenched his teeth but could not hold back the sound of distress. "Yes. I had been badly hurt by Claire, and I found it difficult to trust again, but I learned. From you, my darling, I learned. Now I can only ask that you try to forgive me, that you remember how much I love you. Will you try, Raine?"

"I shall try, Lance, but now I want to be alone for a little while."

Lance did not try to stop his wife as she made her way out of the room and down the stairs to the balustraded veranda. The night was balmy and bathed in moonlight. There was a fragrant breeze blowing in from the gardens, and Raine filled her lungs with the sweet-smelling air.

Walking to the railing, she put her hands on the cooling marble and looked upward to the heavens. Her eyes traced the few constellations she knew and then scanned the brilliant stars on the western horizon. She found the star she had followed the night Lance had been carried more dead than alive to Sacramento.

Her thoughts drifted back to the many times he had forgiven her. She had been suspicious and mean-tempered. She had all but accused him of things he had not done, and always he had been patient. Always he had loved her.

A small smile touched her troubled eyes as she remembered the night Lance had seen her go into Jake's saloon. Even though he had suspected the worst, he had brought a carriage to take her home. There was no thought in his mind of casting her aside even though he made it obvious he thought she had been unfaithful to him.

Raine shook her head and sighed sadly. Despite everything she had done he had forgiven her and loved her. He had taken care of her, and when she had needed it he had protected her.

Then she thought of her parents and their great love for each other. But even their marriage had a few stumbling blocks along the way. As a young child she had not paid much attention to the times of stress and disagreement, but they had been there. Now that she was older she recognized the silences and the averted eyes for what they were. Her parents, the parents she loved with all her heart, had also had their differences, but they had always solved them.

Suddenly the vision of Lance burned and cut and bleeding invaded her mind. She shivered as she had not dared to do that night she and Tom and the Clary brothers had gone to rescue him. Tears streamed down her face as she remembered just how close she had come to losing him. And she thought how little he had said about the Clary brothers. He had accepted her decision to allow them to go free. It was what she had wanted, and it was what Lance had done. Despite his father, despite the job he had been sent there to do and despite all the money he had spent trying to accomplish his task, he had honored her wishes. He had let William and Robert Clary go.

And how many times had she promised to forgive him when the time came? Two? Three? But she had had no idea what it was she would be forgiving when she made those promises. Now she did, and somehow the horror of it all faded as she remembered the nights when her husband had comforted and reassured her.

Then Raine laughed, and with shining eyes looked toward the brightest star in the heavens. "Thank you," she whispered, and turned to enter the house. She loved Lance and the rest did not matter.

It was then that Lance stepped from the shadows and waited for her decision. Raine walked toward him with all the confidence of a woman totally sure of herself and of the man she loved. She put her arms around his waist and rested her cheek against his chest. "Can we go home now?" she asked, and realized that Lance would always be her valiant knight and his armor would always be burnished and bright. It was the way she had first thought of him, and neither time nor circumstance had changed that vision.

Lance held her close. "Yes, my darling," he whispered, and then pressed a gentle kiss on her lips. His heart raced with happiness as he led the woman who had Jay Randall's blood in her veins back to their room. She might be descended from the Randalls, but she was first and foremost a Colter. She had all the capacity for warmth and loyalty and love that her father had passed on to her, and Lance was satisfied. He whispered a forgiving and final good-bye to Claire.

Epilogue

Sacramento, 1855

On a snowy February day Joy Star Randall was born. Her short wispy hair was blond and her eyes Aegean blue. Both her parents fell immediately under her spell.

Lance picked up the tiny bundle that was his daughter and stared at her in fascination. She was so much like his sister when Star had been that age. How well he remembered that tiny, premature baby who had struggled so desperately for life, and now he had a child of his own to love and nurture. His heart could barely contain his joy.

Then he smiled at Raine, who was watching him through eyes filled with love. The past and all the pain that had accompanied it were gone. She had forgiven him completely, and now there was no room in his heart for bitterness or anger. He sighed his contentment and pressed a gentle kiss on the forehead of his sleeping daughter. His world was complete. He had been blessed with both wife and child. Separately and together they filled his heart.

After fifteen years he had at last found the woman who had made it possible for him to love again, a woman of great courage, a woman of absolute fidelity, a woman he would love for all time.

PASSIONATE HISTORICAL ROMANCE BY
EXCITING NEW AUTHORS!

Leisure **Books**

PASSION'S PEAK by Christine Carson. An Indian captive finds love and protection in the arms of a handsome gold miner.

_____2578-7 $3.95US/$4.95CAN

THE HOMEWARD HEART by Kathy Keller. Rorie Shelbourne longs to give herself to mysterious Cameron Deveraux, but is he the man the gypsy seer had warned her to avoid at all costs?

_____2601-5 $3.95US/$4.95CAN

ISLAND ECSTASY by Julia Hastings. Beautiful Haunani must overcome the dark secret of her past to find happiness with a rugged sailor.

_____2605-8 $3.95US/$4.95CAN

DARK CONQUEROR by Mary Christopher. A Norman knight conquered Frey's lovely body, but he could not capture her proud spirit.

_____2592-2 $3.95US/$4.95CAN

AMBER FLAME by Hannah Howell. Spirited Storm Eldon finds herself in love with Tavis Maclagan, her fierce ancestral enemy.

_____2580-9 $3.95US/$4.95CAN

LEISURE BOOKS
ATTN: Customer Service Dept.
276 5th Avenue, New York, NY 10001

Please send me the book(s) checked above. I have enclosed $_____
Add $1.25 for shipping and handling for the first book; $ .30 for each book thereafter. No cash, stamps, or C.O.D.s. All orders shipped within 6 weeks. Canadian orders please add $1.00 extra postage.

Name _____

Address _____

City_____State_____Zip_____

Canadian orders must be paid in U.S. dollars payable through a New York banking facility.   ☐ Please send a free catalogue.

AUTOGRAPHED BOOKMARK EDITIONS
Each book contains a signed message from the author and a removable gold foiled and embossed bookmark.

PIRATE'S LADY Robin Lee Hatcher. Lady Jacinda Sutherland found herself captive on a pirate ship bound for white slavery in Constantinople—unless she surrendered her innocence to its dashing captain.

_____2487-X $3.95 US/$4.95 CAN

SCARLET SURRENDER Sandra DuBay. A fiery novel of ultimate passion that sweeps the reader to the decadent salons of Second Empire France, where a beautiful woman surrenders to a devilishly seductive hero.

_____2555-8 $3.95 US/$4.95 CAN

LOVE FOREVERMORE Madeline Baker. Loralee had a difficult task before her as the Fort Apache schoolmarm—and an even tougher task quelling her desires for a fierce Indian renegade.

_____2577-9 $4.50 US/$5.50 CAN

LEISURE BOOKS
ATTN: Customer Service Dept.
276 5th Avenue, New York, NY 10001

Please send me the book(s) checked above. I have enclosed $_____
Add $1.25 for shipping and handling for the first book; $ .30 for each book thereafter. No cash, stamps, or C.O.D.s. All orders shipped within 6 weeks. Canadian orders please add $1.00 extra postage.

Name _____

Address _____

City_____State_____Zip_____

Canadian orders must be paid in U.S. dollars payable through a New York banking facility.   ☐ Please send a free catalogue.

CLASSIC ROMANCE
By Bestselling Author
Karen Robards

FORBIDDEN LOVE. After a passion-filled night, Megan knew she had given her body and her heart to the one man in the world whose bride she could never be—her guardian, Justin Brant.

_____2549-4 $3.95 US/$4.95 CAN

ISLAND FLAME. Curvaceous Lady Catherine Aldley was furious when pirate captain Jonathan Hale claimed her as his prize, but her burning hatred turned to waves of passion in his muscular arms.

_____2471-3 $3.95 US/$4.95 CAN

LEISURE BOOKS
ATTN: Customer Service Dept.
276 5th Avenue, New York, NY 10001

Please send me the book(s) checked above. I have enclosed $_____
Add $1.25 for shipping and handling for the first book; $ .30 for each book thereafter. No cash, stamps, or C.O.D.s. All orders shipped within 6 weeks. Canadian orders please add $1.00 extra postage.

Name _____

Address _____

City_____State_____Zip_____

Canadian orders must be paid in U.S. dollars payable through a New York banking facility.   ☐ Please send a free catalogue.